T3-BRL-918

RUBY JEAN JENSEN

NIGHT THUNDER

ZEBRA BOOKS
KENSINGTON PUBLISHING CORP.

ZEBRA BOOKS are published by

Kensington Publishing Corp.
850 Third Avenue
New York, NY 10022

Zebra and the Z logo Reg. U.S. Pat. & TM Off.

First Printing: July, 1995

Printed in the United States of America

In the beginning ...

1865

To Jacob Boyd, lying curled in his bed before the last light of the day had gone, the sound could have been part of the thunder. But the thunder rolled away in the increasing dark, going with the black clouds coming over the trees west of the cornfield, beyond his bedroom window, and the other sound came again. *Rummm, drummm* . . .

He leaped out of bed, pulling his overalls up and snapping into place one gallus. He ran barefoot to the window, but saw only the branches of the shade tree in the yard. The sound came again, closer, deeper. Drummm, drummm . . .

Had the war ended?

Were the soldiers coming back home, marching down his own road, beating their drums?

Down on the ground floor the screen door slammed shut. Pa had gone out onto the front porch.

Jacob ran out of his room, down the stairs. His mother stood at the front window, the curtain pulled aside. She peered out in silence. She was wearing her white cotton nightgown, though she hadn't let her hair down yet, as she always did when she went to bed. They had sent him upstairs at eight o'clock, as always, though it wasn't yet dark. Boys needed their rest, she said.

Many people had come through in these years of the Civil War, at times so close Jacob could hear the cannons. Families, old men and women, younger women with children were moving, leaving land that once held homes. They had stopped here often at the farm, where the creek ran just across the road, and there was shelter in the woods the other side of the cornfield. Here, the passage north was easier.

Jacob passed by his mother. She didn't send him back to bed.

He went onto the porch and stopped.

Pa stood at the top of the steps, one hand on a porch post.

Lightning connected the ground with the black clouds just west of the trees. Jacob saw the streak of fire from the corner of his eye as he stared at the small group of people who came closer down the lane. The thunder rumbled. The drum was still.

Not soldiers afterall, Jacob saw with disappointment. Not soldiers coming home from the war that Pa and the other farmers said surely would end soon, but just a group of men and women.

They came to the yard gate and stopped, standing together. They wore similar outer wear, black capes with hoods pulled over their heads. The capes were long, reaching to the ground. Their faces turned toward Jacob's father, shadowed, hidden.

Lightning threw a sudden white light, and within their dark hoods the faces disappeared and became round and wetly glistening, without noses or eyes, but with long, dark slashes, mouths opening, closing, like catepillars that had crawled from rotting flesh and grown huge.

The strange light faded, and the faces became real, human. Handsome men, beautiful ladies.

Jacob stood silent and chilled. The wind was rising, bringing huge droplets of rain onto the porch. What had he seen? Nothing, Pa would say.

The leaders' black capes tossed in the wind.

"Come in," Luther Boyd invited. "The storm is coming, you'll be drenched."

"Thank you, sir, for your offer," the man in front said with a smile. "But we ask only for shelter in the trees yonder."

He pointed to the line of woods to the west of the cornfield, down the road, across from the creek. He was young, Jacob saw more clearly now. The age of soldiers. But he wasn't in uniform. Nor was he crippled, hobbling home on crutches as some of the soldiers did. Men who had accepted the hospitality of Jacob's parents'.

Nor were any of them on crutches. They all smiled, and looked oddly alike, though their faces were different. Jacob found himself frowning as he looked from face to face. He didn't see the drum.

The leader said, "We ask permission to camp on your land, near the trees, for the remainder of the summer, perhaps. We are seeking souls. We would appreciate permission to build a brush arbor, and hold meetings in the evenings. With your permission. Our women will go and invite the farmers and their families while we prepare."

Jacob caught his breath. His heart quickened. Meetings, every evening?

He felt the presence of his mother behind him. Behind the screen door. She would not come onto the porch in her nightgown, but she was listening.

"Revival," Luther said, as if making a statement. Considering, perhaps.

Jacob's parents were members of the Christian church in town, seven miles away. Every Sunday the three of them rode in the buggy, pulled by ole Sally, to the church. Jacob felt it was almost sinful for him to enjoy going as much as he did. After the sermon it was like a holiday, with lunch on the tables beneath the trees in fitting weather, and games with the other youngsters. Hide and seek. Ante over. That was his favorite. Almost sinful.

Mama liked going too. He could see the glow in her face, every Sunday. To have meetings every night would indeed be great fun. It would mean the farmers coming, and the children. Every evening after the chores were done.

Thunder growled, clouds rolled like a wild animal turning in its lair. A few drops of rain fell. The night was rapidly falling. Let them build a brush arbor, let's have meetings. All the farm families would come, and their children. Unlike his own family, who had only one child, the others had many.

From behind the screen door, his mother's voice came softly.

"It will be all right, Luther."

Lightning shot between the ground and approaching clouds, and for a moment it looked as if it would strike the people who stood in the lane beyond the yard fence. They seemed not to notice. Their faces, with features strangely erased again by a sudden shifting of light to dark, grimaced with those long dark slits and waited. There was an odd whiteness to their glossy skin, as if they had never seen the sun.

Luther Boyd nodded his head.

"You're welcome to come in for the night."

Jacob counted swiftly. Eight? Ten? He couldn't be sure how many there were. But even if there were a dozen, there had been more under the roof of the big farmhouse in years past. For as long as Jacob could remember, the war had existed, just as daylight and dark and Sunday church had, and feeding the farm animals and working the farm. As long as he could recollect.

But the leader shook his head again, pledged his thanks, invited Papa and his family to attend their meetings, and turned away. In a group they turned, as if somehow joined. Jacob sighed relief. It was then he saw the child.

She walked behind them, like a small dog following its master.

He stared at her, but could only see her vaguely in the darkness that was punctuated with flashes of lightning. Her hair hung in a long braid down her back. She wore no bonnet, no cape. As if she didn't really belong with them. He couldn't see her face.

He wanted to walk with her, tell her he was eleven now since his birthday last month, ask her how old she was. Ask her where she came from. Ask her if she belonged to those people.

"Papa," he said, "did you see their faces in the lightning? Like—something—" *Inhuman.* He dared not say it.

"Hush your mouth. Go to bed."

The storm passed while Jacob slept, and the night grew still. He rose at dawn, eager to go watch the brush arbor go up, if Papa would allow him to hurry his chores. But already the poles stood in the ground on the edge of the cornfield. Eight poles, three on each side, two at the ends, with poles across the top, the brush roof in place. Even his father was amazed and Jacob heard him say to Mama, "They must have worked all night."

Jacob did his chores with an added zest. At sundown he was ready, his hair combed, his face and hands scrubbed. The farmers arrived, in their wagons and buggies. Wives brought quilts and chairs to sit on. Babies crawled on the quilts. Boys played. The meeting started with a drum roll.

He saw the preachers, men and women in their robes, and in the lantern light they were real afterall.

The little girl sat on the ground near the mourning bench they had built. Still, she didn't raise her head.

While the families attended the meetings, Jacob played with the boys in the field and the woods. He stopped waiting for a look from the girl. She would not be allowed to play anyway. Being a girl, and, he figured, a preacher's child, she would have to attend all the meetings.

Days of work passed slowly as Jacob looked for the setting sun and the arrival of the farm families. It was like a picnic every evening instead of once a week.

On the fourth day he noticed the changes. His father had all at once grown morose and quiet, his mother dreamy and distant. It was something Jacob noticed in the edge of his mind. Then he saw the farmers gathering in the afternoon before the meeting started. They stood in the shadows of the barn and spoke in low voices, their faces dark and serious. There was something in their eyes Jacob had never seen before. Was it fear? What were they afraid of?

He did his chores, and his father's, who seemed not to hear the bawling animals. As Jacob passed by once he heard a farmer say, "Nothin' Godly about them. Not like any preachers I ever heard. What are they?" Jacob didn't understand.

At the meeting that night Jacob stood quietly instead of playing games with the other boys. They, too, came to stand, in the dark beyond the lantern light of the brush arbor. He heard the preacher ask for souls, and was surprised to see his own mother go forward to the mourning bench and kneel. She was already a member of a church. Why would she go to this altar?

Jacob watched, uneasy and tense. She was on her knees, her body bowed, her head down. The preachers gathered around her, men and women both.

Then he noticed that most of the farmers were not in the dim and flickering lantern light of the brush arbor. They hadn't come to the meeting. Only their wives and children.

Jacob grew cold with dread. For three nights now he'd been running and playing, and something terrible had happened during that time. He didn't know what it was.

His mother rose and neighbors helped her walk, as if she had become very weak and ill. Families began leaving, the men appearing at last to take the horses' reins, and the night emptied.

At the house, Papa said, "Stay with your mother." His voice was harsh and angry and filled with that look that had been in the farmers' eyes. A terrible look that darkened Papa's eyes and voice and movements.

Jacob entered the house and went upstairs to his mother.

She asked him to bring her a glass of water, her voice so weak that at first he didn't hear what she'd said. He wanted to ask her what had happened, but he went instead to get the water.

Downstairs, from the kitchen window, he heard the sound of a galloping horse and he hurried out onto the back porch. His father was riding down the lane toward the road, faster than Jacob had ever seen him run one of his horses.

Jacob returned to his mother's bedroom. She lay in bed, her eyes closed. In the lamplight her face was like death. Her breath came slowly, in small gasps. Was she sleeping? He had never seen his mother sleep.

"Mama? Here's your water."

She didn't wake, nor move.

Jacob sat by her bedside staring at her face. For a long time he stared at her, waiting, while the cold dread built in him. Then he saw she was no longer breathing.

He ran, like a wild rabbit caught in a pen. He ran through the house, then turned and ran outside. *Where was Papa?* He ran into the moonlight. The preachers! He had to get them to help with his mother. Something was terribly wrong.

He ran across the lane and into the field, then saw the dark group of horses tied at the railing near the barn. Papa's horse! Other farmers' horses, too. The men were here, somewhere.

Moonlight covered the field like gauze and touched

upon the edge of the brush arbor. In the dark at the edge of the moonlight, figures moved. He saw the men, carrying shovels, picks, sticks of wood, and clubs. They went in silence toward the brush arbor.

Jacob ran into the field. His toe hooked on a clump of soil in the corn rows and he fell. He lay still, staring.

They were bringing the preachers, both men and women into the field. Clubbing, striking, dragging. Jacob lay on his stomach, half raised, stupefied, like a lizard on a cold rock. He watched as the scene played out in silence.

The shovels were used to dig one large grave. As the moon waned the bodies were thrown into the hole and the dirt shoveled into the grave. Dawn broke red in the east, and the men rode away.

Jacob crawled back to the edge of the field, then rose and ran into the house.

He found his mother staring in death at the ceiling.

Neighbors came, as they always did with a death. The house was filled with whispers.

Jacob wandered about in the yard and into the field, stunned by the changes, unable to accept his mother's death, and all he had seen in the last hours of the night. He found clubs, tossed aside, and his father's shovel. He stared, puzzled, horrified. There was no blood, just a strange, glistening, yellowish coating, like slime left by the crawling of slugs.

Then he saw the child.

She lived.

She was kneeling on the grave, busily working with something.

He went closer and stopped near the edge of the freshly turned earth. She was planting a small sapling. A sycamore twig.

She looked up, and spoke for the first time.

"As long as this tree lives, they'll stay buried. Don't ever destroy it, or they will rise again."

He couldn't speak, to ask her exactly what she meant.

In his frozen heart he knew. The lightning that first night had shown their real faces. They were something apart—something inhuman afterall.

She rose, turned and ran and disappeared beyond the brush arbor. He watched the woods where he last saw her, but she never returned.

As he grew older, as the brush arbor fell and became a pile of brush and poles in the edge of the field, he often woke at night, hearing the drum roll.

The sound always faded when he opened his eyes.

He searched the woods, at first, as if the girl would still be there.

But she was gone. Yet the sound kept coming when he slept. Perhaps a part of his dreams, a terrible dirge somehow connected with his mother's death.

He watched the tree grow, from a twig to a sapling, to magnificence.

He watched his son grow, and his son's son. Then his great-granddaughter was born. Her parents allowed him to name her, and he gave her his mother's name.

Beverly.

Then ...

1945

Beverly looked out the car window at the cornfields passing by. In her mind she saw the big sycamore tree in the middle of Grandpapa's cornfield, and she saw him, sitting on the swing, his white beard like Santa Claus.

She sat forward, her arms on the top of the seat between her mother and daddy.

"Daddy," she said, "Do you know what Grandpapa told me when I asked him why there was a tree in the middle of the cornfield?"

He laughed, reached back, and patted her on the head.

"Grandpapa's liable to tell you all kinds of stories."

"He said a little girl planted it a long time ago, when he was just a year older than I am."

Her parents looked at each other. Daddy was no longer laughing.

"He said it grows over a big grave. He said there was something very strange and bad about the people buried there. And he says even now sometimes he hears the sound of their drum, as if it's beating beneath the earth. He said don't ever let anyone cut down the tree."

"Beverly," her daddy said in his most serious voice, "just forget you ever heard that story, okay?"

She looked at the houses they were passing now as they entered town. She sat back.

"Okay."

REVIVALS

There came a perfect family ...

I.

The name on her office door read Beverly Boyd Inness. Everytime she saw it, a cloud of loneliness marred her day for a few minutes, then she made herself get to work. Until three years ago the name on the door had read Clark Inness. In those days, before her husband's death, she came down to the office only when she was meeting him for lunch, or wanted to talk to him or just see him. They had married young, and reared their one child, a son, together in the most traditional of ways. They had taken Mel to church regularly to give him a religious background, although neither of them was particularly religious. They had sent him to the best of schools, and Clark had lived to see Mel become an attorney.

Then the cancer had come.

Clark continued to work. Their real estate holdings grew. The town grew. But slowly he deteriorated, and finally he gave up.

At the age of fifty-five he died, and Beverly had become a widow at the same age.

She stood at the window of the office that had been Clark's and looked out onto the private little garden that she herself had planted and decorated over twenty years ago. The fountain had been a continual source of comfort for both her and Clark. The bird feeder was a place where not only birds came but squirrels too, and lately, a couple of little striped chippies.

Sometimes she felt he was there, in the office garden, sitting on the swing, waiting for her to come out. They had eaten lunch there occasionally, watching the squirrels and birds. Clark would have liked the chippies, she thought.

But there was work to do. She turned away from the window and returned to the map on the wall. Work had saved her. Instead of closing his office, she had decided to come and do her best. She had always worked with him from her space at home. He had never isolated her from the business. She also had studied architecture, and often from her desk at home had drawn the plans for the houses he built. Only after he had gone into larger buildings, had she drawn only for her own entertainment.

The door opened and the secretary who had worked in the outer office for more than twenty years looked in.

"I'll be leaving now, Beverly. It's a few minutes after six."

"Oh, is it?" Beverly glanced at the clock on the wall. Almost six-thirty. "I'm sorry, Glenda, I didn't mean to keep you for so long."

"No problem. I might be a little late in the morning."

A little late for Glenda was usually ten or fifteen minutes. "That's fine. Goodnight, Glenda."

The office building seemed inordinately quiet with Glenda gone. The occupants in other offices of the sprawling, U-shaped, one-story office building, which the Inness Corporation had build twenty-three years ago, obviously had cleared out too. Probably an hour ago.

Beverly looked one more time at the map on the wall. When she was growing up the town consisted of a few major streets, a square with stores around it and a park in the center, a few restaurants, one post office of about five thousand square feet, and three banks. The usual for a town of around 7,000 to 10,000 residents. Big, old houses on large tree-filled lots had been built years earlier near the main part of town, on the square. Beverly had grown up in one of those, and still lived there.

But now the town had quadrupled. The new post office covered an entire block, a Wal-Mart superstore you could get lost in had replaced two older ones. Banks and branches of banks proliferated. The edges of town were blurred, and growing yearly, joining the blurred edges of other towns that thirty years ago were five to ten miles away. Included now in the city limits was part of the old Boyd land, six hundred acres of prime real estate. Another hundred acres was still in the county, soon to be annexed.

It had turned out to be ideal for the new housing developments, with the creeks and trees that had been left undisturbed. Now, the newest Boyd-Inness project was a shopping mall that would not only serve their town, but others nearby. It was being built where the old farmhouse had stood, covering forty acres, including the parking lots, that once were part of the yard, garden, barnyard, and cornfields.

There were times when she was a little sorry about the old farm being covered in concrete, especially the particular site that was now being worked on. She had all the money she would ever need. But there was her son, Mel, who now was an assistant D.A., his fiancée and the children she hoped they'd have. He was engaged to be married to Paula Bowers, a neighbor girl with a background similar to his own. They wanted at least two children. He was in favor of the mall. As he had said, there can never be too much family money. So the work had begun a few weeks ago. The leveling of land for the concrete and the buildings of the mall.

She also had feelings of pride. She, Beverly Boyd Inness, had helped the town grow.

She let the blind down on the picture window that looked out over the small, private office garden, made sure the outside door was locked, and gathered up her things.

The janitorial people were at work in the outer office when she left. She knew them each by name, and mentioned each name as she said goodnight. They knew her name also, but chose to call her Mrs. Inness.

She went out to her car, one of the last in the parking lot, and drove the few blocks home. The moment she turned off the engine, she heard Whiskers and Babs meowing beyond the garage door that led into the house.

Welcome voices in an otherwise silent house.

"I'm coming," she called, and entered the back hall.

She bent to pet the two cats that waited for her. They purred loudly and curled around her ankles. She picked them both up so she could walk freely.

The engine of the bulldozer roared. The large machine spun smoothly around under the guidance of Tom Roush's hand. He pointed the big blade in the direction of the old sycamore tree and then stopped, the engine idling.

He hated to see it go down. It was a great old sycamore, its upper limbs snow white, reaching toward the sky like the bleached bones of an ancient skeleton. But life was still there, trembling on the twigs in the form of new green leaves. He had sat beneath it, this past week, to eat his lunch. The sun, almost out of sight behind the trees across the field, glowed through the limbs of the sycamore, turning its fresh green leaves red and transparent.

The land had once been a large farm, but now the town was eating up the land, and where there had been pastures and cornfields, concrete would soon lie smooth and white, drawing the heat of the sun like a magnet, the cool earth buried beneath it.

Already, to the east, the streets of the town had encroached. Just last week the big old farmhouse that had stood more than a hundred years on this land was torn down. Tom had bulldozed the debris into a pile. He could remember when the farm was a working farm, the barns still standing, the old house still looking good, kept up, new coats of fresh paint as needed, although it was probably a hundred and fifty years old. It had been owned by the Boyd family, and the present owner, Beverly Boyd Inness, was building a shopping mall here where once her ancestor's farm lay. Tom wondered if any of the Boyd family hated to see the land go the way he did. At heart he was a country boy, even if he had lived in town all his life.

The engine hummed in his ears. Over to his left, near their pickups, stood his bosses. Brent Salisaw, a big man with thick dark hair and square jaw, as square as his shoulders, leaned with his arms back, his elbows resting on the pickup bed. Beside him, also leaning, his arms crossed, was Brent's dad, Carl. They didn't resemble each other in the least. Carl was smaller, leaner, fair in complexion with thinning, fine hair, half bald. Off behind, just now driving away, the rest of the crew left machinery parked and silent. The day's work had ended for them.

It should be ending for Tom. This was Friday evening, time to pick up Davey and Ali. Time once again to wrench his heart out, going to the next town down west to a strange house to see for just a moment Adrianne, the girl he had loved and married and who had grown bored with him. Or some damned thing. Anger had vied with heartache these past weeks as Adrianne did her thing, while the kids were torn between her and home. And him, their daddy. Didn't she ever think of him? That he might be important in the lives of his children? Didn't she think of them? The security of their home, of growing up in a family together instead of torn by divorce? What had he done to cause her to leave? There was no answer, only tears.

But now the tree . . .

The sun was sinking, and he had orders from Brent to bulldoze the tree this evening. Get it down and out of the way.

The three of them, Brent, Carl, and he, had stood together, time passing, and discussed the tree. Tom had tried to save it, though he knew it wasn't practical.

"It's a damn shame to take that tree out. A parking lot as big as this one's going to be ought to have room for one old tree. Isn't there any way to save it? Pave around it?"

Carl grunted sympathetically. "I've seen some of the older parking lots with trees left along the sides, but never one in the middle."

Brent laughed. "Imagine the look on Mrs. Inness's face when she shows up, and there's this tree in the middle of her mall's parking lot."

"There's one thing for sure," Tom said. "It'd be a novelty. People might like it."

"You serious?" Brent asked.

Tom shrugged, looking toward the top of the old, tall, spreading tree. "They could fix a little park beneath it, with benches."

Brent turned serious too, and stood with his fists on his hips looking into the upper branches.

"You surround that tree with concrete, even allowing what would seem to be plenty of room, and you've got a slow death. In a couple of years the tree doesn't put on leaves, and the next year it's dead."

"But then, after all the old trees are dozed out," Tom said, "they go ahead and plant a bunch of young ones in fancy little rows here and there."

Carl laughed sardonically. "That's the way it goes. I think they call it landscaping."

Carl was the senior partner, but it was obvious to Tom that he was turning the business over to Brent. Brent now made the decisions.

Brent started moving away. "River birch. Grows fast and easy. They never get very tall, or need much uncovered ground. Let's get to work."

He made a motion with his hand for the work to proceed, turned and walked over to his pickup. Nearby the bulldozer idled, waiting to be used. The angle of the red sun changed, the shadows deepened. The last streaks of red were gone.

Carl gave Tom a nod, and followed Brent.

Tom climbed back onto the bulldozer, revved it up and moved closer to the tree.

Then he paused. But he couldn't wait any longer. The magnificent old tree had to come down. Progress had no room for it. It was just too damn bad that someone who was kind of a tree nut anyway happened to be the bulldozer operator in this case. Maybe it came from bulldozing too many trees as the town grew larger and demanded more ground.

Fortunately, the new housing developments were keeping trees, giving one-half to one acre plats to each house, with the floor plans arranged accordingly. He had recently bought one of those new houses for his own family.

Then, a few weeks later Adrianne decided she didn't want to live with him any longer. *Why?* He wondered if there was another man. She had said no, she just wanted to find herself. He thought that sort of thing had gone out of style, but apparently not. He'd said in reply, without sympathy he now had to admit, "Where the hell do you think you've disappeared to? I haven't noticed you missing lately."

It was definitely the wrong thing to say. Her answer came back to haunt him everytime he entered the house.

"Well you just take a look, old buddy, the next time you come home!"

His fist tightened in bitterness on the gear stick. He was scared to be alone, but he was still feeling these bursts of anger at what he felt was her self-centeredness.

The bulldozer blade touched the grey-flaked trunk of the tree. The top of the tree shuddered. Tom eased the dozer into high gear. The tree trembled, twigs and leaves fell from above. The top leaned slowly.

Tom backed the dozer away, and came at the leaning tree from a slightly different angle. Out of the corner of his eye he saw that Carl had come closer. Roots of the tree had emerged from the broken earth. There were small scurrying movements in the grass as insects deserted the tree trunk.

The bulldozer pushed, its treads rising from the ground and riding the tree trunk. The tree shook as if caught in a storm. It leaned further and further. Slowly, it gave up its hold on the earth, then with a thunderous roar, it fell.

Tom backed the bulldozer away. Beneath the noise of its engine, the sound of the falling tree continued, as if the earth reverberated with an echo. Then another sound rose. The sudden, loud beating of a drum, eerily close. An odd sense of fear slid coldly over Tom's arms. The short reddish hair lifted like spikes.

Tom saw Carl turn, looking around, perhaps, for the source of the drum. Tom's eyes followed Carl's, and Brent's, who stood several feet behind Carl. But there was no one. No marching band anywhere within sight.

The flat farmland stretched to the north, ending half a mile away at the edge of a housing development. To the south across the street where rolling land began, another tree-filled development was occupied with families. Too far away to produce the sounds that he had heard.

Tom eased off the engine, and the drum roll faded,

leaving the evening with only the throb of the idling
motor and the sounds of frogs in a pond to the north.
Leaving, too, the soft echoes of the other sound in
Tom's ears, like a bitter aftertaste.

"Did you hear something?" Carl asked no one in
particular, still looking about as if he doubted his own
ears.

No one answered.

Brent started walking briskly away. "I'm going
home," he said. "Call it a day, Tom."

Tom sat a moment longer on the bulldozer, looking
at the tree. Watching it settle with only a final whisper.

Its leafy green top spread onto the weedy ground.
The huge, long trunk lay still. Tree roots trembled in
the air above the opened hole. He felt like crying.

There would be more work with the dozer tomorrow,
pushing the tree away from the hole where the roots
had grown so that the treecutters could get to it, then
pushing dirt back into the hole to fill it in and level it
for the concrete. Right now the hole was about the size
of the cab of Carl's pickup truck. Half of the root system
had risen into the air as the tree fell, and now shadowed
the hole where the other half of the roots remained.

Tom saw Carl hurry forward suddenly, stopping on
the edge of the crumbling hole to stare down into the
mass of roots and earth cavity. As Tom backed the bulldozer farther away he caught a glimpse of something
pale and round, like fat, white, oily worms grown huge
among the roots that remained in the dark hole.

Carl stepped closer on the unsteady edge of the hole
and bent stiffly forward at the waist as if he were going
to dive in. His mouth made motions of speech drowned
beneath the idling engine.

Tom turned off the switch and heard Carl shout in
the sudden silence, *"What in everlasting hell is that?"*

Brent came forward again from his pickup, walking
through the deepening shadows with long strides. Tom
followed behind him.

Then Carl's voice shouted again, incredulous.

"It's a goddamned grave! There's people in there!"

Something that resembled human bodies were palely visible in the dark hole. As Tom peered down he still had the impression of immense worms, colorless, coiling around the roots.

"Doesn't that look like a grave?" Carl sounded as if he were demanding an answer from someone, somewhere, dumbfounded, his voice still loud as if he hadn't become aware of the silence that surrounded them.

Over toward the trees, in another of the new housing developments, the bark of a dog came joyously with the shouts of children. A wavering and oddly alien sound in the still air of rapidly darkening evening.

Brent stood staring down in silence. Carl too had stopped questioning what he saw. He still leaned forward at the waist as if he had frozen in that position.

The round pale thing that curved around one root took on the shape of an arm as if changing before Tom's eyes into something human. The hand lay palm up. The head was turned, face still half buried in the soil. Hairline tree roots, like thin wires, seemed part of the pale hair. An eerie chill raced up Tom's spine, covered his body. He wanted suddenly to get out of there.

"It's not possible," he heard someone say, and recognized his own voice.

Brent spoke. "I'd better get some help out here on this." Still, he didn't move.

Carl straightened. Tom got a glimpse of his face, almost as pale as that half face in the grave.

They stood together as the twilight deepened, settling around them, closing them into the world of the opened grave. The barking of the dog and shouts of the children ceased. Silence fell.

Tom's nervous thoughts raced to his children, waiting for him. He was supposed to have been there an hour ago, at the rented house where they were now living with their mother. He could see them, Davey, still so vulnerable at age nine, and Ali, still Tom's baby at age three. His babies, both of them. They'd be standing on the front walk with their little suitcases that had "going to Grandma's" in red letters on the sides.

They were an excuse, too, to get away from here. He'd had a bad feeling all the time about uprooting this old tree.

"I gotta go get my kids," he said. "I'm already late. Do you need me, Brent? Carl?" He already had his check for the week's work in his billfold. Brent always brought the checks around in the middle of the afternoon on Fridays.

His question seemed to stir both men.

"Oh no," Brent said, "You go on, I'll get to the truck and call for some assistance."

"Who're you going to call?" Carl asked, following a few steps as Brent turned toward his pickup and the telephone.

Tom saw Brent pause. "I don't know. Police? Sheriff, I suppose. We're in the county here."

Tom felt as if he shouldn't leave them. Not yet. In his ten years of working for the Salisaw Construction Company they had never uncovered anything like this before. But if he didn't leave it would be fully dark before he reached the neighboring town six miles down the road where Davey and Ali were waiting. And if Adrianne had a date, which she probably did, she wouldn't be very happy about him being late.

Yet he felt as if he should hang around even though he wanted more than anything to get away.

He followed Brent and Carl to the pickup. Maybe he could use the phone and call Davey and tell him he'd be an hour late. Hang around and see if he was needed.

Brent dialed, listened, and shook the telephone.

"Of all the damn times for this thing to act up!"

"What's wrong?" Carl asked.

"Damned if I know. It's dead. I have to go find a telephone."

Well, so much for calling Davey. Tom looked over his shoulder. The tree top had stopped all movement, the leaves hung still, the branches gathering darkness.

"Do you want me to hang around, Brent?" Tom asked. "Until you get back?"

He felt that fidgety nervousness that meant he was itching to go, to get finished whatever he needed to do. Yet he hated to walk away.

Carl said, "No, no, Tom. Go on and get the kids. I'll stay here and keep an eye on things till Brent gets back. I don't think there's any hurry. Whoever's in that grave isn't going anywhere."

Tom nodded, yet delayed a moment longer. Brent got into his company truck and started the engine.

Tom turned away, throwing one last glance toward the hole that had become more than the former home of tree roots. The impression of huge worms with faces that materalized in the air stayed with him as he approached his car, parked beyond Carl's truck.

More than one face, half covered by dirt.

As he drove away something occurred to him. The state of preservation. The grave had to be old. The bodies a long time buried. Wouldn't they have decayed by now? Leaving only bones?

2.

Carl sat on the front left fender of his pickup. He had pulled it up close to the trunk of the tree. The hole gaped open in front of him. The bodies were still vaguely visible there in the hole, in the darkness, almost as if they glowed in the dark, like some worms on the bank of a river which he had seen when he was night fishing.

He had tried to understand what he thought he saw. At first, the moment after the tree fell and the hole opened, he had thought they were some kind of strange fungus growth. Or huge worms, soft, glossy and maggotlike. When he first walked up to look, those pale bodies didn't appear to be human. Then he couldn't believe his eyes. Half covered in dirt, intertwined with fine roots, twisted around larger roots, they began to look like human bodies. More than one, it seemed. He saw a foot protruding at one place, an arm at another. It appeared to be soft, round, feminine. The foot was larger, a man's foot, an old shoe half-rotted off.

Brent and Tom hadn't been gone more than three or four minutes, but the light had seemed to go with them. Suddenly. In the east a moon was rising, like a reflection of the sun that had sunk in a glowing ball of red.

Some fine time for Brent's phone to go out, but it

was no surprise to Carl. That was why he hadn't wanted one when Brent got his and offered to get one for Carl. "What do I need with a damned car phone? I can say all I want to say when I get to work." If he wanted to contact one of the guys when they were off work, he called from home. But in the past years it hadn't been necessary. Brent took care of much of the on-the-job business. Nor did he need a phone to call home. There was no one at home to call anymore, since Annie had died. That was going on three years now. Even when she was alive, he had never found reason to call. She always knew he'd be there for supper.

He found himself reaching to his left shirt pocket. With a disgusted, surprised grunt he lowered his hand and placed it flat on the fender beside him. The heat of the sun was still in the metal, slightly warmer than the palm of his hand. Reaching for a cigarette even though he hadn't smoked for ten years? Hadn't even thought about smoking for five or six years, and was half choked sometimes by the guys who smoked around him.

Must be more nervous than he thought. He peered at his watch. The luminous dial reminded him of the things in the hole. Only three more minutes since the last time he checked? Time could drag. Then again, the seasons slid into one another in almost frightening speed, like a snowball rolling downhill, faster and faster the older he got.

How could a grave, that contained more than one person, more even than two or three, have gotten under the roots of a large, old tree? The tree must have been at least a hundred and fifty years old. Trees didn't get that large in less time. The tree roots looked as if they had grown around the bodies. How was that possible?

Carl found himself staring so hard into the hole that his head took on a nervous ache. He could see nothing there now. A dungeonlike dark had filled it. Moonlight slanted across the roots that lifted into the air in a pale, whitish glow, not bright enough nor high enough to throw light into the hole.

Carl lifted his head and made himself look at the dim, twinkling lights through the trees on the other side of the street. The housing development was probably a quarter of a mile away. The street lights were like distant planets seen through the dark trees. People lived there. Not far away. But Carl had never felt so alone.

Nor so nervous.

He had always been a calm-natured person. Taking life as it came. He and Annie had celebrated their forti-eth wedding anniversary just two months before she died suddenly of a heart attack. They had married when they were kids, she eighteen and he twenty, and Brent was their first child, born a year later. The three of them had sort of grown up together, happily, having fun. Then Annie had two more babies, both dead at birth. Life had shown them its serious side, in one of its hardest lessons. Don't ever take anything for granted, Annie had said after that. Still, even with losing their two little girls, life had been easy for them. A hell of a lot easier than it was for some he had known.

The business had done well. Debt had never plagued them, although they'd had to work hard to get things paid for. Then, they'd planned to get a motor home and start traveling. This year, it would have been, when he turned sixty-two. Brent would continue the business. Carl and Annie would be on the road, seeing their own state, neighboring states, parks, mountains, seashores. They had planned to take some of the grandkids now and then. Holly, their oldest granddaughter, who was ten when her grandmother died, was scheduled to be the first. They had been planning to take her and travel up to Canada and around. A two week trip. Annie and Holly had been planning the trip when Annie suffered the beginning of the attack that killed her three days later.

Carl stared at the lights across the way. He saw one,

two, then another, the first blinking out, like stars beyond how many atmospheres? The trees, covering and uncovering the lights. Their leaves moving in the breeze that came like waves from the south.

His mind settled on the grandkids. The number one delight in his life now. He enjoyed getting all four of them in Annie's small sedan, and taking them for special ice cream treats. The youngest, Vinny, a tow-headed boy who was only three years old but talked more than his five-year-old brother, Bryon, was, Carl admitted deep in his own heart, one of his favorites. Although he really loved all of them the same, Vinny was somehow special. Of course, Holly, the oldest girl, was special too. As far as that was concerned, so was the second child, Kara, with her dark hair and eyes and looking so much like her daddy that everytime he looked at her, he was reminded of Brent when he was eleven years old. Kara was more of a tomboy than Holly.

What was a grave doing beneath a tree that was probably a hundred and fifty years old? He hadn't noticed a disturbance in the earth around the tree. He was sure there hadn't been. Grass, unmowed, grew right up to the trunk. The one piece of clothing he had seen, the old shoe, had nearly rotted away. Only a chunk of the sole and a darkened piece of the upper was visible in the dirt, falling away from the pale foot. He hadn't gotten a good look at any of it. The light in the strange grave hadn't been good even then, before the last light had gone across the land.

He had seen what looked like a face, partly covered by dirt, tiny hairline roots growing across the head like hair. Or maybe it was hair. In another spot by other roots nearby he had seen what definitely was a human head. He saw an arm curled around a root. It was almost as if whoever was buried in that grave was working their way out. As if in a month, or a week, they would have risen through the ground.

God!

Strange how the mind worked. It seemed actually to have a will all its own, and took pathways a person didn't want.

What crazy thoughts was he going to have next?

He tried to see the face of his watch again. With the help of the moon he made out that another five minutes had passed. Eighteen minutes since Brent and Tom had left. It seemed hours.

Why wasn't Brent coming back by now?

It was only about a mile down to the convenience store on the corner. Give Brent another five minutes, then surely he'd be back.

Carl peered toward the outlet from the field, the narrow road they had made for the machinery and trucks. No lights turning his way. A few cars moved on the street, their sounds reaching him like streams of water over a distant dam.

He looked upward at the sky. A few stars were beginning to shine now. Part of the milky way appeared overhead.

He began to drum his fingertips on the fender of the car.

The sound, soft and close, grew louder and became separate from the drumming of his fingertips. He grew still, scarcely breathing. His fingers rested, and the sound continued. The same drum roll he had heard when the tree fell. There was a quality about it that shot cold terror into his heart.

He looked around without moving. Moonlight touched the field with its pale whitish light. There were no shadows, no one walking with a drum. The only shadow hung like a dungeon over the hole and in the shelter of the tree.

The beating drum sounded close, muted, somewhere in the darkness that surrounded the tree.

Carl turned and stared.

Faintly he made out a figure standing near the tree top. Tall, formless except for the head, as if whoever it was wore a long robe, he stood in the shadows thrown by the top of the tree. In front of the pickup. Not more than twenty feet away. A draped figure, motionless, darker than the shadows in which he stood.

Carl sat unmoving, his mouth hanging open yet unable to make a sound. He should call out, who are you? What do you want? But he sat encased in a nether-world coldness that made his skin so sensitive it felt as if it had been touched by raw electricity.

The figure in the darkness didn't move either. But the sound of the drum filled the air, louder, closer.

In the dark hole movement began. Pale figures started rising, as if the drum had awakened them.

Without conscious thought Carl found himself leaping off the fender, running to the pickup door and climbing in. He turned on the pickup lights.

The figure was not there. Nothing stood between the pickup and the fallen tree. The top of the tree, lying still on the ground, did not have so much as a leaf stirring.

His stare switched to the hole, slightly to his left, out of the twin beams of the truck lights. His heart pounded against his ribs. A sharp pain spiked up the back of his neck. Figures stirred again, in the shadows beyond the lights.

In the peripheral glow from the truck lights, a human figure rose. Carl stared through the open pickup window. A man, perfectly preserved, reached up, grasped a root of the tree and lifted himself from the hole. Then he walked past the door of the pickup, so close Carl could have reached out and touched him. He wore something long and black that left only his head partially uncovered.

Moonlight glinted on his hair, turning it white. He looked straight ahead as if he didn't see Carl, or the truck, or the lights that partly illuminated his path. Carl saw a straight, perfectly formed nose, sharply etched lips, high cheek bones, a broad forehead. A handsome

man, in that second of vision as he walked past the
window.

The dark hole suddenly erupted with movement. Like
pale snakes, bloated maggots, they writhed upwards. At
the edge of the hole they separated, and like the man,
each took on a perfect human form, visible to Carl in
the pale moonlight, and the teasing edge of the truck
lights. In silence they moved, their bodies draped in
black, their heads lifted. One by one they crawled out
of the hole left by the roots of the tree and passed out
of Carl's vision. Men, women, young, perfect. Strange,
rare beauty, in the face of each one.

Carl stared straight ahead, his muscles paralyzed, his
chin dropped. A pounding thundered in his head.

Brent's pickup bounced over the clods of dirt that
had been turned up when Tom bulldozed a quick road
onto the street. Behind him came the car of a deputy
sheriff. He had called both the city and county police,
but the proposed mall was just outside the city limits,
and the city police didn't consider it their job. An old
grave? It didn't interest them at the moment. Later,
maybe.

Brent had waited at the convenience store to lead
the deputy into the field. He had waited in growing
agitation, checking his watch. Thirty minutes. Forty-five.
The night grew darker, moonlight like clabbered milk.

He kept thinking about Dad out there alone, and it
bothered him. Even though Carl had always been able
to take care of himself. And there really was nothing of
danger there, just the strangest thing he'd ever seen
uncovered in his years in the construction business.

Well, the county had been complaining about being
short of funds to hire more deputies. They wanted to
add a one cent sales tax to help hire more officers. It
was Brent's opinion that if any of those naysayers, the

aginers, ever needed a deputy in a hurry they wouldn't be so fast to vote against the one cent tax.

Brent's pickup lights picked up the tree, and his dad's truck. Carl was no longer leaning against the truck. He was probably taking a nap in the cab.

Brent pulled up and parked, headlights pointed directly at the spidery collection of roots that hung in the air above the dark hole in the earth.

The deputy parked behind and to the side of him, where his car lights further illuminated the hole. He got out of the car, a sturdy flashlight in his hand.

"The moon is almost bright enough not to need lights," he said as he came toward Brent.

Brent waited. Sergeant Crowell, he had introduced himself. He reminded Brent somewhat of Tom, slender, slightly stooped, thin faced. He moved quickly, nervously. His actions said, let's get this over with, I've got the whole damned county to patrol.

"Yeah, right," Brent said, his glance passing quickly over Carl's pickup, the tree on the ground. Where was Dad?

"This the place?" Sergeant Crowell inquired, aiming the flashlight beam at the hole.

"That's it. My dad's here someplace, keeping an eye on things."

He walked with the deputy to the edge of the hole. The flashlight beam swept over the uplifted roots, the clods of dirt, the few small rocks. Bits of dirt fell into the hole from the roots in the air like slow, sporadic raindrops.

"That was some tree," Crowell said, the flashlight beam following the length of the tree trunk, the bushy limbs.

"Yeah, hard to push over."

"A body here, you say." Crowell squatted, and swept the light beam throughout the hole.

"More than one . . . at least three, though it was hard

to tell. Didn't see them clearly. A man's leg, a woman's arm . . ." He stopped, looking puzzled and frowning. Nothing now. Not even the half-rotted old shoe.

Brent saw the dark dirt, roots still clinging, other roots crossing the top of the hole like a seive. He stood in silence staring down into the hole, watching the beam of the light probe every dark crevice. He leaned farther forward, his eyes searching for the bodies he had seen. He pointed.

"They were there!" But then added lamely, "It was getting pretty dark—" They hadn't used a light to look in. They hadn't thought they needed to. How could they have been mistaken? "I could swear . . ."

The deputy said nothing. He continued to shine the light throughout the hole, one side to another, covering every inch. Behind them another car pulled up. Two doors closed.

When Brent looked around he saw that the city police had joined them afterall. Two men walked over to stand behind the deputy, looking into the hole, talking in low voices. He heard someone laugh.

Where was Dad? Suddenly he felt frantic to find Carl. What had happened?

He went to the pickup. Carl sat in the shadows within the truck, his body thrown stiffly back against the seat, his head held high, hands gripping the steering wheel.

"Dad? *Dad?*"

Carl didn't answer. Brent jerked the pickup door open. He reached in and put his hand on Carl's shoulder. Carl seemed not to notice he was there. His body was like wire, tight and tense, beneath Brent's hand.

"Dad!"

Brent saw that Carl's chin was trembling. Drool angled down from the corner of his open mouth. His eyes stared straight ahead.

One word exploded in Brent's mind. *Stroke.*

"Call an ambulance!" he yelled. "Something's wrong

with my dad. I think he's had a stroke! *Call an ambulance!*"

The men stood quiet a moment, looking toward Brent and Carl, then one of them ran back to the city patrol car. The other two hurried over to the pickup.

"Let's get him out of there," Crowell said.

"Dad?" Brent tried again, pleading for an answer. *Not a stroke! God, let it not be a stroke!* Carl didn't respond.

The city policeman shouldered in past Brent and helped Carl out of the truck. Carl moved stiffly. Brent was trying awkwardly to help the officer make Carl comfortable on the soft grass of the field beside the truck when suddenly Carl reared up. He jammed out both arms and shoved them away.

Brent backed off, weakened with relief. At least Carl wasn't paralyzed on one side as so often happened.

"Dad, you okay?"

Carl didn't answer. He reached back, got a hold on the pickup door and steadied himself. He tried to speak, but only a croaking sound emerged.

An ambulance siren suddenly burst through the air. It must have been close, Brent thought vaguely. With its red lights spinning, the driver somehow found the trail into the field.

Brent half expected Carl to shove the ambulance attendants away too, but he didn't. He let the two officers who came out of the cab help him into the back of the vehicle.

At the doors, Brent called in to his dad, "I'll follow you in my truck."

Carl looked toward him, but made no sound. He looked, Brent thought, as if something terrible had happened to his brain, if not a stroke, then a blood clot, an aneurysm. Something. At least he was still alive. He wished he hadn't left Carl alone.

* * *

"Suppose we ought to follow them to the hospital?"
Alton Fullerton asked as Brent Salisaw's pickup bounced
in the wake of the ambulance.

"I don't know. What could we do?"

Crowell was still searching the area immediately surrounding the tree. He had gone all the way around it,
shining his light into the heavy branches. For no reason
other than to see what was there. Nothing but leaves,
limbs, and one bird nest now empty.

"What do you suppose they saw?" Fullerton asked.

"Damned if I know," Crowell said. "I took the call,
and Brent Salisaw was waiting for me at the store down
the road. He didn't strike me as the type of man to
make up stories."

"They claimed there was a grave underneath that
tree? How the hell could there be a grave there, anyhow?
That's nothing but a mass of tree roots that's been in
that hole. Whoever buried someone there would've had
to dig through a helluva lot of roots. Why bother, when
there's a whole field? Doesn't make sense."

Crowell drew a deep breath. He was back at the hole,
shining the flashlight at every root that still clung to
the disturbed earth. Wade Miles, from the city police,
had gone to get his own flashlight. The car lights angled
over the hole and into the huge mass of roots that hung
in the air. There was a mixture of feelings in the air, it
seemed to him. The strangeness of seeing a big tree
down, and the cavern its roots had left in the ground.
Itself like a death. Then the moonlight, so pale, so
inefficient. There was a strange mood, too, like fear.
Behind him one of the men began to laugh again. He
stopped abruptly.

"It'd be funny if it weren't for the old guy getting
the stroke."

Crowell felt the grin on his face, unbidden. His knees
were beginning to ache. He rose, feeling as if he'd been
in a squat for hours.

"Yeah." He turned the flashlight off.

"Well," Wade Miles said, "I didn't see any body, did you?"

"More than one," Crowell informed them. "Supposed to have been a mass grave of some kind."

They stood together, in the edge of car lights, in the light of the moon, each looking over the other's shoulders. In Crowell's view now was the street beyond and the few cars that drifted along it.

"Carl and Brent Salisaw Construction Company, the sign said," Sergeant Fullerton repeated. "This is where that new mall is going up, isn't it?"

"Yeah," Crowell said. "They had pushed over this tree, the last thing they'd done today. It was already past sundown."

Officer Wade Miles turned away shaking his head. "Well, there's no grave. Not beneath that tree. I don't know what they saw, but it wasn't a skull. Probably a rock. With a couple of holes."

He went toward his car laughing. Then again he stopped suddenly. At the car door he paused.

"Kinda weird out here, ain't it?"

The city policemen got into their car and drove slowly out of the field.

Crowell, alone, listened to the silence. A whisper of sound came from the tree. A breeze, stirring the leaves. The street emptied. No cars on the road now, and silence from the areas in the distance where house and street lights glimmered among trees.

Crowell turned his flashlight back on and went again to look into the hole.

Nothing.

Brent Salisaw hadn't looked or acted like a man who imagined things. Carl Salisaw wasn't playing games. And like one of the city guys had said, it was weird out here.

Crowell turned off his flashlight and walked quickly back to his car. Nothing to report, just a call back to say he was leaving the site.

As he drove away he looked back. The old tree was a black hill in the moonlight.

Like Wade Miles had said, it would be funny if it weren't for the old man having to be hauled away in an ambulance.

He decided to call or check at the hospital to see if he was all right.

3.

Brent drove right behind the ambulance. When it parked at the emergency room doors, Brent slammed his truck into the closest parking spot and ran to be there when his dad was helped out. He wasn't surprised to see Carl shoving at the male attendant and trying more politely to get rid of the female. They didn't know what to do with him. Their patient was uncooperative. He wanted no help.

"Sir . . ." the man said.

Color had returned to Carl's face. Instead of looking leached of blood, he now appeared to be flooded. His face and neck were dark red, his hair hanging forward over one side of his forehead. His eyes glittered. They were bright blue, nothing foggy about them. They would be bright blue when he was ninety. He considered himself as capable as anyone. Brent felt drained suddenly of the tension which had driven him.

"I'm all right!" Carl croaked, sounding as if he hadn't used his voice in a long time. "Leave me alone, there's nothing wrong with me."

"Sir . . ."

The attendant put out his hand again, and Carl dodged past.

"Take me home, Brent," Carl said. "Where's my

truck? Take me back . . ." He stopped. Brent saw him blink and waver, and some of the redness leached out of his face.

A couple of nurses had appeared suddenly down the ramp. One of them pushed a wheelchair.

"Come on, we're taking you for a ride."

Carl turned, his expression a mass of confusion. Brent took his arm and to his surprise Carl allowed himself to be led.

But then he balked. "Not in a damned wheelchair. Nobody is pushing me around in a wheelchair. Not yet."

"Go on, Dad. Let's let the doctor look at you. It won't take long."

"I can walk."

A nurse smiled gently at him. "It's just our policy, sir. I'm sure you can walk, but if you didn't ride, I wouldn't have a job."

He didn't argue anymore. He sat down in the wheelchair as if he'd been shoved.

Brent followed behind him. The ambulance attendants went back to their vehicle, probably glad to be rid of this patient, Brent thought. Thank God Dad seemed to be okay, but he wanted to know for sure if there had been a stroke.

The nurses left them in the admittance room. Carl sat in silence, his head bowed, his hands lying limply on the arms of the wheelchair.

"Tired, Dad?"

Carl shook his head. That was typical, Brent thought. If he were tired he wouldn't admit it. Brent himself had been surprised when Carl began to back off from doing so much of the business and began referring customers to Brent. He still worked, everyday, but at times he took off early in the afternoons and went fishing.

Brent always asked him the next morning, "Catch anything, Dad?"

Carl invariably answered, "Naw. Some small ones. Tossed 'em back."

Brent knew. His dad had never been a hunter or owner of guns. His only weapon had been a fishing rod. But as he'd grown older he had stopped actually catching fish. If he got one on his hook, he gently removed it and threw it back to its natural habitat and let it go. It was the river that drew him. The peace, the tranquility, the beauty. The sound of flowing water. The beauty and variety of the fish swimming below the surface.

The admittance took a very few minutes, and by that time the doctor had arrived.

While Carl was being taken up to the room where he would stay a couple of days for tests, Brent told Dr. White, "I was afraid at first he'd had a stroke. He was white as a sheet, sitting in his pickup with his hands so tight on the wheel they looked clamped, and he couldn't speak."

Dr. White nodded, "Sounds like you might be right."

"But then after they got him here to the hospital he didn't want help. His voice had returned."

"Good. Good." He touched Brent's shoulder. "We'll give him a thorough test, and let you know."

Leaving the emergency room area, Brent remembered the day he had come running into this same hospital. His mother had suffered a heart attack, and he was to come immediately, the message Carl left on the answering machine said.

He recalled that feeling of aloneness he'd had that day. Like a little boy who had lost sight of his parents. The child emerging, for a moment, leaving him cold and fearful.

Now, he had to leave his dad here. At least for a few days.

What had happened out there after he went to make

the telephone call? Maybe tomorrow Carl would feel like talking about it.

Brent picked up his car phone and shook it again, when he wound his truck out of the hospital exit driveway. He heard the faint buzz that indicated it might be in order now.

"Why you sonofabitch," he muttered under his breath. Why hadn't it worked earlier when he'd needed it? If it had, Dad wouldn't have been left alone. He dialed his home number.

Louise answered.

"Hi babe," he said.

"Brent! Where are you? I tried to reach you, and all I got was a busy signal."

"My phone was out of order. I don't know what's ailing it. I'm on my way home, but it'll take me a while longer. I'll be a little late, okay?"

"You're already hours late." But her voice was gentle, sounded amused, as if she were smiling. She probably already had the kids in bed, even Holly, whose bedtime when school was out was flexible.

"I know, sorry. It's a long story. Tell you when I get home."

"Okay."

"Love you."

He hung up, then turned right and headed back out of town to the west, toward the site of the proposed mall.

The big machinery sat parked here and there, capped with moonlight, black as pitch underneath. The bulldozer Tom had used wasn't far away from Carl's pickup and the felled tree. A hundred yards away two more big dozers were parked side by side, rigged with land-leveling blades. Near them were a couple of backhoes, and the two long trucks that hauled the machinery, as well as a couple of dump trucks.

He drove around the parked machinery, the big trucks, and slowly over to the tree, the pickup and other bulldozer. He stopped, lights on bright, covering the tree, the pickup, skimming the top of the hole. It yawned like a mouth, filled with darkness. Clods of dirt toppled over its black rim.

He sat still, engine off. The night had silenced even more. A few crickets chirped in the grass. The street was empty. The housing developments appeared to have gone to bed, even the dogs.

Taking his flashlight, he got out of the truck and went to the edge of the hole.

The light beam touched on heavy roots still half buried in the soil of the earth. Clods of soil the size of skulls lay here and there, and a couple of rocks the size of skulls. He tried to remember what they had seen, what he had seen. What it was that had sent him to call the police.

Bodies, he had thought, as pale as if they were bleached, darkened with dirt, entwined with roots large and small, some as small as a hair shaft.

Darkness had been filling the hole even then. In his memory now it was impossible to make out details. Something had looked like a hand. Away from it, part of something or someone else, appeared to be an arm. Two or three. Feet, one with part of a shoe still attached. He hadn't taken time to actually examine anything. He hadn't even shined his flashlight into the shadows that were turning darker by the moment. He had been in a hurry, always in a hurry. The damned phone wouldn't work. He had felt the need to get whatever police they needed, and end this day. Go home, eat with Louise and the kids.

Now he wasn't sure what he had seen.

Whatever it was, it was no longer there.

Rose Merline checked the front and back doors again. She had been nervous since the day she moved into the apartment above the small store. It was all she had been able to afford since the divorce a few months ago.

A housewife for twenty-nine years, she had been plunged suddenly into the working world. She had to go to work outside her home for the first time, and it terrified her. What was she suited for? Housework, babysitting?

Her husband Troy, whom she'd trusted to the ends of the earth, had wanted her to stay home and raise their three kids. Then as soon as Janie graduated high school, Troy told Rose he wanted a divorce. What's more he wanted her out of the house so he could sell it. He also had someone he wanted to marry. The beginning of a new life, with a new, younger woman. Where was the Troy she had known? Gone with her old life.

In something kin to shock she tried to find work, with no luck. Her kids talked her into trying a small business with the meager cash she'd received from the divorce settlement.

So she did. A used-clothing store. In an old building on a side street, with a one-bedroom apartment overhead.

It was a dreary, narrow, dark slice of old-town, and she was scared to death half of the time, and the other half so exhausted nothing mattered. She lived alone in her apartment, sold enough used clothing to enable her to take in garage sales and stock more and more. She made enough money to keep expenses up and to eat.

She started up the narrow, steep stairway in the back room after double checking the back door. A single light bulb above the narrow landing revealed walls stained with old rain water. She tried not to look at it as she began climbing.

The bottom step creaked as she started going up to her rooms above. But tonight the creak sounded further away. Was it at the foot of the stairs? In the back room or the front?

She stepped back and looked around, blinded by darkness in the clothing room.

Where was the dim light that made ghosts of the old mannequins? Had the bulb burned out?

Just her luck. She had to replace the bulb. She didn't dare leave the store dark. A broken front window, and all her inventory would be gone.

She started into the darkness when she stopped again. Terror ate into her like acid.

Dark figures blocked the light in the front. The bulb hadn't burned out. Its light silhouetted heads draped in black.

A cry raged in her mind as she tried to run, to unbolt the back door, to escape. Why would anyone want her pitiful supply of used clothing?

She felt a cold hand press across her throat, then her head was jerked violently backwards, and she knew no more.

4.

The large whitish wormlike creature lifted itself from the black soil, and stood before him, undulating. In the gauzy light of the moon he could make out the thin, wriggling black of a thousand legs down its belly. It stretched upward, growing taller than he, looming over him as he shrank within himself, filled with terror as silent as the withdrawal of the tiny, wiry legs that disappeared into the belly.

In front of his eyes it changed form. A human head grew, shoulders widened, segments of the thing's body separated from the rest and made arms and then legs. A head that was soft, cushiony, palely glistening with no neck, turned upwards toward the moonlight and the neck and features began emerging.

Before his eyes this thing of horror from the inner-earth turned into a woman. Her perfect beauty, increasing like light entering darkness, seemed the worst of all, and threw him into a panic of terror.

He heard himself screaming, or crying. The sound of his voice a gruff croaking, dragging him from the vivid memory of what he had seen, a dream that was a nightmare. Things that he couldn't bear to face in reality, coming back to haunt him.

Carl opened his eyes and stared at the ceiling. A

strange ceiling. A small room, with big windows on his left and a high empty bed on his right. Slowly, the intense, choking fear eased. He was in a strange but normal setting—not out on the site.

The hospital. He remembered now. They had tried to give him a sleeping pill, and he'd refused it. He hadn't wanted to go to sleep, because he'd been afraid of what he might dream. He had tried to stay awake. Yet he hadn't wanted to stay awake either, seeing over and over those strange, pale, human forms rising from the grave and walking past him. They had moved silently. As silently as ghosts.

He sat up. Thank God he had woke himself up trying to scream, before he actually screamed and disrupted the whole hospital. He didn't want anyone running in to see about him. He was afraid his credibility had taken a dive the way it was. He had caught a glimpse of the blank look on the face of the officer from the sheriff's department, when he looked into the hole. The hole that was now probably totally empty.

He wondered about the piece of shoe that had been clinging to the one foot. Would it still be there? Or was it, like the other rotted, tattered rags, now discarded somewhere and would never be found?

He searched the knobs and remote controls around his bed until he decided the light was turned on the way lights in his own house were turned on. By the switch on the side of the bulb socket.

With the brighter reading light turned on, he sat, his knees making a tent of the sheet and blanket that covered him to his waist.

The door was to his right, beside the sink with the long faucets and the small mirror and muted light. His clothes were in the tiny closet. He had seen a nurse put them there.

He could dress and be out of here in a few minutes. He might even be able to sneak past the nurses' station without being seen.

But Brent would be upset. He thought Carl had had a stroke. It wasn't a stroke, it was just plain shock. But he wasn't going to be telling the doctor anything. He probably would never tell anyone, not even Brent, nor Tom, both of whom had seen those bodies in the grave. But not as well as he had. Even before Tom left and Brent went to make the phone call, they'd only glanced in.

A mass grave, he thought now for the first time. People buried sometime in the past without benefit of coffins. Thrown together into one large grave.

Beneath a tree?

Impossible. Impossible to get those bodies beneath that tree, among those roots, in that way.

All of it, incredible, impossible.

He sat frowning at the end railing of the bed, not seeing it, seeing again those pale, perfect faces of the—whatever they were—walking past him in the moonlight.

Brent lay in bed with his arm underneath Louise's head. She slept, curled against him, one leg resting across his belly, her arm over his chest. He felt her warm, even breath against his neck, and knew she had gone to sleep.

He had told her only a partial truth. "We thought we uncovered a grave beneath a big tree Tom pushed over. But it must have been something else. An animal maybe. Too dark to see."

And, "Dad might have had a light stroke. We got an ambulance out there, and I followed it to Saint Mary's hospital. He's there for tests."

"Is he okay?"

"Yeah, I think so. He's tough."

She told him, "Holly helped clean today. She ran the vacuum cleaner for me." And, "Kara was out on her bicycle most of the day. She can't find any friends here yet. Said she wishes we'd stayed in our old place, on the old street, instead of this new place. She doesn't seem to appreciate having a nice new room, like Holly does. With its own deck, yet. How different the kids are."

They had discussed that many times. Ever since the second child was born. Holly had been a perfect baby, blond, blue-eyed, cheerful, smiling, gurgling. Then came Kara. Cranky and colicky. Louise had joked, "She took after her daddy with her dark eyes and hair, and that cranky disposition."

Joked? Was he really cranky?

"Naw, just brusque sometimes," she'd soothed.

It was the job, the pressure, the need to make more and more money to support the growing family. Two girls, then two boys. "We're quitting now, right, Louise?"

The doctor had asked when Vinny was born if she wanted her tubes tied, and she'd said no.

"I thought we were quitting," Brent said. "We don't want any more."

"Right," she said. "We want a new house instead, over in the Wildwood subdivision, with the privacy, the big lots, the trees and curving streets. But I didn't want my tubes tied."

"Then maybe I'd better get a vasectomy."

He lay now with his thoughts ranging back and forth from his dad in the hospital, his mother in her last days in the same hospital, the work on the land where the mall would be built, the hole with what had looked like pale bodies twisted among the roots, to home, this new home, and Louise and the kids. He needed to go get that vasectomy, he reminded himself. Accidents happen no matter how careful they tried to be. Vinny had been an accident.

He wouldn't trade Vinny for anything on earth. Big mouth and all.

But . . .

What had he seen?

What had Carl seen?

He eased out from under Louise. She drew a deep sigh and turned over.

Brent went to the bathroom, looked at the clock on the wall. Well past one o'clock. He wasn't at all sleepy. He had a notion to go make a pot of strong coffee, take it down onto the patio or out onto the kitchen deck and drink until seven. Then he could check the site again before going on to the hospital.

He had to talk to Dad, find out what happened.

He went back to bed instead. Turning over onto his stomach, well away from Louise in the king-size bed, he tried sleeping again. Suddenly he found himself wondering about the children. Were they all right? In this large house it seemed they were so far away. Too far to hear if they cried. "Great!" Louise had laughed when they first looked at the house. "A master bedroom so far away from the children's bedrooms that I won't be able to hear them fight!"

He gave it up, pulled on a cotton robe and went into the hall to the bedroom wing where the children slept. All four doors stood open, the girls' section separated from the boys' by a short hall. He entered Holly's room. Moonlight was like a window in the floor, a path of light from the sliding doors opening onto the girls' private deck. Holly's bed was in the corner deep in shadow. He could hear her easy, slow breathing.

He turned away, not disturbing her.

Kara's room was almost identical to Holly's. Her sliding door opened out on the same deck. Her bed was centered against a wall, giving her a view out onto the deck and across the sloping lawn and down the hill toward the street in the hollow. Moving that bed exactly where Kara had wanted it had caused more than one set of frazzled nerves.

She lay flat on her back in the center of the bed snoring slightly, both arms flung out. He stood looking down for a moment, then his eyes went to the sliding door. It was open, as was Holly's, with only the flimsy screen for protection. He found himself frowning at the door. But if he closed it, he would be closing off the breeze that wafted like a cool drink across the room.

He walked soundless, barefoot, across the carpet and looked out the door. The deck was at least ten feet off the ground. Down below, between the deck and the patio, was Louise's flower garden. There was no stairway leading down from the deck. Getting onto it from below would take some scrabbling, and the dog, Pepper, whose house was underneath the deck, would have first chance at whoever's leg.

It hadn't entered his mind before that the girls might be in danger, with bedroom doors opening out onto a deck. When he moved his family here, within a mile of the site where he was building the new mall, he had felt it was the safest place in the world.

The street down in front of the house, which wound through a seven mile hollow, was quiet and traveled only by the few families that lived on it. Burglaries were unknown. Strangers came only in the form of new families moving in, and soon they were no longer strangers. There was a walk going downhill to the mail box below. But their driveway reached from the double garage on ground level at the back of the house, beneath the kitchen deck to Peachtree Street, more commonly called Ridge Road, which led into town. An easier access than from Shady Hollow Road.

He had been so proud to buy this home for his family, with its generous space, its wooded area and privacy. But now he wished they were back home, in their old three bedroom house where neighbors and kids ran in and out of one another's houses.

Tonight he felt . . . not good about being here. Not safe.

It was the night, the circumstances. It was as if when the tree went down and opened that strange, dark hole with what had looked to him, Carl, and Tom like bodies, a darkness had entered his life.

Crazy thinking.

He left Kara's room and went into the hall to the boys' rooms. They slept in small beds pushed against walls to help them from falling out. Their windows were northern exposure, looking out into a forest of trees that separated house from house. Four-watt bulbs in each room created what Vinny called hills and hollows of shadow and light.

Both boys slept soundly. Bryon was straight in his bed, his covers looking as if they'd just been smoothed. Vinny lay crossways, his head at the edge of the bed, his covers rolled into a knot and tight in his arms. Brent resisted the urge to kiss them both, and slipped quietly out of their rooms.

He went back to the main hall and paused in the kitchen only long enough to get a cup of coffee. Here, too, the house took advantage of the lay of the land, and the sliding glass doors in the kitchen opened out onto a deck above the driveway. Stairs led to the ground.

Indoors, in a hallway between the kitchen and formal dining room, a stairway went to the ground floor and the family room. Brent went down to the lower level, where the utility room, guest room, and family room shared space with the double garage.

He opened the door at the foot of the stairs and went onto the patio. Pepper came stretching from one of the lounges.

Brent sat down on the foot of another lounge and rubbed Pepper's head. "Hey, I thought you said you slept on the rug in front of your doghouse, instead of on the lounge. Somebody's going to be mad when they have to clean dog hair off the lounge."

Pepper rested his head on Brent's knee. Brent rubbed his ear and looked at the spill of moonlight on Louise's flowers. The curved bed took up the space between the patio and the posts of the deck outside the girls' rooms. Through a thin stand of timber at the rear of the house the driveway curled out to Ridge Road, spotted with moonlight as if it had a rash.

Across the hollow in front of the house another new house had been built, similar to theirs but with the garage and driveway on the lower level and leading out onto the street in the hollow. Moonlight touched a new patio there, and glowed off a double-glassed sliding door.

He had never seen this view in moonlight before. The curving street in the narrow hollow, the tall trees, the new house across the way, all took on a surreal aspect that made him feel as if he were in a nightmare.

The only reality was the living warmth of the dog.

"Gotta go in," Brent said softly aloud to Pepper. "Gotta get some sleep."

He climbed the stairs without benefit of light except for the peripheral glow of moonlight that found its way through the glass doors. Silently he went down the main hall, past the living room at the front of the house, and to the small private hall to the master bedroom. It was the only bedroom whose windows were on ground level.

He sat down in a chair, feeling more wide awake than he ever had. What was wrong with him? Anxiety ate at him like a pocket full of worms.

Was he more worried about Dad than he had thought? Was Dad in worse health than he pretended?

It was easy to take one's dad for granted, he supposed. Yet even now that Dad had turned the corner into his sixties, he looked as good as ever, and was always at the site early in the morning. Though he often took off work sometime in the afternoon, Brent could count on him to be waiting at the site at seven A.M.

Since the tree had gone down, opening up that strange, dark hole, it was as if something had changed in Brent's life. A factor he sensed, felt, and feared. Nameless. Featureless.

The spot where he was sitting right now was only about one mile from that tree.

One of the reasons they had chosen this development was the proximity of the new mall, and a new school that was being built just north of it on the same old farm land.

Where he sat in the bedroom he had a view out the long window toward the northeast, toward the level farmland, the tree, the proposed mall. Somewhere there beyond the trees was the street that ran along the south side of the mall site. It continued on to become a county road leading to other towns.

In the trees that grew on his own two-acre plat, very little moonlight penetrated. He looked out into a black world where not even a tree trunk was visible. Yet he had a feeling suddenly that dark shapes moved there, looking through his window and watching him in the shadows of the bedroom.

He got up and closed the draperies on all the windows.

Tom checked again on his two kids. They had both wanted to sleep with him, but he had guided them to the bedrooms where most of their toys still waited, and some of their clothes hung. Their walls were still decorated with various characters that had once meant a lot to them.

He had let them stay up until ten. That was their special treat every Friday and Saturday night. Together, with a big bowl of popcorn, they had watched a cartoon video.

Now, at midnight, he felt an urge to see that they were all right. There was something in the air, it seemed to him. A portent of . . . something.

Ever since he had pushed that tree down, he'd felt depressed, sad, and a little scared. Of course depression wasn't a stranger to him, not since the separation.

Davey slept, clutching his teddy bear. Wasn't that something new? He didn't remember Davey ever hanging on to an object like that before. He was sweating, too. Tom tried to gently pry the large, fuzzy bear out of his arms, but Davey made a sound in his sleep and clutched it tighter. Tom backed away. He stood looking down. Sleeping, Davey's round little face took on a childishness that made him look seven again, not nine.

Tom left his son's bedroom and went to Ali's. An angel sleeping, he thought, and bent to touch his lips against her soft cheek.

They were okay. The windows, open a few inches, let in moonlight and a cool breeze.

He went out onto the porch and stood a moment soaking up the cool air. He lived perhaps three miles from the mall site, and he wondered what had happened.

He hadn't heard from Carl or Brent. Tomorrow he and the kids could drive over and see what was going on.

He frowned, remembering the sound of the falling tree, and that strange drum roll that seemed almost a musical accompaniment to the uprooting of the old tree.

5.

"I feel like a goddamned fool, that's what I feel like," Carl said.

He looked funny, and Brent couldn't help grinning. He sat in bed with a white hospital gown on, his knees spiked beneath the sheet, the head of his bed raised, a pillow behind his back, his arms crossed over his chest in a silent, belligerent "don't mess with me" attitude.

"I've got a damned good notion to put my clothes on and walk out, but just about the time I manage to get over there and grab a few things somebody comes in and hauls me out for another test."

Brent finally gave in and started laughing.

Carl glowered at Brent. "What's so damned funny?"

"It just occurred to me that I've never seen you in bed before," Brent answered.

"Did you order all those tests?" Carl rearranged his arms across his chest and looked up at the television perched on the wall. Figures moved in silence across it.

Brent stood up and patted his dad's shoulder. "You'll be out tomorrow. Just give them time to run the rest of the tests, okay? So far, everything's coming up good."

"I coulda told you that," Carl muttered.

"Dad," Brent said, "you didn't look good last night in the pickup. I was afraid you'd had a heart attack, or a stroke, or a blood clot in the upper story. Take my word for it, you didn't look good."

Carl said nothing.

"What happened to you, Dad?" he asked softly. "Any pains or anything you haven't told me about?"

Carl shook his head. He stared upward at the silent picture on the TV.

"Dad, I need to know. I thought I was getting the police out there because we had uncovered a grave. But when we got back all I found was you, looking white and sick, and nothing in the hole but the roots of the tree. What happened, Dad?"

Carl still didn't answer, although his lips parted and his eyes blinked. A frown settled on his forehead. It was almost like a frown of confusion, Brent thought.

"Don't you remember, Dad?"

Carl shook his head slightly.

If he didn't remember anything, then perhaps there had been a slight stroke afterall, Brent thought. Something.

"Do you remember us looking in the hole the tree roots came out of, Dad?"

"Of course I remember it!"

Brent stood looking down at his father. He sounded angry that Brent had wondered if something was wrong with his memory. Yet, he seemed confused about the rest of it. He had never seen his father act this way. Was it because he didn't want to talk about a mistake that seemed to have made fools of all of them?

"Got anything you want to tell me, Dad?"

"Yeah," Carl said, "Bring my pickup over here and park it somewhere. So I'll have it ready to go when I get out of this hellhole."

Brent opened his mouth and shut it again. He felt like laughing, yet nothing came to the surface. Carl cut a glance up at him from eyes as bright blue as an unclouded sky.

"That's all I got to say."

Brent nodded goodbye and left the room. At the door he peeked back and saw Carl staring upward at the television with that set, strange look on his face of half anger and half fear.

Puzzled, Brent hurried down the hall. He greeted a woman moving slowly within the confines of a walker, with two attendants at her sides. He spoke to a middle-aged couple who carried a bouquet of mixed flowers and ferns and who looked at each doorway number.

At the nurses' desk he saw the family doctor, and stopped, resting his elbows on the high counter. A nurse smiled at him and asked if she could help.

"I thought I'd ask Dr. White about my dad, Carl Salisaw."

The round freckled face of Dr. White turned at the sound of his name. He grinned at Brent and rose from the records desk and came to the counter.

He was a couple of inches shorter than Brent, but his girth well made up for that. He had bright red hair and brown eyes. He didn't waste time with words.

"Brent, I think your dad's tests are all going to turn out great. He's got the constitution of a man in his forties. He's probably healthier than you and I. Says he quit smoking several years ago."

"Uh . . . yeah."

"We're having a hard time keeping him in here long enough to complete the tests."

"So I hear." Brent grinned.

Gerald White reached over the counter and patted Brent's shoulder.

"If he does walk out, I'd say don't worry about it. If he gets a suspicious spell of something again, just bring him back."

He looked down at the folder in his hand, and leafed back a couple of pages. Brent waited.

"When he was brought in last night his heart rate was rapid, but his blood pressure was slightly low, which is actually quite normal for him. There were no other symptoms. Nothing physical. Frankly, I thought he looked as if he'd seen a ghost."

Dr. White smiled. "But he refused to talk, so I have no idea if he had any physical problem we just haven't found yet. He says he feels fine. That's all he'll say. Didn't know Carl was so stubborn."

Brent remained silent. He hadn't told the doctor about the tree, or that they all thought they had uncovered an old grave. But what would that have to do with Dad's problem? A problem, thank God, that seemed to have disappeared.

"In fact," Dr. White said, "I asked him if he had seen a ghost. Just a joke. But his sense of humor isn't what it normally is."

Gerald White sobered and blinked, and folded the papers into the cardboard holder.

Brent felt he should say something. "No, he's not into jokes since we brought him in. He's got the attitude of a bear this morning. But at least he can move and talk now."

Only . . . he almost added, he isn't talking. For the first time it occurred to Brent that Carl had seen something more, after he and Tom left, that had stunned him to speechlessness. That had, actually, pitched him into a kind of shock.

Was that possible?

Brent had started away, and the doctor had turned back toward the desk where he'd been sitting. Brent spun round and moved closer again to the desk.

"Doctor," he said.

Gerald White turned. "Yeah?"

"Could it have been fright? Dad's symptoms?"

The two men stared at each other.

"Fright?" Gerald White asked. "About what?"

Brent shrugged. He wasn't sure he was even on the right track. But . . . "Well . . . could it have been?"

"Beats me."

They looked at each other a moment longer. The doctor's face was alive with curiosity. Questions were ready to spill forth. Before they could, Brent gave him a nod of thanks and walked away. At the elevator he looked back again and the doctor was still watching, his eyes round. Brent could see the curiosity. Fright? his expression queried, out in the middle of a field? Alone?

Brent drove out to the work site on the western edge of town. Before he turned off the paved road out of town he saw some of the men were at work. Two bulldozers were removing top soil from the area where the mall foundation would be built. One dump truck was hauling off the soil. It would go to an acreage farther out where it would be dumped and kept until it was sold, truck load by truck load. It would make some fine flower beds for new homes.

A tree-removing truck was parked near the downed sycamore, whose leaves now were wilting in the morning sun, but the two men weren't working yet. Carl's pickup sat in the way.

Brent parked safely away from the working areas, lining his truck up between the automobiles of the men who had wanted to work overtime. Tom was off this weekend with his children.

The two men with the tree-removing equipment met Brent between Carl's pickup and the uprooted tree. Brent had wanted to get here before anyone else. He had wanted one more good look in that hole, while he was alone.

"This the tree you want out of here, I reckon," one of the men said.

They had done work for Brent before, lots of it. They worked on Saturday, or even Sunday, if they were needed. And sometimes, in the building business, you had to take advantage of the weather no matter what weekend or holiday it might be.

"That's the one," Brent said. "I'll get the pickup out

of your way." Brent snuck a look at the tree hole. It looked like the hole of any tree that had been knocked over. A little larger maybe, more roots exposed, but it was a larger than normal tree.

The two men acted as if they wanted to talk. They had looks on their faces that were close to amusement. Grins, barely disguised.

The one named Harley Albert, a man in his thirties perhaps, who always looked a little as if he needed cleaning up, eyed him with a gleam. A chewed match hung from the corner of his mouth.

"Heard you found a grave there, under the tree."

Startled, Brent demanded, "Where the hell did you hear that?" His mind rapidly followed the possibilities and as rapidly, discarded them. Dad, in the hospital. Tom, at home with his kids. No way.

Harley Albert and Charles Web glanced at each other.

"Heard it down at Lily's Pad, long about midnight?" Harley looked at Charles for confirmation.

Charles nodded, grinning openly.

Lily's Pad? That, Brent well knew, was one of the favorite bars and old-time honky-tonks in the area. When he was a boy it had been in the country. But now the town had engulfed it and it was surrounded by businesses that had tried a few times to get rid of it and had failed. It was open all night, as far as Brent knew, and drew a lot of blue collar workers, as well as some of the white collars. It was the favorite place of his youth. The forbidden, he had thought until he started patronizing it. Where, he then found out, nothing really went on but dancing and drinking and hanging out.

"A couple of cops were talking about it. Said it would be funny if the old guy hadn't had a stroke."

They sobered and blinked. Charles asked, "That wouldn't have been your old man, would it?"

Brent drew a long breath and made up his mind about Carl's pickup. He'd drive it to the hospital, get a

cab to bring him back here. Dad at least deserved that.
It would make him feel more in control if he managed
to walk out and find his transportation sitting there
waiting for him.

6.

Beverly reached for the cup of coffee she'd been neglecting during the long, extremely important phone call, and leaned back in her chair. She expelled a breath she felt as if she'd been holding the entire time of trying to secure one of the best, growing retail businesses in the world. Finally, she had them. They were renting the largest, best display room in the proposed new mall, at the west end. A place designed to catch the most traffic. She had promised the space would be ready in six months.

Not a bad start for a Monday morning.

The phone line blinked and she leaned forward. Her secretary's voice came over the line from the outer office.

"Beverly? It's Mel."

"Thanks, Glenda." Beverly pressed the button that connected her to Mel. She felt the glow of success that combined her son, that handsome young man who was a combination of all he'd ever been, in her eyes, from infant to little boy to big boy to man. She tried to refrain from treating him any of the ways she saw him, except the latter.

"Good morning, Mel, how are you?"

"Morning? Mom, it's noon. Ten minutes past." He laughed. "You've really been tied up this morning, haven't you? I tried over an hour ago to see if you'd like to have lunch."

"Well, I certainly would!" Lunch? He invited her to lunch about once a month now that he had Paula, but that was fine with Beverly. She was used to eating alone much of the time, at home accompanied by her two cats. It was a time of relaxation for her. "I'd never turn down an invitation to eat a free lunch."

"Too late," he said, sounding as if he had his mouth full. "I ordered in fish and chips. I'm eating at my desk."

"Well, why on earth did you invite me to lunch if you already had it in your mouth?"

"I didn't invite you, I was *going* to invite you. See what you missed?"

She leaned back, laughing. Then she told him about the retailer who was renting the largest section of the mall. She was aware of his listening, and it occurred to her finally that he had something to tell her. They'd already had lunch together once this month.

"What is it, Mel?"

"Huh? Oh, nothing much."

She resisted an urge to tell him not to talk with his mouth full.

"Those fish and chips must be pretty good."

"Yeah. Came from Catfish John's, and you know that no one can cook catfish like John."

"Right. Now what's this 'nothing much' you called to tell me? I suspect it had nothing to do with lunch."

"It really did. I was going to ask you if you'd like to take a run out to catfish John's with me. Paula is in a business meeting today and couldn't go. Anyhow, it's what I heard down at the coffee shop this morning. I thought you'd like to hear it, too."

"Sure. What gossip did you pick up? That you think

would interest *me.*" She spoke lightly, yet puzzled. Mel had never carried much gossip to her. Rumors were not really his thing, unless they led to facts and a prosecution.

"You might not like it—it concerns some guys who are working for you."

"Me?" She thought of Glenda as her only employee. Except the janitoral crew.

"Yeah. The new mall."

"The mall?" Her puzzlement increased. Nothing had gone wrong or she would have heard about it directly, not through some gossip passed around at a coffee shop.

She found herself frowning faintly, and put her fingertips between her eyebrows and smoothed the skin. Remember the frown lines, she reminded herself, caused by too many hours over one problem or another. Pucker lines, too, on each side of her mouth. She had a bad habit of pursing her lips when she was concentrating.

"It's this contracting crew," Mel said suddenly, his voice filled with amusement. "The one that's working on your new mall site?"

She stared at the dark wood of the closed door across the room. "Yeah? So? Brent Salisaw has worked for me before. I have no problems with him."

"No problem, that I know of. It's just something to do with a grave they thought they uprooted. Some of the police were laughing about it."

"The police!"

"Well, the bulldozer man who works for the Salisaw construction company pushed that big old sycamore over Friday evening, the one in the middle of the field?"

"I know the one. What about it?"

"It was almost dark. Well, it seems they found what they thought was a mass grave. The two Salisaw men, Carl and Brent, and the bulldozer man, Tom Roush.

In the hole beneath the tree roots they saw bodies. They thought. Tom went home, and Brent left his dad there to guard the grave, while he went to call the police."

Beverly felt her chin droop. The scene was suddenly before her. *The tree . . . tall, huge, reaching toward the sun, the sky. A crow on the very top . . . rose gracefully to sail into the air . . . her great-grandfather tapping his cane on the floor of the porch . . .*

"The police came, Salisaw leading them," Mel was saying. "They found Carl in bad shape—he'd had a stroke they thought, though it turned out he hadn't—"

. . . the corn grew in the field, only a few inches tall, and behind her, Grandpapa began to speak, answering her question. Grandpapa, why is there a tree growing in your cornfield?

She heard his voice answering her. *Don't ever destroy the tree . . . if you do they'll rise again.*

Mel continued, "They called an ambulance for Carl, then the police searched the grave. They found nothing. Just roots and clods of dirt. White roots, you know, that might have looked like people, I guess, in the dark."

She put her hand to her cheek. She'd forgotten the old story. It had completely slipped her mind. She could hear her daddy saying again, "Never mind, Beverly. Forget it, will you? It's just Grandpapa's imagination. Things like that didn't happen, not here in the United States, not even during the Civil War. Forget it."

And she had.

Her voice felt strained with the effort to appear normal. "Brent's father . . . is he all right?"

"It turned out he was, otherwise it wouldn't have been funny. The whole police department was laughing about it. Some grave. Filled with rocks and clods of dirt they thought were skulls. One deputy said that Brent Salisaw said he could even see the hair of one dead body. It was long and blond. Can you believe that?"

Beverly stood up. "Mel," she said, "I'll talk to you later."

She hung up. That was the first time in her life she had so abruptly ended a phone conversation with her son.

She opened the drawer that held her shoulder bag, and slipped the long strap over her shoulder. In the outer office she told Glenda she didn't know when she'd be back. She felt Glenda watching her and expected the question that came just before she reached the door.

"Is something wrong, Beverly?"

"No," she said, and hurried on out.

Wrapped in her thoughts, the frown of concentration showing between her brows and on her mouth, she drove impatiently, faster than her normal speed. The streets were heavy with noon traffic. She drove with the same impatience as the young drivers who usually annoyed her, eager to be out at the mall site.

How could she have forgotten her Grandpapa Boyd's story? She had stood last week and looked at that beautiful old sycamore tree, before giving Brent instructions to remove it. She had felt sorry. Doesn't one always feel sorry when they're uprooting something that took more than a hundred years to grow? But progress . . .

There just *couldn't* be any truth in that old story!

She saw the site a couple of blocks before she came to the driveway. Dust fogged like small dark clouds from bulldozers working far over in the field, smoothing the mounds of dirt. All the trees were gone. The spot where the sycamore had stood looked as if a tree had never stood there.

She drove her Chrysler across the bumpy field, abandoning the two tracks that were most obviously used by the automobiles. She headed toward the man who was walking between the parked pickup trucks. He looked, from the distance, like Brent Salisaw, a big man with wide shoulders. A dark-haired man with a square jaw and a round dimple in his chin.

She pulled up and stopped. He turned and came toward her, nodding a greeting. "Miss Beverly?"

His head was bare. The wind had stirred his hair into a disarray of curls, but it wasn't unattractive. Beverly had never met his father, who she knew was the actual owner of the construction company. Nor had she met any of Brent's family. She knew, though, he and his wife had four children.

He had done several jobs for her in the past two years, and Clark had hired the Salisaw Company before that, many times.

"How's your father?" she asked. "I heard he was in the hospital?"

"He's out now. Went home. I told him to take the week off and go fishing. He doesn't listen to me very well and I wouldn't be surprised if he showed up here before the day's over. Thanks for asking, Mrs. Inness."

"Tell me what happened, Brent. About the tree, the grave."

She started walking toward the spot where she remembered the tree had stood. Brent moved beside her, telling about the end of the day on Friday. The last work to be done was the bulldozing of the tree. The other man had left. Tom Roush was running the dozer . . .

So there were three witnesses, not two.

She listened as she walked. There were a few thin roots still protruding from the ground, a few leaves scattered. But the hole had been filled in. She wished it hadn't.

"Why didn't you call me?" she asked. "Friday night?"

They stood together for a moment in silence.

Brent looked down at his toes in a manner that reminded Beverly of Mel, of the boyishness that remained in every grown man. She felt sorry for him and wanted to pat him reassuringly on the arm, but didn't move.

"Well, ma'am," Brent said. "When I came back . . . with the police . . . my dad was sick. Looked really sick.

All I could think of then was getting him to the hospital. Before that, when I was at the Texaco station waiting for the police, I thought . . . I didn't think, I guess. It was a puzzle. All I thought about was getting back out here."

Beverly stood still, staring at the small pieces of root where the great old tree had stood. Beyond, across the field, was the line of trees where Grandpapa had said the brush arbor had stood. The trees were about a block away. The tree had stood a bit more than halfway between the driveway of the old farmstead and the tree line. The road, now a street, ran along the front about three hundred feet away. None of it was now visible. Grandpapa had died when she was ten years old. The farm house had been rented out for years then, until she inherited the farm. Then, a few years ago, they had sold the buildings. Some of them were torn down, some hauled away on big trucks and set up somewhere else. The driveway was plowed under and different crops planted.

Now there was nothing. Except the plans for a shopping mall, and lots of concrete for parking.

"Tell me what you saw," Beverly said.

"People think we had an end of the week Friday evening syndrome that a couple of beers would have cured. Everybody thinks it's funny as hell."

"I don't. I want to know *exactly* what you saw."

For a long moment he said nothing, then he changed positions slightly. Almost a shuffling of feet. Embarrassment. Uncertainty.

"Well . . . it was almost dark, that's true. And I'm not speaking for Dad, or Tom, but all three of us were looking in that hole. I thought I saw a woman's head, the profile. She had long blond hair, half covered in dirt. I saw a foot. A man's, I think, with part of an old shoe on it. There were arms, legs, that seemed—at first they seemed to be part of the root system."

He stopped. Beverly glanced up and saw that he was

frowning intently at the ground where the hole had been.

"Was the hole investigated thoroughly before it was filled in? For bones, skeletons?"

"Uh—we looked. Police looked. When I got back with them. Whatever it was I'd seen just wasn't there. We even had better light. Several flashlights."

"And?" Getting this out of him was like dragging a log chain through a keyhole. He plainly didn't want to talk about it.

"There was nothing," he ended. "Just rocks and dirt and roots."

"What happened to the skull you saw?"

Another hesitation.

"It wasn't a skull," he said suddenly and quickly. "I don't know where the skull story came from. I saw a woman's head. Face. Hair. At least I thought I did."

"Okay, what happened to it?"

"I don't know. Wasn't there to start with, I guess."

"So it was gone when you came back with the police. But you had left your father here?"

"Yes."

"And he was in shock when you returned," she said softly, half to herself. Was there some terrible truth afterall in the story her great-grandfather had told her?

"Well . . . Dad was—white, not able to move at first. The doctors decided it wasn't a physical problem. By the time we got him to the hospital he had come out of it."

"This Tom you mentioned . . ." She looked around. Three bulldozers running. Two trucks loading dirt. A couple of backhoes doing something equally as dusty. She didn't have any idea which man was Tom.

"Over there." Brent pointed, ready to start running after him, eager to go, to be let off the hook. "You want him?"

"If it wouldn't cause you too much trouble I'd like to talk to him a couple of minutes."

"No, no trouble. I'll send him over."

There was no way she could keep up with Brent. She walked slowly after him, toward the bulldozer out in the field. She watched Brent wave at Tom and motion him over. Tom stopped the dozer, leaped off like a man dismounting a horse.

He met Brent and paused. They exchanged a couple of words. Brent walked back with him, smiled at Beverly and made the introductions, adding, "If there's anything else Miss Beverly . . . ?"

Beverly shook her head. "Thanks for your time, Brent."

Tom was still holding her hand, and she gave it a motherly squeeze before she slid hers away.

"So you're the man who pushed over the tree."

"Never hated anything so much in my life. I mean, I've pushed over a lot of trees, but after a while it's like working in a slaughter house, I reckon, because you get to seeing them as living creatures. And that was a fine sycamore tree."

"I know it was."

At this moment, if she could have returned it, it would still be standing there.

Beverly said, "I just want to know what you saw in the hole, Tom."

A shadow flashed over Tom's face. Not quite a frown. "The same thing Brent saw."

"Tell me."

"I'm not backing down on this either. I saw a face. The guys at the bar were having one damned good laugh. A whole face, or half of a face, they wanted to know. Well, it was half of a face. But I swear it was there."

"More than one body," Beverly said softly. In her mind Grandpapa's words played. *They must have been a*

*dozen of them, or more, men and women, as pretty as any
group of people you'd ever see. Young . . .*

Tom said, "Oh yeah! Several, I don't know how many.
I had to go get my kids. So I didn't stay."

"How were they arranged? I mean, were they laid
side by side? Were there any signs of coffins?"

"You believe—we saw them?" He sounded surprised.

Beverly hesitated. Should she tell the story her great-
grandfather had told her? Not yet. She'd talk to Mel
first.

"I believe you."

"There was nothing there, you know, ma'am, when
the police looked. They claimed there was nothing
there, but roots and clods of dirt. Said there was no
sign anybody had ever been buried there. Not even an
animal bone was in that hole."

"How were the bodies arranged?" she asked again.
"Were there coffins, that sort of thing?"

"No. Not that I saw." He paused. "It looked like
they'd just been thrown in, one on top of the other,
and the tree roots had grown around them."

Beverly felt the skin on her cheeks and the back of
her neck tighten. Yes, that was consistent with what
Grandpapa had told.

"There's one thing that puzzled me, ma'am," Tom
added. "Even then, as I was driving away. If the tree
roots had grown around the bodies, how was it they
weren't decayed?"

*As long as the tree lives, they will stay buried. . . . Don't
destroy it or they will rise again.*

The words of the little girl who had planted the tree.

Beverly remembered being fascinated by that little
girl. She had even dreamed of her a few times.

"So," said Tom, "maybe they're right, maybe we all
needed a beer or two. Maybe we had too much dust in
our eyes and brains."

She turned, her back toward the debris of the tree
that remained scattered on the scraped earth.

What had she done, having the tree removed?

What had Carl Salisaw seen last Friday night, as he waited alone for his son and the police?

"Thank you, Tom, for your information."

7.

"Let me show you the right way to build roads," Kara said. She shoved Bryon and Vinny aside.

Her oldest little brother, Bryon, sat back on his heels. He had been hacking at the dirt with a little hand spade that belonged to Mama. Vinny was chopping with another of Mama's gardening tools.

"Does Mama know you've got her garden tools?" Kara asked.

"Yeah," said Bryon as Vinny said, "No."

"That's what I thought. Make sure you take them back."

"Okay," they said in unison.

Mama had sent her to look for the boys and she'd found them down in the hollow right by the edge of the road. Mama wouldn't like that, even if there was almost no traffic. A UPS truck might come along, and they soared around like frisbees.

The ground beneath the trees here was soft, dark, and moist. Leaves had rotted beneath leaves that were still green. Pine needles lay scattered, from the tall pines across the street. Vines grew over the leaves. Making little roads for their cars and trucks was easy.

Kara had her own collection of cars and trucks, too, though she hadn't brought them along. She'd rather play with them than dolls. Dolls were no fun. What could you do with a doll except change its clothes? A car could be pushed around, and if it were remote control, it could be guided by buttons. She'd rather push, though.

"Okay," she said. "Here we'll make a town, under this root is a garage. Who wants—"

"I do!" they both yelled before she finished her sentence.

"Good grief, guys, there are enough roots for all your cars and trucks." She began working vigorously, cleaning dirt and leaves from under roots that grew above ground.

Vinny looked up at something behind her suddenly. His eyes grew wide. He stared, as if a monster hung in the air just behind them. Bryon looked up too, his face lit by surprise.

"Hey," Vinny whispered shrilly, "Somebody's here."

She whirled, twisting on her heels as she tried to rise.

She looked up into the smiling face of a young woman who stood just at the edge of the pavement. Behind her, still on the pavement where few cars ever traveled, stood a man.

Fear, brought on by the looks on the faces of her little brothers, bled through her body. The faces of the strangers seemed at first the faces of danger. Yet they were beautiful. Both the man and the woman. The woman had long blond hair in coiled braids. She was wearing an old-fashioned, kind of tacky long skirt, which added to the strangeness that Kara sensed about her.

The man was handsome, with a tapered, neat beard. He stood with his thumbs hooked in his pockets.

The woman glanced back at the man, and the man gave her a smiling nod.

"Beautiful children," he said softly.

Kara gawked, unable to tear her eyes away or close her mouth. Frozen in position, squatting on her heels, she was aware of the boys leaping and running like wild deer, in silence, through the trees and up the hill toward the house. A blink of a thought slipped through Kara's mind. The boys had never been afraid of strangers before. Mama used to scold Vinny, especially, for being so friendly. He never met a stranger, they said about him. Anyone could carry him off and he'd go quietly, he was so trusting.

Kara scrambled to her feet, as if when the woman's eyes left her it freed her from some frozen position. She wiped her soil-coated hands down the sides of her jeans.

"What's your name?" the man asked, smiling behind his beard.

"K-Kara." She had never stuttered before. She wanted to run too, but didn't want to make a fool of herself. They had just startled her, that was all. They must have just been out for a walk. They probably lived nearby. Neighbors, maybe.

Through the pines she saw a black car pulled up to the double garage of the new house across the road. One of the garage doors stood open. Inside, it was no longer empty. A garden hose, or something round and snakelike, hung on the wall. Some tools . . .

The young woman saw the direction of Kara's glance. There was a smile on her softly curved lips.

"We're your new neighbors," she said. "We have a daughter near your age."

Kara began to walk backwards. She had never felt so uncomfortable in anyone's presence.

She pointed at the house on the hillside behind her. "That's where I live. I have to go now."

She ran through the trees and into the freshly mowed grass on the sloped lawn in front of the house. She reached the corner near her parents' bedroom, and glanced back once, feeling safer now that she could reach out and touch the brick of her house. They were still in the street below, watching her. She ran on around the house to the bedroom deck she shared with Holly, and looked up. Holly wasn't in sight. Neither was her mother.

She stopped, breathing hard. A sharp little pain in her side caused her to sit down. A stitch, Grandpa called it. From running too fast.

Her heart was still pounding. But rationale was taking over and she began questioning herself and her actions. Why had she been so scared? Just because of her dumb brothers? Because those new neighbors had startled them by coming up behind them so quietly?

Something stupid like that, she supposed.

They were nice people, you could tell by looking, so there was nothing to be scared of.

New neighbors? With a daughter her age? Someone to play with at last? Someone she could talk to, who would understand what she was talking about, who was interested in the same things she was? Wow!

She had to tell someone! Excitement suddenly was eating her up. Now she'd have a playmate her own age. Another girl. Someone she could ride bikes with and stuff. Watch television with. Be buddies with.

"Mom!"

She ran into the family room off the patio, then up the stairs to the kitchen, crying out for her mother every other step.

In the upper hall her mother finally answered. From the front of the house.

At the same time, Holly showed up in the front hall, eyes rounded, but with a little frown that meant she was ready to scream at her to shut up.

Kara didn't give her a chance.

"New neighbors! Across the hollow!"

"Really?" Holly asked. "How do you know?"

Kara put her arms across her stomach as if Holly gave her a great pain. "How do I know! I'm not blind, woman! I met them already!"

"Really? What's their name?"

Mom's voice came impatiently, as if she'd been yelling

and hadn't been heard. It was that way around the house sometimes.

"Kara! What do you want? Where are the boys? Didn't you find them?"

Kara went into the front hall and heard her mother's voice moving further away. She followed.

"Mom! I met the new neigbors."

She caught up with her mother back in the kitchen. Louise stood looking out over the kitchen deck.

"Where are the boys?"

"I was trying to tell you, Mom, about the neighbors."

"Kara, where are Vinny and Bryon?"

"I don't know!"

"Stop screaming and go find them!"

Kara saw Louise draw a long breath, which meant she was about to get herself a cup of tea or coffee and sit down at the snack bar.

"They were down by the road, Mom," Kara said, feeling suddenly very calm and mature. "I was down there with them when we looked up and saw this couple. They've moved into the new house across the street in the hollow below. So the boys ran. I suppose they're in their room."

Louise looked beyond Kara and said, "Holly, go check."

"Okay," Holly said.

Kara looked at her mother. For the first time she really looked at her, comparing her to the lady across the street. Louise had tiny lines at the corners of her eyes and mouth. The corners of her mouth drooped. She wasn't smiling. Her lashes were okay, but were pale brown. The new lady hadn't been wearing mascara, Kara was sure. She was just naturally beautiful. Mama was thirty-four, and the lady across the street must be almost as old if she had a child near Kara's age, but she looked so much . . . well . . . *better.*

Kara suddenly felt guilty and ashamed of herself. She

went over to her mother and put her arms around her neck. Louise hadn't gotten coffee afterall.

"Want me to make you some coffee, Mama?"

Louise returned Kara's hug.

"It's already made, sweetheart. But you can pour me a cup if you want to."

Kara felt a glow of pride. It was the first time her mother had asked her to pour a cup of coffee. She hadn't even been able to pour her own milk without spilling it until just recently.

She stretched up and took a cup from the cabinet, went to the coffee maker, and nearly dropped the whole thing trying to get the coffee holder out of the rest.

"Oh Lord, Kara," Louise said, getting up from the snack bar stool. "That's all I need. Coffee spilled on this carpet."

"Should have had linoleum, Daddy would say," Holly said as she came into the kitchen.

Louise said, "And who did he have in mind to mop the linoleum every day?"

Her mom was in a grouchy mood, Kara thought as she backed away, feeling like a failure. Maybe when she was thirteen, like Holly, Mom would trust her more. Holly got everything she wanted. If Holly wanted a new dress, Holly got it. "It's because I help her, and you don't," Holly had told her. "But I only got one, Kara, one, when you didn't. And if you want it next year, you can have it." Yeah sure, a hand-me-down. Typical. Kara gets the hand-me-downs and the groans and moans when she drops a plate or spills a little something.

"So where were they?" Louise asked, pouring her own coffee, as Holly came back into the kitchen.

"In Bryon's bedroom. Hiding in his bed."

Louise stopped, looking horrified. "Both of them? In Bryon's bed?"

"I made them get off and put the blanket back, Mom."

"What on earth are they playing on the bed for, they know better than that."

"They were scared." Holly smiled. She had a dimple in her cheek that Kara envied.

"For gosh sakes! Scared of what?"

"The new neighbors. I don't know why."

They both looked at Kara.

Kara, caught in the middle, shrugged in an exaggerated way, her palms held out. "Beats me," she said. There was no way she was going to tell how the sudden appearance of the new neighbors had scared her too.

Kara turned away, went to the refrigerator and made a case of looking in, aware all the time that she was being watched.

"Close the door," Louise said. "It isn't lunch time yet."

Kara closed the refrigerator door and started to leave the room. In her bedroom was a small radio she could listen to. She wanted a television, but her dad said no way. Not even Holly was allowed a television in her room.

At the kitchen door though, she could stand it no longer. Even if it did please Holly and their mother, she had to talk. She'd explode if she didn't.

She paused, acting as if something had just occurred to her. Then, dramatically, she turned.

"There is one thing," she said.

She had their full attention. Mom, at the snack bar, her fingers on the handle of the coffee mug, stared intently at Kara, waiting. Holly, standing at the end of the snack bar with her elbow resting on the formica, waited too.

Kara let them wait a second, two, three. Very much longer and they'd both lose patience.

"They have a daughter about my age."

Louise smiled. "Great. Now maybe you can stop complaining about moving here."

Kara shrugged. "I didn't see her." She wasn't ready

yet to like this new place. She hadn't wanted to leave all her friends. The size of the house hadn't mattered to her, even though it was great having her own bedroom. She definitely liked that part. Well . . . she liked other things, too. All the places to ride her bike with so little traffic, for one.

Holly interrupted her darting thoughts.

"Then how do you know?"

"They told me. She, the lady, told me."

"You met them already?"

Nobody ever listened to her, Kara thought with a sigh of disgust.

"Yeah. Uh . . . that's what scared the boys. We were building roads and things at the bottom of the hill, and these people came across from their place, and we didn't see them coming. So Vinny and Bryon just got scared and ran away."

"What's their name?" Louise asked.

"I don't know," Kara had to admit. "But they're nice people."

But never, never would she tell that she too ran off like her scared little brothers.

8.

Kara sat on the front stoop and looked across the hollow toward the new house. She had been watching for hours, it seemed, ever since lunch, and hadn't seen anyone. She'd been watching for the girl to show up. Or even a boy—she was to the point of not caring. Just *anyone* with some brains, someone her own age, someone who knew how to have fun. But no one had shown up in the backyard of the house.

"Shut up, Pepper!" she yelled again. She'd lost count of the times she'd yelled at their small black and white dog. He'd stood barking where the sidewalk started down the slope of the hill toward the mailbox on the street below. Barking and barking.

When she yelled, each time, he'd run back to her, then whirl and take up his stance again, yapping at the house across the hollow. He wouldn't stop barking.

Suddenly she saw a figure moving in the shadows of the open garage across the way. Trees partly obscured her view. She squinted. Then Pepper did something that struck her as being very strange. Just like Vinny and Bryon had, he whirled and ran to her. When someone finally showed up that he could bark at, he shut up and ran.

He sat down against her feet, his ears perked. Kara

stared over him. She couldn't tell if it was the man or woman.

At that moment the front door behind her opened, and Louise came out carrying the cake pan.

"You'll want to go with us, won't you, Kara?" she said. "The boys are staying home. I told them we'd only be a few minutes."

Kara stood up. Pepper took advantage of the open door and disappeared into the house. Holly came out behind Louise.

"Where're we going?" Kara asked.

"We're going to be good neighbors," Louise said, "And take them a welcome-to-the-neighborhood cake."

"Oh, great! Can I go?"

"Well, of course."

Kara let them lead the way. It was almost like hiding behind her mother's skirts, except in this case, it was jeans. She thought about mentioning that the new neighbor lady had worn a long skirt, like some of the really religious people, and maybe Louise should change. But she didn't.

They went down the sidewalk in single file, Louise, Holly, then Kara following behind. Where the hill began a sharp slope, the walk became steps. At the bottom of the hill it became a walk again, ending at the mailbox and the edge of the quiet street.

Holly checked the box and rustled the mail inside, but Louise said, "Leave it until we get back."

They went on, crossing the street, going into the paved drive across the street that led to the open garage.

Tall trees shaded the driveway and the grassy area that reached up to the patio. Like their home across the hollow, trees shaded the house both east and west. In front, on higher ground, there was another street, curving in a cul-de-sac. Kara knew, because she had ridden her bike over there one day, checking out the places and the residents, hoping to find playmates. The only kids she had seen were too little, like Vinny and Bryon.

But it was *her* the lady had looked at when she'd said, "I have a daughter about your size." Not Vinny, or Bryon. So that meant she was ten or eleven, or maybe even twelve.

Where was she? Up in her room? Riding on her bike on the cul-de-sac up in front of her house?

Louise stopped, and Kara almost bumped into her.

Suddenly the door beside the garage opened, and the lady who'd spoken to Kara came out, a smile on her beautiful face. She came forward, her hand out.

Louise balanced the cake pan on her left arm and reached forward with her right to shake hands with the new neighbor.

"I'm Louise Salisaw," she said, "your neighbor across the hollow. These are my daughters Holly and Kara. I guess you met Kara earlier this morning."

"Yes, I met Kara. Hello Kara and Holly, what lovely names you have. I'm so glad you came over, Louise. Here, let me take that. Thank you so much. You're our first visitor."

"We thought we'd bring you a welcoming gift," Louise said, following the neighbor to the patio table, where four chairs were arranged precisely around it. "But we didn't plan to take up your time. You must be very busy getting moved in. We've only been here a few weeks ourselves."

"But I want you to stay. Sit down, please. Oh, I forgot to tell you my name. I'm Joyce Renton. My husband, Albert, isn't available at the moment. But we can talk. Would you like some cake and coffee?"

"Oh no, thank you. The cake's for you."

"I'll take it in and bring back the container. It won't take a moment. Do sit down."

They sat down and waited in silence. Louise said quietly, "Isn't she pretty?"

No one answered her. Kara noticed Holly was staring with a half frown at the door where Joyce had disappeared, her lips parted as if she were deep in concentration. Kara felt as if Holly would leap and run the way the boys had.

Then the door opened, and Joyce and the man came out. He came forward to Louise, his hand extended.

"Joyce tells me you're our neighbor across the hollow."

Louise shook hands with him. Kara could tell by the look on her face that she was impressed.

"He showed up afterall," Joyce laughed. "This is my husband, Albert."

Albert stepped over and took Holly's hand, and shook it as if she were an adult. Kara found herself clasping her own hands in her lap. She had never shaken hands with anyone in her life that she recalled. She looked beyond them, but still saw no child.

"So this is Holly," he said, and looked at Kara. "And we've already met, haven't we, Kara?"

She nodded shyly, wishing their daughter would come through the door. Grownups made her feel uncomfortable sometimes. Especially these two. She felt . . . somehow examined when they looked at her. The man had deep, dark eyes that seemed to know every thought she'd ever had.

When his eyes turned away from her she looked more closely at him. His eyebrows were heavy and thick, yet balanced his pointed beard. He was tall, square and straight in the shoulders. Like her dad, only this man was thin-waisted and had a flat tummy. Not like Daddy's beer belly, as Mama called it.

Joyce remained standing until Albert made some kind of excuse and went back into the house. Kara had tuned the adult voices out, the way she usually did. Disappointment was beginning to take the excitement out of the visit.

Louise and Joyce talked about the weather, about the

location of stores, small talk, boring Kara to the point of twisting in her chair. Holly glared a warning at Kara to sit still. Kara glared back. She saw Louise watching her, and realized she was twisting around almost as much as Vinny, who never sat still for anything. Kara thought of the time she had gone with Mom and Vinny one day to get Vinny a haircut, and she learned why Vinny's hair always looked chopped. He couldn't sit still. He wanted to talk. He wanted to look his barber in the eye when he talked. The barber had said, after asking how old Vinny was, "I never heard a three-year-old talk as plain or as much as this one."

"Moving is quite a job, isn't it?" Louise said, more small talk. "We ourselves moved just as school was letting out for the summer. We didn't want to disrupt our children's school year. Now, this fall, they'll be going to new schools."

Joyce, with her perpetual small smile that at times seemed only to be a facial expression rather than a real smile, asked, "Does a bus come by?"

"Yes, and I'm glad of that. In our other home, they walked to school. We have only the two girls in school at this point. Bryon, who's five, will start kindergarten this fall. Vinny is three. I might start him in nursery school. I think he needs some school discipline to learn that children have to sit still occasionally."

Joyce laughed without changing the expression on her face.

Where was the girl?

Louise asked, "Where did you move from?"

"Not far." Joyce smiled. "It was so nice of you to bring the cake."

Louise was finally rising. "I've left my two little boys in the house. I told them we'd be right back. I'm so glad you chose our neighborhood, Joyce."

"I am too, Louise. We'll have to see each other often."

Kara broke a rule. *Don't interrupt adults with questions.* "Mrs. Renton," she said, "Where is your daughter?"

Joyce looked at her. Yet not really at her, it seemed. Her gaze settled somewhere near the top of Kara's head. At first it appeared she didn't know what Kara was talking about. But then she gave a little tilt of her head and her eyes focused on Kara's face.

"My daughter? She's at a relative's. But she'll be here soon."

"Today?" Kara asked eagerly. "Can she go bike riding with me?"

"Of course you'll be friends. When she arrives."

Louise put her hand on Kara's shoulder. "Kara's been searching the neighborhood for someone other than her sister and brothers to play with."

Joyce smiled.

"How many children do you have?" Louise asked.

It seemed to Kara that Joyce hesitated, as if she were counting kids who had stayed at their grandma's. But then she said, with that curious smiling expression, "Two. We have two. A boy and a girl."

"How perfect," Louise replied, sounding envious.

Kara gave her mother a sharp glance. *Perfect?* Just two kids, a boy and a girl? There were four of them. Did Mama think that was too many? Which of them would she give away in order to keep two, a boy and a girl? Kara knew. It would be her, and Bryon. Holly and Vinny were Mama's favorites. It was like Bryon and she just got lost in the middle.

They went down the paved driveway, between the tall stands of trees, to the street. Kara saw Holly look back, and followed her eyes. No one was in sight now.

"Phew!" Holly whistled softly, and made a wiping motion at her brow. "Weird people!"

"What?" Louise cried, astonishment in her voice and the look she directed at Holly. "How can you say that? They were lovely people."

"Well, yeah," Holly conceded, just as Kara knew she would. She always licked up to Mom. "They looked good. Like models."

"I think they're going to be very good neighbors. And you know how some neighbors can be."

Kara said, "That's for sure," remembering the Criptons, and how mad they got every time Pepper sniffed at their stupid flowers. Pepper never bothered the flowers at home, except to make himself a cool bed on a hot day if he couldn't get in the house, but the Criptons, back on the old street, claimed it was Pepper that dug up all their newly planted annuals. Which was a lie. Pepper didn't dig up Mom's plants, why should he dig up theirs?

"He's really handsome, don't you think?" Holly mused aloud. "And she's fantastic looking. But . . ."

They walked. They crossed the street, and Holly stopped at the mailbox to get the mail. They climbed the steps up the slope of the hill, then continued single file toward the front door.

"But what?" Louise said at the front door, continuing on without giving her time to answer, "For goodness sake, don't say to anyone else that they're weird, Holly. Some people might not know you well enough not to take you seriously."

They went into the shadowed foyer. Kara waited for Holly, and saw her pause and look back across the hollow at the house among the trees.

If Mom had seen her face then, Kara thought to herself, she too might have taken Holly seriously.

Kara agreed with Holly without knowing why. There *was* something different about the Rentons. They were really weird. In a scary way, an unreal way.

But maybe it was because they were trying so hard to be so nice.

9.

Brent had given Beverly his father's home address and phone number, and she dialed it as she drove away from the construction site. She listened to it ring nine times, and finally hung up. She hoped he wouldn't mind drop-in company, because he was going to have some.

She drove through town, reached Carl Salisaw's street in an older section of town on the northwest side, and went down the tree-shaded street slowly, looking for the number.

It was a brown brick ranch-style home, perhaps thirty years old, set back in a fine lawn with shrubs carefully planted in curved beds around the front and side walls of the house. She eased her Chrysler into the driveway and parked behind a blue pickup.

She got out. Neighbors in this area were beyond tall, trimmed hedges, yet there was a home-kept appearance rather than that of a professional gardener. She suspected that one of Carl Salisaw's pastimes was working in his yard.

She closed the car door softly, but it set off a deep-throated barking somewhere in the backyard, beyond the corner of a white picket fence.

A gate in the corner opened, and a man came toward her. Although the Salisaw construction company had worked for her husband in the past, the only dealing she had done was with Brent. She understood that Carl Salisaw was letting his son take over much of the responsibility.

He was a nice-looking man, she thought. He had the build of a thirty-year-old, with muscles well intact. He was several inches shorter than Brent, but she wasn't tall herself, and she found herself looking more directly into his eyes. Brent had found it too easy to stare over her head during her questioning of him.

There was no reason for Carl Salisaw to know her, but she saw from the look on his face that he did. He nodded a greeting, as was common in the area, among the natives, as if he were tipping a hat.

"Mrs. Inness?" he said.

His eyes were bright blue. Behind him the big red head of a dog looked over the fence. The dog had reared up and placed his front feet on the top railing. His paws looked almost as big as his head. Beverly could see his plumy tail wagging receptively.

"Carl Salisaw?"

He nodded.

Beverly smiled. "Is that your watchdog?"

The expression on Carl's face turned tender. "That's him."

"My cat looks more ferocious."

Carl smiled. "Yeah, Bud's somewhat of a pussycat."

"You have a beautiful yard."

"Well, much obliged."

Pleasure glowed for a moment, but only a moment, then the other expression came back. That quiet, disturbed, thoughtful look that he had worn when he came out of the backyard.

"You must work very hard on it." With this man, she sensed, it was necessary to work her way up to serious questions. He hadn't talked to anyone, evidently, and he might not talk to her.

"Not anymore. It kind of takes care of itself now. My

wife, she died three years ago, she's the one who planted the flowers. They just keep coming up every year."

Beverly nodded.

Carl said, "They don't need much care. A little mulching. A little water when it's dry. But we've had good rains this summer."

"Yes, we have."

Carl turned toward the gate. "Would you like to see the flowers?"

"I would. Thank you."

The dog stood back, big and shiny red and friendly. Beverly patted his head and he pushed close and looked up at her with adoring brown eyes.

"Behave yourself, Bud," Carl said calmly, and Bud walked away as if guiding her toward the flower bed.

There was a small birdbath fountain in the backyard, with a pebbled walk leading up to it, and surrounding it. At the edges were borders of flowers, all colors and sizes. Several bird feeders were scattered over the yard, in the trees at the borders, and on poles near the birdbath. All of them were serving birds, from cardinals to blackbirds and sparrows.

"You must like birds," Beverly said.

"The squirrels eat with them, and the chipmunks."

"Bud doesn't mind?" Beverly smiled over her shoulder at Carl.

"Oh, sometimes he minds, and chases them all out. But they get to eat often enough they keep me running down to the feed store for fifty pound bags of sunflower seed."

She stood still a moment. There was a feeling of peace in this backyard that she hadn't known in quite a long time, not since she and Clark used to sit quietly in their own little garden at the office.

"Come up onto the porch, and I'll bring you a glass of tea."

She started to tell him no thanks, she hadn't come for a social call, but stopped herself. She had a feeling

Carl knew something he hadn't told Brent. If they relaxed with a drink, perhaps he could more easily talk to her.

She sat down on the open porch, in a swing that reminded her of her great-grandfather's swing. She hadn't thought of Grandpapa much in these later years. He was part of a long ago past, a pleasant time when she, her mother and father, used to go out to the farm sometimes on Sunday afternoon. Her own grandfather had lived in a newer house on the same farm, so they usually ate dinner with Grandma and Grandpa, and someone always brought Grandpapa over. Until he began to refuse to leave his own house. It was during the last year of his life that he'd told Beverly the story of the revival meetings in the brush arbor, the strangeness of the ones he had called the "preachers," and the night massacre.

The story her dad had laughed at and told her to forget.

From this point, it sounded as if a terrible wrong had been done to innocent evangelists. But she remembered other things he'd told her. There was no blood, only a yellowish, slimy substance. Then, the girl who had planted the tree, and her warning.

The coincidence of three sensible men feeling they had uncovered a mass grave was too much. Her daddy had told her the story wasn't true. Just an old man imagining things.

But—she couldn't help but wonder.

What, exactly, had these men seen?

If there actually was a massacre there during the Civil War, and a mass burial, then the skeletons should still be there.

But the police had found nothing.

The laughter that was invading the town troubled her. Especially in light of the fact that something had caused Carl Salisaw to go into shock to the point where he had to be rushed to a hospital.

As Carl came out the back door with a couple of glasses in his hand, she wondered if she should tell him that story.

Carl sat down in a chair nearby.

"I don't suppose you remember much about me," he said.

She looked at him, surprised. "Remember you? We have done business with your company for years, but Clark always handled it as long as he lived."

"No, I mean back in school."

"In school . . . ?" As if the old comic lightbulb burst in her mind, she suddenly remembered. Not Carl, but . . . "Checkers!" she cried, feeling all at once like a teenager again. Remembering how she had stood on the sidelines of the ball field and yelled with the rest of her friends.

"Yeah." He grinned, leaned forward and rested an elbow on his knee. "I knew you the moment I saw you awhile ago, but I could see you didn't remember me."

"You were pitcher." She laughed. "You'd wind up and throw that ball like a pro."

He glanced up at her. "And you had the shiniest, prettiest hair I ever saw." His gaze caressed her hair. "It's still shiny and pretty, but a whole lot shorter."

She touched her hair, cut short, around her ears, boyish in back, bangs in front. "That's for sure. At one time when I was about seventeen, it hung to my waist."

"I remember that. You were a couple of years younger than me. Too young to ask out on a date."

"I can't believe I knew you then, Carl. It's like meeting an old friend."

"Not a whole lot of us around this area anymore that went to Northside school."

"No, I suppose not."

"Both of us went the whole twelve years there. I remember when you started. I was in the second grade. You had that long, shiny hair hanging in curls. I thought you were the prettiest little thing I'd ever seen."

"I didn't know that."

"No. I was too bashful to talk to you."

There was a moment of silence. Beverly wasn't aware that it was an awkward moment until Carl made a clearing sound in his throat, and sat back in his chair. He would be too polite to ask her why she had come to see him, so it was up to her.

"I came to see how you're feeling." She wondered the best way to approach the subject without startling him to silence. "Brent told me you'd been in the hospital."

Carl squinted out toward the birdbath. Bud came up and settled down at his feet.

"I got up and walked out of that place, brought myself home. There wasn't a damned thing wrong with me, and I don't have time to waste in a hospital."

"Right," she said. "I understand."

She didn't return the look she felt directed at her. The injured belligerence in his voice clued her in that he probably wouldn't talk to her either. Why should he talk to her? He wouldn't talk to his son about what he had seen. Beverly would have bet that he hadn't told anyone.

"You know, of course," she finally said, at a loss how to start, how to approach the subject with Carl. He seemed like an old friend already, but she could only guess at his reaction. "That I am the uh—the owner—the builder of the mall."

"Yeah, sure."

"Uh . . . ummm . . . I don't know where to start, Carl."

From the corner of her eye she saw him lower his head and look down, the same gesture Brent had used. The same dropping of the head Mel had used when he was a little boy, and ready to be sorry for something, or had a serious question to ask. The moment of getting ready to talk, or avoid talk.

"Let me help you," Carl said suddenly, lifting his head. "You heard the story of the grave underneath the tree that turned out not to be a grave, and since you own the land you want to know what the devil is going on."

"Not just because I own the land, Carl," she said softly. "But because I feel responsible."

"Why the hell do you feel responsible?" he demanded with surprise in his voice.

"Because . . . I could so easily have told Brent to leave the tree standing. He asked me. It was there alone, and it could have been left, I suppose."

"We talked about it," he said.

She looked at him and saw he was staring with his eyes narrowed off into the trees in the backyard. She sensed he was seeing the tree in the field. Or perhaps, the opened hole beneath it. She didn't interrupt his reverie.

"It made a strange sound when it went over," he said. "I thought at first it must be coming from that housing development across the road, but it was a quarter mile away, too far to hear a drum like that. And the sound was right there—kind of soft and close and deep."

She felt a ripple of trepidation. *And I think at times I hear it yet*, Grandpapa had said to her that day, *sometimes in the night I hear the beating of the drum.*

"The beating of a drum," she said breathily, feeling a pressure in her chest, coldness creeping into her heart.

"Yes," he said. "I keep having these nightmares. I see . . . things, and hear the drum roll. Getting to where I hate to go to sleep."

"Carl . . ." She made up her mind instantly. "I have a story I want to tell you. And then, perhaps you'll tell me what you saw that night while you were waiting for Brent and the police."

She saw his attention on her, serious, steady, waiting.

"It happened when I was nine years old. My great-grandfather owned that section of land where you're working on the preparations for the mall. He had been born in the house he lived in all his life. Like most of my family, he was a single child, as my father was, as I was, and my son is. We're not a prolific family." She smiled, but Carl didn't. He said nothing.

"It was my Grandpapa, as we all called him, that told me this story."

She repeated the story, every nuance of it that she remembered. Carl sat without moving, his eyes on her. In the backyard the birds began coming back to the feeders as if no one sat on the porch. The squirrels returned, their bushy tails high. They sat on the porch of the feeder prepared for them and picked up sunflower seeds in their sharp-clawed little hands and ate them, dropping the hull where they sat. They paid no attention to the dog asleep at his master's feet.

She finished the story. Carl said nothing. He continued to stare at her, as she stared at the birds, the squirrels, only partly aware of them. One part of her mind lingered with the picture she had presented to Carl. The only person she had ever told the entire story to. The only time she had mentioned it since her daddy told her to forget it.

Was Carl blaming her now for letting the tree be destroyed, or was he thinking she was totally mad if she believed for a moment that crazy old story?

She looked at him.

There was a strange, sorrowful look in his eyes. Almost misty. Slightly squinted. He wasn't questioning her beliefs, she saw, or asking why and when she had become so gullible. The look on his face was difficult to read, but it wasn't critical.

"The thing is, Carl," she said. "I had forgotten. It was just one of those things that slip a person's mind. Until my son called me and said people were laughing about this—this grave beneath the tree. Then it popped into my mind."

Carl's voice was almost a whisper. "You had never told anyone."

"No. Well . . . of course I tried to tell my mother and

dad on the way home in the car, but I assume Dad knew because he told me to forget it. That Grandpapa . . . umm . . . in so many words that Grandpapa had a wild imagination and couldn't tell fantasy from reality at his age. He was ninety or more, I believe."

Carl changed his position. He crossed his legs and leaned back, and she heard a sigh. He gazed out at the peaceful scene of wild things eating and drinking and bathing. Water splashed in the birdbath as a bright red cardinal took a bath. The droplets carried miniature rainbows into the air and dropped them to the ground. But the scene belonged in a different reality. Beverly felt removed from it, as if something dark and terrible stirred just behind her, just beyond the edge of her vision.

"You didn't tell your son?" Carl asked.

"No, I didn't. As soon as he hung up I went in search of Brent. I talked to him, and talked to Tom. Both of them were about to decide they'd been seeing things that weren't there. Because nothing was found in the grave. Not even that old piece of shoe Brent thought he had seen."

Carl looked down again, his head lowering. He said nothing.

Beverly said gently, "He was very concerned about you. He said you were—ill. He was afraid you'd had a heart attack or stroke."

Carl grunted. It was close to a snort of derision.

"He said it turned out you were okay. But—it could have been shock."

"He said that?" Carl looked at her sharply.

"Not exactly. Not in those words."

A moment of silence came, interrupted by the soft snoring of the dog.

"I think, Carl, that you must have seen far more than you've told. Would you tell me?"

Carl was silent a long time, then he looked at her. She knew if he saw the slightest expression of disbelief or amusement on her face, he'd never say another word. But she felt nothing but a growing dread, as if a masked danger were entering the garden, and bringing an early dark.

"I don't know what good it would do to tell you, Beverly. I think it would just worry you."

She made a sound of dismay in her throat. "Don't protect me, Carl! What do you think I am now? Unworried? Amused, like those others? I've never been a believer in things I can't see. But something happened while you were alone there. You *were* in shock, weren't you?"

He moved uncomfortably, obviously recalling his hours of near helplessness. Carl Salisaw would not want to be helpless, Beverly saw, not for a moment, not for anything. Admitting it would be admitting a weakness. Totally against his self-concept.

"I guess it was something like that," he finally said.

"What did you see?" She leaned toward him, her elbow on her thigh. "I believe, Carl, that Grandpapa told the truth. That something very alien was buried that night long ago. A group passing themselves off as evangelists, but not, perhaps, even human. Grandpapa certainly believed it. I think now he had tried to warn both my grandpa and my dad, but they only laughed at him."

She had spoken the right words: *only laughed at him.* Carl nodded earnestly. He edged over to sit close to her, as if he were afraid of being heard by someone beyond her. His worried eyes stared into hers.

"Damned if I know what it was, Beverly," he said in a loud whisper. "*Goddamned if I know!* And pardon the language, but that's how I feel. For the first time in my life I'm scared. I mean *scared.* There's something out there. Now. Since Friday night. I saw them . . . *them.* They came out of that hole like—like something working out of the ground, one after the other. Then they rose to their feet and walked past me, their faces as human as any you've ever seen. Perfect faces. Women, men. In pairs. Several of them. Maybe a dozen or more, like your grandpapa said.''

He drew a long, exhausted breath and leaned back, looking weak and drained for just a moment before he squared his shoulders. She understood he had told her more than he had told anyone, or had ever expected to tell. He had been prepared to carry that disturbing experience in silence, probably trying to figure it out.

He looked at her again, and said, ''They're out here, Beverly, among us. Somewhere. Walking the streets, the stores, maybe. And I don't know what they are, or what they're after. Like those old-time farmers, they—whatever they are—they scare me.''

They sat together another hour. They went over again all she recalled of her grandpapa's story, but it revealed nothing of the source of those buried beneath the tree.

He described the faces as he remembered them. ''I couldn't believe my eyes. They weren't naked. They didn't wear rotted rags. They wore long black robes. I think. With hoods. Their faces were shaded, but two of them I saw—I saw the features clearly. They walked right past my truck lights. The man had a straight nose, a beard, and seemed to have dark eyes and hair. The woman that was with him had long, pale hair. It was— they were—young—as if—as if they'd walked from a magazine. Like models, you know.''

Beverly listened, trying to visualize what he had seen.

''It was dark,'' he said. ''But the lights were on. These weren't people walking across the field from some— some cult gathering or something in the woods. I definitely saw them rise from that hole beneath the tree.''

He grew quiet. She reached for his hand, and felt his fingers grip hers tightly.

''But what could I have told the police?'' he asked. ''That it wasn't dead bodies afterall? In rotted garments? That they should be on the lookout for several pairs of good-looking—,'' He stopped, then added, ''It could have been maybe they did come out of the woods. And just happened to walk by. A witches coven. Something like that."

She shook her head.

"I've been thinking and thinking," Carl said. "It would seem they might have been harmless. They didn't seem to see me. Or they didn't care. I didn't know the old story, of course, and looking back on it, it might seem those folks were plain traveling preachers afterall. Themselves persecuted and killed. Except for the sickness of his mother, which evidently his father, and the neighboring farmers, blamed on them. . . . So what was their purpose? What were they preaching that caused the farmers to react the way they did?"

"But what about the child's warning?" Beverly asked.

Carl nodded in silence.

"You don't feel they're harmless," she stated.

He gave a short, sardonic laugh. "God no. You should have seen them, Beverly. They're not part of our world. Nothing of our world stays buried for a hundred and thirty years and then rises like they did."

Carl was silent again. Beverly held his hand as tightly as he held hers. "We're alone with this, aren't we, Carl?"

He didn't answer. The sun was gone, perhaps behind a cloud, or the trees.

"I have this feeling," Carl finally said, "that even though that group on your grandfather's farm set up a revival meeting, and pretended to be preachers saving souls for Christ, they were something out of hell itself." He paused and added so quietly she barely heard. "And your great-grandmother was—"

He didn't put it into words, but she felt she knew. The ancestor for whom she'd been named, Beverly Boyd, had become a sacrificial victim.

10.

Holly opened the sliding door off the family room and called to Pepper, "Shut up!"

The little dog came running to her, looked up pleadingly.

"What's wrong with you, Pepper? Shut up your barking."

He immediately ran back to the front west corner of the house, peeked around, and started barking again. His stance cried *boogerman*. Holly muttered under her breath and went to look.

Maybe there was a bobcat or something in the shrubs. Out here, where it seemed so far out of town even though they were still in the city limits, it was as if they were living in the wild, wild woods. There were so many trees between the houses that the only house visible was the one across the hollow. It was too dark now to see anything. The new neighbors must not even be home because there were no lights.

Pepper darted back to Holly nervously, then became braver and more ferocious. Fur lifted rigidly all along his back. Holly felt a similar chilling on her own backbone.

She wished Daddy would come and look.

She stood at the corner of the house, where shrubs

had been planted in a curving line that softened the sharp corners.

Her gaze swept the slope of the front yard. Only the walk was partly visible, from lights shining through windows. Pepper stood against her leg and growled, his nose pointed toward the hollow. She looked down at him, and across at the new neighbor's house. A street light down at the end of their driveway showed the white concrete dwindling to darkness. Nothing else was visible. Yet it seemed now that Pepper's yapping was aimed somewhere there.

"Do they have a dog over there that you haven't met yet?"

Pepper sat down, shivered, and whined.

"Or a cat?" She sighed. She didn't feel like laughing. "You're an awesome watchdog, Pepper."

She turned to retrace her steps to the sliding patio door. She called to Pepper. "You can sleep in my room tonight."

But Pepper had sat down at the corner of the house. His tail made a sound in the grass as it wagged. The pale edge of light from the living room windows outlined his small body. He didn't move. Holly could hear him growl.

She went into the house, up to the kitchen and helped herself to a glass of chocolate milk. She carried the milk to her bedroom and set it carefully on the desk.

"Hey!" Kara stood in the doorway, "You can't do that! You'll spill it on the carpet. Or your bed."

"I can too bring milk to my room. I don't spill," Holly answered in her new, quiet voice. She was learning to speak more carefully so that she didn't sound as if she were squealing or yelling all the time like Kara.

"Since when!"

"Since I turned thirteen," Holly replied. "Chill out, okay?"

"Thirteen. Big deal. Just because you're suddenly a teen makes you real cool, hey? Holly gets to do everything. I'm going to tell Mom." Kara disappeared down the hall.

So, Kara was irritated again. Holly felt at times she couldn't do anything that didn't irritate Kara.

Holly yelled, "Just because you haven't earned the right to take anything but water to your room, don't blame me. So I've grown through the spilling stage. So you haven't!"

Holly heard a grumbling complaint. "You get to do everything."

But it came from next door, not the hall. That meant Kara hadn't gone to tell Mom afterall.

Sometimes Holly could strangle Kara. Sometimes she felt sorry for her, even when she was whining or complaining. It made her furious if another kid so much as looked cross-eyed at Kara. But, she had carefully explained, as had their mother, when Kara got older and her hands larger and steadier, she too could take a drink to her room. Holly was still spilling when she was eleven, too.

She left her bedroom and went down the hall to the living room. Her parents had come upstairs and were watching television and reading. Mostly they seemed to be reading, looking up occasionally to see if anything was going on. Kara came in and sprawled on the sofa, her legs over the arm, a pout on her face. The little boys had been put to bed at eight.

"Dad," Holly said, "I couldn't get Pepper to shut up. I think something's out there."

"Yeah I hear'im," Brent muttered from deep in his concentration on the newspaper. "He's okay."

Kara said moodily, "No neighbors close enough around here for him to bother."

Holly understood what she meant. Back home on Crescent Street, the houses were so close you could hear the neighbors' televisions sometimes. You could hear mothers yell for their kids. You could especially hear people arguing, because their voices were always raised.

"I wish we were still there," Kara muttered.

"I guess it didn't bother you to share a bedroom," Holly said.

"The company was rotten, but all I needed was my own bed."

"I'm not going to get into that." Holly liked her new bedroom, and she knew that deep down, so did Kara. "Goodnight, everybody."

She went by their chairs and gave Louise and Brent a kiss goodnight. She paused near Kara just to tease her.

Kara covered her face with her hands, drew her legs up and squealed, *"Yukkkk!"*

Holly went down the hall laughing.

Outside, Pepper began barking again.

She loved her corner room, with windows in front and the sliding door opening onto the deck. She wasn't afraid to leave the door open with nothing between her and the night except the screen door. She felt so safe here now. At first, she had been afraid of the owls that cried in the woods at night. She hadn't even known they were owls.

She had heard the strange screaming, that loud cry that sounded like a soul lost in hell. That was the way she thought of it. It reminded her of some of the paintings she'd seen, done long ago, of people in purgatory. She had even gone running to her parents' bedroom one night and woke them.

Her dad sat up and listened, then he collapsed again, his voice muffled by his pillow. "It's a hoot owl," he said.

Holly stood there in her short white nightgown, probably looking like a ghost, in the muted light of the master bedroom. Mama turned over on her side of the king-sized bed and groaned.

"Hoot owls hoot!" Holly said, listening to the scream that was definitely not a hoot.

"Not all hoot owls go who-who all the time, Holly," he muttered. "Especially when something disturbs their nest. It's an owl, take my word for it."

Louise mumbled, "Go to bed, Holly."

So that had been Holly's introduction to the owl that screamed. Pepper hadn't barked at it. It hadn't bothered him, even though he'd never heard one before either.

She had gotten used to the owls, and in fact now enjoyed their cries, as well as their murmurs. She left the drapery on the sliding door open, and the window blinds up.

She drank the milk, went to the bathroom she shared with Kara, and brushed her teeth again. She had bathed earlier.

Her plans were to lie in bed and read, but the moment she adjusted her pillows to lean against, her eyes drooped. She turned off the light.

A cool breeze flowed through her room. She heard Kara go down the hall. A door closed. Then came silence, broken only by Pepper's occasional barks, and the scream of one owl, the hoo-hoot of another, soft and nearby.

It was incredibly quiet here, even with the birds and dog. There was no car noise. It was as if they lived miles away from the city, instead of the outer edge.

She curled on her side almost asleep, then images of the Rentons bore down behind her eyes. She tried to frown them away, but they remained, fantastic looking, fabulous bone structure behind unblemished skin. Both of them. They had the most unusual eyes. So pretty. Though she couldn't remember the color.

Yet, they gave her the creeps. Shudders. Shivers. And she couldn't dislodge their faces from her mind.

What was it about them?

Mama had seemed to like them. There was a glow about her that replaced the sullenness that had come over her lately. A distance, since she had met the Rentons, as if she were deep in thought. Holly knew she loved this new house. She was planning a big dinner, in which she was going to invite down some relatives that lived in other towns. Mom's parents were both dead, but she had some aunts and uncles that she visited a couple of times a year. Now she wanted them to see her new house. So Holly knew she loved it. But maybe the move had tired her. She just wasn't acting right lately.

Maybe Mama missed her old neighbors, just as Kara missed her playmates.

Maybe Joyce Renton could help Mama adjust. But just the thought of Joyce, the sight of her behind her closed eyes, made Holly want to pull the blinds, close the sliding door, and pull the covers over her head.

Louise stood in the master bathroom nude and looked at herself in the full-length mirror. Was her belly rounding again? Yes, she thought so. She had been too fat around the waist and hips ever since Kara was born, so it was hard to tell. Her periods had been coming fairly regularly, but scant and brief until the past month. Then none at all. She had thought it was because of the move. The excitement. The rush, rush. Even good things can be stressful.

She had ignored the faint feeling of nausea, and the sharp little pains in her nipples.

But yesterday she had felt movement in her belly. Not gas. Not that kind of movement. She could swear it was movement of another baby. Hadn't she felt it often enough to know? Four pregnancies, and now a fifth?

She hadn't once missed taking her birth control pills.

And for Lord's sake, it seemed she and Brent never had time to make love anymore. He was either too tired, or she was. But if this was real movement she was feeling in her belly, and not the roll of gas which she had tried last week to convince herself of, then she was about five months pregnant.

She felt like crying.

She dropped to her knees on the bathroom carpet and lowered her face to her hands.

"Please God, no, let it be something else."

She slumped, feeling as if she were crumbling inside.

The only planned child they'd had was Holly. Kara came before they were ready. They were stopping, they decided, with two little girls. But when Kara was five, Louise found herself pregnant again. That was fine with Brent. He was proud of all three of the children. Their family definitely was complete. Two girls and a boy.

Louise thought she could handle the birth control now. Her doctor had told her, "You must have missed one." She hadn't, she was sure.

Then Vinny came. Louise had been miserable through the whole pregnancy and had planned to have her tubes tied at birth. She did not want more children. She wanted to rest.

But when the doctor asked her about having her tubes tied she'd said no. Not until she was out of the hospital had she wished he'd asked her when she wasn't groggy.

There was something about Vinny, though, that was special. Right from the start, this squirmy little creature, the most miserable of her pregnancies, was the most precious infant. Maybe it was because she had not wanted him, that made him so precious. She didn't know what it was. She knew only that she did not want to go through another pregnancy.

If she were only two months along could she consider an abortion?

No. She would not have an abortion. She couldn't stand the thoughts of killing a baby, even one still called a fetus. They were, afterall, living creatures.

She had to make an appointment to see her doctor.

She pulled herself up and made herself go to bed and sleep. Fortunately, she'd had no trouble sleeping. She was always so tired these nights. Days too.

Brent leaned over to kiss her goodnight. "You okay?" he asked, as he did every night.

"Yes. Goodnight."

She had no intentions of telling Brent her worries. Not yet. She wished she could have an abortion, without feeling like a murderess. She might feel guilty, but if it were only tadpole size and shape, as early fetuses were, could she handle it?

No, no. It was her fault after all, and Brent's. Permanent prevention would have been so easy, since she knew temporary birth control had failed her before.

It was her feeling people should not make a baby if they didn't intend to take care of it for eighteen or twenty years, and love it forever.

It was so easy for Brent. He saw a pregnancy as a child. They could always manage. She saw it as months of misery, ended by the dangers of giving birth.

Holly woke.

Wide awake she stared upward through the darkness of her room. She listened. The night was silent. Pepper was silent. No owl hooted or screamed. Katydids and crickets were silent. But she sensed that a sound had awakened her, and a sense of danger had entered her room like a rapist, sneaking, wearing a black mask.

She sat up, and as if her movement stirred it to life, she heard the sound again.

A *drum*. Nothing, no one in her room afterall, but someone walking along the street in the hollow? Carrying a drum?

One beat, a deep rumble, followed by a rapid drumming, then slowing to a steady *drrruumm, drrrumm*. It came, closer, closer, yet never louder. Just a feeling of approach.

She looked out the window, puzzled, disturbed at this sound in the deep of night, but saw only the trees and the dark beneath them. She ran to the sliding door, opened the screen and went out onto the deck.

Moonlight touched half of the deck, the half that was outside Kara's room. In the dark half, Holly leaned over the railing and looked toward the street in the hollow.

The drumming stopped. The night seemed deadly quiet in contrast.

Then she saw the figure.

He stood in a path of moonlight in the middle of the street. Tall, shapeless but for the head, he wore something flowing and long and as black as the night beneath the trees.

The hidden face appeared to be looking up at her. She had an impression of paleness, surrounded by black, as if he wore a black cape over his head. She felt the white featureless face staring directly at her, and fear burst like vomit rising in her stomach. She wanted to run and hide, but she couldn't move.

Suddenly the moonlight disappeared. Darkness was everywhere. She felt helpless in the dark, no longer able to see someone that could still see her. But still she couldn't move. Her hands clung to the railing that surrounded the deck. There were no steps down, but she felt vulnerable, reachable.

The moonlight returned as suddenly as it had gone. It shone on the other half of the deck, and along a narrow path in the street.

But the man—the *person*—was gone.

In the silence Holly heard her bare feet making soft sounds on the redwood floor of the deck as she ran back inside her room.

She closed and locked the sliding door.

Then she hid in bed, clutching the sheet to her chin, and stared at the pale outlines of her windows.

Everything appeared distorted. Her room looked strange and dark and frightening, but she was afraid to reach out and turn on the light.

When he was a boy, so many years ago he could no longer be sure how long, they had called men like him bums. Or hoboes, if they rode the trains. He used to stand in the wheat field in the Nebraska sand hills when he was ten or so years old and watch the slow-moving freight trains going like long, segmented worms across the prairie. On the top, or in empty, open box cars, those old hoboes rode.

Loners, as he was.

One would ride here, the other there, box cars away.

It was all so long ago he had forgotten not only the number of years, but had almost forgotten his name. Dave, he thought, maybe David on his birth certificate. His mother had called him Davey.

He had planned to go back to see her. Long ago. But the sunset kept beckoning, the sunrise pushing him on. Or pulling him back. He kept thinking he'd go back. Then it dawned on him that he had probably waited too long.

His hair had turned white. His beard was long and white. Kids stared at him, as did their parents, when he came within their sight, which he tried not to do.

Sometimes, when he was caught in the cold, he had to search out the soup kitchen and a dry place to rest. It was in one of those that he learned people like him were now called the homeless. Not old bums, or hoboes.

It was, he supposed, a better name. But, call a spade a spade. Calling it a rose don't make it a rose.

He had known even when he was watching those hoboes on those freight trains that he would become one of them. The problem now was there weren't many trains anymore that could be ridden.

He walked, keeping as much out of sight as possible.

And at night he bedded down in private places. Such as old cemeteries and graveyards. Here, he was never bothered.

Country graveyards were the best. Neglected places, where leaves piled up against old tombstones, made good, warm, soft beds.

On a summer night such as tonight he sat against the old, leaning stone and gazed at the stars while he smoked his last dribble of tobacco. Time passed, growing silent.

He stretched out, leaves rattling beneath him. Stars winked and blinked and he wondered, what kind of homeless live there? But he wasn't much on reading or thinking, and he closed his eyes.

He had barely drifted to sleep when the sound woke him.

Footsteps, through the leaves.

He lay still, listening, eyes tight.

Not animals. These steps had a different rhythm.

He opened his eyes, and lay still. He had learned, in his long years on the road, to stay hidden. Never reveal himself when footsteps woke him in the dead of night.

The footsteps drew nearer, more than one person, more even than two or three, coming with a strange regularity, as if marching. They stopped, not far away, then started again, stopped again, and started once more. *What were they doing?*

He heard his own breath, and the rattle of a leaf in front of his chin. He eased his breath in and held it.

The footsteps moved nearer. Something dark and flowing swept into view. He stared. Long robes? Brushing the ground, the leaves. Black robes?

He silently cursed the lack of shadow upon him, his own carelessness in choosing a spot to sleep. Moonlight, starlight, outlined his legs. He could see his own worn shoes by casting his eyes down.

What were the witches doing? They must be witches. Who else wore black robes and came into an old graveyard on a still night?

They paused at a gravestone less than fifteen feet away and he heard the low murmur of voices. Then, they began to dig. Using shovels and hands, they quickly removed the packed soil. Their faces hidden by the hoods of their robes, he saw them bending into the open grave. In silence several figures bent into the grave, and when they rose, they held a small figure.

A child.

The body of a child, long dead. He saw her white dress, and the flow of long hair that looked silver in the faint light.

His eyes bulged, and his lungs burned. He almost sat up, then caught himself and lay still. They hadn't seen him. They must *not* see him.

Others who had been out of his vision came forward. The body of the child was placed on the ground, and the robed figures began a strange, soft chant. Hands touched the body, the mummified skull where the dead hair grew.

The child moved. Her breast lifted as if she'd been shocked. The robed figures stood back, their voices silent. The girl, long dead, sat up, and raised her face. It changed before his eyes, fleshing out, shriveled features returning.

The witches began to dance. He heard the words, "Success! She rises."

As if the dark woods beyond pulled at him, as if the dim light of stars and a dying moon reached out and filled him with terror of the very light, he plunged into movement.

He tried to stand, to run. His arms reached for the safety of darkness, of escape from whatever had entered the graveyard to bring up from the dead a child from another century. He tried to scream, but his voice was no more powerful than the death cry of a bird at night.

The hands grabbed him. They carried him face down to the empty coffin in the open grave.

He felt himself drop into the darkness. He felt the hard bottom of the coffin and smelled the mustiness of material long rotted, of flesh that had rotted away to cling to the satin within.

He heard the slam of the coffin lid.

Clods of dirt fell above him, striking the hard surface of the lid, becoming muffled as more and more fell. Until at last the falling could have been the death roll of a faraway drum.

His scream died in the silence that held him.

II.

Morning came, slowly, a grey arrival in which every flower, every tree seemed colorless and cut of the patterns of a dark and frightening night. Then the sun rose, but a thin layer of clouds obscured its brightness. No hummingbirds came to the red salvia Holly had helped Mom plant in the bed by the patio.

Holly thought about the night before as she made her bed and tidied her room. Finally she had slept, but lightly, as if a warning within her told her to watch, and listen. The sound of drumming did not return, but even with the day, she felt dread, as if its message, which she didn't understand, had been left to linger in the air.

She dressed for the day, went to the kitchen and ate a bowl of cereal in silence. Kara was at the table, but she was quiet too. Mom sat sipping coffee and staring out the sliding door onto the kitchen deck. Just staring.

"Did you hear the drumming in the night?" Holly asked. Her question sounded oddly to herself as if she'd asked, *did you hear the calling in the night?*

Calling?

For a while it seemed no one would answer. She heard Vinny's voice, chattering something to Bryon somewhere in the backyard, down below the deck.

Then Mama asked, "What drumming?"

Holly wished she'd said nothing. It was too weird.

"Somebody down on the street in the hollow, had a drum—"

She stopped, the vision of the dark-robed person returning more sharply now then it had last night. Now that she wasn't so afraid. He had stood in the moonlight. He had carried no drum. None that she saw. Where had the sound come from? The bass beat, as of a radio far away turned too loud.

"I didn't hear anything," Kara said. She rose, took her breakfast things to the dishwasher.

Louise returned to staring out the door.

The boys were going to their play area. Holly heard their voices, Bryon occasionally getting a word in. They had a sandbox in the side yard, near their swing set.

She returned to the bedroom, and smoothed the bedspread. As her mind had clung last night to the faces of the Rentons', now she thought of that strange drumming sound. And the phantom. Yes, phantom. As if he, or she, had been unreal. Not human at all. A real person wouldn't have been dressed like that, walking at night down the center of a street mostly obscured by darkness. He wouldn't have stood looking up at her in the dark part of the deck as if he—knew her.

A scream shattered the stillness of the morning. At first Holly thought of the owls she often heard at night. The figure in the long cape flashed through her mind again. Then she knew who it was.

Vinny. Screaming.

Holly ran to the door onto the deck, fumbled with the locks, and finally pushed the screen back and ran out.

Bryon came running hard across the yard in silence, and went out of sight below the deck.

Vinny stood on the slope of the hillside in the shade of trees staring down toward the street. The scream rolled from his chest, appeared to consume him, leaving him breathless. He made no effort to run, as Bryon had.

Holly looked over the deck. It was about ten feet to the ground. She climbed over at the corner, looking down. A splinter dug into her palm. She turned loose and, letting her body sag to protect her ankles, dropped. She fell into the edge of the flower garden where the soil was soft. Cushion mums beneath her were like pillows. The flowers were crushed. She rose to her feet and started running.

Behind her a door slammed and Louise's voice came on the verge of hysterics.

"Vinny! Vinny, what's wrong?"

Holly reached him first. The moment she touched his shoulders he whirled and threw his arms around her. Footsteps pounded the earth behind Holly, then Louise was pulling Vinny away and lifting him, crooning comforting sounds and words. Vinny's screams settled to sobs. He pressed his face against Louise's shoulder.

Holly looked. She saw nothing. The slope of the hill leveled off below and the neatly mown lawn continued on to the blacktop of the street that was now a light and dark mixture of shade and sunshine. Across the street was the driveway of the Renton's. The garage door was now closed, but both of the Rentons had come out to stand in the shade on their driveway and stare toward Vinny.

Holly looked behind her. Louise held Vinny, patting his back. He only sobbed now, his face hidden against their mother.

Kara stood with parted lips, her skin strangely pale. She too stared downhill.

Holly looked again.

Bryon was not here. She suspected he had gone to his room to hide in a corner, the way he had yesterday.

Another family member was missing.

"Where's Pepper?" she asked. Pepper who had barked half the night. He hadn't even wanted to come in. Sometimes he seemed to prefer his doghouse, especially when the nights were warm. Now that she thought of it, Pepper hadn't barked at the dark phantom in the moonlight, nor the strange sounds of a drum past midnight.

Vinny shook his head back and forth, mumbling incoherently.

"Vinny," Holly demanded, "Where's Pepper?"

The Rentons were coming across the street, Albert gaining a lead with his long, fast steps. Behind him came his wife, almost running.

Vinny's voice quavered. His small hand knotted into a fist with a finger pointing. "P-Pepper . . . my doggie . . ."

He pointed down the hillside.

Kara began to run down the slope. Holly followed her. The Rentons had reached the edge of the street.

At the lower corner of the lawn a trio of shrubs had been planted. The one in the center was a columnar evergreen, the other two round and thick. Before Holly had gone ten feet she saw the dark little body beneath the edge of a shrub.

Kara reached the shrub just before Albert Renton. By the time Holly had run to the foot of the hill Kara had gathered the dog's body into her arms.

Albert Renton said, "A car hit him. His neck is broken. He's been dead several hours."

A car! On this quiet street where only the home owners drove? And the mailman at noon? Only an occasional service truck? To Holly, the remark was oddly out of place.

Kara began to weep, holding the dog in her arms. Pepper's head drooped over her arm, his brown eyes flat and empty, no longer soft and warm and filled with life. Holly reached out to touch him, and Kara drew back, holding him closely against her.

Joyce Renton stood in silence in the center of the street.

"I'm sorry, children," she said.

Holly glanced at her in appreciation, and then stared.

Joyce's face was fixed with that same smooth, expression-less look that was almost but not quite a smile. Both their faces, Holly saw, had the same expressions they'd had yesterday afternoon. It was as if although both of them expressed regret, neither felt it.

Louise had come walking slowly down the slope still carrying Vinny.

"Poor little Pepper," she said.

"A car didn't hit him," Kara sobbed. "Somebody killed him."

"Let me take him," Albert said, reaching beneath his body and lifting him from Kara's arms.

Joyce said, "We'll take him home and bury him for you."

Vinny lifted his head. "No, no!"

"That's very nice of you," Mama said.

Holly was aware of the sudden tenseness of Kara's body. They had left a small pet cemetery at their old home. Their pets were always buried at home. The flower bed where she had crushed the plants would be a perfect place.

Bryon came running suddenly from nowhere it seemed. Usually quiet and unassertive, he now tugged at Holly's shirt.

"No," he whispered loudly. "Don't let him be buried. He's not dead. He's not dead."

Vinny kept wailing, "No, no, no . . ."

Holly reached out for the dog. It seemed as if Albert was ready to walk away, taking Pepper with him. But after a hesitation he placed the body of the dog in Holly's arms.

He smiled down at her. "Are you sure you want to do this?"

Joyce said, "You really should let Albert take care of the dog."

"Thanks anyway." Mama turned, blocking Vinny's view. "My kids like to take care of their pets, even in death."

"A car definitely hit him," Joyce said.

"Yes," Albert repeated, "a car."

Holly started climbing the hill. Why had they kept saying that? She'd heard Pepper barking for a long time, but he wasn't down at the road. She couldn't imagine Pepper going down to the road alone when he was acting so scared.

She held him closer, feeling the coldness of his body. He was still limp. How long did it take for stiffness to come? Rigor mortis. Or had it come and gone already? Had he died early in the night, or later . . . when the figure in the cape stood there, not far from the shrubs?

She carried Pepper, his body so cold. Hot tears swelled from her heart and eased down her cheeks.

Kara and Bryon walked beside her. She knelt at the corner of the flower bed into which she had jumped, and laid Pepper down.

"Don't bury him!" Vinny cried.

Mama came near, holding his hand. He pulled away and ran to kneel by Pepper.

There was no mark on Pepper. Holly turned him over. No blood on his mouth or nose. She felt his legs. None of them broken. His head hung, as if his neck had been broken.

"Mom," she said, sitting back and looking down at him. "Let's take him to the vet and see what caused his death." She heard in her mind the unexpected roll of the drum in the deep of night. As if it heralded the arrival of death.

Pepper hadn't barked.

Holly began to weep, her head bowed over the little dog that had been a tiny puppy five years ago. A little spotted wiggly lovable being. He would never hurt anyone.

Bryon sobbed a question that seemed to Holly to describe her own feelings, "Why did they kill him?"

"Can I bury him here, Mom?" Holly asked, wiping tears from her eyes with the back of her arm.

"Not in the flower bed, Holly. Take him to the woods. The ground is soft there, and easy to dig."

"No, no, don't bury him," Vinny cried. "He's not dead yet!"

Holly tried to soothe him. "Vinny, he's dead. See, his eyes are blank. Like the mouse last winter, remember? We buried the mouse. You helped, remember?"

Vinny nodded. "But Pepper's not dead!"

Louise picked Vinny up again and carried him toward the back door, saying over her shoulder, "Holly, you and Kara take care of it."

"It," Kara muttered, reaching down to slide her hands gently under Pepper's body. "She could at least say his name."

"She meant the burying, Kara."

Kara said nothing.

"I'll get the shovel," Holly said.

Daddy usually buried the pets, while she and the other kids performed the service. Vinny had been interested in a story about mouse heaven, and had given the three-year-old pet a last gentle rub. He had calmed before the burial, being assured the little mouse was in a perfect meadow where he ran and played with other mice.

But this was different.

Pepper was not a mouse. He had special ways of communication. Sometimes he even tried to talk, using different vocal sounds. He seemed to understand what they said to him, and considered pros and cons. He obeyed a command only if he thought it warranted effort on his part. They loved him. He was part of the family. A warm, furry, affectionate part. They all took turns getting affection from him. When Holly had her moods, feeling as if no one else loved her, she could always depend on Pepper to cuddle with her awhile, lick her face once, then lay his head against her chest.

Holly had seen Kara hold him that way. Often, since the move, Kara and Pepper sat on the hillside in the edge of the trees, with Pepper leaning against her.

When Bryon was scared, he wanted Pepper with him. At those times Dad always left the dog with Bryon, on his bed, until Bryon went to sleep. Then Pepper was put outside.

Holly wished she had made Pepper come into the house last night. He could have done his barking from the deck. He would still be alive.

That reminded her of the Rentons, being so sure he'd been hit by a car. She looked for them, but the house across the hollow was dark with shadows and shade. No one was in sight.

Bryon came dragging the rug from Pepper's bed, and something else. Holly took another look. Bryon had his old comfort blanket, the one he had carried with him for three years. He met her eyes in silence. His eyes were dark brown, and expressed sorrow easily. But he was no longer crying. He held his chin in a pucker of determination.

"He *is* dead, isn't he?"

"Yes, Bryon, he's dead."

"I'm going to put my blanket over him."

They spent the morning preparing Pepper's grave, arranging the rug in the bottom and sides to be sure no dirt would fall in his eyes. They carefully laid his body into the grave.

"To rest," Kara said after a long silence in which she had worked quietly.

"Do dogs have heavens too?" Bryon asked.

"Of course they do," Kara answered.

"Well," Bryon said, "when I die I'm going to Pepper's heaven."

"Everything is together," Kara said, "In one beautiful endless world where nobody hurts anybody else, where if a sun isn't shining a dozen moons are. Where the trees never die, and where bad bugs become good bugs. Even Jiminy Cricket will be there and little Mighty Mouse. We'll all be together again, Bryon. And Pepper will come running to greet us."

"He'll be waiting?"

"Yes, he'll be waiting."

Bryon leaned down and carefully spread his old blanket over the dog's body.

As Holly put the first shovelful of dirt onto the blanket over Pepper, she wondered if Mom knew Bryon had brought the blanket.

It didn't matter, she decided, looking at Bryon's face. Although she usually told her mother everything, she wouldn't tell her about the blanket.

12.

It had been an almost sleepless night for Beverly. Much of it she had spent standing at the window looking out at objects familiar to her all her life. Large trees, neat lawns, decorative fences, and the house next door—old, well-kept, large. But this night it was only a large, dark bulk, the street lights and the moonlight cut off by sheltering trees.

Her driveway below was lighted at each end by electric lanterns. Nothing walked or moved there. The dog next door was quiet.

Yet, she felt watched.

She resisted the urge to call her son. He had moved into his own place after law school. His fiancée, Paula, was probably with him, even though they didn't live together. Their wedding was three months away. Beverly suspected she spent many nights there away from her apartment, which was small. There was no point in disturbing them. What could Mel do?

What could anyone do?

What *should* anyone do?

She slept at five A.M., and woke at eight, relieved the night was over. She dressed for the office, but stopped at the kitchen phone to make a call to Carl. She greeted him with forced cheerfulness, then expressed one of her worries.

"Anymore nightmares?" she asked.

"Not enough sleep for nightmares."

"Insomnia?"

"Just couldn't quit thinking."

"That's why I'm calling, Carl. I can't quit thinking either. And I was wondering something."

"What?"

"Would you know those faces if you saw them again?"

There was silence on the line, then Carl said softly, "A couple, yes. I think. I'm not sure of anyone. Sometimes I still see them, and I think how could I ever forget them? Then, I don't know."

Beverly felt her heart beating in her throat. "Then maybe we can find them. I'll drive, you look. We'll scout the town and look. We'll find out the new people who have moved in. Want to give it a try?"

There was another hesitation. Then a soft, "Yes. Why not?"

"I'm on my way over."

Neither of them had said, and then what? Then what, if they found them, would they do?

Beverly thought as she got into her car and turned the switch that she should talk to Mel. Being an assistant D.A., he was well acquainted with judges and the prosecuting attorney, the Chief of Police, and officers of the law. Yet the thought of going to Mel with his most logical mind, after he'd been laughing at the grave that had nothing in it, made her hesitate.

No, not Mel, not yet.

She knew no one else she could talk to. Certainly not the minister of the church she sporadically attended, nor her doctor. Both of them, whom she had known since they were all young parents, would probably look at her with the same look she could imagine on Mel's face. *What, woman, are you crazy?*

Carl hadn't told his son. Carl wouldn't have told

her, if she hadn't told him the old story her great-grandfather had trusted her with. Trusted her. And she had not listened.

Beverly saw Carl when she turned the corner onto his block. Waiting in front of his house, he was walking back and forth along the sidewalk, hands in pockets, head bowed, deep in thought. She drew up beside him, and he came alert, gave her a small salute and climbed into the car.

She pulled away from the curb, going slowly toward downtown.

Carl was comfortable to be with, she thought. She too was given to moments of silence when she needed to get something straight in her mind. But she also liked someone to whom she could talk. And she hadn't had that in three years. Neither, she guessed, had he. Their mates had died the same year, only a few months apart.

"Where do we start?" Carl asked.

Beverly shook her head. "I don't know." She paused. "We need someone to check records for us."

"City hall? Chamber of Commerce? The records department? A private detective?"

Beverly felt the beginnings of a frustration that she sensed would be part of her for an indefinite period. She tried to smile, to relax. "Have you had breakfast? Why don't we start with a cup of coffee?"

He nodded. "Sounds good."

Everyone was so quiet, Holly thought as the day drifted along. It was so lonesome without Pepper. It didn't seem possible that he wasn't out there sleeping. She wished she could hear him barking at the corner of the house again.

Louise reminded her it was time to clean. Holly had been helping her mother clean the house since she was six years old. On Tuesdays they ran the vacuum.

Kara was supposed to vacuum her own room, but

sometimes Holly would rather do it than wait for Kara to finish her grumbling and get it done so that she could put the vacuum and attachments away again. When Kara put them away they were usually left sprawled across the floor of the hall closet and Holly was tired of telling their mother about it. She had grown to not like the way Louise looked when she scolded Kara. As if somewhere deep in her lay a wish she hadn't had children.

Today Kara was down on the hillside, just sitting there, not far from Pepper's grave.

After the cleaning was finished in the afternoon, Holly went to her room and tried to read a new mystery novel. She lay across her bed, the book on the floor, her chin resting on the edge of the mattress. The sound of the drumming she had heard in the night came back like the memory of a terrifying dream. She stared at the wall. She tried to get interested in the book. She read the same paragraph again, and wondered what she had read.

The sun had gone beyond the trees. Mom would be cooking supper soon. Then Dad would be home.

Holly got up and walked to the sliding door and looked out onto the street where she had seen the strange figure last night. Her gaze switched to the area where Pepper's grave was hidden among the trees. She started to turn away, then paused. A movement there, dark and quick, blended into the shadows of the woods. Kara? Was it good that she brooded over Pepper's grave? She'd have to ask Mama.

She went into the hall and back to the kitchen. Louise was at the sink jabbing at potatoes with the potato peeler. Part of the time she spent looking out the wide windows over the sink toward the driveway.

The boys played quietly in the corner of the dining area.

"Mom," Holly said, "Kara is—"

Then she saw Kara on the deck outside the kitchen,

stretched out on the bench, her legs draped over the railing. Her feet dangled, bare and tanned.

"Kara is what?" Mama looked out the window, but Holly sensed she wasn't watching for Dad.

"Nothing," Holly said.

Louise kept peeling potatoes. The voices of the little boys were soft mumbles. Kara changed positions, sat up and leaned her arms on the railing, chin cushioned. She too seemed to be watching the driveway.

"Is everybody waiting for Dad?" Holly asked, getting from the drawer another peeler and moving to stand beside her mother and help with the potatoes.

"I guess we are."

"Is he coming home early?"

"Who knows? The regular time, I guess. He hasn't called and said otherwise."

Holly peeled potatoes in silence a moment. "Mom," she said, and waited for the invitation to talk. It was always easier to talk to her mother when they worked closely together. Most of their serious conversations had taken place when they were preparing vegetables, or sewing, or cleaning the same room.

"Hmmm?"

"Mom, you know that drum I heard in the middle of the night?"

"Drum?"

"Yes. I told you. This morning. It woke me."

"Somebody practicing, maybe."

"It scared me. It sounded so out of place. I got up and ran out onto the deck and Mom . . ."

"Yes, Holly?"

"There was somebody in a long cape, standing down on the street looking up at our house. At me. The drumming had stopped. But—Mom—I had a feeling it had something to do with him."

Holly felt her mother's eyes on her face. Her hands grew still. Her left hand held a potato, and her right the peeler. But she was so still, so quiet. Holly glanced up.

"It was late—I mean like maybe two or three o'clock."

Louise said, incredulity in her voice, "You saw a man in the night wearing a long cape and carrying a drum?"

"No!" Holly said quickly. "He wasn't carrying a drum. At least, I don't think he was. I could just barely see him. And he was wearing something long and dark, like a cape. But Mom—"

"Then who was doing the drumming?"

"I don't know. It just—accompanied him. He was just standing there, looking at me, at us."

"Holly, how did you see all that when it was dark?"

"I don't know . . ." Louise was making her feel like a little kid who was trying to explain something that hadn't really happened. "The moonlight. It was shining on him. Then it turned dark and I couldn't see him anymore. It scared me, and I ran inside and locked my door."

"Why didn't you call Daddy?" Louise dropped the potato and the peeler and went to the refrigerator, emergency over.

"I don't know. I just went back to bed."

"I didn't hear anything at all. Are you sure it wasn't a dream?"

"Mom!" Holly cried in frustration, "I'm old enough to know when I'm dreaming."

Louise went to the door and said to Kara, "Come in and set the table."

"Mom—" Holly ventured, "Do you think it had anything to do with Pepper's death?"

"Holly, what kind of books have you been reading lately?"

Holly turned away. "Well, jeeze," she muttered.

Through the window Holly watched Kara drag herself off the bench with a total lack of energy. She came into the kitchen and in silence put the plates, flatware, and glasses on the table.

She said, "Can I go now?"

"Yes," Louise said.

She hadn't put the napkins on the table. Holly opened her mouth to remind her just as she left the room, going into the hall where the stairway went down to the ground floor. Kara was going to Pepper's grave again. But let her go.

Holly put the napkins on the table.

Kara went out onto the patio that was sandwiched between the wall of the garage and the posts of the bedroom deck. Mom's flower garden was a triangle, edged by the patio. Beneath the deck was Pepper's doghouse.

Kara sat down against it and leaned her head against the cool vinyl that sided it. Tears came again, sliding hot and wet down her cheeks.

She had spent the morning crying. Sitting at times on the grass near his grave. All day she had tried to think of something else, and couldn't. Pepper had been her puppy when she was just a little kid. They had pictures and videos of him playing in the wading pool with her and Bryon before Vinny was born.

He'd been Holly's puppy too, of course. Holly always brushed him. Sometimes she got mad because he wouldn't stand still. He liked being brushed so much that he wiggled and twisted and tried to lick her hand or face. But nobody ever got really mad at Pepper. Who could get mad at a dog, just because he was trying to have fun? Not even Mama got very mad—even when she chased him out of her flower bed with the broom she used to sweep the patio. Kara could see her grinning as she turned away, because Pepper had a way of tucking his tail and looking upwards from a lowered head as if he were really, really sorry.

Then he'd wait until she was out of sight and go right back to his bed in the flowers.

There was a hole there against the wall that he had dug out to lie in and cool off. Mama had left it.

"One bed, okay," she had said. "Two beds, no way."

You made a rhyme, gonna see your lover before bedtime.

That was a very old saying Kara had been told by Grandpa Carl. It was used to tease people, long ago, he had told Kara.

Shadows lay heavily in the woods now. Cool air came from among the trees as it came from the mouth of a cave. A gentle flow of coolness.

She stood in the edge of the trees looking toward Pepper's grave. Then she stared, and a frown slowly implanted itself between her eyebrows. She began to walk, then to run, toward the grave.

Something was different. Pepper's grave wasn't the way they had left it. Each of them had lovingly left a handprint on the soil, and something had ruined it. The soil they had carefully smoothed and patted down was now mussed and rifled, as if something had been digging there.

She came to the edge of the grave and stared down, dropping to her knees.

The grave lay open, like a wound. The blanket Bryon had covered Pepper with was lying crumbled in the grave, but Pepper was gone.

Beverly drove slowly through another housing development. Neither of them had spoken in the past few minutes. Carl looked to the right, and Beverly to the left as often as she could, as they passed slowly by the new houses, some of them occupied, some with "for sale" signs in their front yards, others still in the construction stage.

They had been everywhere they knew to check on newcomers. The Chamber of Commerce had given them statistics. The last counting, two years ago, gave a population number of 49,276. "But of course," said the lady who tried to help them, "many are not counted. Those who don't want to be counted manage not to be. They're usually people who are living with someone else, or in apartments rented by friends or relatives."

Newcomers, they found, were next to impossible to know about. People moved about, place to place, in many cases.

They had gone away discouraged. Back in the car Carl drew a long sigh, and Beverly knew how he felt.

They went for a light lunch that neither of them finished.

Now they were looking at another of the developments.

"But they wouldn't be here," Beverly finally said, and felt like slapping herself on the side of the head. "Not this soon."

She pulled the car to the curb in front of a house that had a "for sale" sign. The front yard was still bare. A few shrubs had been planted, softening the corners of a house that stood in the open, with no trees.

Carl looked at her, weariness crinkling his eyes.

"It happened only last Friday. They wouldn't have had time to . . ."

She didn't finish her thought. She wasn't even sure where the thought had been leading her.

They looked into each other's eyes.

"They're probably not even here," Carl said. "They could be miles away by now."

"But we can't give up, Carl. They're somewhere."

"Why don't we just go home," he suggested.

She nodded, and used the driveway of the unsold home to turn around.

Holly finished slicing the tomatoes and arranged each slice neatly on a small platter, placing radishes around the edge, and tiny onions across the middle. She was playing, wasting time, as Louise would ordinarily say.

But today Mama wasn't noticing anything, it seemed. She kept staring out the window. Over the deck. Toward the driveway. At first Holly had thought she was looking for Dad, but now she decided it wasn't that at all. She was just staring. When the boys got in a small fight in the corner, with Vinny screaming at Byron about something, Louise hadn't even noticed.

Kara came quietly into the kitchen and stood still just inside the doorway. Holly saw her, but didn't really look until Kara kept standing there, saying nothing. Holly glanced up.

Kara looked as if all blood had been drained from her. She stood like death, staring blankly, and Holly felt a chill of premonition.

"Mama," Holly said.

Louise turned.

"Kara, what's wrong?"

They went toward her, all of them. The boys came quietly from the corner.

Kara looked up at Louise.

"Pepper's gone," she said.

13.

They were silent, stupified. No one understood. Kara, pale and trembling, stared up at their mother.

"He's gone," she said again. "His grave is empty."

Vinny cried out, "He's alive! I told you Pepper wasn't dead!" He pushed past and ran out. Holly heard his footsteps thumping on the stairs. Bryon took out after him without speaking.

Holly paused only a moment, then she too followed Vinny. It's not possible, she was thinking. Pepper *was* dead. She had seen him, with his eyes staring and his body cold. He *was* dead. She had to see the grave for herself.

She was aware that Louise and Kara were following. In front of her, already halfway across the back lawn to the trees, Vinny was crying out, "Pepper? Pepper?" His short legs worked like some mechanical toy—up, down, up, down. He ran faster than he'd ever run. Bryon couldn't catch up with him.

They were both already at the grave when Holly caught up. Vinny took only one look, pulled Bryon's old blanket out of the small grave, and went dragging it back toward the lawn, calling.

"Pepper? Pepper? Where are you, Pepper?"

His voice, babyish yet very clear without a lisp or

mispronunciation, carried in a high-pitched song. Bryon just stood looking into the grave as if mesmerized by it.

Holly didn't know Louise was standing behind her until she said, "Something dug up his body."

Kara cried, "But who would do that?"

"Not who, Kara, what," Louise said. "Probably a wild animal, or another dog dug him up and dragged him away."

Holly heard her walk back toward the house, her footsteps whispering in the leaves. Kara sat down on the disturbed soil of the grave and began crying audibly. Holly saw Bryon put his arms around Kara's neck, and Kara's arms go around Bryon.

"It's okay, Tara," he murmured with his lisp, "It'll be okay. Pepper, he's gone up to heaven."

Holly slipped away. She had never seen Kara hug Bryon before. Usually if Bryon got close to her he got an elbow in his face.

Louise called, "Come on in now. Daddy will be home soon." She had Vinny in her arms. He had stopped calling and was beginning to cry in frustration. Mama had made him quit calling.

She went out of sight through the back door at the stairway up to the halls and kitchen above. Kara and Bryon rose, and walking together, heads down, followed Louise.

Holly stood looking through the woods. Shadows were deepening, and it gave her an eerie feeling. She wanted to run to her room, and view this woodland from her exposed deck. But she stood still, looking.

Through the trees, not far away, she glimpsed the wall of the house next door. So far as she knew those neighbors, a retired couple, had no dog, only a couple of cats that she had seen out on the driveway when she had ridden out in the car.

On the far side it was the same. A few hundred feet

of woods, then another house. Their dog was tiny. She could hear it yipping sometimes.

There were no closer neighbors. Only the new couple across the hollow.

Pepper's grave had been robbed sometime since they'd buried him this morning. But there was no dog running loose in the area that she'd seen. The thought of a wild animal that would dig up a corpse in the daytime, as Mama had said, might be believed by Vinny, or Bryon, but not by Holly. She had studied the habits of animals in biology and knew it wouldn't have happened like this. Wild animals came out mostly at night. Nor would many wild animals dig up a dead dog and drag the corpse away.

Mom knew all that, Holly suspected, because the look on her face at the grave was filled with a strange curiousness, a frowning uncertainty.

Holly circled the grave, looking closely for any sign of disturbance to indicate which direction the grave robber had gone. A sprinkle of fresh-turned soil, a disturbance of the leaves and vines that coated the woodland floor, but that was all. There was nothing other than their own pathway through the leaves and vines. The vines that had been inadvertently kicked aside were already falling back to their natural growth and covering their path.

The long, pale streaks of sunshine that had lain across the mowed grass of the yard a few minutes ago were now gone. Heavy shadows were growing in the woods, and the night insects were beginning to buzz fitfully here and there.

Holly walked into the yard and stopped, her eyes drawn to the figure across the hollow.

A little girl stood at the end of the Renton's driveway, watching Holly. Chills slipped like melting ice over Holly's body. She felt the skin on her face tighten, and goosebumps pop up on her arms.

She stood returning the girl's stare, unable for a few moments to breathe or move. The girl was too far away for Holly to see her features, but she saw the pale blond hair that hung loose over her shoulders in long curls.

The girl didn't move or look away.

Holly turned, the inexplicable fear increasing to panic. She yearned to run—*run* and hide, the way she had hidden from the man in the cape last night . . .

. . . the sound of a drum . . . the man in the hooded cape . . .

Death.

And now a strange little girl staring.

Holly ran. In the shadows of the woods to her left, not ten feet away, the girl suddenly stood. Holly almost screamed, then she saw it wasn't the strange little girl afterall, but Kara. She had come out of the house again to look at the empty grave.

Kara turned at the sound. Holly, running, had stumbled. She paused, steadying herself.

"Come on in the house, Kara," Holly said, breathless. She ran on, and out of sight around the house.

Kara started to follow, then her eyes caught the flash of color down in the Renton's backyard. Someone wearing pink walked slowly into the middle of the street.

Not the lady, but a girl. The Renton's daughter must have arrived. She had walked toward Kara as if she wanted to talk to her, but she stopped. She didn't speak.

Kara walked partway down the lawn. She returned the girl's long stare.

Then she noticed the girl's dress. It was the same dress one of her friends at school had worn last year. Her mom had taken it to a used clothing store. Did the Renton's buy used clothes?

Weird.

"Kara!" Holly stuck her head out the front door only

long enough to give the order. "Come on in!" She slammed the door shut.

Kara turned, paused and waved at the girl in the street. Then she hurried on around toward the back door.

Carl sat with his newspaper. He had opened the paper after his small supper, the way he always had. But since he had seen what he had seen climb out of the hole beneath the tree roots, he hadn't been able to lean back in his recliner and rest. He hadn't been able to relax and read the newspaper. His nights were filled with brief episodes of sleep and long periods of wakefulness. Going to bed seemed almost a waste of time.

He fought an urge to walk the floor, thinking, trying to figure out whether he had seen what he thought he had, or was he crazy? He knew the opinion of the police who had investigated, and the laughter that was circulating in some groups. He had known, beneath his shock that night, what their opinions would be. Afterall, there was no longer a body or a grave, was there?

But what was there?

He had finally, before it was even dark, brought his dog into the house to lie on the rug near his recliner. Then he had tried again to read the paper.

There were a couple of killings, caused by a mixture of jealousy and booze. They were getting to be common lately, it seemed. One was at a bar, and the other at a trailer house on the edge of town. Four banks had been robbed sometime during the past few nights, entry unknown, amounts taken undetermined.

He read and reread the parts about the banks. They had been in neighboring towns. Odd. Odder still was the murder of the woman on Basil street. Someone had entered her store somehow after it was closed, and killed her by breaking her neck. There was no specific inventory to tell if anything had been taken. Clothing was still on the racks, and a few dollars remained in the cash register.

An apparently motiveless murder.

He found the other item on the third page.

"Graves Robbed in Roller."

Beneath the headline was a short article stating that three graves in the old cemetery called Roller, which was in the county by a small white church that hadn't been used in years, had been opened by some unknown persons. The coffins were still there, interiors rotted. But the bodies that had been buried in them were gone.

The graves were those of children, all girls, ages eight to ten, who died in 1867, 1875, and 1891.

The names weren't mentioned.

Carl sat frowning at the fireplace mantel across the room. Why would anyone want to rob graves that were more than a hundred years old? All female children, in an area that had never been wealthy? If they were looking for jewelry, the robbers would not have picked a child's grave.

What was the purpose? And there must have been a purpose because it wasn't random. A random destruction would not have seemed so deliberately chosen.

It disturbed him deeply, as if somewhere in the depths of his mind a connection was building. He didn't have any pretentions toward being in touch with anything that he couldn't reach out and feel. He wasn't sure he believed in anything.

Yet . . . since the big tree went down, his whole world seemed to have turned around. Too many strange things were happening, and many of them concerned graves.

The phone rang, and he jumped out of his chair and cried out involuntarily. His heart pounded. Bud leaped up and gave one deep woof.

Feeling weak and ready to cave at the knees, Carl sat down again, laughing without humor at himself, and with more humor at Bud's reaction. He reached out and laid his hand on Bud's silky head for a brief caress. "We're a couple of fine ones, aren't we Bud?" The dog settled down again, his eyes cautiously open. The phone went on ringing, loud and shattering.

It sat on the table beside Carl's recliner, and he reached over and lifted it, glancing at the clock on the mantel. 10:10. No one called this late. Maybe it was Beverly, and maybe she had learned something she wanted to share.

"Grandpa?"

For just a moment the child's voice seemed distant and ghostly. "Grandpa? Is that you?" He recognized Kara. She sounded weak and weepy.

"Kara, sweetheart! What's wrong?"

"Oh, Grandpa, Pepper is dead. We found him dead this morning. Mr. Renton said a car must have hit him. I tried to call you, but you were gone."

"Pepper is dead? I'm sorry. I'm sorry about Pepper, and that I wasn't here. Did you bury him?"

"Yes, this morning. Then I went out to see his grave again this evening, and it was empty. Pepper was gone."

"What?"

"It's empty. What do you think happened, Grandpa?"

Empty graves. "Sweetheart, I don't know."

"Vinny thinks that maybe he dug his way out like that little dog did—you know the story about the little dog that actually did dig his way out? He wasn't really dead? But I know Pepper was dead. I saw him. I carried him, and he was cold when we buried him."

He started to ask if she shouldn't try to rest, to sleep, because sleep was restorative, but said nothing. The newspaper was on the floor beside Bud, open to the page about the empty graves of the little girls.

Kara went on talking.

"Daddy came home late, and looked all around. But he didn't find Pepper."

"Well, honey . . ."

"Mama said Pepper was dug up by a wild animal."

"That's very possible, Kara. That must be what happened."

He made his voice soothing, but his eyes gazed steadily at the headlines of the short article.

Graves Robbed in Roller.

He was aware of his deep frown, the squint of his eyes, and was glad Kara couldn't see his face.

"You'll feel better about it tomorrow, Kara. These things happen, sweetheart, when a dog gets out into the street . . ."

He heard her sob, and tried to think of a way to distract her. "How do you like your new home? Big new bedroom all your own, with a door out to a private deck and everything!"

"I have to share the deck and bathroom with Holly."

"That's better than sharing your room too, isn't it?"

"I guess so. I don't know."

"Have you found any playmates yet?"

"Well . . . I haven't met her yet, but I saw the new girl across the street. They just moved in across the hollow. Their driveway is right across from our mailbox, down front."

"Yeah?" He stopped breathing.

A new housing development . . . of course there'd be new families moving in. The—people—whatever they were—he had seen rising from the hole beneath the tree had all been adults. There were no children. He felt smothered, and drew a deep breath. It came with difficulty.

"So," Kara said, "Mama, Holly, and I took them a cake yesterday."

"I thought you said you hadn't met the girl. Wasn't she at home?"

"No, just the parents. I think she was staying with her grandparents until the moving was finished."

Carl looked again at the article in the newspaper. Graves robbed very recently. Possibly last night. A woman's neck broken for, perhaps, a few articles of used clothing? Banks robbed. No forced entries anywhere. No suspects.

"But tonight," Kara was saying, her voice slow and sad, "when it was almost dark, I went out to see the grave again, and the girl stood in the street by the driveway."

"Kara," Carl said slowly, "what do these people look like?"

Kara hesitated a moment, obviously puzzled by the question. "Look like?"

"Yes, you know, blond—brunette—Hispanic—African American?"

"Oh, no. Mrs. Renton is blond. And so is the girl. Mr. Renton has dark hair and a beard, but he's white."

"Were they real young?" Carl queried. "The parents?"

"Yeah—I guess. Younger than Mom and Dad."

"Try to describe them, Kara."

She sighed. "Well, he has this funny beard. Not like Daddy used to have. I don't know if her hair is bleached."

"Is it long and flowing?"

"Uh—her hair? No, it was braided. I guess it's long, though. Why?"

Carl felt the edging upward of the same cold shock he had felt Friday night while he waited alone at the old grave for Brent and the police. He saw again the pale movements within the dark hole, the almost phosphorous glow of the figures.

Then, the lovely skin and features, the almost waxlike appearance of those that came one after the other from the old grave. He'd never forget that long, flowing hair, some dark and glossy, others as pale as if they'd been bleached by long years within the darkness and dampness of the earth.

"Were they—are they," he asked slowly, "exceptionally pretty? Good-looking?"

"Uh . . . yeah, I guess so."

"Kara, I think I'll come over to see you tomorrow, all right?"

Her voice lightened. "Sure, Grandpa."

"I have a lady friend I want you to meet."

"Okay, great."

"And I would like to meet your new neighbors."

"Great! Then I can meet the new girl."

"Now Kara, you do me a favor, go to bed, and go to sleep, all right?"

"Well, goodnight, Grandpa."

"Lock your door, Kara."

"Okay."

Carl hung up and sat back in his chair. Ten-thirty. He was tempted to look up Beverly's number and call, then decided to wait. He didn't know but that she might be one of those people who like to go to bed with the chickens, as the old saying went. Meaning sundown.

He didn't realize he was tapping his fingers against the chair arms until Bud lifted his head and looked to see what the noise was.

14.

Brent went out onto the front stoop. Narrow wedges of light escaped from beneath the blinds in the master bedroom and competed with moonlight on the lawn. Moonlight bathed the sloping yard in front of the house and fell in patches on the street below. He had walked the perimeters of the two acre lot in growing darkness earlier in the night. He had carefully examined the grave. He had covered enough of the wooded areas to feel the dog was not on the property.

Although he had tried not to reveal his edginess and perplexity to the kids, he hadn't been able to relax. All of the children, naturally, were upset because of Pepper. Each, in his or her own way, had shown their unhappiness. Vinny had whined and complained and been short of temper, until finally Louise took the boys to bed. Even Bryon, usually very mild, had thrown something at Vinny. Kara was weepy. Holly stared. Brent was glad the evening was over and everyone in their rooms.

He walked down the path toward the mailbox. The racket of katydids and other busy, buzzing insects rang in his ears. He stopped, hands in pockets, and looked at the darkness in the trees across the street.

People had moved in there, the kids had said. He

hadn't had a chance yet to talk much to Louise. They never talked until the kids were settled down.

Kara said a new girl was there now. She hadn't been quite as excited as Brent expected. Probably because of Pepper.

Yet now, for the first time, his attention was drawn to the house that was invisible in the dark. He hadn't thought of it earlier, but while lights were on in his own home, slashes of bright triangles in the dark, there was no light across the road.

He knew there were twin lightposts at the bottom of the driveway, on each side. Just as there were on his driveway. Those lights came on at dusk and went off at dawn. Automatically, as soon as the electricity was turned on at the home.

The lights across the road weren't burning. There was no light anywhere among the trees where the house stood. So, obviously, the new neighbors hadn't finished moving if they hadn't had the utilities turned on.

Farther down, a dot of light glowed softly like a firefly. Another home. A light somewhere, wherever there were people and houses.

He looked once more at the darkness across the street, then turned away and circled his own house once again.

He couldn't figure this thing about Pepper. What would dig a dead dog from its grave? Especially in daylight. There were too many incidences lately having to do with empty graves. His thoughts slipped back to the other empty grave, and to his dad. He hadn't shown up at work since Friday. Yesterday he had said he was feeling fine and would probably see them today. But he didn't show.

Brent tried off and on all day to call him. Then, when he left the site, he drove over to see about him.

Carl was in the backyard pouring sunflower seed into the bird and squirrel feeders. Claimed he was fine. Brent asked him if he'd gone fishing today. Carl said no, he was just out and around. Brent had a feeling Dad was still keeping things from him.

It was destined to be a short conversation. Brent was overdue at home, and in a hurry as always. So he'd left.

"See you tomorrow?"

"Is there anything you need me to do?"

"No . . ." Not exactly. Just liked to have him around, like to talk to him about work now and then, get his approval.

"Then you probably won't."

Carl didn't offer any explanations. Brent hesitated only briefly before he left. Patted the dog, inquired again if Carl was feeling all right.

The short visit tumbled through his mind in conjunction with arriving home and being met head-on by his four teary kids. All of them tried to talk at the same time. He had finally heard a strange, terrible story about Pepper. Killed sometime last night, they had buried him this morning but now he was gone from his grave. All of it, from the kids and Pepper, to Dad, combined with minor problems that had occurred at work. Yet his thoughts kept winding up back at the place across the street. The one where a family had moved in, but the electricity appeared not to have been turned on.

Moonlight softly touched areas of his own house. The girls' bedroom deck was dark, shaded by trees and the roof of the house. Lights were on in both bedrooms, blinds and draperies pulled. It must be eleven o'clock, he thought. But the girls were allowed to read at night if there was no school tomorrow.

The boys' rooms were only faintly lighted.

Brent stopped at Pepper's doghouse. A deep anguish felt for a moment as if it would crush him. The little black and white shepherd had been with them since he was six weeks old. Ordinarily, he would have been walking with Brent through the night. Sniffing. Alert.

What had killed him? Even stranger, what had robbed his grave?

Vinny was certain that Pepper had climbed out of his grave. Then he cried because Pepper had run away. Brent had only held and hugged him. Was it better for Vinny to think Pepper had somehow rescued himself from death and the grave, and then chosen to leave the only family he'd ever known?

At the back of the house Brent paused, looking at the dusk to dawn lights at the end of the driveway. They glowed dependably.

After a few more minutes he returned to the front door of the house and let himself in.

He had bathed and changed to pajamas and light cotton robe before he went outside. Now he entered the bedroom and sat down on his side of the bed to remove his house slippers. He tossed his robe toward the bedpost at the foot of the bed, and didn't pick it off the floor when it slithered down.

"Where've you been so long?" Louise asked.

"Oh. You still awake?"

"Yes."

"I just walked around the house again."

"Didn't see anything?"

"No."

He arranged his pillows so that he was slightly propped up. The only light on in the bedroom was within reach. The blinds were still up, windows open. He felt a cool rush of air. It was like a drink of fresh water.

"Are you sure he was dead?" he heard himself saying.

Louise turned her head and looked at him. "Yes. I'm sure."

"What do you think killed him?" They hadn't talked of the cause of death in front of the children. They hadn't talked of anything, actually.

"The Rentons next door . . . the new neighbors, came over. They thought he'd been hit by a car. His neck was broken."

"Maybe somebody killed him," Brent said, surprising

himself with this sudden thought. Pepper had been barking a lot, earlier, at something or someone. Then he'd grown quiet, and barked no more.

"I don't know what happened, Brent. I just want to go to sleep." She turned over.

He stared at the ceiling, his mind veering from disturbed ramblings to blank depression.

"Brent," Louise said suddenly, after he thought she had gone to sleep, "Did you look at the grave?"

"Yes."

"What was your opinion of what happened?"

"I think it was opened by someone with hands or a shovel."

She sighed. "I wondered. But I told the children a wild animal had dug him up."

"If an animal had been digging there, the dirt would have been scattered. It was piled in a neat little mound. It was deliberately scooped out and piled to one side."

They were quiet for awhile.

Then Louise asked with anguish in her voice, "*But why?* Why would anyone want to do that?"

"I don't know."

He leaned over and kissed her. There were shadows beneath her eyes, and exhaustion. "Go to sleep," he said.

She nodded and turned onto her side again, her back toward him.

He hadn't told her the reason why Dad had gotten ill Friday evening. About uncovering what they'd thought was a mass grave beneath the tree. Then, the disappearance of the bodies. He was glad now he hadn't.

He turned out the light and cushioned his head on his pillows, staring toward the moonlight at the windows.

Empty graves.

If it hadn't been for Pepper's disappearance from his grave he could have accepted what the psychiatrists called the—the whatever. The mass hysteria? Of three men who'd never had delusions in their lives? Not even under the influence, would any of them have imagined they saw bodies where there were none. But, he would have accepted that it had to do with the light, the shape of the roots, the color and all that. Especially since he saw for himself no more than an hour later that it wasn't a grave afterall.

Yet . . . what happened to Pepper brought it all back, and enforced a feeling that weird things were happening lately.

And it had something to do with graves.

15.

In Carl's nightmares the solitary drum played an eerie march and the bodies glided past, large, colorless, pulpy wormlike beings. Human features erupted as they approached him, noses, lips, chins, forming faces of rare beauty. A terrible beauty that left him shrinking in fear as they drew closer.

He woke, trembling and cold. He went to the kitchen, warmed a small glass of milk, drank, went back to bed and had the same dream, changed only in that the faces swarmed around him, laughing, chanting in a language he didn't understand.

He woke at last to find a grey dawn filtering through the darkness. He was ready to abandon the effort to sleep and rest, those two conditions he had taken for granted less than a week ago.

At dawn he went out to work in the flower beds, looking for weeds to pull. He did a little digging, making the earth soft and receptive.

He fed Bud. Gave him a full can of food. Bud stood looking down into his dish of food, then, tail wagging only slightly, looked quizzically up at Carl.

Carl remembered. He always fed Bud at night, not in the morning. Bud had no appetite in the morning.

Carl patted the dog's head, and Bud settled down to guard his unwanted food from flies.

Carl puttered about the clean kitchen. He had surprised himself with his housekeeping abilities. When Annie became too ill to keep the house, he had found that he could. In the beginning he had hired a lady to dust, vacuum, wash the bathtubs, and all that sort of thing. Then gradually he had taken over. But this morning the housework had been done, the house was clean. All he could do now was look at the clock, sip coffee, and wait. He wasn't sure what time he should call Beverly. Or if he should. He wanted her to go with him to see Louise and the kids, and to see what kind of neighbors had moved in across the street. But perhaps he shouldn't ask Beverly this time. Not without Louise's permission. He, alone, could just drive over. His visits were always short and spent mostly with the kids.

He watched the room grow lighter. Outside on the patio he heard Bud growl and leap, shooing away flies, or perhaps a junebug that inadvertently flew too close to Bud's food dish.

Louise showered, feeling as if she'd been beaten. She was so tired.

As she dried she considered planning the day, but slumped instead onto the vanity stool, rested her elbows on the counter and her head in her hands. Why did she always have to think out each hour of the day? First, see to it that Vinny and Bryon were properly dressed. Then, see to it that all four children had a proper breakfast. Then . . . laundry, shopping. Grocery day? Something for dinner. Sweep the decks and porches and patio. The driveway needed to be blown free of debris too. The bigger the house, the more work, she had discovered.

Oh God . . . so tired.

But she had to get moving.

She stood up and the nausea came. She hung over the wash basin until the sickness eased away.

Now she knew. She needed only to have the doctor confirm it.

Her tubes would be tied, definitely, after this birth.

If she only had the guts for an abortion! Brent would never need to know anything about any of it. She could just hear him. "That's okay, Babe. One more. What's meant to be, you know."

Yeah.

But maybe, she thought as she pulled on a duster, she only had a virus. Maybe she was just so afraid she was pregnant that she was imagining her symptoms.

She went to the kitchen to find that Holly and Kara had already eaten. Holly was rinsing her cereal dish. Kara had gone out to sit on the kitchen deck and stare off toward the woods and Pepper's grave. The boys were at the table, dressed acceptably in shorts and shirts. Vinny was yelling, as usual. Thank God he sounded as if he had regained his appetite. He'd been so sad since Pepper's death. Too sad for a little three-year-old boy.

"Cocoa Puffs! Cocoa Puffs! Somebody get me Cocoa Puffs! Can I get my own Cocoa Puffs?"

Holly cried, "Mama make him shut up! Vinny, get down from that cabinet! Right now!"

"I want Cocoa Puffs!"

"I'll get you Cocoa Puffs! Just give me time! Gosh, I'm never going to have any kids," Holly muttered, reaching for cereal boxes.

Louise brought out bowls and milk. Kara came into the kitchen.

"Mom, can I go over and see the new girl?"

Louise glanced at the clock. It was scarcely nine o'clock. She had overslept a little. "No," she said.

"But why not?" Kara wailed. "I won't go to the house. I'll only go to the driveway."

"No. It's too early. Holly, make some toast, please."

Kara was still begging to go visit the new neighbor girl.

All at once Louise felt she had to get away from the kids or commit mayhem. "Just shut up, will you, Kara?" Louise heard herself scream. Tears came to her eyes. What was wrong with her?

She went into the den and closed the door. The room was small and shadowed, and very private. She dialed the number of their family doctor. The appointment nurse gave her an appointment, two weeks away.

"That long?" Louise asked.

"If you need to see him sooner I might be able to get you in next week. It will be an early appointment. Eight-thirty."

"Okay, I'll take it."

A week away. Of course she could take a home pregnancy test, but what good would that do? They weren't foolproof. She wanted to know for certain.

She had never felt so depressed, so lost, in her life. It was an emotion new to her, as if a dark shadow had skewered her soul.

She heard the children yelling, and pushed back the drapery to see what the hell they were into now.

Vinny went running past the window, his arms out, a look of delight on his face.

It meant only one thing. Grandpa Carl was here.

Good. She hadn't seen him since he'd taken himself home from the hospital. She had gone in while he was still sitting grumpily in his hospital bed and given him a peck on the cheek. He looked fine to her though he seemed distracted and nervous. He had jumped and stared at her a moment without recognition it seemed to her when she entered the room. He claimed nothing was wrong with him.

She loved Carl almost as much as Brent did. He took the place of her own dad, who walked out on her mother and all the kids, with Louise the oldest of seven at age ten. She never saw him again. Her mother had become so discouraged a few years later, trying to keep the kids together, that she too had disappeared. Since then, Louise had rarely seen the other kids, who were reared by family members, as she was. At sixteen she was out on her own. Later, she'd heard both her parents were dead. So Carl and Annie had been the parents she'd never really had.

Just going out to heat the coffee again and have a conversation with Carl lifted her spirits.

Kara paused in the hallway and listened. Voices somewhere in the house? Vinny? As always. And a deep voice, like Grandpa's.

Her feelings soared. He had promised to come over. He said he wanted to bring a lady friend. How long had he been here? When Mom had told her no she couldn't go over to meet the new girl yet, Kara had decided to wash her hair. She had shampooed, then used the blow dryer. He had come while she was making her own racket. Why hadn't they told her Grandpa was here?

She hurried toward the kitchen. She heard their voices as she approached. Everyday stuff, like the weather. Kara pushed open the swinging doors into the kitchen. Grandpa had come alone. The lady friend wasn't with him.

He sat on a chair near the sliding doors that led onto the deck. Vinny was on one knee, and Bryon on the other. Vinny fiddled with the pocket watch Grandpa always carried in his shirt pocket. Why, Kara had asked once, didn't he wear a wristwatch? Because something around his wrist made him feel he was handcuffed, he told her. She didn't know if he were joking or not. It was hard to tell with Grandpa.

She went around behind him and put her arms around his neck. She kissed him on the cheek, then hung there, her cheek pressed to the top of his head.

"Good grief, guys," Holly said from somewhere on the kitchen side of the room, "Get off Grandpa and leave him alone."

"I can remember when *you* sat on his lap!" Kara retorted, giving Grandpa's neck one more squeeze before she moved away.

"Well, that was when there were just two of us."

Grandpa Carl said, "Ah, they're all right. They'll be like you one of these days, Holly, too old to want to sit on my lap."

Mama sat at the table sipping coffee, and Holly showed up with a platter of sliced coffee cake.

"You shouldn't have done that for me," Carl said. "I just thought I'd come by a minute. Don't mean to stay long. I was wondering about your new neighbors, Louise. You've met them, I guess."

"Yes. Lovely people."

"Do you know anything about them?"

"Ummm . . . not much, really. We met briefly. They're very nice. A young couple with two children."

"But," Holly offered, "the children weren't with them. They had stayed at their grandparents'. Then yesterday I saw the girl was there. She was weird." Holly frowned.

"How can you say that?" Mama asked. "You didn't even meet her."

"I mean, she was weird in that she just stood down at the end of the driveway looking over here. And later, she was still there. I mean even when it got dark, she was still there. I thought that was kind of weird."

Mama said, "It is rather odd the parents didn't call her in. But maybe the child is lonesome for a playmate, like Kara."

"Yeah!" Kara agreed eagerly. "We could walk over there, couldn't we, Mom?" Kara had her, she saw, when Louise looked at Grandpa. She wouldn't tell him no. Kara added, "Then Grandpa could meet them himself."

Mama said nothing. Wrinkles formed in the corners

of her mouth. It was the almost-smile that meant she felt someone had put her on the spot.

Holly came to the table, sat down, and starting munching on a tiny square of coffee cake. Vinny got down off Grandpa's knee and helped himself to one, but then offered it to Grandpa.

Holly said, "Oh Lord, Vinny, look at your dirty hand. Grandpa doesn't want that. It would probably poison him."

Vinny dropped the coffee cake on the table, believing Holly explicitly. He looked at his hand, grubby with dirt, fingers spread.

"Go wash," Mama said. Then, "If Grandpa wants to go with you, I suppose it will be all right. But I need to get busy around here."

Carl eased Bryon off his knee, and stood up. Kara was first out the kitchen door into the hall. She waited at the top of the steps while Carl was coming, saying his goodbyes to Holly and Mama.

When Grandpa Carl came into the hall with both boys, Kara asked, "Are the boys going along?" She heard the whine of objection in her own voice. "Why do they want to go along?"

"We won't go up to their house. We'll just walk over and talk to them if they happen to be out in the yard."

Kara led the way down the stairs to the back door. She remembered something. "Grandpa, you didn't bring your lady friend?"

"No. It was a bit early, I decided."

"What's her name? Where'd you meet her? Are you going to bring her over sometime soon?"

Vinny asked, "Are you going to marry her?"

Kara scolded, "Vinny! For gosh sakes, he just met her."

They had reached the yard, and Bryon paused at Pepper's empty house and began to speak slowly in his soft lisp about Pepper being dead. "But he rose up from his grave," he added, his eyes round and large.

"Who told you that, Vinny?" Kara demanded. "He was *dug* up, that's what! And Grandpa knows all about it. I told him last night."

They went on, the boys detouring over toward the trees, pointing out Pepper's empty grave. Carl followed, and spent a moment frowning down at the pile of dirt outside the hole.

Kara waited in the grass. She didn't want to see Pepper's grave, nor even think about him. When she thought of him, a hollow feeling opened in her chest.

Carl and the boys came back and Kara led the way down to the street.

At first the Renton's driveway and backyard looked deserted, as if they'd moved away in the night. Then Kara saw a movement at the trunk of a tree. The girl stood pressed against the trunk, as if trying to hide. Kara slowed, her eagerness leaching away, disappointment rising. What was wrong with her? Was she scared of them?

Grandpa Carl stopped in the middle of the street. Overhanging trees shaded him and the boys. Vinny was quiet for a change. He reached up and grappled for Grandpa's hand. Kara's attention was split between the actions of the boys, suddenly bashful, and the shady driveway where the girl stood against the tree.

But Kara could see her face now. She was beautiful. The most perfect face she had ever seen. Her eyebrows were straight and high, dark against her pale skin. Her eyes were bright and dark. Her hair in contrast was pale blond and long. The thick strand over her shoulder hung to her waist.

She was like a girl from a long time ago. She wore a new dress today, but it was long, halfway between her knees and ankles.

"Hello," Grandpa Carl said. "Do you live here?"

The girl said, "Yes."

They stood in silence. The girl stared at each of them in turn. Kara decided she was maybe ten years old. Really childish and immature, like Kara hadn't been in three or four years. Well, two.

She looked, though, as if she'd be almost as tall as Kara herself. And, like Kara, she was totally flat chested. Holly was into her first bra, and Kara kept watching her own chest for some signs of growth but nothing, absolutely *nothing*. When she'd complained, Mom had said, "Well, thank God." No understanding there. She'd been hoping for a growth shot or something magical.

Grandpa Carl asked with a smile, "When did you move in?"

"Yesterday."

"Your parents, too?"

Kara looked back at Grandpa. Why was he asking these questions? He already knew the answers. She'd told him.

"No," the girl said after a hesitation.

Kara waited, Grandpa waited, expecting more information, but the girl said nothing.

"What's your name?" he asked, speaking in that tone of voice that he always used with children or pets.

"Heidi."

Heidi! The name of the little girl in the book. Kara had never known a real live Heidi.

"That's a very pretty name," Grandpa said, and motioned toward Kara. "And this is Kara. She's been waiting for you to come so she'd have someone to play with."

Heidi's stare switched to Kara. She stepped out from against the tree. Then, to Kara's pleased surprise, Heidi smiled faintly.

"Hi," Kara said.

A flicker of something crossed the girl's perfect features. She answered softly, "Good morning."

They stood awkwardly, staring at each other. Grandpa and the boys were quiet. Kara could believe they were no longer there, and it made her feel a little scared.

She glanced back to make sure she wasn't alone. She swallowed and moistened dry lips.

"I'm eleven," Kara said. "My birthday was just last month. How old are you?"

Heidi opened her mouth, but it was a long moment before she answered. That same flicker, like a shadow, crossed her face. At first Kara had the impression that she didn't know what to say. That she didn't even know. Was she retarded?

Then Heidi spoke, as softly and slowly as she had before. "Ten. I'm ten. My birthday is . . ."

Kara waited, but she never finished. The shadow moved across her face, like streaks of shade among the sunshine when a breeze swayed a tree limb.

The boys began to talk, to move about in the street. They went back to their own lawn. Grandpa Carl, Kara noticed, gazed with narrowed eyes toward the Renton's house, shadowed and partly hidden by the trees. But no one was there. Except Heidi.

He asked, "Are your parents working?"

Heidi seemed so hesitant and bashful Kara ached for her.

Then, "My father's a minister. He's building a church."

Grandpa turned his head quickly, staring hard a moment at Heidi. Kara didn't understand. He looked at her house again.

"Are they home?" he asked.

This time Heidi didn't answer for a long time. She stared as if she were looking at something far, far away. Then she said, repeating, "He's building a church. My mother sometimes helps."

Kara waited for the next slow sentence. She had such a strange way of talking.

"We're going over there soon," Heidi finished almost in a whisper.

Kara felt disappointment again. That meant Heidi wouldn't be home to play.

As if Heidi's voice had called Joyce out, the back door of the house opened and closed. Joyce came walking briskly down the driveway. Kara saw she was wearing a skirt and blouse. The skirt was gathered very full and ruffled at the hem. It, like Heidi's dress, hung halfway down her calves. On her feet she wore sandals. Her pale hair had been braided the way it was before, and pinned up on the back of her head.

Carl went up the driveway to meet her.

Kara looked at her again, and noticed even more this meeting how beautiful she was. Her face, like Heidi's, was perfect. Yet they looked nothing alike.

Carl couldn't be sure if this face was one of the ones he had seen. Like her daughter, Joyce was exceptional. He couldn't help but think their skin was abnormally perfect, like a baby's skin. Or, like skin that had been buried in the darkness, never decaying, but becoming more and more perfect.

Those he had seen in the darkness, rising from the grave beneath the tree, had long, flowing hair. Like the child's. Joyce's hair was done up, but it could have been the right color of several of those he had seen. Her size was right. Slender, medium height.

Hearing from the little girl that her father was a minister had struck him with that sense of shock, the chills, the cold dry skin, that he'd had Friday night. The man claiming to be a minister, tied in completely with the story Beverly had told him.

He asked the young woman who hadn't offered her hand, "Your daughter tells us your husband is a minister."

Joyce nodded and smiled. "Yes."

"What denomination?"

There was no shadow or expression of hesitation on her face as there had been on Heidi's.

"Oh," she said smiling, "we don't belong to any

special group. We'll be naming our own church. Yo
must visit us.''

He hadn't known how to ask without sounding as i
he were giving her the third degree. Which, in fact, h
was. But she, friendly, seemingly open and honest, ha
given him the opening.

"Thank you," he said. "Maybe we'll all come. Wher
is your church?"

"I'm not sure of the address, but we'll certainly le
you know."

She put out her hand toward Heidi. The child move
toward her, but Joyce's hand fell before the chil
reached her.

"It was very nice to meet you, sir. I'm sorry we nee
to leave now." She said to Heidi, "Come dear, Daddy'
expecting us."

Carl nodded, and backed off. Standing on the gras
of Brent's lawn, he watched as she got into the blac
car, turned around in the wide driveway and drove dow
the street.

Well, she could drive. Outside her style of dress, he
old-fashioned looks, long hair, no makeup, sh
appeared very modern.

He watched the car disappear around the corner
shaded by trees. She could drive expertly, it seemed
She already had a car, a house, everything a norma
person would have. Would she, if she had been one o
those, be here, living the human life, the American life
So soon? He didn't think so.

Whatever he had seen, where would they be now? A
he turned he looked into the woods. Hiding places
behind trees, as the little girl had hidden? In caves and
hollows?

Was he getting paranoid? Would he see in every new
arrival in town, possibilities of horror? What kind of
horror?

Maybe they were harmless, those that had crawled

out of that hole. Those that had been buried long ago. Maybe they were the persecuted, as it might seem.

But even now the coldness, the fear and dread that ate at him and pushed him to search, told him they weren't harmless. They wanted something, something they were beginning to get in that old-time revival back during the Civil War.

He wanted to talk to Beverly. They could discuss it over coffee in some little place, and maybe eventually everything would make a little bit of sense. Or maybe, it would all just drift away, like any nightmare.

16.

Carl kissed the three children goodbye. From the kitchen deck Holly called goodbye and he waved. "See you later, Holly." He motioned the children out of the way of the pickup. They stood together, each a head taller than the next. Little Vinny still looked like a baby. They all did, he decided, looking from one baby face to the other. Even Kara's face was still round-cheeked.

He backed into the turn-around section of the driveway among the forest trees, then started to pull away.

Three innocents. Four, five, counting Holly and Louise. Across the road from strangers who might be very fine neighbors or . . .

He had a dread suddenly of leaving them. A fear he would never see them again as they were now.

He slammed on the brakes. The kids, still standing together, came running toward the pickup.

"Are you staying, Grandpa?" Vinny asked.

"No, baby. Grandpa just stopped to tell you to—to—" How could he put it without giving the children nightmares? "To tell you to stay away from the road until I see you again. Okay? The street down front."

They looked at him, puzzled. He read their thoughts.

That road? Where only the neighborhood people drove? It went on east about a mile before the hollow came to an end and the street climbed a shady hill where big trees came together above the pavement, and then on the level above it joined busier streets and became part of town. Between here and the end, streets every quarter mile or so came down the hill through shady lanes. A good place to live, ordinarily.

Carl looked directly at Kara.

"Be careful of the strangers," he said pointedly. "Across the street. *Be careful of them.*"

Kara said nothing. He saw her frown. Puzzled. It came and went like a heartbeat. He was confusing her, scaring her. She wanted to play with the little girl across the street.

He said, afraid that his deep concern might harshen his voice again as it had before, "Just watch out for strangers. Play on your side of the street."

He left them. They stood together. Holly was leaning over the railing. She had heard him, he saw.

"Bye kids," he motioned a wave that included Holly. "See you in a day or two."

They all returned the wave but Kara. She still stared at him, puzzled. Hurt in a way, he thought, and wondered if he had been wrong to advise her. It wasn't his place. Yet neither Louise nor even Brent knew what Carl knew.

Brent hadn't seen what he had seen, and he had been unable to tell him.

He wondered if the time had come that he should tell Brent.

Carl drove into the driveway of Beverly's house. The house was in the area of homes that used to be called mansions, in the days before the houses in the subdivisions became larger and more elaborate. It was a fine old house, rising above the tree-sheltered driveway, many porches indicating a style a century old. The lawn in front was small compared to his own. A sturdy wrought-iron fence, very decorative, encircled the front lawn and had been there he surmised as long as the house had. A gate opened onto walks both out front by the sidewalk, and here in the driveway, leading to porches.

He sat still, feeling out of his element. But wasn't that why he had never spoken to her in school? The little rich girl, Beverly Boyd would never speak to him, whose father was a construction worker. Beverly's people owned most of the land of the area, as well as banks and businesses.

Yet Beverly seemed not much different from Annie, one of the sweetest women he'd ever known. The girl who had made him forget the beautiful Beverly Boyd.

He had called Beverly on his way over. Not choosing to keep a phone in his truck, he'd had to stop at Quik-Stop and use the pay phone. She hadn't gone to work. She didn't intend to go to work. "I'm taking some time off, Carl," she had said softly. "We have to concentrate our efforts on this thing. I tried to call you at your home. Since then I've been biting my fingernails wondering if I should go over and see how you were. I was just ready to leave the house when you called."

Carl had felt something when she said that. An emotion almost forgotten. That old feeling of being cared-for, being understood by someone. Of being not entirely alone.

He had barely turned off the engine and opened the truck door when Beverly came out of the house. She was dressed in a casual pantsuit, his favorite shade of blue. A small brown bag hung against her side, the strap over her shoulder. Her dark hair was brushed back from the sides of her face, and fluffed into bangs on her forehead. She looked cute as a button, younger than fifty-nine or sixty, which he knew she was, since she'd been only a grade behind him.

But her face was set and serious.

He hurried around and opened the door for her, and was ready to help her up into the pickup. She didn't give him a chance. She pulled herself up into the seat and sat looking ahead. He hurried back to his own seat and started the truck.

"I've been calling around, driving around," she said, "I asked my son Mel to check on newcomers to town. He wanted to know what for, he said that was some job I'd assigned him."

She gave Carl a quick smile, reached over and put her hand on his forearm as he backed the truck out into the street. The touch almost threw him off, and he nearly backed into a car that he hadn't seen because of shrubbery. He stopped quickly. The car went on by.

Beverly said softly, "I'm so glad to see you . . . to see that you weren't . . . well, that you're here."

Carl returned her smile, then put the pickup into drive and headed forward.

"I've been over to see my grandkids."

He told her about the family across the street.

"I don't have a good feeling about the woman. She's too perfect. No blemish, nothing normal and human, it seemed to me. Too perfectly beautiful. Yet, would she be able to drive? If she was one of them?"

They had passed the square and were headed out toward the site before Beverly attempted an answer.

"We make the mistake of thinking of them as people, Carl. Somewhat like the rest of us. They aren't people. They can take human form. Evidently they choose perfect human form. Who knows what other powers they have? What abilities?"

They rode in silence for a few blocks, moving from older, smaller homes in the edge of what was once the old town, into new areas of shopping centers, businesses on one or two floors, and new homes, getting larger and larger.

She added, "Or what dangers."

"I don't know if it's because of what I saw," Carl said, "But it seems to me people can sense their presence, in some ways. It's a feeling of not being safe anymore, of feeling that something is out there, in the dark, in the night. Even in the open day."

"I know," she said. "I haven't felt safe since Mel told me about the tree, and the grave. It's strange how we take for granted the reality of our world. The sun rises, sets, things grow. Then suddenly . . . it just isn't the same. The kind of things we worried about no longer seem important."

"Did you read about the grave robbings?" Carl asked.

"I beg your pardon?"

Carl told her about the childrens' graves at Roller cemetery. He told her also about his grandchildrens' dog.

"Carl!" she cried so softly it was almost a whisper, "Those can't all be coincidences. What does it mean?"

"I don't know. My brain seems to be on overload, and it leaves me blank. I don't know what it means. I do know it scares the—well, it scares me."

They rode in silence again. He noticed she leaned closer to him, and found himself responding by leaning a bit her way. Here they were, the only two people who knew. He felt emotionally closer to her than he ever had any woman other than his mother and Annie.

"I was thinking about telling my son Brent, about what I saw. I thought if you told him your story, then, it would help. Not to understand, but to see why I'm worried about the new people in his neighborhood. The kids are going to be together."

"But you changed your mind?"

It was almost as if Beverly could read his thoughts. "Yeah, I did. For the time. If I told him that, after what he himself saw, he'd be worried to death. And what could he do? What can anyone do?"

"You're going to the site," Beverly stated when they came to the more open areas west of town, and nearer to the little trail into the field.

"I'm going to talk a little bit with Tom."

Dust fogged in places over the field where the Boyd farm had been, indicating the places where bulldozers and smaller machinery were at work. The pickup bounced over a few clods of dirt, raising its own fog of dust. The trail across the field that once had been worn into grass, had now disappeared into ragged, but smoothed earth. Tufts of dislodged grass mixed with the dried dirt. There was nothing to indicate where the tree had stood.

Carl parked safely away from the dustiest areas.

"Want to stay in the car, Beverly?"

"Absolutely not," she said, opening her own door and getting out. Then she came to meet him at the hood. "But, Carl, I don't think we should say much yet to Tom, or anyone else, do you?"

"No. I just want to ask him if he knows of any new people moving into his area. He lives in a development about two miles from Brent."

One of the bulldozers stopped, and a lithe, young man jumped down and came walking toward them, wading through the dust clouds made by other machines.

"That's Tom," Carl said. "I could tell that walk of his on a crowded street at midnight."

They went to meet him.

Tom came closer, using a big red handkerchief to wipe dust from his face. Still, he looked as if he'd been powdered. Dust clung to his eyebrows, eyelashes, hair, and circled his mouth even though he rubbed vigorously. He looked embarrassed.

"Excuse my looks, Miss Beverly."

"You're fine, Tom."

"Looking for Brent, Carl?"

"Not especially. Just wanted to talk to you a couple of minutes. We'll try not to keep you too long."

Tom grinned. "You're the boss."

"How do you like your new home, Tom?" Beverly asked.

Tom glanced down, smile gone. "It's okay, ma'am. It was our first home. Of our own, that is."

Carl prompted, "A lot of new people moving in, I suppose, since the development is just being built."

"Oh yeah."

"Have you met any of them?"

Tom gave him a squinted, curious look. Carl could see he thought the questioning was peculiar.

"I don't have time to meet anyone, but there is a new couple moving in right across the street from me. Came this week. Couldn't help but notice that. And there are several on the next street."

"We're checking out the newcomers," Carl said lamely, wondering if eventually he would have to enlist the help of both Brent and Tom.

"I can tell you this," Tom reached up and replaced the cap he'd had in his rear pocket. He pushed it to the back of his head and stared off across the street toward the wooded area of another housing development a couple of years old. "This place where I go to have a few beers in the evening, it's getting to where there are a lot of people up from Mexico. It's a mixture of languages in there now. I don't know what they're saying," Tom grinned. "And I don't suppose they understand much of what I'm saying. But everything's friendly after a while."

Carl exchanged a glance with Beverly. They could certainly discount Hispanics. Those he had seen emerging from the ground were pale-skinned. As white as you could get and still have color.

"Have you met the new neighbors? The ones across the street?"

"Oh, well, yeah, I guess you could say that. They moved here from up north. Came driving one of those U-Hauls. The missus drove the car. They don't know anyone here, just wanted to get away from all the kids and grandkids, the way it sounded to me. They're only two hundred miles from home, close enough for easy visits, but . . . but hey, Carl, what's going on?"

Carl hesitated. Beverly said nothing at first. Then she said, "It has something to do with the tree, Tom."

She had spoken softly and slowly. The tone of her voice had made her words seem ominous and chilling. Tom stared at her intently.

Carl said, "You saw the grave, Tom, beneath the tree."

Tom said, "I had almost convinced myself that I didn't see anything. It was getting pretty dark."

"Well . . ." Carl didn't want to talk. Something stopped him. The incredibleness of it, perhaps. It was the stuff of nightmares, not of reality.

Beverly made a move as if to leave, or look away, but said nothing. Carl put his hand on her back, gently, and felt the warmth of her. It was the first time he had touched her.

"We'll talk to you later, Tom," Carl said.

They walked back toward the pickup.

As Carl got into the truck, he said, looking across the way at Tom, who was still watching them, "I just couldn't."

"No," Beverly said. "Not yet."

Carl started the truck, and turned toward the street.

Tom watched them go. What was that all about? There was something about the questions that made him feel the same way he had that night after driving away from the damned tree and what he thought was a grave, leaving Carl and Brent to handle everything. As if he could have done more.

Suddenly he remembered. The new young couple that was moving in right next door to his place. The two best-looking people he'd ever seen.

He hadn't mentioned them to Carl and Miss Beverly. But why would they be interested?

17.

"Mom?"

Oh no. Louise covered her head with the knitted throw she had drawn across her arms when she closed herself into the quiet, darkened, master bedroom. Maybe, she thought, if she stayed quiet, Kara would think she was asleep and go away.

While the three smaller kids were occupied with Carl, she'd slipped away, telling Holly that she was going to lie down for awhile and if Carl came back into the house to let her know, but otherwise leave her alone. It had been so long now, she had even dozed a little. But still, she didn't want to be bothered. She was so tired these past few days.

The door squeaked. That annoying little squeak that she couldn't remember to spray. She uncovered her head. Kara stood just inside the door.

"Mom, are you sick?"

"I just don't feel really well, Kara. But I'm not sick." She sat up. No use trying to get anymore rest today. "What is it?"

"Mom, Grandpa said for us to stay away from the Rentons. He called them strangers."

"Carl said that?"

Surprised, Louise looked at Kara for confirmation, as

if she hadn't heard right. Kara nodded, emphasizing her silent answer. Louise sat up and folded the cotton throw she'd bought a few weeks earlier at a flea market. She hung it on the footboard without looking, using her hands to feel that it hung evenly. It wasn't like Kara to scare the children.

"Why would he tell you that?"

"I don't know." Kara answered with a worried look on her face. "But they're home again now. I saw their car drive in. Why can't I go over and see if the girl can play?" Kara's voice was a soft wail of disappointment. "Heidi's not a stranger, Mom. I met her already, and so did Grandpa."

Louise shook her head in disbelief. "I can't imagine why your grandpa would say to stay away from them. Maybe he isn't as well as the doctor and Brent thought he was."

"Do you think then it was just because he'd been in the hospital? The reason he was scared of the neighbors?"

Louise managed a small laugh. "I doubt that he was scared of them. He probably warned you against strangers in general. And that's all right, you should be wary."

"Then can I go over?" Kara inquired with hope.

"You can go close enough to ask if she can play. But only," Louise added hurriedly as Kara started running, "only if they're outside! Hear me?"

"Great! Bye, Mom." Kara slid to a stop in the hallway. "Will you make the little boys stay home?"

"*You* make them stay home," Louise said, and immediately regretted giving Kara that much authority. "Kara!" she yelled, ready to retract her words, but Kara had already pounded her way out of the front door.

Louise paused at the dresser to run a comb through her loose, blunt-cut hair. She no longer had perms, or kept her hair long. She liked it thick, soft, loose. Running her fingers through it helped her think, relax, or took her mind off things she didn't want to dwell on.

She didn't feel she looked very good with it so flat on top, but the comfort of easy care outweighed looks. Now. At her age.

At her age. Thirty-seven. Too old to have another baby. At the moment she could welcome menopause.

Oh no.

Then what? Come to think of it, the rest of her life.

She went to the chair by the front windows and sat down.

Kara stood on her side of Shady Hollow Road and waited. The black car had driven in several minutes ago. Heidi would be coming out, she hoped. She hadn't talked to her much at all. Once, Kara had seen Heidi come down into the driveway, but before Kara could reach the street, she had ridden out again in the black sedan, with her mother and dad. All of them had waved, but hadn't stopped.

Kara waited. Shadows grew along the street. Sunshine that had streaked the road had inched away, replaced by shadows, in the minutes Kara waited. She pretended to play alone, swinging on tree limbs and thick wild grape vines, like Tarzan of the Apes while she waited for Heidi.

Why wouldn't Mom let her go to the Rentons' door and ask if Heidi could come out?

Why had Grandpa said stay away from them because they were strangers? He had made her feel somehow afraid. For awhile.

Where were the Renton's? They were so quiet.

She had seen the car drive in. Like a black ghost it had slipped beneath the trees in the driveway, as silent as fog. She'd caught a glimpse of it before the garage door lowered. Yet a long time had passed and still Heidi didn't come out. Disappointment leached away her energy, and finally she sat down with her chin cradled on her bent knees.

Then she glimpsed a figure on the patio. Someone not very large bounced a ball. Heidi playing with a ball? No, it didn't seem like something Heidi would do.

Kara walked into the middle of the street. She heard a car coming slowly and moved on to the edge of the Rentons' driveway. A lady who lived somewhere on down the hollow waved at Kara as she passed.

When Kara looked again at the child, she saw it was a boy. Not Heidi.

He stopped playing suddenly. He seemed to be looking her way, although she couldn't be sure. She was ready to call out to him, when Holly's voice yelled from behind her.

"Kara! Come on home!"

"Oh darn," Kara muttered under her breath. She lifted her arm in a wave at the boy, who, she supposed, was Heidi's brother.

He didn't respond.

She ran back across the street and up the lawn to the house.

Holly stood at the corner of the house, her hands hooked in the front pockets of her jeans. Kara heard her give that deep sigh that meant she was getting impatient and feeling put upon.

"Mama called for you to help set the table, and you didn't answer."

"Heidi's brother has come home."

"Oh yeah? Well, you'd better get in there and do your part. I've made the salad. It's your turn now."

Kara went on. Ordinarily, she would have stopped to argue a while with Holly, who could be a smart mouth sometimes, crabbier than an adult. But things were looking up in the neighborhood. Maybe now that both kids were home, they'd be around more. Kara would definitely have someone to play ball, ride bikes, and speak *her* language.

* * *

Holly started to follow Kara, but stopped short. Across the hollow a door slammed as someone entered the house. But the object that caught her eye was a movement on the ground among the trees. She stared hard, wishing she had the binoculars. It was a dog. The size and color of Pepper.

She walked down the hillside, hurrying against the increasing shadows. When she reached the street she could see the dog nosing about in the leaves near the Renton garage. It was the size of Pepper, but even more, it had the movements of Pepper. With quick little scoots he pushed his nose into the leaves and vines. The only difference was his tail didn't wag wildly high over his back. This dog's tail drooped, the way Pepper's did when he'd been scolded.

"Pepper?" she called, barely loud enough that the dog might hear. It just couldn't be possible, could it, that he was alive afterall? She kept walking, across the street where the driveway lights remained dark.

The dog raised its head and stared. There was no friendliness. No running to greet her.

He looked exactly like Pepper . . . and yet . . .

Someone stood behind her. She sensed the presence. A sudden fear that a hand would drop to her shoulder chilled her to the depths of her being.

She whirled.

Nothing. Nothing visible. But the feeling of a presence near remained.

The street stretched east and west, shaded, cool, darkening fast. Terror held her stomach in a tight grip. The air in the hollow seemed suddenly very cold, hard to breathe. She still felt as if *something* hovered behind her.

Turning, she looked all around.

No one stood within sight. The dog, like the robed phantom in the moonlight, like the eerie drumming, was gone.

At home, on the rise of the hill, lights began glowing softly in windows. A dusk to dawn yardlight came on faintly, greenish-white, brightening to white even as she watched.

Feeling that a strange, evil presence followed closely behind her, Holly ran across the street to her own yard.

She looked back once more, her heart aching for the little dog who had faithfully answered her call during his lifetime.

All she saw was the hover of dark trees.

Tom Roush traveled the Shady Hollow Road twice a week, when he went on Friday nights down to Highway 12 to pick up the kids, and once again when he took them home. Otherwise he used 34th Street to go to work, and to the grocery store and the hangouts he most enjoyed on lonesome nights alone.

Shady Hollow Road, where Brent and his family lived up on the hill above farther east, was a two-lane blacktop strip that followed the hollow, a narrow dip between two shelves of land. Once, eons ago, a stream had rushed here, revealing small outcroppings of stone and bluffs. Trees had grown on the slopes, creating a shady haven for small wild animals. In Tom's youth it had been a place to go for picnics. In one place a spring rushed out from beneath a bluff, and flowed through a narrow little valley of grass and wildflowers. A narrow dirt lane drifted along the hollow. In the wider places, where there was parking room, teenagers gathered, necked, and partied.

Then, about two years ago, the city grew to the point that the old dirt road was changed to the present street. Acreages began to be sold. Custom homes were built. The old parking places became people's yards. The mail carriers began to drive Shady Hollow Road.

The complexion of the hollow changed. But there were still a lot of wooded areas where no houses nestled unexpectedly. Especially down his way. He hadn't been able to afford one of the custom built houses, like

Brent's, so he'd chosen a new development on the hill
where the smaller houses were on smaller lots. They
were still good houses, and he was satisfied with what
he had. It was a three bedroom brick, with two bath-
rooms, and a yard big enough for some privacy. The
back was fenced for the kids to play safely. Or a pet dog
to stay loose, but safely confined.

He didn't have a dog. That was the next surprise he
had planned for the kids, a puppy of their own, now
that they had a safe place. But then, Adrianne had
suddenly taken the kids and left. Maybe, if she had told
him why, he could have dealt with it better. She had
no reason that she would give him.

It was true that he wasn't at home a lot. But he had
to work. Sometimes the work took in Saturdays and
Sundays because he needed all the overtime he could
get. He was, afterall, going into debt to buy a house
they really couldn't afford yet. It was for her and the
kids. He could have done with less.

He didn't know though, if he was getting used to the
situation, or just turning numb. The new schedule was
growing on him. Work all week, go after the kids Friday
evening. Spend a busy weekend with the kids, take them
home Sunday evening, go back to work.

Last Sunday night, when he had taken Davey and Ali
home, there had been a woodland of trees standing
between Roselawn and Clipper Drive, on Shady Hollow
Road. But this Friday evening, a little road had been
made through the trees, curving up the slope from the
hollow toward a clearing on the top of the hill. In the
clearing was a building.

He almost ran into the bank staring at it. It wasn't easy
to see. It hadn't been painted, was intended probably to
remain rustic, the color of the trees that stood behind
it. At first glance it could have been one of the custom
homes. But it was too plain, too tall and square. The
height was caused by a sharply angled roof.

Long, stained glass windows suggested a church. A

cleared area suggested a parking lot. There was no steeple, no cross at the top.

Tom parked at the side of the quiet street and gazed up at it. Light changed in the windows as he looked. There was something about it that disturbed and puzzled him. A church, he'd bet. But it either wasn't completed, or it was a very private church. He saw no name, no sign. The walls were natural pine, it seemed, unstained, unvarnished. Darkness began to swallow it.

Unfinished, he decided, and drove on.

But, he thought, it was within walking distance of home, if a person didn't mind a half-mile walk.

He speeded up. At the end of the hollow, where the land flattened out into the bottoms along Beaver river, he turned right and joined the traffic on Highway 12. The sun was down, lights were on, the kids would be waiting.

18.

Kara threw the bedspread up over the mattress. She wished school would start. Having kids across the road hadn't helped at all yet. They were always gone, or something.

Saturdays at home were no different from the rest of the week except they usually went out for lunch before they went shopping. Today, however, it didn't look as if Mama was going anywhere. She had gone back to her bedroom, saying she didn't feel well, and had closed the door.

Dad was at work. As always. Sometimes he came home during the day and they did something special. But he hadn't been around much since they'd moved to the new house. The only difference was on Saturdays he didn't leave so early.

This morning as Kara was on her way down the stairs to go outside, she had heard him and Mom talking about graves that had been robbed. It was in the newspaper, he said. Kara paused to listen, wondering if it was Pepper's grave. But who, at the newspapers, knew what had happened to Pepper?

Dad said to Mom, "It's the second rash of grave robbings in a week."

Pepper's and who else? Kara wondered.

But then Mom said, "Who would do a thing like that? Did they know who or why?"

"No. Dad told me about the first ones. Out in a small cemetery called Roller. Three little girls' graves. They had died back in the eighteen hundreds. This one, robbed sometime this week, was at the Latimer Cemetery. A young boy, buried in nineteen-forty-three."

Not Pepper after all. It was weird, but didn't interest Kara. She got a doughnut. Neither Mom nor Dad even noticed. She hurried out and returned to her bedroom to finish making it neat, and where she could eat the doughnut without being seen.

When she heard her dad's truck leave, she went into the hall just in time to see Mama going toward her bedroom.

"I don't want to be disturbed, Kara," Louise said, going on without even looking at her. Mama could make her feel literally invisible at times.

Kara wandered back to the kitchen wing. Too quiet. She went on down the steps and outside.

The boys were playing in the sandbox. She heard Holly making noises in her bedroom above, sliding doors open and shut. Music played.

Kara felt at loose ends. She wandered around the house and the yard, feeling lonely. She went back inside and sat on the bedroom deck for a few restless minutes, listening to Vinny's voice drifting up from below, and Holly's music. Bored, sick of Holly's dumb music, she went to the kitchen deck and sat there. Nothing happened. Nobody came to talk to her. She wished she had told Heidi to come over whenever she wanted. She wished she knew the Rentons' phone number. She'd call and ask Mrs. Renton if Heidi and her brother could come over and play.

She went into the kitchen and called information,

and asked for the Albert or Joyce Renton phone number. The operator told her there was no listing.

She went to the foyer, looked out the glass panels beside the door and saw both of the Renton kids in their driveway below.

Well great! Finally, somebody looked alive.

She ran into the hall of the master bedroom. But the door was solidly closed. She paused a moment. Mama didn't want to be disturbed.

Kara turned back toward the hallway to her and Holly's bedroom. She put her hand on the doorknob of Holly's room, remembered how Holly had yelled at her the last time she'd entered without knocking, and lifted her fist against the door.

"Holly? You busy?"

"Yeah! What do you want?"

Kara opened the door. Holly lay across her neatly made bed.

Her room was peach and green. She had a fat, quilted cover with a matching skirt on the bed, and draperies of the same print on the windows and sliding door. There were no posters on the wall, or anything really cool like Kara's own poster-cluttered room. But that was Holly, getting more and more boring the older she got.

"Holly, come with me, okay?"

"Where to?" Holly twisted, leaned her head on her hand.

She was dressed in her stone-washed jeans and a blue pullover. Her light brown hair was pulled back in a ponytail. She hadn't put on any lipstick—it was the only makeup Mom and Dad let her have—but unlike herself, Holly looked good anyway, Kara thought. Her lips were pink and full with defined edges. Kara's own lips sort of drifted into her face. But even though she needed to use lipstick to define them, Mom said no.

Holly said impatiently, "Well?"

"Over to the Rentons'. Both Heidi and her brother are out on the driveway."

Holly started to say no, Kara felt sure, but got off the bed instead. "Okay."

Kara grinned her thanks, and danced down the hall toward the front door. She waited for Holly on the front stoop. When she saw that both of the kids across the street looked her way, she lifted a hand in greeting.

Both of them waved back.

The day suddenly began to look better than it had.

Holly came out. Kara hurried ahead of her, eager to cross the street. She told Holly about the kids waving. But Holly didn't smile or answer. Kara saw that Holly's eyes were narrowed and exploring the trees. Then they stopped and stared at one point.

Kara's eyes followed the direction of Holly's intense gaze. She saw a small dog sitting at the edge of the driveway pavement, near the garage. Her heart leaped. Pepper? *Pepper?*

"Is that Pepper?" Kara whispered. Holly didn't answer. She walked across the street, pausing at the edge of the driveway.

Kara came up beside her. Heidi and the boy came together down the driveway, but the dog didn't move.

"Is that your dog?" Holly asked.

The boy said, "Yeah."

Kara, watching the dog, her heart pounding, scarcely looked at the boy. This meeting, at last, when she'd be able to talk to her new neighbors and see if they wanted to play, was shadowed by the little dog that looked just like Pepper. Yet he wasn't running to them. He stayed back in the shadows, sitting the way Pepper used to, and looking their way. He even had a white stripe down his face to his nose. His ears were peppered black and white, resulting in a grey-blue look.

"Where did you get him?" Holly asked.

The boy shrugged and bounced a small ball on the pavement.

Holly kept on. "Have you had him very long?"

The boy played, ignoring Holly. Heidi answered, "Yes . . ."

Heidi's hesitant way of speaking reminded Kara of a boy in class who was learning to talk slower so he wouldn't stutter. What kind of problem did Heidi have?

Holly kept questioning. "Where did you get him?"

"Our parents—got him—for us. So we'd—have a dog."

"How long ago?"

Kara offered, "He looks just like—" Holly poked her.

They were quiet. Kara saw that Holly still stared at the dog. Kara's gaze wavered from it to the faces of the kids. The boy was darker than Heidi. His eyes were dark, his hair dark and trimmed short, leaving bangs on his forehead. He bounced the ball. Then he pulled a toy out of his pocket and began to swing it up and down on a string. His hand barely moved, but the round object moved up and down the string smoothly and rapidly. Kara stared, hypnotized at it, trying to remember what they were called.

"What's your name?" Holly asked. She sounded like a teacher.

The boy finally said, "Monte."

"How old are you?"

A yo-yo! Kara remembered suddenly. A yo-yo, and he was really good at it. But now he stopped playing with it suddenly and put it back into his pocket. He looked at the ground, then cut a glance sideways at his sister.

Like Heidi, the first time Kara had talked to her, he didn't seem to know how old he was, either.

Heidi said in her strange, careful voice, "He's nine."

"A year younger than you," Holly said, as if confirming something in her own mind.

"Yes."

Holly started to walk away, and Kara was glad. Enough of this big sister stuff. Kara wanted to do something interesting.

Holly looked a last time at the little dog before she started across the street. Then suddenly she stopped and turned back. She bent foward and called, patting her knees, "Here, Pepper. Come Pepper."

"That's not his name," Monte said in a snotty voice.

"What is his name?" Holly asked, straightening slowly, her eyes still on the dog.

Monte hesitated a long time it seemed to Kara. Then he said with a shrug, "Dog. Just Dog." He pronounced it with an odd emphasis, almost like contempt. Kara watched Monte. Didn't he like his own dog?

Holly called softly, "Here, Dog. Doggie."

The dog didn't move for a moment, then it melted into the shadows beside the garage. Kara stared at the spot where it had been. What an odd dog, she thought. Pepper would have been bouncing and jumping all around. He loved a gathering of kids.

And how odd that Holly had tried to call him to her, as if she felt he really was Pepper.

Louise heard voices, faintly. Children's voices. She reached back and opened the draperies.

At the bottom of the lawn Vinny and Bryon were standing in their own yard. Kara was out in the street looking back, yelling at them to go home. Across the street the two Renton children stood, silent and waiting. Vinny and Bryon came walking back up the hill. Louise smiled. Kara would handle it. Across the street, the boy moved, as if he didn't intend to hang out with the girls.

Kara and Heidi met at the edge of the Renton driveway.

Louise started to let the drapery fall, then saw Joyce Renton. She came down the driveway, stopped for a couple of seconds with the kids, then came on over toward the walk.

Louise stood up. Company, at last. The first neighbor in this new neighborhood to drop by.

She took another look at her hair. Compared to Joyce Renton's lovely, shiny hair, her own hair was dull. She turned sideways and checked her profile. Had her belly suddenly bulged even more, or was it always that way?

She pulled her blouse out of her jeans and let it hang loose. Joyce, as she had been everytime Louise had seen her, was wearing a neat dress, gathered in close at her slim waist, hanging full in the skirt and long.

Maybe, she thought, she dressed that way because her husband was a minister and didn't approve of pants on a woman.

Louise went to the front door feeling tacky, fat, guilty about something vague and dark.

She was trembling slightly as she opened the door. It reminded her of the day the Welcome Wagon had come, bringing three of the town's matrons, to welcome them. They brought a few gifts from various stores downtown. Louise had been obligated to invite them into a living room that wasn't arranged yet, and offer them a refreshment. They were so dignified, so proper. But then when she said, "I don't feel we deserve gifts. I've lived here in town for years. We just moved, that's all." One of the women said, "Anyone who moves, anywhere, deserves a gift." Then she gave her movie passes. They had been nice afterall, and the four of them had a nice visit. So why was she trembling and nervous now? Her condition, she decided. Being pregnant had always changed her for nine months.

Joyce's eyes seemed almost glittery bright. For just a second Louise wondered if she might not be the essence of perfection that she seemed to be, and wore contacts. But no, of course not. It was just a feeling, but Louise knew in her heart Joyce would wear nothing for its effect.

"The children told me you're not feeling well," Joyce said in a soft, sympathetic voice.

Surprised, Louise blinked at her. Then, to her mortification, her eyes filled with tears.

Joyce stepped uninvited into the house. "Oh, my dear," she said, "I'm so sorry. Want to tell me about it?"

She put her hand just behind Louise's shoulder and guided her down the hall toward the kitchen. The tears flowed. Louise couldn't stop them.

"The kitchen is much more cozy, and I can make you a glass of iced tea," Joyce said. "And you can cry on my shoulder all you want to."

Joyce's hand urged Louise on past the hallway that branched off toward the boys' rooms, and on to the kitchen. As if she'd been in the house before. She took Louise to the kitchen table and pulled out a chair for her.

"There, I think you need to be waited on a bit. Now you just tell me."

Like a child Louise found herself jabbering, talking so fast her words blurred in her own ears. Meantime Joyce worked in the kitchen as if she were totally familiar with it.

"It's the move, I think, partly," Louise heard herself say, and wondered where her feelings had been buried. Not once had she thought the move might have something to do with her depression. "It just hasn't become home yet."

"It takes a while."

"And there's so much work . . . getting everything done, so much work . . ."

"Yes, I know."

"That's right, you do. You just moved too."

Joyce came to the table with a tall glass of iced tea. There was even a slice of lemon stradling the edge of the glass. Where had she found it? Louise hadn't remembered to buy lemons since Kara had used them all making lemonade.

"Aren't you having any?" Louise asked.

Joyce sat facing her, at her side, her chair turned so that her knees almost touched Louise's chair. Louise had to turn her head to look at Joyce, but Joyce was situated to look straight at her. Louise was aware of some discomfort, of being exposed in some way, but the tears kept running down her cheeks.

Joyce pulled a tissue from somewhere and gave it to Louise.

"Tell me," she urged.

"I'm pregnant!"

Joyce smiled faintly. "That's marvelous."

Louise wept harder. "No. I already have four. I hadn't planned—"

Joyce patted her shoulder. "Ah well . . ."

Louise put the tissue against her face a moment. "I've thought about an abortion. For the first time. A week ago I'd have said never, never would I kill my unborn. But now—if it's not too developed—"

Joyce's light brown arched eyebrows rose slightly. "And your husband? Does he agree?"

"He doesn't know I'm pregnant."

Joyce's eyes briefly checked out her figure. "I see. You don't look very pregnant yet."

"I'm one of those people who never show until I'm almost six months along. Also, I think . . . I might be farther along that I had first thought. My periods . . . I haven't missed but two. Others were light. I thought it was the move causing it."

She made up her mind suddenly to go this afternoon to the clinic and have whoever was on call check her. She had to know if it was too late for an abortion. It would be a relief to find out she was. The decision would be made for her.

She confided to Joyce suddenly, "If I'm too far along

for an abortion, it would save me from having to make that decision."

"Come to our church, Louise. You need us."

Louise's tears dried suddenly. She turned her head to face Joyce. She had spoken so insistently.

"It will solve all your problems, dear," Joyce said. But though her voice was barely audible Louise began almost immediately to feel soothed.

Yet, she couldn't answer.

Joyce asked, "Do you have a church? Do you belong anywhere?"

Louise sighed. "That's one of my failures as a mother. I've really wanted to see to it that the kids have a church, but . . . weeks will go by and I find excuses not to take them to Sunday school. Sometimes I drop the two girls off and pick them up later."

"Are you a Christian?" Joyce asked.

Louise blinked back a tear that came inadvertently, and looked at her. "Why . . . uh . . ."

She thought, as if the thoughts came from a voice within her, That's one of the reasons I don't like some churches much. First they welcome you, then they ask if you're a Christian, then, if you've been saved. Then, they tell you if you haven't, if you don't believe exactly as they do, you're going to hell. If she spoke those thoughts aloud to Joyce, the distant expression would cross her face, that holier-than-thou, you-poor-soul mask, and that would be the end of the friendship.

On the other hand, if Joyce and her husband were fundamentalists, Louise didn't want anything to do with their church.

"Oh, come on and go with us," Joyce said, as if she had understood something Louise hadn't openly expressed. "You need us. We need you. Our church isn't far away. Less than a mile down the hollow, on the north side of the hollow, like your house is. It would be a lovely walk. Shaded and cool. Of course we have parking space if you want to drive."

A strange sense of peace flowed for an instant through Louise. "I've always longed for a religion I could fully accept. I do want contact with God. I really do. I want to raise my kids in church. A church without . . . prejudice, I guess is what I mean."

Joyce nodded sympathetically. "I understand exactly what you mean. You're the kind of new member we want. You and your family. Come with us, and you'll see your feelings about life change totally."

Louise nodded. "What time is Sunday school? I guess I could start with that. Maybe I could bring the kids."

"We don't have Sunday school. We have services, every night. Why don't you come tonight? Alone, at first? Then we can arrange to bring your children."

Joyce rose. Louise also stood up, ready to follow her to the front door.

"You can ride with us," Joyce offered, "Or you can follow us in your car."

"I'll follow." Louise surprised herself at such willingness. "What time?"

"When dark falls."

Louise, still oddly at peace, followed Joyce to the front door. She closed the door behind her new friend.

Then she hurried to tell Holly that she was going to be gone for awhile, and Holly should watch the children.

"Where are you going?" Holly asked, looking up from the book she was reading.

"Just—to the store. You'll all be fine here without me. Joyce is right across the hollow. If you need help, run to her."

Holly said nothing. She left her book and stood up, then waited as Louise gave her a last look.

Louise's mind didn't linger on the kids. If she hurried, she estimated, she could have the pregnancy exam over in a couple of hours.

After she had backed the family station wagon out of the garage and turned it around and headed toward the street, it occurred to her that she had never done this before. Never left Holly alone with the little kids. Had never put that burden on her before.

But Joyce was right across the street.

Louise sighed, leaned back, and speeded toward the clinic.

19.

"Yes," the young doctor-on-call said. Louise felt his withdrawal, saw him turn away. At a metal waste bin he stepped on a lever that lifted the lid and peeled off rubber gloves, dropping them into the bin. "You can get dressed now."

"How—" She asked hesitantly, "How far along?"

"I'd say almost six months. The movement you're feeling is definitely the fetus. It's possibly viable by now. Occasionally these hidden pregnancies do occur, when the period continues. But I wouldn't worry. It doesn't seem to hurt the baby."

He left her, hurrying on to another patient.

Alone, she sat up and hung her head. He hadn't reacted much one way or the other. He hadn't said, "Congratulations." Maybe it was because when he came into this examining room she had told him, "I have to know. Quickly. I have an appointment to see Dr. White next week—he's the one who delivered my other babies—but I need to know now."

The only question this young doctor had asked her was, "How many do you have?" When she told him four, the youngest only three, the oldest thirteen, he had nodded.

She probably wouldn't see him again. But it didn't

matter. Her records would reveal whatever Dr. White would need to know.

She dressed. A nurse showed up. "Doctor Aubry suggested you keep your appointment with your regular doctor and begin prenatal care. You're in good health. There should be no problems." She smiled, gave Louise the sheet of paper that stated the care given and cost, and left.

Kara struggled with the bicycle down the lawn in front of the house. Mom was gone, and Holly wasn't her boss. She hadn't asked Holly if she could go bike riding, she'd just gone out and started riding around on the level surface of the driveway, and had even ridden out to the street behind the house. But she didn't want to ride alone. So she pushed the bike around the house and down the lawn to the hollow.

A car came slowly along, and she moved out of the way, choosing to ride across the street and stop again in the Renton driveway.

No one was out.

The strange little dog slunk out of sight around the corner. She watched him until he seemed to turn to shadows, disappearing within them.

She rode the bike on up to the patio. Still no one.

She knew they were home because it hadn't been long since she'd seen them. Joyce Renton had gone over to visit Mom, then when she left, Kara had been called in for lunch.

But after lunch she'd seen all of them. They were sitting around the patio table, as if they were having lunch outdoors, except they were just sitting, hands in lap, so still. The dog had been there too, sitting off to one side, as if he didn't dare go closer. As if he didn't really belong to them. Then, she'd seen something really terrible. The boy had gone over and kicked the dog. No wonder the poor dog seemed afraid of people.

Kara had noticed Holly watching, looking that way, and that was why Kara went to stand beside her, on the deck.

Holly had said, "Little bastard. Wish I was over there I'd kick *him*."

Kara didn't threaten to tell Mom that Holly was cussing, because she felt the same way Holly did. She didn't like Monte. Period. But . . . she had to put up with him if she wanted buddies.

At that moment Mom had called and told them she was going to town and that Holly should watch the younger children.

So Kara had gone bike riding.

She couldn't remember her Mom ever going off before without leaving someone in charge. A neighbor or babysitter or Dad or Grandpa. Someone.

She didn't feel really great about being left in Holly's care, she felt kind of—deserted? Why hadn't Mom asked *her* to go along?

She waited, holding her bike, in the shade at the edge of the Renton's patio. The round table had its chairs pushed precisely into place. There were no signs that a lunch had been eaten.

The patio had no leaves on it. Neither did the driveway.

She probably should just ride away.

Mom wouldn't like it if she rang the doorbell.

Feeling suddenly self-conscious, as if she were being watched, Kara got on the bike and rode down the driveway, spun around with the front wheel in the air, eased it down, and rode back up the driveway.

She sat.

They were here. She could feel their presence.

Mom was gone. So she wouldn't know if Kara rang the doorbell.

Kara went to the entry door between the garage and the patio with the sliding doors, and put her finger on the doorbell. Nothing. She looked up at the second story of the house. If the doorbell had rung, she would have heard it herself. But it hadn't.

She went over to the sliding doors. One panel was open, and she could see through the screen into the room beyond.

It must be a game room, instead of the family room like theirs at home. The floor was linoleum. A couple of chairs sat in one corner with a table between them. There was a lamp, but it wasn't like the lamps at home. It had a glass globe like a kerosene lamp.

She backed away, embarrassed that she had looked in. She glimpsed a stairway as she moved. It came down the wall, not enclosed like the stairway at home that came down from the kitchen, but open to the room with the linoleum. The regular door with the doorbell opened at the bottom of the stairs.

She started back toward her bicycle. Maybe they weren't home after all. The black car could have gone out when she was riding on the driveway behind her house.

Disappointment dragged her spirits down. No one to ride with afterall.

She looked around for a bike stand. None. Of course the bikes could be in the garage. She started away.

The screen door opened suddenly.

Kara whirled.

Monte came out, with Heidi behind him. She didn' slam the screen door. Door slamming was part of life at home, with Mom yelling, "Stop slamming the door!"

"Hey!" Monte cried. "You've got a bicycle."

He came over to look at it.

"That's pretty," he said.

Kara blinked at him. Pretty? Not neat or cool or awesome, but pretty? She took another look at it. It had been blue and yellow, but the paint was scratched, and there was a rusted place, and the cover of the seat had a hole that was getting bigger. When they moved Dad had gotten a good look at it and scolded her for being so rough with it. "It's only a few months old, Kara," he'd said. "Can't you take better care of it than that?" In contrast, of course, was Holly's bike. Older than hers, but still in mint condition.

"Wanna go riding?" Kara asked. "We could ride down the hollow and back. Would your folks care?"

Monte still was admiring her bike. But he looked at Heidi for the answer.

Heidi smiled softly, her head tilted to one side like a little bird.

"I'm sure it would be all right. Only . . ."

Kara waited impatiently. "Then why don't you get your bikes out," she finally said.

They both looked at her. For the first time she noticed that even when they seemed to be looking directly at her, their gazes appeared slightly off, kind of cockeyed, as if they really couldn't see her. There was no connection between her eyes and theirs. No real connection. Kara fidgeted.

"Come on, let's go. Unless your folks don't want you to?"

Monte said, "I don't—think I have a bike." He turned that indirect gaze on his sister.

She shook her head, still smiling.

"No bikes?" Kara cried. "*Why?*"

Heidi said, "Maybe we will get some."

Monte looked enviously at Kara's bike, from one wheel to the other. He touched the finish gently, caressing it with his hand.

"Pretty," he said again.

Kara held it, but stood away. "Want to ride it?"

"Oh yeah."

He took it and straddled. He wasn't quite as tall as she, Kara saw when he tried to sit on the seat. He put one foot on a peddle, turned the bike down toward the street, and began wobbling away, almost falling, as he tried to ride. Kara ran after him instinctively, as she would have one of her little brothers, afraid he'd fall and get hurt. Then, of course, she'd be blamed. All the adults would be mad at her.

The truth was, it didn't look as if Monte had ever ridden a bike before in his life.

He almost fell. Kara grabbed the bike and steadied it.

Monte got off, his face showing something deep and curious. It was the most expression Kara had seen on his perfect face. He was, like Heidi, only in a different way, very beautiful. The only flaw was a small mole on his chin, close to the dimple in the center.

"I guess I don't know how to ride," he said.

Kara felt sorry for him. She could almost forgive him for kicking the dog. "That's okay," she offered quickly, "I'll teach you."

He stood back, shaking his head. That puzzled, wondering look stayed on his face. There was something else that Kara couldn't define. It was as if his brain didn't really work.

She turned toward Heidi. The girl stood with her fingers linked together in front of her, watching, smiling just a little, as if unaffected by any of it.

"Do you want to ride?" Kara asked.

"Oh no," Heidi answered. "That wouldn't be ladylike."

"*What?*"

"It wouldn't be ladylike," Heidi repeated sweetly.

Kara stared at her. Well, so much for that. Monte couldn't ride, and Heidi didn't feel it was ... what? Ladylike?

"Who cares?" Kara muttered. She offered the bike to Monte. "You can practice if you want to."

"No," he said. "That's okay."

Kara fidgeted. "Wanna play something?" she asked.

"Yes!" Heidi cried with more animation than she'd displayed so far. "We could play ring-around-the-rosy."

Kara repeated what she'd said in emphasis. "Ring-around-the-rosy? What's that?"

Heidi smiled.

Monte said, "How about hide and seek?"

"Hide and seek?" Kara answered. At least she'd heard of that. "Well . . ."

Heidi offered, "There's also eye-spy. It's a very good game."

"That's an indoor game," Monte said. "I want to stay outside. I like the air. Doesn't the air feel good?"

Kara frowned from one to the other. "I was thinking something like Nintendo."

They stared at her. Neither of them smiled.

"Don't you have television?" Kara asked, and received no answer. She added, "Dad says you don't have your electricity on yet. But we could go over to my house."

No answer.

Oh well, her mistake, Kara thought. If they didn't have electricity they didn't have television, so they wouldn't have a Nintendo game either. And they didn't seem eager to go to her house. Maybe it was against their religion, the way with some friends she once had, to watch TV or play card games or Nintendo.

"Okay," Kara said. "Let's make up a game."

She waited for suggestions. None came.

Pulling the small ball from his pocket Monte turned away, bouncing it along the concrete of the driveway.

Kara paused awkwardly, looked at Heidi, and then looked away. Surely there was something they could have fun with. Maybe they just had to get acquainted first. "You've got a neat name," she said. "Are you named after Heidi, in the book?"

"What book?" Heidi asked.

Kara gawked at her, then blinked upward at the trees. "I thought everybody had read *Heidi*," she said, "and seen the movie. I've seen the movie a dozen times. More, maybe. Haven't you even seen the movie?"

Heidi said nothing. She smiled faintly, her round, blue eyes looking out from beneath incredibly long lashes. Was standing around and gazing out from beneath her lashes like a cow all she did?

"Maybe we can just talk." Kara offered, trying to find a subject that both of knew well. "What school do you go to?"

Heidi opened her mouth. Her gaze wandered. Kara anticipated the answer. *I don't know.* Well, maybe she really didn't, yet.

"Haven't been enrolled yet?" Kara asked. "We haven't either. It isn't time yet. But I bet we go to the same school. The bus will stop here at our mailboxes, probably. We were told by the real estate man that a school bus came by."

Joyce's voice made Kara jump.

She said, "The children will be going to private school, Kara. We must go now. Come children. Visit us again, Kara."

"Oh. Okay. Thanks."

Kara kicked the bike stand up. She said, "Bye Heidi, Monte, Mrs. Renton."

"Goodbye, dear," Joyce answered. She went back to the garage door, stooped, gripped the handle at the bottom of the door and lifted. The door opened.

Kara stared. There were handles on the bottom of their garage doors too, but they didn't lift the doors. They were locked, and lifted only from the remote device inside the cars, or from the button on the inside. Unless, of course, the electricity was off.

She reminded herself to ask Heidi the next time she saw her if they didn't believe in using electricity.

Kara rode away. Up the hollow was a street that connected to the street on the hill behind her house. She rode toward it, the cool air in the shady hollow brushing softly against her flushed, heated skin.

She looked back, but the street was empty as far as she could see. Hadn't they gone afterall?

Holly's words came to her mind. *Weird.*

Yet it made her a little angry that Holly would talk about her new friends that way. Because they were going to be friends. Maybe. There was no one else around to be friends with. She didn't care if they had some odd-ball religion that kept them from having bikes or electricity or whatever.

Beverly got out of the pickup. Carl waited, his hand offered. She had sat a moment longer than she usually did after Carl parked, but she felt a little hesitant to go uninvited to his daughter-in-law's. He hadn't even called. When she suggested he call, he'd said, "They don't mind me dropping in, they really don't. I've never gotten a bad reception there."

But that didn't include a stranger, she'd told him.

The two little boys came rushing out from somewhere, and Carl lifted them both in his arms at the same time, gave them hugs and kisses, then put them down.

"Where's your mom?"

A teenage girl came out of the house. She was almost as tall as Beverly herself, but obviously very young. Her brown-blond hair was long, curled on the ends, and held back with barrettes. She had a pretty face.

"Hello, Holly," Carl said. "Where's your mom?"

"She's gone to town."

"Kids, this is Mrs. Inness. Beverly, this is Holly, Bryon, and Vinny."

"Hello Holly, Bryon, and Vinny."

"Where's Kara?" Carl asked.

Holly shrugged. "Oh, who knows?"

At that moment another child showed up riding a bike down the driveway toward them. In total contrast to Holly, Kara was sweaty, obviously younger. She tumbled off the bike and ran to Carl. She kissed him on the cheek.

She had short, dark hair, very fair skin with freckles

scattered like tiny brown stars across her nose. Beverly held back an urge to reach out and wipe the child's sweaty face with a tissue. She instantly liked Kara.

Kara grinned at her widely as Carl introduced them.

Holly asked politely, "Would you like to come in and have a glass of iced tea?"

"Thanks Holly, but we just dropped in for a minute," Carl said. "We—uh—" He glanced at Beverly. But she couldn't help him. There was no way to tell these kids that they wanted to meet the new neighbors, or why. "We'd like to take a walk around. I was just showing Mrs. Inness your new neighborhood."

"Oh, don't you want to come in and look at the house?"

Beverly decided to take over. "Maybe you'll have a housewarming some evening, then we'll come in."

They walked into the narrow strip of lawn on the west side of the house. Vinny showed Beverly Pepper's house. Then he ran to the woods to show her the empty grave.

Holly said, "There's a dog over at the Renton's that looks just like Pepper. But he wouldn't come to me when I called."

Bryon tugged on Carl's hand. "It's not him, though, is it, Grandpa? Pepper rose from the grave and went to heaven."

Kara said, "Bryon, he was dug up by a wild animal."

Beverly exchanged a look with Carl. Graves of children being robbed in isolated cemeteries, and the grave of a dog also robbed? There seemed to be a connection, irrational though it was. Children and dogs.

She looked at the grave, and felt a strange sense of doom. The dirt piled so neatly to one side, as if it had been taken out handful by handful. Not dug out by a wild animal, which would have scattered it. The grave had been carefully emptied. Carl had told Beverly about it. The dog had been buried in the morning, and in the evening the grave was empty. So whoever, or whatever, had done it worked within easy sight of the house, within sight of a deck where two sliding doors opened, within thirty feet of the house. And weren't seen.

They went on down the hill, and to the street. Carl walked into the street as if they were all taking a stroll along the edge of the quiet two-lane blacktop.

The garage door stood open. Beverly saw the back of a black sedan.

"They haven't left yet," Kara observed. "I thought they were going somewhere."

A boy stood in the driveway, bouncing a ball.

"Hi, Monte," Kara called, waving.

He came toward them, and stopped about halfway down the driveway. Beverly saw him clearly. A handsome boy nine or ten years old, with dark, curly hair, golden tan skin, almost a deep ivory, as if instead of being tanned it was his natural color. Dark eyes. Dimple in his chin, and a distinctive mole just to the side of it.

He stared at Carl, then at Beverly. He didn't answer Kara, or speak to the children. His gaze moved unblinking between Carl and Beverly, back and forth.

A young woman's voice called, "Come, Monte, we have to go."

She was in the garage, opening the car door. On the other side a little girl got into the back seat. The young woman had one of the most beautiful faces Beverly had ever seen. She smiled and waved.

The boy ran to the garage and got into the front seat with his mother.

Beverly and the children followed Carl's lead and moved back to stand near the walk on the other side of the street. The black car backed around in the driveway and drove out. The children and their mother waved goodbye. Beverly was struck by the beauty not only of the mother but both children. Yet there was no resemblance among any of them.

The car moved almost silently down the street.

Beverly suddenly knew she had seen the boy before. Somewhere, long ago, in her childhood.

20.

Davey looked around for Ali. She wasn't on the slide anymore. Where had she gone? He had to watch her, keep her close and safe. Ever since Mom and Dad got their divorce, Davey had felt a need to keep Ali in sight as much as possible.

He looked over his shoulder and saw the gate stood open. Ali had gone out of the fenced backyard.

He ran to find her, his heart feeling as if it clogged his throat. In the workshop a saw was buzzing. Dad was working on something. Yelling at Dad would be useless.

He went out of the gate, leaving it open. What if someone had kidnapped her? She was only three. She wouldn't know to try to escape.

Then he saw her.

She stood on the corner of the front lawn, a couple of feet from the sidewalk and the busy street. A man and woman were with her, their backs to him.

The woman bent and took Ali's hand. Neither the woman nor the man looked at Davey. Both of them stared at Ali. That was all right, up to a point. Davey was used to people staring at Ali. Mom always dressed her in cute clothes, and her blond hair was curly and long, and she had dimples in both cheeks. Davey was proud of her, but she was just a baby and didn't know about bad things the way he did.

"Isn't she a little doll?" the woman said, the same thing all women said. "She's the most perfect little girl I ever saw."

"She is," the man said. "Certainly perfect. Perfect for us."

Davey slowed, puzzled. They were talking about Ali as if she were an object.

"She even looks like me, don't you think?"

"She does indeed."

Davey saw it was true. The woman had hair a lot like Ali's, long and softly curly. Her face was heart-shaped, with dimpled cheeks. Kind of like Ali's.

"And the boy—did you see him? He somewhat resembles you. Can we have them?"

Davey looked at the man. He had dark hair and wore a beard that hung down to the second button on his buttoned-up shirt. What boy? Who were they talking about? He didn't trust them.

What had the woman meant, *can we have them?*

Davey wanted to grab Ali and run, but he could hardly move he was suddenly so scared.

He threw a glance over his shoulder toward the little building that his dad had made into a shop. The saw was still buzzing.

He looked for a car parked on the street, one that might belong to the strangers, but there was none. Where had these people come from?

"What's your name?" the woman asked Ali.

Ali answered the woman shyly. Even with all the praise she'd had all her life, she was still bashful.

The man asked, "How old are you?"

Ali held up three fingers.

"Do you live here?" the woman asked, nodding at the house behind Davey and Ali. Ali nodded.

Davey looked again at the shop. Why didn't Dad

come? Davey wanted to run to the shop and scream at him, but was afraid to leave Ali with these people.

Then the man said, "And this is our house." He motioned toward the house behind him.

They lived in the house next door! They were even standing on their own lawn. Maybe he could chance running to tell Dad, afterall. He whirled away, calling back to the strangers, "I'll get our dad."

He sprinted through the open gate of the chain link fence and across the back lawn behind the house, but before he was halfway there, the saw stopped and his dad came out of the shop.

"Dad? People are with Ali!" Then he ran back to stand beside Ali.

The man and woman smiled at Davey, but he didn't smile at them, nor answer when they said, "Hello."

Tom came toward them, wiping sawdust from his face.

"Hello there," he said, smiling. "Looks like you've just met my kids."

Dad knew them? He even acted as if he liked them, which should make it all okay. But he didn't understand what they'd meant by all the things they'd said about Ali and him.

He heard the man say, "We're having services tonight in our church, and were coming over to see if you'd like to go."

Tom answered, "Well . . ."

"We promise not to ask you for money," the man laughed.

The woman said, "And do bring your children."

"Well," Tom said again. Davey saw Dad begin running his fingers through the back of his hair the way he always did when he was undecided about something.

Tell them no, Dad, please. Dad, please, say no, Davey prayed in silence.

"Well," Tom said, "I guess."

* * *

Louise drove down the hollow at a slower speed than she usually drove. The black car had gone out of sight, but she knew the way.

Her thoughts reran the evening that had preceded these firsts for her. She had never gone out at night without Brent, or some of the kids, with her. Before this, she had never even gone to church at night, in all her life. Only on Sunday mornings, and then not often, and certainly never alone.

She wasn't sure right now why she was doing this.

It had to be the power of persuasion. Joyce was very persuasive. Louise had a feeling she had met the woman who would be the best friend she'd ever had.

Joyce had come over after Louise had returned home from the doctor and invited her again to ride along to church. But Louise preferred her own car. She could leave then, if she wanted to. They had walked together down the lawn, and Joyce explained that the road up to the church was the only unpaved driveway that climbed the hill.

"We're very poor," Joyce had smiled, "and can't yet afford to pave. But we'll grow. We have many churches planned, some already in progress."

Louise had made dinner and they ate without her mentioning the invitation. After dinner, Louise left the girls to clean up the kitchen while she joined Brent in the family room downstairs. While he sat with the newspaper and the news muted on television she had told him, "I'm going to church, Brent. Can you stay with the kids?"

"*What?*" He dropped the newspaper.

She explained about the Rentons. "They really seem eager that I go. And I like her . . . I just feel like I want to go."

She didn't tell him about the visit to the doctor, or her need for something spiritual at this time in her life. She saw the puzzled frown on his face. Then he shrugged slightly.

"If you want to." He rustled the newspaper. "I was thinking that since we've all been so upset since Pepper's death, and it's Saturday night, we might take the kids to a movie and then someplace for ice cream afterwards. They've been pretty sad lately."

"Great," she said, trying to muster something Brent wouldn't question. "You take them out, and I'll go to church."

So now she was here. Joyce and Albert, with their children, had waited for her in their driveway, as if they knew exactly the time she would arrive. From her own driveway on the hill she'd had to go a block east, then down the street that connected the ridge road to Shady Hollow Road, then turn west. When they saw her coming they waved and pulled out onto the street where yard lights were coming on in the evening dusk. All but the lights at their own driveway.

She drove slowly, feeling guilty that she hadn't gone with Brent and the kids. They had been so eager when they heard they were going to be taken out. And so puzzled that she wasn't going along. At one point Louise almost drove into a driveway and turned around, ready to follow them to their favorite theatre. But then she saw ahead of her the rear of the black car. As if the Rentons were waiting for her to catch up.

She speeded a little, driving out around a couple of kids on bicycles. When she caught up with the Rentons their car drove on, taking a sharp righthand turn into a makeshift drive up the hill to the church.

She bounced along behind them, slowly, and came out into a parking area where the trees had been thinned. The church had soft, dim lights shining in the stained glass windows. There were several cars parked haphazardly.

They waited for her. She wished suddenly they wouldn't.

There was a single step up to the double doors. She

entered ahead of Joyce, Albert, the two children, and stopped. The interior looked like any smaller church she had ever entered, with long wooden benches and isles. But there the similarity ended.

There was no pulpit, no minister in sight. There was, at the front, beneath a tall stained-glass window that, she suspected, would tranfer dark, varied colored lights during the day, a solid structure that resembled a long, low table, or bed, draped in black velvet.

The soft, shaded lights came from lamps in brackets along each wall. Tiny flames licked upwards in glass globes, producing just enough light to show the way.

Several people had arrived and sat in the pews. In the pew nearest the exit sat Tom Roush and his two small children. She felt surprised without knowing why.

Tom nodded as she spoke softly. "Good evening, Mrs. Salisaw," he said. His son, Davey, she thought his name was, looked scared half to death, his eyes big and watchful.

At the outer ends of the pews, men and women dressed in black robes stood quietly. The women were all beautiful, young. The men, like Albert, wore beards of different lengths, all neatly trimmed. Silence suddenly filled the room. No one spoke.

She had to get out of there. She wanted to shout at Tom and the kids to run, hurry, before it was too late. Fear iced her skin and tightened her stomach and muscles. She tried to speak, to call Tom, and couldn't. Her throat felt paralyzed.

She turned.

The door had closed. She looked into the faces of Albert and Joyce. Their eyes seemed to have taken on the strange lights of the windows. They barred her way.

Joyce put a hand on her shoulder.

"You need us," she said in a whisper.

The touch calmed Louise, as if a drug had entered her brain. Somewhere in the back of her mind a tiny voice cried, *No, no, this isn't right*, fading, disappearing as Joyce and Albert led her toward the front pew, their hands on her shoulders.

It was, some sense of rationality told her, like a wedding march.

The chanting rose softly, like a song. The people in black robes began to move among the people. A voice rose above the others. A man, talking now. Louise closed her eyes and tried to concentrate. She felt as if she were moving in space.

"Life," the voice said. "This is the church of life. A better life that you have ever lived. We lead you to never-ending life, Come with us, be one of us. The world is ours. Our movement will spread. Each of you will become one of us and carry the word.... Come ... come ... we are Aeternita!"

"Life everlasting ... Aeternita ... death is only a state of mind.... Let us show you the way.... You can become one of us ..."

Euphoria entered Louise as other voices took up the chant. Like a strange, rhythmic music it calmed her, and she felt her body swaying, her own voice beginning to murmur.

Someone draped one of the robes over her head and shoulders. Hands helped her up. They led her to the table beneath the tall window at the front. The room seemed almost without light, dimmer, further away, cathedral ceiling lost in darkness.

The robe was opened in front by the hands that had guided her. She felt the caressing hands on her bare abdomen, gently, yet there was a sensation of pain. Then the pain became part of the euphoria that drugged her.

She heard nothing of her own body, no rushing blood, no beating heart.

She glimpsed a tiny baby, perfectly formed, lying silently on the palms above her.

Moving, finally, but not crying. It was placed in the

arms of another—and was soon draped and sheltered by the black velvet robe the young woman wore—then it was gone.

All, gone. The pain. The fear. All of her.

Holly was about to fall asleep when finally they drove into the garage. It had been a fantastic evening. Dad had kept them out longer than he ever had, and let them have all kinds of treats they ordinarily didn't get. Like greasy hamburgers and fries and candy bars.

Holly saw with surprise that Mama hadn't come home yet. Her car was not in the garage. Holly said nothing. One of the other kids would ask.

It was Vinny. "Daddy, where's Mama?"

"Remember," Dad said, "she went to church."

They were all sleepy. Even Holly. Did church last so long?

In the upstairs hall she said goodnight to the others and went into her room. She heard Kara in the bathroom. Dad had taken the boys toward their bedrooms.

Daddy had acted as if he wasn't worried, but she had seen the puzzled look, as if in examining the empty place in the garage he would understand more about Mom's absence.

Holly changed to pajamas and went to bed. Soft, cool air entered the open sliding door. Moonlight touched the deck, moving away even as she watched. The night seemed very still.

She closed her eyes and made her head more comfortable on her pillow. It was the first time in her life she'd gone to a movie with the other kids and Dad, but without her mother. She felt uneasy.

She closed her eyes and listened to the silence of the night. Not even the bugs, tonight. Nor the owls. If only Pepper were here, to watch the night beyond her door.

She dozed, slipping gently toward sleep.

The drumming came softly, like a car easing along

the hollow road with its music tuned so loud that only
the bass thump was audible.

Terror jerked her wide awake. She lay stiff and still,
listening. The drumming drew nearer, louder, yet still
soft. It was near the house, down on the street in front.

Like the other time.

She slipped from bed and went to the door onto
the deck. At first glance, among the waning, changing
moonlight and shadows on the black street, it seemed
a parade of figures in black. Then suddenly all were
gone but one.

He stood in a dim pattern of light, as if he wanted
to be seen.

She clearly saw the black robe, the outline of the head
and shoulders. The figure seemed again to be staring
toward her.

She stepped back, out of sight, too afraid to reach
out and close the door. Only a screen, and the deck,
stood between her and the person in the black, hooded
robe.

The drumming had stopped, she realized suddenly.
She slipped silently to the door again, staying back in
the shadows.

The street below was empty. Only the moonlight
moved among the shadows.

It was like the other time. But this time she was more
afraid, because she knew now what it meant.

Death.

The death of someone close to her.

Beverly stirred restlessly in her bed. She was aware of
turning from side to side, never quite being soundly
asleep. Yet not dreaming. The face of the boy—the
Renton boy—kept coming to disturb her.

Then suddenly she woke and sat up.

Morey!

Morey Chapin!

She had gone to school with him. He had died during their fifth grade.

He'd had a mole on his chin, near the dimple! Everything about the boy she'd seen today, was that boy of fifty years ago.

She turned on the light and looked at the clock. Midnight. How ironically appropriate. She reached for the telephone, then drew her hand back. Surely it could wait until morning? Let Carl get some rest?

She got up, too anxious to stay in bed.

She went to the library downstairs and looked for the old school albums. In the storage section she found her fifth grade album. The picture could easily have been the same child. Monte Renton, Morey Chapin?

Carl would want to know. Perhaps he too was awake, waiting for the day.

He answered on the first ring.

"Carl? I apologize—"

"I wasn't asleep. Haven't gone to bed. Is something wrong, Beverly? Are you all right?"

She visualized him leaning back in his recliner, eyes focused on the ceiling fan, it whirring on low. Carl unable to sleep. Thinking, thinking, trying to make sense of the senseless.

"Carl, I woke up knowing where I've seen that boy. One who looks exactly—"

He interrupted her, "Where?"

"He was in school. My grade. He died when we were in the fifth grade. It was the first funeral I'd ever been to in my life. I have his picture here, Carl—"

"Morey Chapin!"

She heard a faint metallic squeak, as if he had leaned forward suddenly.

His voice was soft, shocked. "My God, Beverly! After I got home, what you'd said about him looking so familiar kept going through my mind. I began to think I'd seen him too, but I couldn't remember where or when. Got your clothes on? I'll be over there in a few minutes."

He hung up, and she began quickly to dress. She chose a pair of old jeans and a pullover knit shirt.

She grabbed a flashlight on her way out, a shoulder bag with her keys and other essentials. Her cats purred and wrapped themselves around her ankles as she opened the door. She hesitated, then let them out into the yard. "Behave yourselves," she admonished, then went to wait on the sidewalk.

When Carl pulled up to the curb and started to get out of his truck, she called softly to him as she ran, "Don't get out. I can let myself in."

He closed his door, leaned over and opened hers.

"Where are we going?" she asked as she settled in the truck. She had the school picture in her purse. She answered her own question, "He was buried in that old family cemetery out by that little church that was once a one-room school, right?"

"Right. I don't remember what they called it, but I know where it is." He put the car in gear. In the dash lights she saw him look at the flashlight.

"I have the school picture, too. Are we crazy, Carl?"

"I don't know."

They drove through quiet streets, and onto a state highway that had little traffic. The pickup clock changed numbers. 1:12. Most traffic was gone. Houses they drove past had lights only in the yards except for an occasional dim light in a back or upstairs window. Cows in fields were lying down, dark blobs beneath the starlight. Woodlands beyond pastures were black, their tops spikes against a star-sprinkled sky. It was summer, yet there was a chill in the air. Something dark and dangerous in the black woods. When something moved, just out of her vision, she was startled by it, and her heart pounded. When Carl spoke, she jumped. But he didn't notice.

"I was thinking," he said. "What . . . is their purpose? I keep wondering, what are they? Was it they who dug up the graves of the children, and why? Was it they who dug up Pepper's grave? Holly and Kara told me there's a new dog across the road that looks like Pepper, but doesn't act like him. They can't bring back to life the dead and buried, can they, Beverly?''

She opened her mouth, but then only sighed.

"And if, by some miracle they do, what harm is it? I mean, it was they who were buried back then, in your great-grandfather's day. Are we afraid of them because they're not like us? Is that one mark of the human condition?''

He was silent. Her thoughts had been running a similar channel, yet she had not once thought of them as harmless.

"Do you mean," she said, "that you think if we understood them better we wouldn't be afraid of them? That they're harmless?''

"No. Even though they passed right by me that night, and didn't harm me, or even look at me, I sure didn't think of them as harmless. It—they—it was the worst nightmare I ever had. I was never so scared. But," he added quickly, "I sure as hell wasn't asleep.''

He turned onto a county road, unpaved. She didn't remember the neighborhood at all. Ahead of them was another collection of trees, and a building. He drove into the weedy driveway beside the old one-room schoolhouse. He turned off the engine.

"Here it is.''

They sat still.

Beverly opened her door at the same time Carl got out on the other side. She turned on the flashlight, pointing it at the ground, and went to the front of the truck. He took her arm. He carried a large flashlight from his tool box.

Beyond the line of trees that grew by the driveway, tombstones stood irregularly, as if time and weather had tipped them. Even the cemetery was weedy. They walked from tombstone to tombstone. Darkness dripped from the trees like dead insects. Carl checked the dates on the stones. 1910. 1920.

He motioned with the light beam toward the far side of the graveyard. It touched the stones, turning them a sickly bluish-grey. An owl screamed somewhere in the woods beyond a field of grain. A breeze rattled leaves in the trees and moved the tall grass so that it looked as if something crawled.

"The newer graves must be out that way. I can remember the grave being at the edge of a field."

She couldn't remember that at all. Perhaps she hadn't come to the cemetery. She recalled a church, and the small casket with the flowers. She had been surprised at how pretty the coffin was, but how sad it was that he would never rise from it. Morey had not been one of her friends, only a classmate. She probably had never spoken a word to him during their years in school.

Carl led her carefully between stones. The grass hadn't been cut in years.

Carl stopped abruptly.

There it was. His light shone down into the open coffin.

The interior had grown dark with mold. It was eaten and torn with only a darker trace of where the body once had rested.

21.

Carl drove slowly. There was no traffic to rush him. The clock on the dash read 1:47.

"I'd say that grave robbing hasn't been discovered," Carl said. "It didn't look as if anyone had been there in years."

They drove on in silence for awhile. Beverly stared into the night, deeply disturbed, with no answers.

Carl said, "What do they want with those poor little corpses? They'd be nothing but skeletons now, especially those from the last century."

Beverly heard herself saying, "To form the perfect family. Man, woman, and two children. A boy and a girl." The answer seemed to come from beyond her conscious mind, and stunned her. Yet it somehow made a curious sense.

Carl added, "And a dog."

They reached for each other's hand and held tightly.

"No," Carl said. "It's not possible."

"No," Beverly agreed. But then, trying to make sense of the senseless, staying within the same premise, she said, "Let's just suppose it's true. Why? The couples must be incapable of reproducing. They somehow . . . restore life to the dead."

"Thank God they choose the dead. I have four live
grandchildren . . ."

Right across the street? Was that what he was going
to say? Their speculations had not helped, it had only
made the puzzling terrifying. She felt acid rise in her
stomach, and was afraid she was going to be sick.

"And they had a little dog," Carl added, his voice so
low she could hardly make out the words, as if he were
thinking aloud, "It died. And it was removed from its
grave. And the kids tell me the Rentons now have a dog
that looks like Pepper. But doesn't act like him."

"How—what killed him, Carl?"

"They didn't know what. But they said his neck was
broken."

They drove into downtown and around the square
toward Beverly's home.

She asked, "What are we going to do, Carl? Should
we talk to someone? The police laughed," she recalled
aloud. "Where can we go from here? Call on the arche-
ologists? Other scientific groups who might listen? Find
out what the purpose of these people are? As long as
they aren't killing, robbing, harming, what law are they
breaking?"

"They might be the ones robbing the graves—" He
stopped abruptly, then slapped the steering wheel.
"Have you read about the bank robberies? There were
two or three, in towns not far away. And a woman here
in town who owned a used-clothing store was murdered
that same weekend—"

He suddenly grew quiet again. She looked at him,
and saw a look of tightness on his face. He stared straight
ahead.

"Why didn't I think of that?" he said. "I heard about
those things on the news when I was in the hospital,
but I was so concerned with getting out of there—I'll
check the newspaper again. That woman's neck was
broken, I'm sure, and so was the guard at one of the

banks. That happened the weekend the tree was uprooted!''

"Carl! My God! I remember hearing something about that, but murder and robbery are becoming so common that I didn't make any connection.''

He shook his head, again and again. "It was just—pushed back in my mind, I guess. There have been other things too. I read the newspaper, but what I've been reading kind of drifts away even as I read it. I keep thinking about what *I* saw.''

He drove into the driveway at the side of her house.

For the first time she felt afraid to get out, to walk through the shadows, to find whatever might be waiting in any of the dozen rooms in her house.

He squeezed her hand tightly. The slight pain was a welcome change from the torture of her confused fears and thoughts.

"Carl—stay the night with me.''

He nodded.

They sat in the living room on a soft sofa, holding hands. They grew silent because their efforts to understand and solve this horror that had invaded their lives, their town, and threatened their families and friends had no answers.

She finally said, as dawn replaced the night, "Carl, we have to tell someone. Mel. We'll start with Mel.''

They finally slept, their heads together on the back of the sofa.

Holly woke, surprised that she had fallen asleep. After the sound of the drum in the night she was afraid to go to sleep. She had lain in a tense knot until she heard her mother's car drive in. Even then a deep dread kept her awake, listening, she had thought, all night. But now the sun was shining.

The house was deadly quiet.

In her pajamas she ran, her footsteps silent on the carpet. Without knocking she pushed open the rooms of Kara, Bryon, and Vinny. They were all asleep. All safe, all alive.

She ran to the master bedroom. The door was closed. None of them were supposed to open their parents' door without knocking.

"Mom?" she called, frantic to see that her parents were there. Alive. "Dad?"

Louise's voice answered, sounding asleep, or heavy with drugs as if she'd taken a sleeping pill.

"Yeah?" The word was drawn out, barely audible.

"Mom, are you okay? Dad?"

"Dad's gone to work." Her voice suddenly became louder, the tone nasty. "Go away, Holly."

Go away? Mom had never said that to her before. Holly had never heard her use that tone of voice, even when she was yelling bloody murder at one of the kids. Holly backed away, feeling only slightly better.

Then, on the way back to her room she stopped. Dad? Gone to work on Sunday morning? No—something was wrong.

A new terror clutched her. Daddy, equal with Mama in her heart, in a way the most important person in her world. Daddy—what would she do without Daddy? What would any of them do? He took care of them, protected them, loved them . . .

She ran back to the telephone in the foyer and dialed the number of her dad's truck telephone. It rang and rang, and Holly became colder though the morning was warm. She tightened her free arm across her stomach.

When she was about to hang up her dad's deep voice answered, "Salisaw Construction Company."

"Dad!" She sat down on the floor, weak and trembling with relief.

"Holly? What's wrong?" His voice changed, becoming anxious. "Is your mother all right? The kids?"

"Yeah. Sure. We're all okay." She hadn't told him

about the drums in the night, or the strange, dark-cloaked figure that she now thought of as the devil, or phantom, bringing news of death. "Are you okay?"

"Yeah," he said slowly, obviously puzzled, and again, "What's wrong, Holly?"

"Dad, you're not working today, are you? This is Sunday."

"I had some things to check on, honey. I often come to the site Sunday mornings to check the machinery, you know that. Vandals and thieves seem to get their first wind on Saturday nights. I'll be home early this afternoon. Isn't this pretty early for you?"

"I don't know. I just woke up. I guess I had a bad dream . . . or something."

She didn't want to tell him her fears. That a death-carrying phantom was appearing to an eerie drum roll, and warning her in silence that someone she loved was going to die.

If she put it into words it would make it happen.

Pepper had died that other night she had heard the drum, seen the—the phantom. She could tell herself it was some kind of coincidence. Even if she didn't believe it was a coincidence. But if she told Daddy, it would be because she had accepted that it was going to happen, and she was asking for help.

"You'd better go back to bed," Daddy said. "Wake up again."

She giggled nervously. "Yeah, okay." Already she felt better. Daddy's voice—calm and gentle, but authoritative.

"See you later, sweetheart."

"Okay, Daddy."

She hung up the phone and started toward the hall to her room, then stopped again. Through the glass at the front of the foyer she had caught a glimpse of movement across the hollow at the edge of the street and the Rentons' driveway. She went closer to the glass panel.

The little dog was there, sitting, looking toward her house.

She opened the front door and went out onto the stoop. The dog continued to sit looking toward her.

Holly went out to the walk and slowly down the hill, step by step. The dog didn't move. She came to the bottom of the lawn and the end of the walk. She didn't call to the dog, but continued on across the street, careful not to startle him into slinking away as he had before. He sat still, a small statue of fur, like a stuffed animal skin. She sat on her heels in front of him. "Pepper. Yes," she whispered. It definitely was Pepper. The spots on his nose were the same. The blaze on his face, and the ring around his neck. His ears were perked the way they used to be. Yet . . .

How had he gotten out of the grave? How could he be alive after he had grown cold, his eyes glassy and flat?

She stared into the dog's eyes. Glassy and flat with death . . . the way they were now.

They seemed to be looking toward her, yet they weren't focused. There was death there, afterall—flat, cold, unseeing. He didn't seem to know that she had crossed the street toward him. He sat, like something artificial. Yet . . . he was capable of movement.

She yearned toward him though she felt smothered with fear. He was her puppy. She used to sneak him into her bed on cold nights, though his house was insulated and filled with warm blankets and cedar chips. It had always been her job to feed him and be sure his water dish was filled.

Maybe that was why he appeared now more to her than to the other kids. She didn't know. She only knew this was Pepper.

How could she be afraid of him?

She put her hand out and said pleadingly, "Pepper?"

He didn't move.

She touched him.

The coldness stunned her. Again. The way it had when she picked him up after he'd been . . . *killed*. The softness and the warmth was gone.

She moved back abruptly, unable to control the terror icing her own body, compressing her heart, strangling her.

She stood up slowly, and slowly walked backwards until she felt the steps of the walk behind her. Carefully, she continued walking backwards, climbing from step to step. Her bare heel scraped the edge of a step and she turned briefly, looking down.

When she looked up again, the dog had disappeared. She ran into the house and locked the front door. She wanted to tell her mom. She had to tell her mom. The master bedroom door was still closed. She dared to enter without knocking.

Louise was still in bed, her back toward the door. She turned when Holly closed the bedroom door. Holly stopped, dazed at the look in Louise's eyes. Anger. *Hatred?*

"Don't ever open that door without knocking."

Her voice was soft and even, but vicious. Holly stared at her. For the first time in her life she felt afraid of her mother's anger, and petrified by her own fear.

Louise sat up and pressed one hand to her face. When she removed the hand she blinked at Holly as if she'd just awakened.

"What do you want?" she asked, her voice normal, the strange cruel look gone from her eyes.

Gone. But Holly would never forget it, she knew, as long as she lived. She had never seen her mother that way. Nor anyone else.

"Mom," Holly said quickly, afraid Louise would somehow revert to the *other*, as Pepper had somehow come alive in a terrible, frightening way. She was afraid Louise would send her out without listening. "Mom, I just saw Pepper. It's the dog the Rentons have now. It's Pepper. I know it is."

Louise stared unblinking at Holly. The light did something strange to her eyes, as if they reflected different colors from a flat surface. Holly wished she hadn't come to her mother's room.

"Of course it isn't Pepper," Louise said. "Pepper is dead. His body was dug up by other dogs or racoons or something, that's all. You really need to get hold of yourself about this, Holly. You know that animals do die."

"Mom . . ."

"I don't want to hear anymore of that nonsense. Now go see to it that the kids are dressed and fed, and don't mention the Rentons' dog to anyone else. Ever. Not," she lowered her voice and hissed the words, "*to your dad!*" The look she turned upon Holly held cold hostility.

Holly stepped out of the room and closed the door. Her eyes filled with tears. Her heart felt as if it were bleeding.

What was wrong with Mom?

What . . . had happened to Pepper? His death had not been as awful as this strange, moving, living death he now existed in.

Louise held her head for a moment. Her mind felt shattered, jumbled, yet oddly numb. No pain, just a sense of unconnectedness. She recalled Holly coming into the room. She recalled her feelings of irritation, of wanting her to be gone. She had felt so peaceful here alone, before Holly had entered.

She stood up, and swayed, her head feeling as if it floated without a body. She clutched the headboard and steadied herself. It wasn't exactly dizziness, but a strange feeling as of not knowing how to stand or walk. She looked across at the door to the bathroom. A dozen steps, maybe more. She couldn't judge.

What had happened?

She felt as if something had been removed from her brain. She didn't remember going to bed. . . . Had she taken more than one sleeping pill? She didn't remember taking any. She didn't remember the evening before, or—

Then suddenly it came back in vague, dreamlike movements. She had driven somewhere—alone—she had followed a black car up a hill. A rough, trail-like road that angled through the woods.

Oh Lord! Yes!

Church.

She suddenly felt high and free, as if she were soaring. She felt the smile on her lips. She remembered how the church had looked on the inside. She vaguely saw in her dreamlike memory the table beneath the long, elaborate, stained-glass window. Someone had put a long robe on her and led her to the table.

But there her memory faded.

She didn't remember what happened after that.

She didn't remember driving home, or going to bed.

The walk to the bathroom was easy afterall. It was as if she floated.

She stripped and showered. The marvelous feeling of being out of her world of worry and anxiety disappeared and she was Louise again, mother of four, pregnant with her fifth. Yet her hands, soaping her belly, felt flatness. Hipbones.

She rinsed and dried, and stood in front of the full-length mirror. Yes, her stomach was much flatter.

Frowning, perplexed, she turned sideways, looking at herself. She not only looked flatter, she looked slimmer. Better shaped than she had been since Holly was born. Her large breasts, which had drooped in ugly bags, were firmer, younger, uplifted as they hadn't been since she married.

What was happening to her? It was as if nature were turning backwards.

She had to talk to Joyce, Louise decided as she finished cleaning the kitchen. She had sent the girls to clean other parts of the house, and the boys to clean their room. For the first time she had felt as if she couldn't stand to have them underfoot when she was trying to put the kitchen in order.

Without telling anyone that she was going, she went down the stairs and out of the back door. She walked briskly around the house, at times feeling as if she weren't touching ground, that marvelous feeling of euphoria she recalled from last night returning. Then she would hit reality, painfully, realizing her situation all over again.

What was wrong with her? Was this the way manic depression felt? Was she mentally ill now? Had this pregnancy done this to her?

Or was she no longer pregnant?

She stopped, her memory opening again, briefly.

She was on the table beneath the dark, colored panes of the window. She was surrounded by people in black robes. Hands caressed her belly . . . her belly that had somehow become exposed. There was a pain . . . a terrible pain . . . somehow more in her heart, or head, than in her stomach . . .

Then, hands that weren't hers held an infant, tiny, not crying. It moved, finally. It lived.

Though it was too immature to be born, it moved. It came alive in the other woman's hands.

Her memory closed again. She had a feeling she would never know what happened next. How she got home.

What had they done to her?

She almost turned back toward the safety of her own door, but then heard her name called.

Joyce stood in her backyard below. She lifted an arm and waved Louise to come over. Even at the distance Louise saw the welcoming smile on her face.

Louise continued on, feeling drawn, unable to turn back. She went down the lawn and across the street.

Joyce took her arm. "Come on, let me make you a cup of tea."

For the first time Louise entered Joyce's house. She didn't see Albert or the children.

In Joyce's house, which appeared to have a floor plan similar to Louise's, the stairway up to the hall on the first level was inside the family room. A railing protected it.

The stairs came out directly into the kitchen, separated from it by the railing. Joyce guided Louise to a kitchen table that was oak, much like her own, only smaller.

"Sit," Joyce demanded in a friendly order.

She served a cup of tea that had already been prepared and waiting. Then she sat across the table from Louise and smiled slightly at her.

"How do you feel?"

"I don't know," Louise said. "I have this feeling I'm not pregnant anymore. My—all my symptoms are gone."

"Great."

"Great?" Louise cried. "What happened to me last night, Joyce?"

"You're in the process of joining us."

"I—joining—you?"

"Yes, exactly what you need. And you're what we need. Many, many more just like you. Strength lies in numbers. Power in control."

"But—that part on the table—what happened?"

"You were partially delivered of the onuses of life, the kind of life directed by nature."

"*What?*"

Joyce smiled at her in silence. Then said, "You're soon going to be free, Louise. Natural death will no longer be a fear, or part of your future. You should be feeling very good, very euphoric."

"I do—at times. I do. But, I don't feel pregnant anymore."

"Of course not. That was what you wanted, wasn't it? You will never be pregnant again."

Louise stood up. "I don't believe you! I never asked you to—to—" What had they done? Louise turned. Trapped. Looking for an escape. She didn't want *not* to be pregnant again, *not* to ever have another baby. *Not what she wanted . . . not what she wanted.* Not—not the irretrievable. That was why she had refused to have her tubes tied. Subconsciously, she had known.

She had to leave. She had to get out of here.

Joyce didn't try to stop her, but she followed.

At the foot of the stairs at the door, Joyce commanded, "Be sure to be at services this evening, Louise. You haven't completed your transition. In order to fully become part of us you'll need to depart this life violently—you will understand better later on. When you've accepted, you'll start feeling much better. You're part of us now. You needed us, and we needed you. You can't go back or change the direction, you can only finish what has begun. We'll give you time to make the transition, before we'll be forced to do it for you. We have many things for you to do for us."

What was she talking about? Transition? Violent death? What in God's name was the woman talking about?

She must have misunderstood. Surely she did. But she didn't want to pause to ask, she only wanted to go home.

As Louise left the house she saw the two children sitting in the shadows beneath the trees. The dog sat separated from them.

None of them moved.

22.

Beverly felt a twinge of guilt when she sat down in the conservative vinyl chair in her son's office. He was busy, she understood that, and deserved Sundays off. As an assistant district attorney he was always loaded with work, especially as the town grew beyond its budget. She had used her status as his mother to interrupt whatever plans he had for resting or going to church this morning, and asked him to meet them at his office.

She had introduced Carl, and watched as they finished shaking hands over Mel's desk. She felt a little headachy with lack of sleep. After their couple of hours sleeping together on the couch, sitting up, both of them too exhausted to even know they were propping each other up, they had grabbed a cup of coffee and arrived at Mel's office. They both were wearing the same clothes they had worn to the cemetery last night.

Beverly promised, "We'll just stay a few minutes. What we want is for you to investigate the newcomers in town." He frowned, perplexed, but she hurried on. "Especially at this address. And look into the church that was built recently at this location."

She pushed toward him a sheet of notepaper with the Rentons' name and location of the church.

"Their house is right across the street on Shady Hollow Road from Carl's son Brent Salisaw. This is his address. The Renton's address is two-forty-one Waldron Circle, a cul-de-sac on the hill across from Brent's."

"I know the old Shady Hollow Road fairly well."

Mel took the small sheet of paper, glanced at it, looked up at Beverly and Carl, and said nothing. It wasn't like Mel to say nothing.

"Carl, as you might know," Beverly said, "is one of the men who was present when the sycamore tree was bulldozed. Remember you called me, telling me what you'd heard? Everyone at the hangouts, wherever that is, was laughing, you said."

She noticed Mel was trying to give her a couple of eye signals without cluing Carl in. He had raised his eyebrows, frowned slightly, did a thing with his eyes that he'd always done when someone was about to give something away. Beverly smiled faintly.

"It's all right, Mel. Carl knows he was laughed at. Brent and Tom were also laughed at. Carl, as you know, was hospitalized overnight. It was thought he'd had a stroke. Certainly the shock was enough to give almost anyone a stroke."

Mel looked suddenly sympathetic. That was one of the inborn traits of her son that Beverly loved. He had always been compassionate toward people, animals, bugs, anything that moved and much that didn't. Also, for her, his expressions were easy to read.

"Mr. Salisaw, I apologize," Mel said. "You're obviously doing well . . . ?"

Carl nodded and murmured, "Thanks."

"You understand, Mom, Mr. Salisaw," Mel said, "that I don't have the foggiest of what the hell you're talking about. What have these Rentons done? Why do you want the church checked on? And what shock are we talking about?"

Beverly and Carl exchanged glances. They had agreed to bring Mel in on only enough to convince him to check on newcomers to town. They would possibly be invading privacy if they investigated much on their own, and they needed help. Carl also had asked Beverly to do the talking. She knew her son, how much he could, or might, believe. How far she dared go.

"Mel, you know about the graves of children being robbed."

"Of course," he said. "They're being investigated."

"We found another one last night."

His eyebrows raised. "Yeah? Where?"

Beverly indicated Carl should answer.

"An abandoned schoolhouse turned into a church years ago out in the Malvin community. The cemetery hasn't been taken care of. The church hasn't been used in years."

Mel's frown had returned. "You were out there last night? Looking in an old cemetery? Why?"

"Mel," Beverly said, "I first have to tell you what my great-grandfather told me. Then Carl will tell you about the grave beneath the tree . . . and it goes from there."

She talked fast, abbreviating where she could. Mel stared at her and then at Carl. Flickers of disbelief came and went in Mel's eyes. When they came to the robbed graves and the children of the Renton's, she found herself hedging, saying only, "We suspected the children were the purpose for the robbed graves—in some way."

Mel leaned back in his chair and tossed the pen he'd been holding onto the desk. "That is the craziest thing I ever heard, Mom!" He sat forward and glowered at her. "Mom! You're telling me this for the truth? Mom!"

She said nothing. Carl was silent, his lips tight. He had spoken reluctantly, telling very briefly what he had seen emerge from the hole beneath the tree.

Mel drew a long, deep breath, rested his head in his hands for a couple of seconds.

"Of course it's not likely that both of you are nuts on the same subject, so, I don't know. I just don't know. I never heard anything so preposterous in my life. Just give me a plain old secret in the closet, please. Tell me you murdered somebody back in the fifties or something and let me get busy with that."

He stopped talking. The worried look that had gradually come over his face grew deeper.

"I'm sorry," Beverly said softly, wishing at the moment that she'd left her son out of it. She stood up. "Maybe we should just go, Carl."

Carl was up and halfway to the door ahead of her, ready to hold it open. He hadn't wanted to share this with her son, or his. Not yet. She had talked him into it.

Mel came quickly behind them, and put his hands on their shoulders, holding them back.

"Look," he said, "I'll find out about those people, and the church. They probably moved here from another location just like other newcomers. I don't know what you saw, Carl, but . . ."

"I understand." Carl shook hands with Mel. "Thanks for listening."

They were going out the open door, into the empty front office when Carl stopped and looked back at Mel.

"There've been some pretty strange murders lately," Carl said. "A woman here in town who owned a used-clothing place was murdered and robbed, clothes taken, but no one could say exactly what. Right? Why would anyone take used clothing?"

"Nobody knows," Mel admitted. "It's under investigation."

"Then some area banks have money missing. No one knows who or how, right? Used clothes—money. Is there any news on those crimes?"

"Well no, but . . . the missing money is assumed an inside job." He ran his fingers through his hair. "It's being—" he stopped.

Carl took Beverly's arm and guided her toward the

exit. Behind them, when they reached the outer door,
Mel spoke.

"Be careful, both of you. I'll be in touch as soon as
I know anything."

"Daddy, please," Davey pleaded. "Let's don't go to
that church this evening, please." The little boy leaned
over the edge of Tom's chair. Tom ruffled his hair.

"Hey, what're you looking so worried about? Was it
that bad? If I remember right you were asleep most of
the time."

Tom had been reading the Sunday comics to Ali. She
sat nestled in his lap like a little bird in its nest.

He was going to keep the kids again tonight because
Adrianne had somewhere she was off to for the weekend. He supposed it was with a man, though she'd said
only, "Friends." But he was coming to the place where
he didn't care anymore. He felt as if he'd been freed
last night from a terrible burden. He had awakened
this morning not caring. Just not caring anymore if
Adrianne never came home.

Tomorrow morning he had to get the kids back to
their mother before he went to work. In time for her
to take them to the Christian daycare center where they
stayed while she worked.

He hadn't particularly wanted to go church last night,
he'd gone only because of the new neighbors. They
were nice people. He hadn't been to church since he
was a kid going to Sunday school, so he didn't know
much about services. He did know enough to see this
church was different. He hadn't particularly liked those
black, hooded robes the members wore.

He had felt better when he saw some familiar faces.
And especially after he had seen Louise Salisaw enter.
He was surprised, though, when she went up to the
altar. He hadn't seen any of the rest of her family. He

would have thought she would want her husband with
her when she went to the altar—if that was what it was.
If it meant saving her soul, as it used to mean when he
was a kid.

But he didn't know her very well. He wouldn't have
known her at all if she hadn't used to bring the kids
and come to whatever site they were working on, bringing iced tea, soft drinks, sometimes sandwiches.

"*Please*, Daddy?"

Tom put an arm around Davey and hugged him close.

"Sure. What would you like to do instead?"

Davey's face brightened. "Anything, Daddy. Anything
else."

"All right, how about the city park? We can play a
little ball. Maybe go swimming."

Davey buried his face against Tom's chest. He nodded
okay. His small, smooth hand, fingers still chubby, held
to Tom's wrist.

Next week, all week, every night if he wanted to, Tom
thought, he could go to church. They had services every
night, and they wanted him to come. He didn't remember any specific beliefs they had preached, but it had
sounded good. He had *felt* good. Better than he'd ever
felt in his life, maybe. Almost as if he were on a drug-
induced high.

He also had the sense of vague memories, the lack of
anything definite happening, the spots of forgetfulness,
like an induced high could leave. Yet he had taken
nothing. Not even a beer.

So they must have something going for them.

The afternoon had been great. Holly couldn't remember when she and Mom had gone shopping alone
before. Mom had taken her to stores in the eastside
mall and let her pick out a couple of outfits for church.
The only catch was, she was supposed to wear them to

the Rentons' church. Holly didn't tell Louise she didn't want to go. She felt just a wee bit guilty for her feelings. This afternoon had been very special—with a special feeling of closeness to her mother. She didn't want to ruin it.

Kara hadn't wanted to go. Dad was home, mowing the grass, and Kara wanted to stay with him and the boys. Holly knew why. She probably wanted to play with the Renton kids.

Louise drove the car into the garage, and Holly got out. Louise carried the two bags of new clothes.

Holly had noticed that Mom hadn't bought anything for anyone else, except a little knit shirt for Vinny that had printed on the front, "MAMA'S BOY." It also had angels flying. Holly didn't like it, but she didn't voice her opinion. Louise hadn't asked for any.

She remembered, when she saw the kids running toward the house, that Mama hadn't asked Kara if she wanted to go along. Holly herself had. She had been relieved when Kara said no, because she had a feeling Louise didn't want Kara.

This was *their* special time—hers and Louise's. Holly had even wondered if Mom wanted to talk to her about sex. But she hadn't mentioned it.

The kids burst up the stairs behind them, pushing for space.

Vinny cried, "Did you bring anything for me?"

Louise handed Vinny the bag that held the shirt. A feeling of sorrow tugged at Holly's heart. Bryon ran with Vinny toward their room. But he wouldn't find anything in the bag for himself.

Not until now did the unfairness of it strike Holly. Mama had never been this way before, buying something for one without buying something for the other. Had she?

Going shopping alone with her mother no longer seemed good.

She and Kara followed Louise to the living room.

Kara asked far less confidently, "Did you get me something too?"

"Show her the clothes, Holly. They're for Holly. Things to wear to church."

Holly saw the shadow of hurt on Kara's face. Her arms hung at her sides.

Holly drew out the red silk blouse.

"You can wear this sometimes," she offered, knowing as soon as she said it how condescending it sounded, and how it would hurt Kara.

Kara drew back, her face twisted into a grimace, her hands behind her. "Yuk!" she cried. "Silk! It came from a worm's rearend, and it's slimy! I wouldn't wear it if—"

Louise reacted swiftly, hand lifting. She slapped Kara on the side of her face and head. The sound popped in the room, like something broken. Tears whipped to Kara's eyes. She fell backwards, over the arm of the sofa, and to the floor.

Holly stared, paralyzed. She had never seen Louise lift her hand to any of the kids before.

Kara lifted herself half up, her hand against her face, tears streaming from her eyes.

"Can't I even say what I think anymore?"

Louise bent slightly and struck her other cheek, hard. The sound again stunned Holly. She was unable to speak, or move. She was aware, in a still, waiting, painful way, of each movement of both Louise and Kara. She saw the fear now in Kara's eyes, heard her cry, her half-scream, then her soulful weeping. Holly held herself tightly, her breath held. *No, no, don't say anymore.*

Kara crawled a few feet then rose, bent forward, and stumbled and ran from the room. The sound of her bare feet on the carpet reminded Holly of the drum in the night.

Holly stared at Louise. Mom's eyes looked oddly

blank. There was no expression at all on her face. She had no feelings for what she had done to Kara. She calmly went to a chair, picked up a magazine from the table beside it, and began to leaf through it.

As Holly turned away, still so stunned she couldn't speak, Louise said, "You can fix dinner tonight, Holly. Make Kara help you."

Holly ran from the room, dropping the sack of new clothes in the hallway. Kara's door was closed. Holly didn't pause to knock, but pushed her way in.

Kara had huddled in the corner, her eyes wide and terrified. Her cheeks showed the white marks of Louise's fingers. Red streaks ran from the white like blood.

She was like a wild animal, cornered. She shrank even from Holly.

Holly fell to her knees in front of Kara, and approached her on hands and knees, talking softly.

"Kara, Kara, it's me. Holly. Kara, *I'm so sorry.*"

Kara threw herself into Holly's arms. She squeezed Holly's neck so tightly that Holly felt choked, but she didn't try to release herself. She pulled Kara onto her lap as if she were Bryon's size, and held her as tightly as Kara clung.

She listened in silence to Kara's sobs. Her heart ached. She felt as if it too had been struck, with the white leaching away the blood.

Outside the window the lawn mower chugged along, its sound close, then drifting on.

Holly held Kara until she quit crying. The lawn mower came by, went on past, came by, went on. Shadows grew long across the deck outside the bedroom door.

Kara had been still several minutes. Her arms weren't so tight around Holly's neck. Her face was hidden against Holly's chest.

The lawn mower moved toward the garage and stopped. Vinny's voice drifted up, then Dad's. Holly wanted to run and tell him what Mama had done, but she didn't dare. If Mama could do that, what would she do after Dad asked her about it? What would she do tomorrow, when Dad was gone?

Holly had never felt so frightened in her life. What was wrong with Mama? She had turned into a stranger.

"I have to go, Kara," Holly whispered. "I have to fix dinner."

Kara moved away. Her head still hung in dejection. "What did I do, Holly?" she asked softly. "Just because I don't like silk?"

"I don't know. Honest to God, I don't know. And—I don't really like silk either. I'd rather have poly-cotton."

Kara said nothing more.

Holly stood up, but hesitated. "Kara. Mama said you were to help me. You don't have to do anything. But maybe it would be better if you came to the kitchen. So Mama . . ."

Kara nodded, rose and followed.

In the hallway Holly saw the bag of new clothes, the red blouse falling out. It hadn't been her choice. Louise had chosen everything.

She picked up the sack and stuffed the clothes into a ball at the bottom, a bitter anger building. She wanted to rip each garment apart, the two silk blouses, the cotton skirts.

Instead, she wadded it all.

"I hate this stuff!" she said. "I'll never wear it."

She opened the door to her room and threw it in.

She wanted to put it in the trash can, but didn't dare. The time would come, she knew, when Louise would insist she go to church, and wear the new outfits. Then a puzzling and unsettling thought came to her mind.

The clothes were chosen to make her look like Joyce Renton.

23.

The doorbell rang at eight-thirty, and Beverly nearly jumped out of her chair. She had just finished a bath, dressed in a soft summer gown and robe, and sat down to lean back in the chair by her bedroom windows.

She got up, went to the front windows of the master bedroom and looked down on the driveway. Mel's cherry-red BMW sat just outside the entry gate. The yard light in her driveway was coming on. Dusk had settled around the trees along the driveway, making it seem as isolated as the cemetery last night in the midnight dark.

Beverly drew a deep sigh of relief and hurried out to the stairway. She and Carl had each gone their different ways a couple of hours ago. He had a home and animals to care for, and so did she. She had found herself exhausted when finally she had a chance to sleep. Too tired to climb into a bed that was still unmade from the time she had left it in the middle of the night.

She didn't have to dress to let Mel into the house, thank heavens.

She opened the door. Always a pleasure, she thought, to see your kid. Always.

"Come in. I'll get some coffee. Or would you rather have iced tea on the back porch?"

"Were you in bed?" he asked, following her down the hall to the kitchen.

"No." She entered the kitchen and went to the refrigerator, thinking that there was less caffeine in tea. "Actually, I felt too tired, or maybe too tense, to go to bed. You didn't bring Paula?"

"I haven't even seen Paula today. Let's go to the porch?"

She poured iced tea from a pitcher. She had let it brew in the sunshine yesterday, and hoped it was still good. "Was that because of Carl and me? That you didn't see Paula?"

"Yes, it was." But he grinned tenderly at her.

"I'm sorry."

He took the tray from her and they went onto the back porch. Here there were rockers and porch furniture as well as a swing. They both chose the swing. The scent of four o'clocks wafted up from their bed beyond the railing.

She asked, "But what could you find out so fast? And on Sunday when so many offices are closed?"

"Not much, but you really gave me something to think about. It's not easy gathering information on any day, you know. Even for an assistant D.A."

His tone of voice was gentle, holding a smile somewhere in the depths. She didn't feel like smiling. Her sense of humor was rapidly eroding.

She said, "It's like being overwhelmed with something. It's like having your idea of reality turned bottom up. I'm getting really scared, Mel. I didn't want to bring you into this, but I didn't know what else to do."

"Do you want me to move home for awhile?"

"No, of course not. What did you find out?"

"Not much. Except, of course, that the church appears to be their source of income. They have what appears to be legitimate social security numbers. It will take me a while to check on those any further. Maybe when the work week opens up I can get more information. But I went to the city hall and checked records. The purchase of the house was made in cash. And—"

Beverly stared at the side of his face, interrupting, "Where would they have gotten the cash?" She realized she was assuming they were the—whatever Carl had seen emerge from the old grave beneath the tree. "Could they be the bank robbers—the—"

"I don't know. I don't know where they came from. Where they got their money. A former church somewhere, maybe. Some of those organizations make a lot of money. They do have some large accounts, under the name of Aeternita. I called the postmaster, Jim Hawks, and he went down to the post office and checked for former addresses, but there were none."

"They had to come from *somewhere*. If they're not . . . ."

"I know. In fact, their names weren't listed at all. He didn't know anyone had moved in at that address you gave me. No utilities have been turned on."

"No lights?" she asked incredulously.

"No lights, no water, no sewer, nothing."

She had no answer. She could only gaze at him, waiting.

"I did check on that church, and the land it's on was purchased recently in cash, under the name of Aeternita. He didn't see the buyers. Neither did the real estate agency. The check was written on the Aeternita account, of course."

"These people live across the hollow from Carl's grandchildren," she said.

"Yes, but I wouldn't worry about that. They wouldn't dare do anything to harm anyone. I'm sure they aren't killers, Mom. They may have seemed to come from nowhere—and that old story is weird, but . . ."

She sipped tea, and felt cold, colder than the ice that floated in it. She set it aside and hugged herself.

"Any suspects on the murders Carl mentioned?"

"No. But . . ." Again he didn't finish his thought.

Beverly sipped tea she didn't want. The cats came onto the porch and sat looking into the darkness.

"Thought I'd come by and tell you."

She nodded. "Thanks. Sorry it ruined your day."

They sat in silence. She heard ice clink in Mel's glass. The swing squeaked softly as he moved, shifting his position. Neither of them rocked.

He said, "Mom, I've been thinking about this. I know you like this Carl Salisaw. You've done business with him, and trusted him. But, maybe you ought to just get back to work and let him get back to his work. Have you thought that maybe this guy is—maybe—off his rocker?"

"Carl?" She looked at Mel's profile in surprise. He drank tea calmly, looking out over the gathering dark in the backyard.

"Like I say, I know you like him. I don't mean to knock your friends. But . . ."

"Mel—" She didn't know how to convey her fears. And, in fact, didn't want him to feel her fears. She wanted the world safe for him, for the children of everyone.

"He must have had a stroke, Mom, though the doctors dismissed him. You haven't really talked to his son, have you?"

She opened her mouth to object, then closed it. Better to let it go at the time, maybe.

"Mom. Mother." He turned toward her. She felt his eyes on her profile now. "You look tired. Do me a favor, okay?"

"Okay," she acquiesced. "What?"

"Go to bed and sleep. You were up all night last night weren't you?"

"Not quite."

"Out wading through the weeds in some old cemetery."

"And we found an empty grave, too," she said softly.

"The coffin open. A *fresh* empty grave, Mel. It was a terrible sight."

"But graves are being robbed lately. We don't have a clue who's doing it, but we will. We have some extra men out patrolling, keeping an eye on the cemeteries. But what I want you to do, Mother, is stay at home a couple of days. Rest. Don't talk to anyone but me. Okay? I'll make an appointment for you to get a checkup."

"I'm not sick!" she said with sudden vigor. "I just had my annual checkup three months ago."

"Just do me that favor, okay?"

"No," she said. "I can't hang around the house doing nothing."

"All right then, go back to work. But don't talk to anyone but me, okay? I mean about this other thing."

"In other words, stay away from Carl."

"Well, yeah," he said lamely. "Something like that."

Anger fired her rush of words.

"Haven't you wondered how we happened—just happened—to go to that particular cemetery, looking for *that* grave, at midnight?"

She knew by the way he looked at her that even though it might have seem odd to him, he hadn't really considered why.

"I'll tell you," she said without invitation. "It was the Renton child—the boy, Monte. Carl and I went over there, to the Rentons, with his grandchildren. The boy, Monte, looked very familiar to me. To me, not Carl. Then it popped into my mind—at midnight—when I'd seen that boy."

She took a breath. She'd been talking so fast she was breathless. Mel's gaze had become steady.

"I went to school with Monte, Mel. He died when we were in the fourth grade."

Mel was still trembling when he got into his car. He had waited on the porch long enough to hear his mother bolt the door. Now, he pressed the button that locked his car doors.

He backed slowly out of the driveway, reluctant to leave her alone.

There was something else too—something he hadn't told her. About Paula.

She hadn't been around much this past week because she had started going to a church that had services every night. Revival meetings, she had called them.

It was the church called Aeternita.

Holly stood on the kitchen deck and watched her mother's car back out of the garage. Dad was sittiang in the kitchen, eating a late snack with Bryon and Vinny.

Kara had been so quiet earlier at dinner that Holly wondered if Dad would notice and say something, but he had come up the back stairs after Vinny went to call him, sweaty and with grass bits on his clothes. He had gone to shower, and then ate in silence himself. It hadn't been a pleasant dinner. No one had eaten much. Vinny never did. He was at that age. But Bryon, who usually had an appetite, only messed around, and Mama had gotten after him. Holly had been afraid for awhile that she was going to hit him, too. But she didn't.

She had left the table instead, and Holly knew it was up to her to clean the kitchen. She hadn't asked Kara to help.

It was a relief to be alone in the kitchen. She hurried, running the dishwasher, and wiping the kitchen cabinets before Mama returned and saw the little dirty fingerprints on the white paint.

She was still in the kitchen when Dad and the boys came back for a snack. And when she heard Mama's car going out the driveway.

She remained standing on the deck, looking into the

night. In a way it was a relief to have Mama gone. It would give her a chance to talk to Dad in private.

Yet she didn't go back into the kitchen just yet. She stayed, watching the driveway lights come on through the trees. She found herself listening for Pepper. Pepper at the door whining, scratching to get in for his evening with the family.

The dark deepened, and came toward her. The light from the kitchen splayed out upon the deck, revealing her to whatever hovered in the dark woods. Whatever had killed Pepper, and then removed him from his grave.

And brought him to a strange kind of half-life again.

It was Pepper, she was sure of it. Yet, it wasn't.

She went into the kitchen, closing and locking the sliding doors. The night beyond the wide panes of glass looked black. She pulled the draperies.

"Daddy," she said. "Did Mama go to church again?"

"Yes."

She swallowed a lump in her throat.

Brent rose from his chair and held out both hands. "Come, guys, time for baths and bed."

Holly started to ask him if she could talk to him later, but held her voice. Alone in the kitchen she put away the box of corn chips, and the bottles of fruit juice. She rinsed the glasses and put them on the sink to drain dry, and wadded the paper napkins they had used for plates into the waste bin.

She closed all of the blinds in the kitchen and dining area, shutting out the black night and whatever it was that was trying to enter their home.

She turned on the television for a few minutes, but it was a rerun she had seen before. She didn't bother with a different channel.

When she left the kitchen she saw a light on in the den. The door stood open.

Dad sat in his chair reading the Sunday newspaper. The television was dark.

Then, she noticed, he wasn't reading the paper afterall. He was staring over it at the blank screen of the TV.

"Dad?" she said from the shadowed hallway.

He jumped slightly and lowered the newspaper. His head swiveled toward the doorway. "Yeah? Holly?"

She entered the room and sat down on the end of the sofa nearest him, her legs drawn up, her sandals kicked off. The clock on the mantel tick-tocked slowly. It was an antique Mom had bought at a garage sale. Holly, Kara, and the boys had been with her that day. Holly felt her eyes fill with tears. It had been so good then. Mama had seemed to love them. They had just moved to the new house, and she was so happy.

"Daddy . . ." *Mama slapped Kara. She hit her so hard, Kara fell . . .* "Daddy, there's a dog over at the Renton's that looks exactly like Pepper."

Only, perhaps, somehow more gaunt, hollow in the cheeks, if a dog could be hollow-cheeked. Blank eyed. *Different.*

"Yes," he said, surprising her. "I saw him."

"I think it's Pepper," she blurted. "Daddy, I really think it is! And yet, he—it—scares me. I called him, and he wouldn't come. He didn't know me at all." *I don't know Mama.* Not the mother that hit Kara.

Her dad leaned back in the chair, his head resting on the top cushion, the footrest going up. He closed his eyes.

"Daddy," she cried desperately. "What's wrong?" *Don't you change too, Daddy!*

He opened his eyes.

"Just tired, sweetheart. Why don't you go to bed?"

She got off the chair, stooped, and picked up her sandals. At least Daddy had an excuse for being tired. He was okay. He wasn't changing.

She leaned down and kissed his forehead, and felt his pat on her hand.

At the doorway his voice stopped her.

"Holly . . . don't go close to the dog across the hollow. Just remember, it only looks like Pepper. Pepper, our dog, is gone."

"Okay," she said after a long hesitation. His voice hadn't carried conviction and she knew—he didn't believe his own words. It was Pepper, somehow revived from the grave, and Daddy knew it.

Davey's eyes popped open and he listened. He'd been asleep. But like a door opening, all at once he was wide awake. Somewhere, coming along the street, was a lone sound. Music. No, not really music, but the background of music. A car must be coming, creeping along, getting closer and closer, and the thump, thump of the bass was gradually louder.

Davey's bedroom hung in shadows, with the spooky sound coming toward him. He looked past the dresser against the wall, the desk, the chest, the posters he had left here. He looked in his mind outside the house to the street that was empty and silent this time of night. He saw a dark car coming, the music coming ahead of it, yet never really breaking into music. He heard the drumming, and he felt enclosed in it. That awful ghostliness, that somber movement into his area.

A drum. Not just the bass of music unheard, but a drummer, coming, closer and closer. Walking, perhaps down the street or sidewalk.

Davey threw back his cover and ran to the window. He pulled aside the curtain and put his face against the screen beneath the opened window.

A tall, dark figure stood just across the lawn in the middle of the street. He was all covered in black, even his head. It was like a cape that fell to his feet.

The drumming had stopped. The night was silent.

Davey stared at the figure. There was no face. Only a dark head beneath the hood. But it looked straight at him.

Davey wanted to scream for his dad, but his throat froze. Street lights glinted on the pavement. A wind blew suddenly and a black shadow from a moving tree swallowed the figure.

Davey stared, stared so hard the night blurred, the light changing places with the shadows. He stared, but the figure had hidden itself somewhere in the dark.

Maybe he had come closer to the house. Maybe at this moment he was trying to get into Ali's room, or Daddy's.

Davey ran into the hall, and into Ali's room. She was still there, asleep in her little bed with the side railings.

With fear so frozen in his chest and behind his eyes the tears wouldn't flow, Davey ran to his dad's bedroom.

He heard the snore even as he entered the room. Davey stopped, breathing hard. Light came dimly through the windows. No dark shadow hovered there, trying to break in.

Davey stood still a moment, then went back into the hall. He stood, listening. The drumming . . . gone. Nothing now, but silence.

It was late. The time of night through which he had always slept. In all his life he hadn't been awake now, this time of night, even when Mama first took him away from Daddy and made him sleep in a strange room.

He crept back to bed and huddled with his sheet pulled high beneath his chin. He would run and tell Daddy about the man in the street, but Daddy would go out to see, and he might never come back.

Shadows moved in his room, reaching long fingers. The bad feeling came and wouldn't go away. He was afraid . . . afraid the bad person in the black cloak was going to come and get someone. Take away someone he loved. He was afraid to go to sleep. Because if he did, when he woke in the morning, he would find that it had happened while he slept. He had to stay awake and watch, and listen. Listen, as the shadows moved ever so silently in his room.

* * *

Adrianne drove through the night on a nearly empty highway. Starlight glossed the fields. Cows rested, black lumps like boulders. Black, lacy treetops traced a paler night sky that sparkled faintly with tiny stars and planets. She had put her window down, though she drove fast. It was a good feeling. It was freedom.

The weekend had been good, but not as good as coming home. She had made up her mind while she was in the mountain resort with five other people, one of whom she'd been dating for a couple of months, that she was going home. It was three-thirty in the morning. If she kept her speed at seventy, she anticipated she would reach home around four o'clock. Only thirty minutes.

What would Tom do when she turned up on his doorstep?

She knew she had a lot of explaining to do. She didn't know what to say except that being on her own hadn't turned out as she'd expected. She was no longer a twenty-two-year-old looking for excitement, she had discovered, although she'd been acting like one.

She wanted to go home. To Tom, the kids, the new house he'd bought her.

Maybe it was the thirty-year mortgage that had scared her away. Maybe it was knowing that money would be tight just to pay for the house, and if they ever managed a vacation it would be because she'd gone to work too. But Tom didn't want her to go to work. He had the idea that rearing children at least to school age before the mother left the house to work was the most important job in the world.

She hadn't agreed until she'd seen for herself how the kids reacted to the changes in their lives.

She didn't want to date anyone anymore. She was ready to grow up and join Tom in the job of providing a solid base for the kids.

A large sign to the right of the interstate gave the exit she wanted. She slowed to sixty, let an eighteen-wheeler whip past, and drove onto the exit.

Beneath the interstate the exit joined a two-lane highway that passed beneath the interstate. There was a stop sign, but no traffic on the highway into town. She didn't bother to stop. Beneath the viaduct she drove through darkness, her headlights on dim.

She speeded up again on the empty road into the west side of town. Trees grew thickly for a ways before they thinned. She had come this way many times. Ordinarily she would have gone west instead of east, toward the house she rented in the adjoining town. But tonight she was going home.

She drove into the darkness beneath the trees, her headlights throwing a twin path near her car. Not far enough ahead for her to see someone walking beside the road, or an animal about to walk into her path. But then, what person would be walking at this hour? Only possums would be out—

He was there, suddenly, in the street ahead of her.

She saw a flat, colorless, featureless face, surrounded by the darkness of a strange, black cape that hung to his—*its*—ankles.

She heard her own gasp of horror as she swung the car to the right sharply.

The tree stood within a few feet of the road.

She heard the crash, felt the jolt against her, the opening of the car door. Through her mind flashed the images of her children, Tom, their home, and the seat belt which she had undone because it was confining . . .

24.

"Tom's wife was killed last night," Brent said.

"Oh yeah?" Louise answered. She went on working calmly, filling plates that would go into the microwave.

Holly watched her, waiting. Her mother didn't react in any way to what had happened to Mrs. Roush. Holly thought of the little boy and girl. The girl was only about Vinny's age. The prettiest little girl Holly had ever seen. But her memory of the few times she had seen Ali, from the time she was a baby until Mrs. Roush moved away and took the kids with her, was tainted by Louise's reaction. The lack of compassion in her own mother's reaction seemed paramount, somehow.

Holly looked at her dad. He had come in from work earlier than usual, probably because of the death, and sat down in a kitchen chair. He had washed in the utility room, but he hadn't changed clothes. He looked so tired, and sort of disheveled.

Kara was bringing out flatware and placing it on the table, slowly, as if she had no energy. She glanced at Holly, and Holly saw her own horror and fear reflected in Kara's eyes. Somewhere down the hall Vinny was talking as the boys came closer to the kitchen. Mama had sent them to wash their grubby hands and faces. "And not in the utility room, either!" she had said.

"I'm not in the mood to clean up your messes. Go to your own bathroom."

"He didn't come to work today, of course," Brent said. "But it was noon before I knew why. I thought we should go over after supper."

Louise said nothing. Now, the past few evenings, since she had started to church with the Rentons, she put individual servings on plates and heated them in the microwave. By the time all the plates were on the table, the first two were cold. No one complained though. No one was ever hungry.

Holly asked, "How was she killed?"

"Car wreck," her dad said. "For some reason she had driven in this direction from the interstate instead of going home, and she crashed head-on into a big tree just this side of the viaduct. The crash woke a couple in a house nearby, and they got to her about four o'clock. She was already dead."

The flatware clinked as Kara arranged it. Holly thought her hands were shaking. She knew her own were. Was this the death that she had felt was coming? Yet she hardly knew Mrs. Roush. She wasn't even sure what her name was.

"Kara," Louise said, "fill the water glasses." The microwave began to hum. "Holly, keep an eye on this. Warm the others."

She left the room. After a couple of minutes her voice rushed back, words jumbled and fast, angry, muffled by distance and walls. Bryon screamed once, then began to cry.

Holly saw the frown her dad directed toward the hallway. "What the hell happened?"

Kara stood beside the table, her head lowered. Now Holly saw she was trembling all over. She didn't know whether to go to Kara or pretend she didn't see her agitation. With a deep, sickening dread Holly guessed what had happened to Bryon.

Brent made a move to rise, but Holly said quickly as she hurried from the room, "I'll go see."

No, no. She couldn't let him know what Mama must have done, what she had done to Kara. *He must not know.* He would be angry. Furious. He might even want a divorce. Holly had friends whose parents were divorced, and she didn't ever want that to happen. She'd hide whatever Mama did as long as she could. Maybe tomorrow, or next week, Mama would be sweet and kind again, loving them as always.

She ran, going toward the hallway where Bryon now cried, on and on. He stood trying to hide his face against the wall, hands up for protection. Vinny stood nearby, stunned to silence.

Holly picked Bryon up, and felt his weight soft and limp against her shoulder.

"There, there, you just fell and hit your head on the door. Just fell."

Vinny followed, his blanched skin making his eyes look too large for his face.

"Huh-uh, Mama hit him. Real hard. I saw Mama hit him."

"Shhh. Don't ever say that, Vinny."

She entered the kitchen, carrying Bryon, whispering in his ear, "Shhh, don't cry. *Please.* Don't tell that Mama hit you."

She put Bryon on Dad's lap. Bryon leaned against him, sobbing, trying to stop crying. Dad asked, "What happened?"

Holly said quickly, "He fell and hit his head against the door."

Bryon said nothing.

Not Vinny, though, never Vinny.

"Huh-uh, Daddy, he didn't, Mama pushed him. She was ma—"

Holly hastily put her hand down and covered his mouth. She felt him flinch slightly, as if he had feared

Holly was going to hurt him as Mama had hurt Bryon. His big blue eyes almost leaped at her.

"Shhh!" she hissed. Then kissed his forehead to soften her demand that he shut up. She started to take her hand away from Vinny's mouth.

"But—" he began.

She clamped down harder again and gave him a serious frown. *Shut up, Vinny!*

Kara moved. She went to the microwave, removed the hot plate and put another in. Then stood and waited, looking at the glass door as if it were a television screen.

When the plates were finished they saw only five, not six. Holly looked at them, and toward Kara. The boys sat quietly now at the table. Vinny had finally caught on. Holly had never known him to be so silent when he was awake.

Bryon's left cheek was white outlined in red. Mama's handprint there was as sharp and clear as it had been on Kara's face. But he sat with that cheek away from Dad, unseen, so far, by Dad.

Kara had barely spoken a word in the house since Mama had struck her. She had spent most of her time out riding her bike, or somewhere. Maybe across the hollow with the Renton kids. Holly didn't know. The laundry and vacuuming had fallen on Holly's shoulders. She hadn't had time to look for Kara, though she'd wanted to. All day she had worked, doing the things Mama used to do.

It didn't matter. Mama wasn't well, she was beginning to think. She had a health problem, maybe. At least it would excuse what she had done. Didn't people always use health problems or addictions for excuses? She wasn't sure she approved, but it was better than the other. That Mom herself was responsible.

Vinny spoke up, looking at Holly as if for approval. "Isn't Mama going to eat?"

Brent finished pouring glasses of milk and sat down. "Just eat your food, Vinny," he said.

They had almost finished when Louise came to the doorway. She was dressed in a long skirt and blouse. She looked, Holly thought, a lot like Joyce. Now. In that outfit. Even her hair looked vaguely different. Brighter, soft curls around her face.

"I won't be able to go with you to Tom's," she said. "Just buy something at the grocery to take over. I'll go to the funeral, whatever."

"Mama!" Vinny cried, getting off his chair. "Mama, where are you going?"

"I'm going to church, sweetheart."

She sounded normal. Happy. From the corner of Holly's eye she saw Kara lift her head and give Mama a look. A hopeful look? The way Holly herself felt, as if Mama had come home again? Even as she was leaving?

Vinny began to cry and started toward her. "Mama! Take me with you."

She bent and kissed him.

"Not tonight, baby. But soon. Very soon."

Bryon watched them with a wistful look on his face. That wasn't uncommon, Holly thought, her heart feeling as if it would break. A knot gathered in her throat. Mama had always seemed to like Vinny better than anyone. Better than Bryon.

Vinny came back to the table, his tears halted. They glistened on his cheeks, catching the kitchen light with tiny rainbows.

"She's going to take me with her," he said. "Maybe next time."

Louise felt her body sway with the musical chanting of the voices. Soft, surrounding her, everywhere. Within her, lifting her from all her former worries. "Life," they whispered, sang, "Unending life. It has come to you, now bring it to others. Bring your loved ones to us. Make them part of us. Step outside the existences that surround you. Bring us your children. Bring us your children. Let them become immortal as you who are part of us are immortal. Bring the young and the beautiful, so they can stay young forever. Those who fight you—can never touch you. Those who would shun you—don't matter. They can never touch you."

They spoke to her within her mind even as the service ended and she drove away. In silence they left, one after the other, filing out the door, yet connected in a way she had never felt connected before. The person in front of her, the person in back—all a part of her.

The voices continued in her mind as she drove home. Make your children immortal. Bring them to us. *Kill the life that is within them, and bring them to us.*

Kill the life that is within them . . .

Kill the life that is within them . . . it is not real . . . not good . . . not good . . .

Something within her cried out in rebellion. She saw herself in the shadows at the side of the road, keeping pace with the car, leading her on.

She saw herself going up the stairway from the garage, going ahead, going into the hall toward the children's rooms.

"No, no!"

The whisper was in the air. Harsh, crying out for something that had once existed within her. Suddenly the image that moved ahead of her disappeared.

She leaned against the wall, weighed down in depression. She pressed a hand to her belly. "I'm pregnant," she whispered to herself. "That's what's wrong with me. I'm going crazy. Please . . ." But the words wouldn't come to her lips. Please God help me.

Her appointment to see her doctor was still days away. Did she dare wait?

Exhaustion suddenly swamped her body. Her legs ached. Her head felt numb and faintly dizzy. She felt as if she had no blood carrying oxygen to her heart. Breathing was . . . wasn't necessary. When she tried to take a deep breath some part of her that seemed far away drew even farther away, slipping from her reach.

The master bedroom drew light only from the half-open door of the bathroom. She went toward it, feeling an almost total lack of energy. Brent was in bed. She hoped he was asleep. She didn't feel like facing him, or anyone. She went into the bathroom and stood, wondering why she had come here. What had she wanted in the bathroom? Then she remembered. Remove clothes, put on nightgown . . . robe . . . bed . . .

She found herself back in the bedroom, going toward the bed, the light from the bathroom trailing her, trying to hold her.

"How was church?"

The voice broke upon her harsh and loud. It crushed her skull, entered the silent darkness of her mind.

She stopped. Yet the other part of her went forward, toward the bed. She saw the hand of the figure that looked exactly like her reach for the drawer where the small revolver was kept when he was out of town. She opened the drawer, and paused, looking.

Then the strange other part of her was gone.

Brent turned, looking toward her.

The drawer stood open.

"What are you doing?" he asked.

She pushed the drawer closed.

"Where's the gun?"

"You know it's locked in the safe. When I'm here it's always in the safe."

She got into bed. What had that other person . . . whoever she was, who looked exactly like herself even to the pink nightgown . . . what had she meant to do with the small handgun?

She knew.

She wasn't sure if she was glad it hadn't happened.

He touched her and she recoiled, moving nearer to the edge of the wide bed.

He drew away and turned onto his back. From the corner of her eye she saw his profile in the near-darkness of the room. His nose was silhouetted against the mint-green drapery at the window beyond.

He asked again, his voice closer, softer, not so intrusive. "So what happened at church?"

What happened? She didn't know. On looking back, she couldn't recall. Only the feelings. The oneness, the sense of belonging.

They must die. The voices sang rhymically, in her ears, in her mind. Returning. *To make your children immortal, they must die and be brought back to life, as you have been. They must be entered into the Way of Aeternita. The natural life that is within them must be destroyed to make room for the new life that will last forever . . . forever . . .*

"Oh," she said aloud, hearing her human voice as from afar. "Nothing unusual."

She turned away from him, to sleep.

It's my pregacy, she thought. I misunderstood.

His voice came again.

"Don't you think you're overdoing it? Every night?"

She snapped, "It's not exactly as if I'm leaving my kids alone! You're here."

"I can't always be here. Sometimes I'm delayed at work, you know that."

She drew a deep breath.

"I'm going to be taking them with me . . . before long."

She smiled faintly. Yes. Before long, her children would be going with her. Forever.

25.

Brent was gone when Louise woke. The master bedroom was bathed in silence. She lay still awhile, her gaze roaming the recessed ceiling, the fan, the dark oak molding around the edge of the ceiling. It was as if she'd never seen it before. Her gaze fell to the large double dresser and the twin mirrors. She didn't like what she saw.

She got up and went to shower and dress. She had designed the whole house, in a way. She had chosen it from a selection of floor plans. Now she hated it all.

Brent was going to give her trouble. He wouldn't want her to go to church tonight, and she must go. He didn't understand. He would never join her. She sensed he would object to all it stood for. It didn't matter. He was older—too old to become one of the members. In his forties, he was years older than any of the other men, who were mid-thirties at most. He had lost his handsome young body, his smooth skin.

She needed to talk to Joyce.

The rest of the house was quiet too. At first she thought the kids might still be asleep, but then she saw the time on the hallway clock. She had slept twelve hours.

She listened, and heard the murmur of the boys'

voices in one of their bedrooms or somewhere down the hall. She resisted an urge to go after them and make them go outside and play. The television, she thought. That wicked, terrible box that was ruining their minds.

She stood in the doorway to the bedroom hall and saw herself move forward, toward the boys' bedroom. Satisfaction settled within her like a full stomach. She waited.

The part of her that was apart, yet so visible, walked into the room where the boys played. She saw them look up, happy smiles turning puzzled, then afraid.

She saw herself grab an arm of each child and drag them out of the bedroom. Her voice screamed, "Go outside. Keep that noise out of here!" She couldn't order them to turn off the television because there was no television in the room. That was odd, she thought. She had thought those wicked boxes were all over the house, in every room.

One of the children began to cry. The larger one. She shook him viciously, and his cry turned to a scream. Hatred boiled in her.

She had to release one of them in order to open the front door. The child screamed. The larger one began to sob.

She heard her voice saying things she didn't understand. Wicked children. Wicked. They must be released from the wicked life that lived within them, and brought to the life that was good.

She kicked open the door.

"Leave them alone!" the voice screamed.

She turned. A young, lovely girl . . . so right for Aeternita . . . *Holly?*

She dimly recognized her firstborn, but the anger pushed aside all other emotions. She saw her shadow, the shadow that was more real than she who watched, drop the smaller children and attack the girl.

Her hands went around the girl's throat, squeezing,

choking. The voice of the thing in her hands had no words, only a gasping, gasping . . .

Suddenly it was she. Not a double that she watched in cold anger. She felt in her hands the warmth, the being of her beloved first child. Her face had turned blue, her eyes bulged in fright. Vinny and Bryon screamed and clawed at her clothing.

"Oh my God!" she cried, and pulled Holly into her arms. *"Oh my God, what have I done?"*

Holly gasped for breath. Louise bent her forward and pounded her back, crying, crying, *"Holly! My God, Holly, speak to me!"*

The boys had fallen back, weeping, holding each other. She thought of Kara, of all her children. She loved them more than life. Didn't they know? They were becoming afraid of her. She could see it, feel it.

Not her . . . the double. Whatever it was that separated from her and did things she would never do.

Holly began to breathe and weep softly. Louise held her, rocking side to side, patting the back of her head, whispering, "I'm sorry. Baby, I'm so sorry."

She gathered the two little boys to her and held the three of them. She longed for Kara. But Kara didn't come. Riding her bike somewhere, Louise thought vaguely.

She drew them down and they huddled together on the floor, and gradually the children hushed.

Louise kept murmuring, "I'm sorry. I'm sorry. I don't know what's wrong."

Holly said, "It's okay, Mom. We love you. We'll always love you."

The boys nodded, their heads warm against her, their eyes looking up into hers.

They sat in silence. Louise's heart began to beat again, it seemed, after a long delay.

She had to do something. She had to see her doctor.

"Holly . . . I think I'll go see Doctor White. Can you watch the children?"

"Yes. Don't worry about us."

It was said eagerly, anxiously. Holly wanted her to go for help.

They stood on the kitchen deck and watched their mother's car drive away. A cool breeze from the trees at the end of the house fanned against Holly's hot face. Hot and cold, she had thought strangely when Mama's hands were around her throat. Her skin, her body had felt as if it were both burning and freezing.

Mama's fingers had been so strong. Holly, trying desperately to loosen their hold, had found them inhuman. Unreal.

But it was okay now.

She squatted and pulled both boys against her. "Don't tell," she warned, pleaded. "Don't tell Daddy. Or Grandpa. Or anyone. Vinny, don't talk about it."

His eyes examined her neck. "Mama's going to the doctor," he said, for the tenth time.

"Yes."

"Then she'll be better."

Bryon pointed. "Kara," he said.

Holly stood up. Kara came riding down the driveway. She turned the bike around in a circle then rode out again.

Everything looked so normal. Now, when Mama got back, maybe it would be.

Louise dressed and waited. Dr. White had said nothing during the examination. Although the waiting room had patients with appointments waiting, they had let her come on back. Maybe the nurse had seen that she was desperate.

Dr. White came in and sat down. He looked at her chart, then at her.

"When did you have the miscarriage?"

She stared at him, stunned.

He said, "You were in last week. The doctor who examined you found you five or six months pregnant. You're not pregnant now. What happened?"

She searched her mind. She had thought it was a dream. The removal of the fetus, the tiny baby, at the church. *She had thought it was a dream.* It must have been a dream. It couldn't have happened that way.

"Is something wrong, Louise?"

She licked her lips. They felt dry and rough. "Uh— there were no scars, or anything?"

He shook his head. "Your cervix is enlarged. It indicates that you have recently been pregnant, but there's no way for me to know what happened."

He watched her closely. She felt herself withdraw.

Tell him, tell him, tell him about the voices you've been hearing, and the double that separates from yourself and does terrible things.

She stood up and gathered up her handbag tightly to her chest. "I don't know. I don't know. I haven't been feeling very well."

Only in church. Only in the building that was the Way of Aeternita. With the people who surrounded her, who wanted to make her part of them.

Yet now, she remembered so little of it. It all seemed like a dream.

She left his office, and went out onto the sidewalk.

Go back. Tell him about the voices, and the double. Let him make an appointment for you to see a psychiatrist.

A hand touched her back gently, yet felt glued there, a permanent part of her. She turned.

Joyce stood smiling at her.

Louise looked into Joyce's eyes and felt the bond. She had made the transition, she now knew, from one world to another.

"Hello, Joyce," she said.

"Let's go home now, shall we? Don't forget the services tonight. We have to go prepare ourselves. We have to prepare the children. They are needed. Many couples need the children. We must save them.''

"Yes.''

The euphoria came, surrounded them, separated them from the people walking by.

"We have much work to do,'' Joyce said.

"Yes.''

They smiled at each other. People looked, stared, then walked on around them. A couple frowned, others smiled too. But it didn't matter about them. Not yet. Not until they became one with the Way of Aeternita.

As Joyce had said, they had much work to do.

Holly looked at herself in the bathroom mirror. Her throat was sore, inside and out. She felt as if it had been torn from her body. She felt as if she were taking a bad cold. She swallowed, and cringed with the pain.

She leaned a moment over the sink, nausea rising, receding.

Someone stood in the bathroom. They must have slipped in while she stood with her eyes squeezed shut. Her heart nearly exploded with fear. Silent, shadowy movements frightened her. She whirled.

Kara stood looking at her, lower lip drooping, chin dropped.

Her saddened eyes examined Holly's neck. Holly put her hand up to hide it. Kara's eyes met Holly's. Sympathy, understanding. Holly felt closer to Kara at that moment than ever before. She fought tears rising, blinked them back.

Without speaking Holly turned and looked again in the mirror. She slowly moved her hands. Her neck looked dirty. She wet and soaped a wash cloth and began to scrub. It hurt, but she kept scrubbing.

"Holly,'' Kara said softly, "tell Daddy.''

Holly whirled. "Oh no! Don't ever say anything to anyone!'' Her voice rasped unnaturally. She turned her back, dropping the useless washcloth in the sink, lowering her head. "It's okay, I'm just taking a cold. My throat hurts a little."

The sudden sense of helplessness was worse than any physical pain. The pain of anguish that her mother had done this to her, done what she had to Kara and Bryon, those things hurt deep inside her. Her heart cried, shedding blood tears. Her body felt shrunken, drawing into itself as if she had some terrible malady.

"Vinny told me," Kara said simply.

Holly lifted her head, a mixture of impatience and amusement bringing a quirk to her lips. "Vinny talks too much."

Kara laughed a little, "Yeah."

Then they both were laughing. They stood looking at each other, tears running down their cheeks, laughing. Suddenly they were in each others arms weeping, crying their hearts out. They sank to the floor and cried until they both were exhausted. They continued to sit together, silent, leaning head against head.

In the silence they heard the soft murmur of sound, the garage door rising. Mama had come home.

In silent agreement they rose and left the bathroom.

Kara rode her bike out the driveway and down the street behind the house. Homes along the hilltop street had larger yards, fewer trees. But it seemed to Kara they were all occupied by old people who worked in their yards, or middle-aged people who were seldom home. She hadn't seen any kids along the block to the street down to the hollow, or along the street in the other direction. A couple of teenage boys lived in one house. They had a car that seemed never to run. Maybe their dad had gotten it for them on purpose, so they'd be busy but could never go very far, because they were always out working on its engine, or working on something beneath it.

This afternoon they had it chugging. One of them was inside, the door open, one long leg out the door, foot on pavement. The other had his head under the hood as usual.

"Rev it!"

The one inside revved it. It roared, then sputtered to a stop. Both boys cussed some dirty words, but by that time Kara had ridden past.

She came to the street down the hill.

No houses here at all. It was like riding through a wilderness. She just sat back, kept the brakes pressed just enough to keep the speed under control, and flowed with the gravity.

This was her favorite street of all. Here she was in a world where only squirrels, chipmunks, birds, and butterflies lived. Trees shaded the road. She had never met a car here.

She came to Shady Hollow and turned right. The afternoon was warm. Sweat had begun to pop up on her forehead when she reached the Rentons' driveway. She kept to the shade, and stopped her bike, one foot down, the other on the peddle.

No one was in sight. Only the dog that sat like a statue at the side of the patio. It didn't bark at her. It had never barked. It couldn't be Pepper, as Holly seemed to think, because Pepper was a good watchdog. She had decided that because it helped her to hurt less when she saw him.

"Kara," a voice said, "come on in. There's someone here who wants to meet you."

Kara looked up. In the shadows of tree limbs above the patio was a deck similar to the decks on her own house. She had never noticed it before. Joyce leaned slightly forward over the railing, her fair hair hanging loose and falling over her shoulder. She looked almost as young as Holly, and very beautiful.

"Just come on up the stairs, dear, to the living room."

"Okay."

She approached the lower entry door hesitantly. She didn't know where the living room was, and she felt as if she should turn and run away. The dog sat still as she crossed the patio. He didn't seem aware that she was getting ready to open the door.

Something whizzed past her and landed with a small crack on the dog's head. It cringed.

The boy's voice came sharply right behind her. "Get away, you cur! I hate you!"

Like a dark little shadow the dog slunk away, his tail between his legs, and his spine lumpy and thin. The ribs showed through, the fur thinning. Monte ran after him, throwing rocks, yelling, "I hate you! You stink!"

Kara ran after Monte. "Stop it! Stop it!" She grabbed his arm and jerked him round. Hastily, she moved her hand away and put it behind her.

The coldness of his flesh felt as if it had rubbed off onto her hand, like something evil and slimy. She wiped her palm.

Monte stood with an expression on his face that made Kara afraid. His tongue darted at her, not pink but thick and squishy. His eyes gazed flat and colorless past her, as if he weren't sure exactly where she stood. She stepped well away from him.

Her voice shook when she spoke. "Don't throw rocks at him!"

"He's a cur. I hate him."

She stepped backwards, farther away. "Well, I hate you. You're mean."

The boy darted his tongue at her again, and bent to pick up another rock. When he looked up his face was gone. There were no eyes, no nose, no dark curly hair. His mouth was now a long slit across a round mush, glistening wet . . .

Kara stumbled backwards, and blinked her eyes wide. His face was there again, bronzed, beautiful—as if something had played a trick on her—a strange light maybe—or part of her own mind going bad, maybe.

At that moment the screen door opened. As if the sound had made him into a different person, Monte smiled. His face became pleasant, bland. Like Heidi's.

Heidi held the door open.

"Come in."

Kara climbed the stairs with Heidi. The living room was at the top of the stairs, beyond a fancy, knobby railing. Kara stood with the railing separating her from the two women who sat smiling at her.

Joyce said, "Kara, dear, this is Bertha."

"Hello, Kara."

Kara mumbled greetings, wishing she hadn't come. Why did she keep thinking that Heidi and Monte might make good friends? She had nothing in common with them, even Heidi, she realized as she stood there looking into the face of the stranger. She didn't like any of these people very well at all, not Heidi, and especially not Monte. She was going to stay only long enough to escape politely. After this she'd ride her bike alone in the shade.

Bertha stared at her in a funny way. Kara felt as if she were being examined, like a vegetable at the supermarket. The woman was beautiful, in an evil way. Her dark hair was so glossy it looked artificial. Her eyes were deepset and very bright blue. Brighter than any sky, yet with no flecks, no depth.

"Heidi," Joyce said, "you can take Kara into the kitchen and have a treat."

"Yes, Mother," Heidi said, and smiled at Kara, waiting for her to follow.

No, I can't, Kara wanted to say. But her weakened will pushed her along. She couldn't leave yet, it would be impolite. Joyce would probably tell Mama . . . and Mama . . .

Kara followed.

The kitchen was dark. A window faced over the garage, and a tree limb filled with large, dark leaves hung in front of the glass.

Without turning on the light, Heidi went to a cabinet and opened the doors, as if the darkness didn't bother her. Kara looked around. There was a table with four chairs drawn up beneath it. There was no decoration of any kind. Nothing sat on the cabinet counters. The room reminded her of a show room set up in a furniture store.

Voices from the living room across the hall drew Kara's attention. Her name had been mentioned. Kara listened.

"She's the one I want," Bertha said. "She'd be a perfect addition to my family, with her dark hair and lovely eyes. She's the right age to be a lovely big sister for Ali."

"Great. I'm sure Louise would be delighted to give her to you."

Heidi asked, "What would you like? We have fudge. We have carmel corn."

Sensations of cold and heat, freezing and burning, covered Kara. Trapped by fear, as if she were dying, she stood unable at first to move. The voices in the living room went on, but Kara's heart pounded in her ears, deafening her. She was aware that Heidi had spoken and now paused, looking at her. Heidi's lips moved, words inaudible beyond Kara's terror.

"I have to go now," Kara finally managed. She wished she could leave through the window, through the floor, any way except past the living room. "I don't want anything."

She hurried out, managing to mumble some kind of goodbye as she passed the smiling women. Whatever they were saying now, she didn't understand. But she heard her name, and Vinny's. And other familiar names. Ali. Davey. Kara ran.

Monte was not in sight, and Kara sucked in a breath of relief. She grabbed her bicycle, but when she tried to balance, she fell.

Running, she pushed it across the street and up the

yard at home. She pushed it through the grass around the house and to its stand.

Praying she wouldn't see anyone, she hurried into the house and to the bedroom hallway. She started to pass Holly's door, then stopped. Holly sat on her vanity stool polishing her fingernails.

"Can I come in?" Kara pleaded.

Holly looked up. Her face whitened. She ran to Kara, pulled her into the room and closed the door.

"Kara, what happened?"

Kara told her, beginning to tremble. "She said—she said that Mama would—would be glad to give me away, Holly."

"Hey! *No way!*"

Kara felt her hand pressed tightly between Holly's. Together they went out onto the deck. Kara held back. The Renton house was visible, in part, through the trees.

"What if they're looking?" Kara whispered.

She saw that Holly was staring across the hollow.

"Maybe—maybe this Bertha person just meant it as a compliment. That you, added to her family, would make it . . ."

"Perfect," Kara said. She *knew.* Now. Somehow. Like the Rentons with their perfect family. They never fight or argue. Nobody over there ever yells at anyone else. Only Monte—at the dog. Not like here at home. But . . .

"And," Holly went on as if she chose not to hear Kara, "Maybe Joyce was just joking. Like, you know, sure, Louise will give her to you. Like that. They were probably laughing."

"I didn't hear anybody laughing."

"Kara, it was just a joke."

Kara drew a deep breath and felt some of the tension and fear go away.

"It wasn't a very funny joke."

"Well, maybe not to you." Holly shook her a little. "Hey, you don't think we'd ever let you go, do you? No

way! Who would I fight with? I can't fight with Bryon or Vinny, they're too little. They're no fun."

Kara couldn't buy Holly's attempt at joking. She couldn't lift her eyes to Holly's for fear she'd see sympathy and real worry and start crying again.

"Mama—Mama doesn't really like me, Holly. She never did."

"That's not true! She loves you!"

"Me and Bryon. It was me she hit, and Bryon."

Holly was still a moment. Then she whispered, "What about me, Kara? She tried to choke me, remember? But Kara, what do you do when somebody breaks a leg or an arm?"

Kara raised her eyes to Holly. "What's that got to do with Mom and us?"

Holly said softly, "Mama isn't well. Something's wrong. Can't you see that? If one of us had broken a leg, or an arm, she'd help us, wouldn't she?"

Kara nodded, puzzled. "Yeah—but—I don't understand."

"Well, it's like something is wrong somewhere in Mama, and we try to understand and help her get through it. We don't tell on her, to anyone. We love her and protect her, just like she'd do if it was one of us."

Kara looked out the sliding door. The woodland held deep shadows and dark movements, no longer a sanctuary of privacy, or a place to play and explore. The walls, the house around her, had changed, and all safeness was gone in her world.

She nodded. "Yes, we'll take care of Mama."

But she had a fear now that Mama would no longer take care of her.

26.

Holly had hoped, three years ago when she'd had to go to Grandma's funeral, that she would never have to go to another one. She remembered telling Mama then, crying and repeating, "I'm not going to another funeral. Ever!" At the time she had really thought it might be that way. Deaths and funerals weren't what life was made of. The people in her life were supposed to be there forever, never leave her. Life was a constant. But she'd been only ten years old. She'd had no real concept of the truth.

Now, she sat with her white-gloved hands tightly clutching the neatly embroidered handkerchief, wadding it and wadding it. Mama had insisted they dress in their best clothes, including the Easter bonnets, and that she and Kara carry handkerchiefs in their little handbags, not tissues. Just getting ready to go had been traumatic.

They sat on the front pew. The family of the dead woman was beyond a drapery, but it was only half pulled, and Holly could see the little boy, Davey. His face was pale and his eyes huge, as if he were scared to death. His mother lay in the casket not far away, surrounded by flowers. The odor of the flowers was too overpowering to be fragrant, as in a garden.

She longed to go to Davey and tell him . . . what could she tell him? What would make the death of his mother easier? Maybe she'd just tell him to call her if he needed someone to talk to. She'd always be there. Always?

She looked down the row of her own family and saw her mother's face.

Mama wore a faint smile on her face, her eyes gazing dreamily. She appeared to be blankly estatic. Her eyes were fixed on the raised lid of the coffin in an unblinking stare.

Cold moved in waves through the funeral home, on the smell of the flowers. Cold fear moved through Holly. The odor of the flowers became nauseating. The funeral home seemed too still, too dark, too enclosed, too cold. As if they all were already in their graves. Holly fought an instinctive need to leap and run . . . *run*.

Against her side, as if she were feeling the same way, Kara trembled. The two little boys, who sat between Holly and Louise, fidgeted, then sat still again. Beyond Dad sat Grandpa and Miss Beverly. In the pew behind were the other men who worked for Dad and Grandpa. The work on the ground at the mall had mostly been shut down for a couple of days, in deference to Tom Roush.

The minister began speaking in a soft voice, telling where Adrianne Marshall Roush was born, where she had gone to school, married, lived, and the names of the children she had left behind . . .

Holly's thoughts went back to Kara. Kara, yesterday, coming to her in tears, white and trembling, afraid Mama was going to give her away. To that—that person who was part of the church Mama went to now. Bertha?

Twice last night Holly had almost told Daddy. After the boys and Kara were in bed, while Mama was still gone to church, she had gone back to the den and tried to tell their father. Kara needed him to tell her he would never give her away.

But she couldn't. It was crazy that Kara would even

feel the way she did. Tomorrow, next week, she'd forget about it. When school started again, she'd be busier. Though they'd never get back with old friends now because they would be going to different schools.

So she hadn't told. She had gone to bed, lying tense and awake, waiting for Louise to come home. Why did she need to stay away so long at night? And every night? Not until the car drove in, the lights flashing through the trees for just a swift sweep of the bedroom deck, did Holly draw a sigh of relief and close her eyes.

Mama didn't come to check on her as she always used to do on the rare occasions when she was out. Back then, of course, she and Daddy always went together, and there would be a sitter in the house. A neighbor, or a relative. Someone other than Daddy.

The minister had stopped speaking, Holly noticed, and the usher was motioning for them to walk past the coffin, view the body, and leave by a door over in the far corner. Kara went first, following a lady beyond. Holly followed.

She didn't want to look at the face in the coffin, but her eyes were drawn. She stared. The skin had been heavily made-up, and looked perfect. Softly blushed at the cheekbones, softly roughed on the lips. The blank mask of the face looked familiar. Then, like a shock wave, it struck Holly.

Mama.

Holly moved on blindly, holding to Kara for leadership. *Mama.* That was the way Mama looked most of the time now. As if as her skin became more waxy and superficially perfect, her expression became more blank. More blank, and more dead.

I'm not doing this, Brent told himself as he took his car keys down off the hook on the letter holder. I'm not the kind of man who follows his wife when she goes somewhere by herself at night. I don't have the kind of wife who has to be followed. I'm not doing this.

"Holly," he called into the kitchen area where he'd last seen her. "I'm going out for awhile. Lock the doors. You and the kids will be okay."

She came to the door with a dishtowel in her hands. At thirteen she was having to take over her mother's responsibilities? She looked as serious as she had when they'd left the funeral this afternoon. All the children had been more quiet lately. Home was changing.

Holly looked at him. Behind her the boys and Kara sat at the kitchen table. Bryon and Vinny were coloring or pasting, or something very quiet. Kara only watched.

"I'll be home soon," he assured Holly.

"Okay, Dad."

He drove around the block and down into the hollow, his headlights on dim. The only signs of human civilization was the pavement that curled ahead of him and the occasional yard lights. All the homes were hidden among trees, built on the rise of the hill.

He'd almost had to force the location of the church from Louise. In the beginning she might have wanted him to go. He wasn't sure. Then she had stopped talking about it. She had stopped talking at all. When he came home from work she was always busy with dinner and then hurrying away to her church.

Church? Churches promoted family, it didn't draw family members away. Did it? Not if it were a real church.

A lover? The distant look in her eyes, so different from any he had ever seen, didn't it speak in silence of some ecstasy he had never shared? She was running out on him and the kids, and he was a mixture of anger and dread and anxiety. He understood now more how Tom must have felt when Adrianne left him.

But she had taken the kids.

Brent forced his mind away from those thoughts. He watched closely on the right for something that looked like a church. How could he find it in the dark? On the hill, she had said. Accessed from the ridge street? he had asked. No, she didn't think so.

One of those half-assed conversations that happen when one person is in the bathroom and the other in the bedroom. Question, answer session. Neither successful. She hadn't asked him if he wanted to go with her.

His mind slid back to the funeral, to Tom and the kids. They would be with him now, permanently. But Tom hadn't wanted it that way. That he would ever have it that way had never entered his mind. Life could end so abruptly.

A sports car slipped passed him so fast and silently it was almost like a ghost. He jerked his car to the right and sat with his heart thumping. Like that, he thought. He hadn't been watching his business, hadn't seen the car coming until it was there.

He noticed a trail up into the trees. He leaned to the right and looked out the window.

Pale lights, rainbow lights, in long tapered ovals, such as would come from the stained glass of a church, glowed dimly on the rise of the hill. He eased the car onto the trail and climbed. The dirt road switched to the right, and to the left, along the steep slope. Not far up the hill leveled off.

The church wasn't large. It looked to be only one room, perhaps eighty feet long and forty wide. The best he could tell by the windows misting the dark.

Cars were parked on both sides. He angled his car so the lights would shine off into the woods, then got out, leaving the engine idling softly.

The night seemed filled with katydids and crickets, and off in the trees the soft sob of owls. A rhythmic sound of voices came distantly from beyond the walls, the few widely spaced windows. He walked closer. Not singing, but . . . chanting? He heard no words, only the murmur and the rhythm.

There were two long windows in front. Narrow, small-paned colored glass through which only a pale light showed. On the left side of the building four windows, long and narrow, hid whatever was within. He didn't go around to the back of the church.

He walked toward his car, and paused. Louise's station wagon sat among a group of cars beneath the oak trees.

She was here, afterall.

He felt sick with self-disgust. He had doubted her. Had he seen something in her that . . . was in himself instead?

He didn't know what the hell was going on in his own mind. He just knew he had to get out of there.

But he was too restless to go home.

He drove back down the hill, checked the clock on the dash and turned toward town. Holly would have the kids in bed. She was dependable. One beer, one whiskey, that was all he'd have.

Somewhere.

Holly sat on the bedroom deck, her robe pulled around her shoulders. The moon sinking, shone over the roof of the house on the other half of the deck, but she huddled in the dark near the glass door and screen. Here, she could see the end of the driveway behind the house, and the street below.

Here she could watch for Daddy to come home, and for Mama. And she could watch the street below . . . for what?

Tonight she longed most desperately for Pepper. To sit beside her, his eyes and hearing and nose sharp and watching. Far superior to her own.

She saw the lights before she heard the murmur of the car engine. It turned into the driveway and came toward the garage. She stayed still, hidden in the dark.

It was Dad's car.

He had been gone hours.

His entry into the house was silent, too many walls

beyond her. She imagined him opening the door from the garage to the entry hall at the foot of the stairs. Now he would be climbing the stairs. Going down the hall now, maybe into the boys' wing to see if they were okay.

Holly waited, barely breathing, listening. He didn't come into her and Kara's hallway.

The night grew silent again. Bug sounds softened. It seemed hours longer before the station wagon made the quiet turn into the driveway and the garage door rose.

Now, at last, she could go to bed. She took one more look at the street below.

The dark cloaked figure wasn't there tonight.

Sometimes it seemed as if she were dreaming. That all her existence now was ethereal and dreamlike, with small bursts of nightmare intensity. She didn't remember leaving church. She didn't remember arriving home. Only the voices . . . chanting . . . softly . . . in her mind . . . over her shoulder.

Bring us your children. Bring us your earthly family. Let them not slip away. To make them immortal even as you are immortal, they must come to us. Kill the life that is within them. Kill . . . kill . . .

Louise lay on her back staring at the ceiling, seeing nothing.

Brent sat up and blinked at the clock on the table at his side of the bed. Almost four o'clock. Dark. Even the moonlight was gone. He got out of bed and felt his way to the bathroom. He turned on the light. It almost blinded him.

He went back into the bedroom, looking toward the bed.

Louise lay close to her edge of the bed staring upwards. Her eyes were open.

"What's wrong?" he asked, feeling sorry, sorry for everything. For suspecting her of—he wasn't sure what. Just suspecting her. He was sorry he had followed and checked up on her. He was sorry he had gone for one beer and stayed for . . . how many?

She didn't answer.

He went closer, sat down on the end of the bed. "What's wrong?" he asked again, "Can't you sleep?"

Still she didn't answer.

He looked at her, and then stared. She was lying unnaturally still, her arms straight down at her sides. Her head was straight, facing steadily toward the ceiling. Her eyes were half open.

He stood up, staring down at her. *Wrong—all wrong.* The image of Adrianne in her coffin came to his mind.

He started to speak again, then instead held his hand above her eyes. She didn't blink.

Sleeping with her eyes open?

He touched her arm. Icy cold, as if blood no longer flowed through her veins. He felt himself panicking.

Oh my God. Louise . . . dead . . .

Then he saw her chest rise and fall slowly. Softly a breath expelled.

He touched her wrist, searched for her pulse. He found none. Then, as he started to panic, a flutter, like a struggling butterfly, pulsed beneath his fingers. Of course her heart was beating. She was asleep. Only asleep.

He stumbled back to the bathroom and pulled the door almost shut on the light, leaving just enough to make a trail toward the bed. He followed the thin streak of light and fell into bed.

Cold too, inside and out, he lay without touching his wife.

27.

Everytime he turned, it seemed to Davey, they were there. The lady had brought a cake and pie, the day of the funeral, and she asked if she could do anything. Davey heard his dad say they were great neighbors, and the fear that had burrowed into Davey the first time he saw them ground deeper each time.

They came to the funeral. Afterwards they brought something in a dish. When Dad opened it at suppertime, Davey refused to eat. He chose plain bologna instead, slapped it on a slice of bread and choked a couple of bites down. Ali had cried and asked for Mama.

As if the lady heard, she came again and knocked on the door, lifted Ali into her arms and walked with her into the yard, talking in a low voice, whispering words that were beyond Davey's hearing. *Taking Ali away with her.* Davey ran after them, and the lady brought Ali back.

Later, when they were alone, Davey asked Ali what the lady had said. Ali looked at him with her big eyes, and answered, "She said not to cry." She looked thoughtful. "She said I have a mama. A real mama who will never die."

Davey didn't know what to say to Ali. Yes, they had a mama, but she was dead now. It sounded as if the woman meant another mama. Herself?

When Ali was busy playing in the corner, he told Dad, "The woman told Ali she has a mama, Daddy. She's trying to take Ali away."

"Davey, the lady's name is Mrs. Petersen. Bertha and Sydney. I want you to stop being so rude to the Petersens. They've been kind enough to look after you two, while I work, and they won't take any money for it. That means a lot, Davey."

"No! No. They're going to take Ali! *I* can look after Ali!"

Ali looked up, alarm on her face.

Tom grabbed Davey by the arm and shook him.

"Stop that! I don't know what's wrong with you. You should be thankful!"

"I can take care of Ali! Right here at home!"

"No, Davey." Tom drew a long breath, turned his arm loose and patted him on the shoulder. "Nine-year-old boys are too young to take care of a three-year-old."

Tears of fear and anger popped into Davey's eyes. He felt as if Dad were still shaking him, though he wasn't even touching Davey now.

"I'll run away! I'll take Ali and run away!"

Tom's eyes turned on him, stern and direct, with that look that could make Davey back off. He had gone too far. In his heart he knew he wouldn't take Ali and run away from Daddy, but he couldn't say so.

Tom pointed his index finger at Davey like a gun. "Don't you ever say anything like that again! Don't you even think it. You start treating the neighbors with respect. If you don't want to stay over there you can stay at home, but the minute you leave this yard, unless it's to go to the Petersen house—," he didn't voice his threat. He didn't have to. The look, the pointing finger was enough. "And I don't want to hear one more objection about church, understand?"

Davey nodded.

"Now go to bed."

Davey was glad to go to bed, to lie in the dark with

his fear and trembling. It was like Daddy was blind. Blind. That he couldn't see they wanted Ali—and maybe him, too.

Dad took off from work the next day, and stayed home with Davey and Ali, and the Petersens came over.

The lady brushed Ali's hair with her hand, running her long fingers through the curls as if trying to comb and arrange. Maybe Ali's hair wasn't as neat as it had been when Mama took care of it, but that didn't mean the strange lady could take Mama's place now.

"I suppose you'll be going back to work tomorrow," the man said.

Davey held his breath, listening.

"Yeah," Tom replied. "I have to."

"Well, Tom," the man said, "don't worry about the little ones. Your children are safe with us."

Tom cleared his throat, and surprised Davey by saying, "I think my boy is old enough now he can hang around the house and yard here."

The lady hurriedly said, "Oh, but Davey can stay with us, too."

Tom rubbed his chin. "If you'd just check on him now and then—he'll be fine.

She went on, smiling, talking in her velvet voice, "Ali, though, she's just a baby. She needs full-time care."

Tom nodded. "I appreciate it."

So Dad was going to let him stay at home—but not Ali.

"Come to church, Tom. You need us now."

Again Tom nodded.

"Come tonight, Tom. Every night. We can help you."

They put their arms across his shoulders and Davey could no longer see his face. It was as if they had taken away not only Ali but his daddy.

"All right, we'll come."

Davey broke and ran into the backyard. He pushed the swing as high as he could reach then hopped on, hanging with his belly over the seat. He kicked wildly, swinging, trying to work off that feeling. Dad was giving in. They had to go to that funny, scary church, and *they* would be taking care of Ali. And he ... he couldn't stop them.

When they were gone, Dad called to him.

"Come on, Davey, we'll go to MacDonalds for supper."

A treat then, Dad was offering him a treat. MacDonalds, his favorite place to go, where there was a playground, and the kind of food he enjoyed. A treat this evening, the day before his dad went back to work, a day after his mother's funeral.

He'd try again. Away from the house, away from those neighbors. Yet they seemed to *be* there, somehow, everytime he turned around, their eyes eating up Ali, and sometimes him too. And Ali going to them like a baby chick. Couldn't Dad *see?*

No, Dad seemed surrounded by his own dark cloak, like that man in the street the night Mom was killed.

Kara moved through the woods kicking leaves. Nothing had been any fun since they had moved. No, that wasn't quite right. It had been fun for awhile.

But now it was no fun. Heidi wasn't much fun. Much? She wasn't any fun at all. And the boy, Monte, Smonte, whatever, Kara couldn't stand him. Not since she'd seen him being mean to his dog.

She paused and looked across the hollow. They were sitting at the round table on the patio. Heidi, Monte, their parents. Together.

The way her family used to be.

She turned away and went back up the hill, until when she looked back the Rentons were no longer in sight. It was growing darker in the woods, the sun going down. It was time for someone to yell at her to come and help in the kitchen. Mama would probably be mad, the way she was lately.

Kara dragged her feet through the leaves, going back toward the house. Before Mom yelled.

To her left was Pepper's grave. She paused. Then she went closer, looking down at the grave.

Someone had filled it in. The hump of dirt no longer sat at the side of the hole, but had been smoothed into it. Once again it looked the way it had after Pepper was buried.

"Kara!" came the voice from the house. Holly calling.

Kara ran to the grave and fell to her knees. She began digging with her hands, digging, digging, frantic, her heart pounding, seeming to expand to fill her whole body. A mass of quivering vessels and roaring rivers of blood.

Her hands dug, dug, and touched cold, rough fur.

She uncovered him. Pepper, dead, really dead, his open eyes filled with dirt. His open mouth filled with dirt. She brushed it away, gently. She brushed him from his nose to his tail. From somewhere far away a voice called.

"Kara!"

The voice came closer, and she felt less alone in a dark and frightening world.

"Holly, come here," Kara cried.

The footsteps rattled leaves behind Kara. Then there was silence. Kara turned and looked up. Holly stared into the grave with horror in her eyes.

"They did it," Kara said softly, feeling that they were hearing her every word. "Those people. He was mean. Monte. He threw rocks at Pepper . . . it was Pepper. Holly, what did they do to him?"

Kara ran. Holly wasn't behind her, she saw, when she reached the edge of the woods. She was still staring at Pepper's cold, dead body.

Kara ran into the back entry and up the stairs to the kitchen. Louise stood by the kitchen sink looking in her new dreamy way out into the trees toward the driveway.

When Kara entered Louise said without turning her

head, "Your father will be home soon." *Father?* Kara didn't pursue it. It didn't matter.

"Mom!"

Louise didn't move.

"Mama!" Kara went to the counter and tried to see into her mother's face. A month ago she would have grabbed her arm to get her attention, but now she felt oddly repelled at the thought of touching her.

"Mama! Pepper's in his grave again! Mama! He's back. He's back in his grave!"

Louise turned slowly and looked at her. There was no expression on her face. None at all. Kara wondered if she had heard.

"Mama, Pepper's back!"

Holly entered the kitchen and stopped just inside the door. Kara saw her from the corner of her eyes.

"Mama," Kara tried again. "They have put Pepper back into his grave. *They* did it, Mama, I know they did. It was him over there. He wasn't dead afterall . . . maybe they drugged him or . . . something! They got him out of his grave, but Monte was mean to him, and killed him, and they buried him again!"

She stopped, backing away. The expressionless face of her mother changed rapidly, and became cruel and filled with fury. Exactly the way Monte had looked when he was being mean to the dog.

Kara backed into Holly, and stopped.

Louise picked up a butcher knife and put the point close to Kara's nose. Her voice was carefully controlled, soft, words spaced precisely.

"Don't you ever say that again. Now you girls go out and cover that grave. Don't say another word about it to anyone. Not me, not your father."

Holly's hand gripped Kara's arm and pulled her out of the kitchen. Together they went down the stairs and back into the woods. Holly knelt on one side of the grave and Kara on the other. They began brushing dirt over the still body.

"Holly, what did they do to him? Mama says . . ."

"I don't know, Kara."

"Do you think they did it?"

"Yes I do."

Neither spoke again until the dirt was spread smoothly over the grave. Then Holly sat on her heels, her face softening from its horror, tears sparkling in her eyes.

"I'm glad he's back," she murmured.

"Me too."

It was as if a prayer had been spoken over Pepper's grave.

"We'd better go help Mama," Holly said, and rose from the grave. Her voice was so soft it was almost a whisper. "Daddy will be home, maybe, soon."

Kara said, "You notice how she calls Daddy 'father' to us now instead of Daddy?"

Holly shook her head and didn't answer.

Kara followed her back to the kitchen. Mama stood at the counter dumping a variety of vegetables in on top of a caserole of cooked noodles. She slapped at the stuff with a wooden spoon as if she were still angry.

Kara said, "More of that? We've had caseroles for supper for three nights now." She wondered immediately why she'd said anything at all, with Mama in a mood.

Louise tossed the spoon into the sink. It bounced.

She said, "Holly, go find the boys. Take them to their rooms and clean them up for dinner."

An instant vision of herself alone with Louise chilled Kara. She started to ask, "Why can't I—" But Louise directed a cold, steady stare at her, and she choked the words off.

She heard Holly walk away. Her footsteps led into the hall and faded. Kara stood alone in the kitchen with Louise. She was not Mama, Kara thought suddenly. She only looked like Mama . . . a resemblance that was fading away. Kara was so scared she couldn't breathe normally.

She wanted to run. But she didn't dare act afraid. She opened the flatware drawer.

"Get steak knives," Louise said in a calm, soft voice.

Steak knives? When they weren't having steak? Knives with sharp, serrated edges?

Her hand hung over the drawer, trembling. . . . *No*, instinct warned. *Don't* . . .

The hand reached past her, picked up a knife from beneath Kara's own nerveless hand. The other hand pushed against her, shoving her toward the open sliding glass door onto the deck. The hand with the knife pushed the screen open.

Kara felt herself shoved with a series of hard pushes out of the kitchen and through the door. One of her sandals came off. The redwood boards of the deck felt cool to her bare foot. She gasped the shaded air, smelled the dampness of leaves from the woods. She threw a desperate look down the driveway for Daddy, for Grandpa, and saw nothing but long shadows and emptiness.

She almost fell, and as she righted herself she looked back for Holly. But she had gone after the boys. As Mama had told her to do. Holly would always do what Mama told her.

Another hard shove sent Kara against the railing. It struck her back like a blade. All her breath expelled sharply, and she gasped for air, weakened, shaking, terrified.

In front of her Mama stepped closer, the steak knife lifting higher, higher.

"*Ma . . . maaa,*" Kara heard her voice whimpering, whining, that voice Mama had always hated. "Mama . . ."

A terrible smile came to Mama's lips. She looked excited and happy. The smile softened, no longer angry. Her face held instead an almost gentle peace. Her voice sang softly.

"It's all right, Kara . . . it's all right . . . you'll thank me . . ."

The knife plunged. Kara felt the pain, heard it tear into her throat. *No Mama, please . . .*

Louise's point of self, of consciousness, was still in the kitchen. She watched her physical image on the deck with Kara. She tried to scream. *No, my God, no.* She wanted to stop that part of her that was physical, that other part that moved beyond her own wishes. She wanted to stop, but she no longer had a voice or a will of her own. The knife had entered Kara's body as if she were as tender as a baby. The physical self of Louise, that part she no longer knew, lifted Kara and threw her over the deck railing.

She watched Kara—helpless, terrified Kara. Falling through the air, so slowly it seemed . . . blood soaking her blouse. In the kitchen behind her Holly suddenly appeared. Her scream rent the air, hollow and useless, as if it came from Kara.

Kara, who hadn't once screamed.

In this helpless moment of realizing what she had done, Louise heard Kara's head strike the concrete below with a loud crack. The knife was embedded in her throat.

28.

Call for help . . . Dad . . . Grandpa . . . 911!

Holly felt as if she were only dreaming as she moved, as if to follow her own mental orders seemed an impossible task. Though she now stood in the middle of the deck she was able to see Kara on the cement below.

The vision showed a still body, severed repeatedly, as if she'd been cut by the cracks in the deck into narrow strips. No longer Kara, Holly saw her body there, blood pouring from her throat, nose, mouth.

Yet Kara tried to rise, her eyes coming to Holly on the deck, her lips moving as if she were trying to tell her something.

Mama almost fell as she stumbled down the steps. Holly wasn't sure if the screams were Mama's or her own, or maybe even Kara's. Mama fell across Kara, her body hiding from Holly Kara's face. At first it seemed horribly as if Mama were pushing Kara down again, and holding her. Didn't she know her body would push the knife even deeper into Kara's throat?

Help . . . they had to have help . . .

Holly felt as if she were running, taking great, bounding, floating steps, yet the telephone seemed farther and farther away. The world had grown silent. It seemed there was no sound at all within it. Then below the deck a thin, childish scream rose. Kara! Thank God! Kara was able to scream.

But . . . it was all wrong . . .

"Kara!" the thin voice wailed, like a winter storm rising faraway. *"Kara! Mama, Kara's hurt!"*

Bryon screaming, not Kara. Vinny's screams joined Bryon's.

The telephone was within Holly's reach at last. She grabbed it. It fell, bounced away. She chased after it, grabbing. With deep sobs in her throat she sat on the floor and pushed 911.

"My sister . . . hurry . . ." she cried. A voice on the phone was trying to get more information. Holly shouted at it, "Just come on, will you?" They had the number and the address. She had to go to Kara.

She found herself on the deck again, looking down. Mama was no longer there. The boys had fallen near where Kara lay. They were on their knees, screaming, crying. Kara had turned, or been turned, half onto her stomach, and her eyes stared toward the boys. The knife now penetrated her neck so deeply only the handle showed.

Holly ran through the kitchen into the hall looking for her mother. Mama must come back. She had to help Kara. She ran through the house, breathless, silent. *Where was she?*

The front door stood open. Holly stopped, staring. Mama had come around the house and entered the front?

Holly hurried on toward the master bedroom. The door was closed, but Holly threw it open. The bathroom door stood partly open. The shower was running. Scattered on the bathroom carpet was the clothing Mama had worn, crumpled, bloody.

The sight of the clothing so hurriedly discarded and the sound of the water spraying from the shower head brought Holly to the apex of horror.

That sound of her mother showering, the clothes on the floor, brought to Holly's mind a picture of dark horror. Mama, running down to Kara, and throwing herself across Kara. As if she were deliberately pushing Kara down, pushing the knife deeper into her throat. Not to help but to finish killing.

She tried to push away the thought, but it persisted. *Mama killed Kara.*

No, no, no. She couldn't be sure. How could she think this of their mother?

Holly pushed the bathroom door shut and whirled away. Why had she followed her mother? She didn't know.

Mama was so different lately . . . but that didn't mean she would kill one of her children.

The boys' screams came like the cries of owls at night. Holly ran back through the halls and down to the cement beneath the deck. Streaks of light shining between the widely spaced deck boards made stripes on Kara's body. Blood spread darkly from beneath her, easing out, making new borders.

Vinny and Bryon clung to each other crying, screaming. Helpless. As helpless as Kara.

Holly's heart burst for Kara. Kara the sister she had fought with, talked with, and was beginning to align with against the whole world. Holly had to touch her. To hold her. Somewhere in the back of her mind was the warning never to touch an injured person, but Holly sank beside her, Kara's blood making the concrete slippery and sticky. It coated Holly's bare legs and clung to her knees.

She lifted Kara off the ground and cradled her. The point of the knife erupted from the back of her neck like the tip of a needle.

Sirens grew closer.

"Kara," Holly wept over her, seeing her eyes wide and staring, and so utterly blank, as if a vital curtain had been drawn over them. Kara was gone. Holly felt like lifting her face to the sky and uttering a primitive howl.

Several automobiles slid to stops in the driveway and pulled into the woods where there was room. Holly, glancing past the people who came to lift Kara from her, saw the familiar color of her dad's pickup.

She heard Louise screaming, and saw her coming down the deck stairs again. Someone held her back from going to Kara. With her hands over her face she appeared to weep, but Holly glimpsed her eyes and saw they were dry. She wondered if anyone else noticed. Suddenly she knew she must protect her mother, above all. Holly's own mind had gone mad. Louise would never hurt, really hurt, Kara.

Dad came running, breathing in hoarse gasps.

"My God, what happened? *What happened?*"

They kept him from going to Kara. He turned, as if he had suddenly been blinded, then he gathered the little boys into his arms. He reached toward Holly and pulled her into the nest of his arms with the boys.

A police car sat at the edge of the driveway, lights rotating. Two more officers joined the scene, looking up at the deck, around at the ground, talking, making notes. The slow-motion nightmare continued.

The paramedics worked only briefly with Kara. Then their actions slowed. They backed off and let her lie in the dark lake of blood. It had stopped running and was now congealing, the edges turning black.

Brent put the children away from him and rushed to Kara.

"You can't quit! You've got to do something! Can't you get her heart started for Christ's sake? Do something! Aren't you even going to take her to the hospital?"

A paramedic said, "I'm sorry, sir. Your daughter was gone before we got here."

"How is that possible? Can't you take her to surgery? *Can't you try?*"

For the first time in her life, Holly saw her daddy crying.

More police cars were driving in. Men dressed in plain clothes got out. One man wore jeans and a demin shirt, as if he'd been on his way to the river to fish, or to a bar for a drink. They showed badges to Brent, and introduced themselves as detectives.

"What happened here?"

Holly saw her dad's suddenly stooping shoulders. He shook his head, no longer yelling at them to do something. Somebody spread a sheet over Kara's body. The knife that hadn't been removed from her neck made a peak beneath the sheet.

"Can't you—get that—Goddamned thing—out of her?" Brent bellowed, sobs jerking his words. "Can't you at least get her—off the ground?"

A woman in a white uniform took his arms and turned his back to the body. Holly could hear her voice, low and persuasive. He let her lead him over to the patio.

The little boys, Holly noticed, were pressing against her. They had stopped crying and seemed wide-eyed and stunned, just the way she felt. One of the men began taking pictures of Kara. Someone dressed in a dark suit, who had been kneeling by Kara a long time now eased the knife out. Holly let out a sigh of relief, as if it had been in her throat too.

Then, at last they were lifting Kara and taking her away in the ambulance. Somewhere in Holly's heart was a prayer. A hope that Kara wasn't dead afterall. That she'd come alive at the hospital.

Lights were on. Holly hadn't noticed when night came.

"We have to know what happened," One of the officers said to Holly. "Were you here when it happened?"

Louise's quivering voice came from behind Holly, answering for her.

"Kara was a very lively girl," she said. "And careless. She'd been dancing around with the knife. I told her to be careful. She must have fallen over the deck railing. I was in the kitchen at the time."

The officer looked at Holly. "Were you a witness?"

They waited. She tried to speak, to tell them Mama had sent her to get the boys, but she had returned to the kitchen to tell Mama they weren't in their room, and Kara had already fallen. Or . . .

But she could never say that terrible thing that was in her mind. Never. She felt nauseated with the thought that wouldn't go away.

She managed at last to shake her head no.

"She had gone to get the little boys," Louise said, her voice soft but steadier.

"Anyone else see the child fall?"

"Not that I know of. The boys were out playing somewhere. They might have seen her fall."

Holly caught a glimpse of others moving into the group. The Rentons. Joyce, Albert. The two Renton children stood over beyond the flower beds beneath the bedroom deck.

Joyce put her arms around Mama, and Mama buried her face against Joyce's shoulder.

There were murmurs Holly didn't understand, and then faintly audible words that added to her sense of total horror.

"Why didn't you call us instead of the police, Louise?" Joyce said softly, meant only for Mama to hear. "Why didn't you call us?"

Louise answered, "I was going to . . ."

Albert said, his voice a low buzz, barely audible to Holly. "Come first to us, the next time . . ."

The next time . . . the next time . . . the next time . . .

* * *

In her nightmares that night Holly heard the words repeated, repeated, time and time again.

The next time . . .

The next time . . .

She woke, hearing again the running shower, and saw the bloody clothes on the floor. She saw her mother running again down the steps outside, in clean clothing. Why? It was as if she wanted to separate herself completely from Kara's death. Was that why she had changed? Because she couldn't bear the truth? Or because she wanted to hide the blood from falling across Kara? Splatters, or drops, she might have received if she had actually stabbed Kara before Kara fell.

Holly lay coiled in a knot, frozen in terror.

Kara had been taken away, alone. So alone. And the family left here without her. Grandpa had come and sat with them for a long time, silent, leaning forward, his hands clasped between his knees. When finally the boys fell asleep, long after midnight, Grandpa left. Holly couldn't recall if he had said one word.

She slept again, and heard the music in her dreams. Distant. The background thud, thud, and voices in a strange, discordant harmony. She came suddenly awake, her heart pounding. The music faded away. Gospel music? No. But maybe. A song in minor key, so . . . not sad, but frightening. Different. Music she'd never heard before.

Now the music was gone, and only the background beat was left. It came nearer slowly, along the hollow road, like a car moving silently, only the background beat of its music loud enough to hear.

Then as it drew nearer it became the drum. *Drum, drummmm,* the sound carrying clearly, deeply.

She threw the covers aside and was running, halfway across the room before she stopped. She'd been going to see if Kara was okay. Now Kara's room was empty.

She sank onto the floor and sat weeping into her hands.

The silence in the night brought her awareness back and she lifted her head and listened. The drumming had stopped. It had come closer, louder, then stopped.

She knew what she would see.

She stood pressed against the screen of the open sliding door and looked down to the street below.

The dark cloaked figure of death stood with his shadowed face staring up toward her.

She stepped back into her room, so that he couldn't see her. As she moved he disappeared. The deep shadows beneath the trees on the street behind him swallowed him as if he'd never been there at all.

How could they get up, eat, make beds, vacuum floors, do laundry just as they always had? How could Mama give orders the way she always had?

"Holly, see that the boys are dressed for the day."

Dad was home, of course. That was different too.

He said softly, "I'll take care of that."

"So when is the funeral?" Louise asked.

"I don't know. There has to be an autopsy."

"Why?" Louise demanded, voice rising. "I don't see the necessity!"

"Because it was an accidental death."

Murder. Mama killed her. The words came to Holly's mind as if spoken softly by someone at the back of her head. She went on cleaning up the table, moving as if each step, each reach had to be planned ahead of time. Another part of her mind responded. *No, you don't know that.*

Louise cried, "I do not want my daughter left lying like that! I want her in her grave! As soon as possible!"

Holly heard, and cringed further within herself. No one else seemed to notice how odd her words were.

The telephone rang and rang, friends calling to express sympathy. Mama took the calls. Holly sensed her displeasure. She wanted the funeral over immediately. *Why?*

"I'll be going to services tonight," Mama said to Daddy. He didn't say a word.

But it was as if she had answered a question not yet formed in Holly's mind. If Mama wanted the funeral to be over quickly, it couldn't be because she felt it might keep her from services. There was another reason, but Holly didn't know what it was. How could Mama want Kara buried quickly? Holly wanted to hold to her, however she could.

She was alone in the kitchen when a police car drove in. At the moment of their arrival Holly heard Pepper bark. Her swift response, her heart lifting eagerly, plummeted as soon as she realized she must have been mistaken. She walked onto the deck, and saw in the car down in the driveway a police dog, his head stuck out the window.

One of the officers looked up at her. Both of them stopped.

"Holly?"

She nodded.

"Can we talk to you?"

She unlatched the gate at the top of the steps and went down.

One of them said, "Nice deck." He looked at the exposed edge of the bedroom deck around the corner. "Nice house. How long have you lived here?"

"Just since last spring. May, I think. Mom—Dad would know."

The other officer went over to the place where Kara had died. A tarpaulin had been thrown over the spot and, Holly knew, the blood that was still there. She couldn't bear the thought of washing it up.

"You don't mind if I ask a few questions, do you, Holly?"

She shook her head, not sure if she should say yes or

no. Her mother and dad would probably disagree. Her mother would say no.

"Where were you when Kara fell?"

Her lips moved in silence. The sound lay buried within her for a long moment. Then she said, "I must have been in the hall."

"Did you hear anything? Any conversation, any cries?"

She knew then they suspected her mother.

"Why?" she asked, looking from one to the other. They both smiled a little as if trying to reassure her.

"We just always need to ask questions like this when there's an accident such as your sister's."

"Oh," she said. Then tried to cast her memory back. Had Kara cried out? No . . . but Mama had said something . . . something—she hadn't caught. But she had heard Mama's voice.

"I think," she said slowly, "I think I heard Mama tell Kara to be careful."

They looked at her and she returned the looks in silence. They suspected Mama, but they must not take Mama away. They were wrong. She was wrong. Mama could never do that.

She added, "Kara was careless. Mama often told her to be careful."

Kara was careless. Mama's words.

29.

Nothing in the world is sadder than a child's funeral, Beverly thought as she sat with bowed head. The eulogy had been spoken, a brief prayer, a lovely poem Holly had written for her sister. Mourners were gathering at the casket.

It had been kept small. Only a few close friends and family. She was honored to be included. Her son Mel had declined when she had asked him.

"They would have asked me, Mother," he said. Mother, she thought now as she heard the weeping in the small room. He called her mother only when he was very serious, and lately, he'd been calling her mother.

She had a feeling he wanted to talk to her about something, but when she asked, he said, "Later. I'll be over later."

"For supper?"

"No, no. I'll just drop in. Maybe coffee."

She rode with Carl following the slow-moving hearse as it wound through streets toward the cemetery. Police led and cars parked in homage along the sides. Some of the passengers bowed their heads in prayer. Beverly found herself feeling sentimentally grateful that they would take this moment from their busy lives to say goodbye to someone they didn't know. Perhaps they knew it was a child's furneral. Perhaps not.

The cemetery was a lovely, cool, green expanse on the top of a hill. Large trees stood just open enough to make it look like a park. Old tombstones further to the north indicated its age. They stood tall and green, mossed with age. The narrow streets that wound into that area were made of cobblestone and had never been changed.

The hearse took a newer street and drove to the northwestern corner. An area was marked off with scalloped cement. Within it stood scattered tombstones. One of them bore the name of Carl and Annie Salisaw.

His plot was ready beside his wife, just as her own plot was ready beside her mate. Still, she felt a tinge of something . . . jealousy? It wasn't permittable. But she knew now, here, for the first time, during all this sadness, that she was in love with Carl Salisaw and wanted to spend the rest of her life with him.

She stood back. When he took her hand and tried to pull her into the family that surrounded the small silver coffin, she shook her head and smiled tenderly. *Not yet.* It wouldn't be appropriate yet. The family had only just met her. A few days ago. Much of the more distant family didn't know anything about her but her name, and probably had forgotten that.

But she stood behind him. And finally, while he stood with bowed head and trembling shoulders as once again the Methodist minister spoke over the casket that soon would be lowered forever into the ground, he put his hands behind him, fingers entwined. She slipped her fingers into his, and he held onto them desperately.

When it was over and he turned, it seemed right that he would lean on her, his arms around her shoulders. She held him tight, this man she loved as she had never dreamed she could love again. She held him, and wanted to be part of him for the remainder of their lives.

But she drew away.

Now was not the time.

She rode back to Brent's house sitting beside Carl. Then she got busy with the mountains of food brought by neighbors and friends and she, with other women, fed the children and men, washed and put away dishes.

Until finally she was the last in the kitchen, doing up last minute things. She looked around once more.

Carl came in for another uncountable cup of coffee, and saw that she was preparing to leave.

"Won't you stay?" he asked, plaintiveness in his voice. She finished wiping up the last crumb, and put another closed item into the refrigerator. But it was getting dark, and she had to go.

She paused, wiped her wet hand on the towel at her waist and touched his cheek. She longed suddenly and urgently to draw him into her arms and hold him. The little boy in his eyes pleaded for comfort.

But how could she comfort a man whose granddaughter had been buried just two hours ago? There were children in the room. She didn't give in to her urge to kiss him.

He said before she could form an answer that would suit both of them, "Of course, you have your cats."

"My cats always have feed and water available automatically when I'm not home. So it's not that. It's that the family should have this evening alone."

"You're part of family," he said. "To me, you're part. You belong here."

She shook her head. "Not yet," she whispered. "I have to give you time with the children. You alone. Goodnight, Sweetheart."

She saw a flicker of something in his eyes. He started to kiss her, but Vinny came into the kitchen and climbed up on a stool at the counter.

"Can I have something, Grandpa?"

Beverly said, "Sure, Grandpa will get you milk and cookies."

She took advantage of Vinny's entrance to leave. She exchanged a warm look with Carl. She saw the incredible sadness in his eyes and wished she could magic-wand it away. But Vinny, with his demands, would do more good than a wand.

She drove home in a blue daze.

Thinking over the funeral she kept coming to one person. Louise. The child's mother.

Not once had she seen tears in Louise's eyes. Usually she sat with her eyes closed, her chin lifted, and a strange look of peace on her face. Peace, or nothing? A blankness? As if she were struggling to stay calm, or as if she felt nothing?

Of the strange new people Carl and she had traced through town, the only visitors to the funeral were the Renton's. They had sat directly behind Louise. And often, Beverly had noticed, it was Joyce Renton who seemed always there to touch Louise, hold her hand, or lean forward in the pew and lay her hand on Louise's shoulder.

If a word was spoken between them Beverly had not been close enough to hear it. But when the services were over she had seen Carl staring, his eyes narrowed. She had looked, and saw Joyce murmuring to Louise.

Had they become friends?

The Rentons were beautiful. Each one complementing the next as if they were creations of art. The handsome man, the beautiful woman, beautiful children, Monte, Heidi. Heidi carried a small collection of wild flowers tied with a rainbow of ribbons which she laid on the casket.

When the child stepped back Beverly saw on her face that look of . . . *nothing*.

Long chills ran over her body, and she rolled the car windows up although the night air was sweet and cool.

* * *

Louise had gone out, Carl didn't know where. A short trip to the grocery store, perhaps? She hadn't told anyone goodbye that Carl had noticed.

He too should leave, he thought. Feed Bud. Feed the squirrels and birds. But he kept putting it off.

Bryon and Vinny sat on the floor in the corner by the toy box, and Vinny alternately cried and talked, dragging toys out, putting them back in. Bryon sat watching in silence. It was as if Vinny were desperately trying to find in the toy box the world that had been his.

Holly stood looking out the window into a dark night.

Brent sat with his head bowed, leaning on his legs, one leg bent with ankle resting over his knee. A prop. A frame for the man that had been. He hadn't shaved, Carl noticed, in surprise. Was he letting a beard grow again? Something to hide behind? His skin had taken on the color of an untouched palette.

"I'd better go," Carl said. "Anytime you need me . . ."

Brent lifted his head a little and wriggled the toe of the foot that rested on his ankle. He cleared his throat, as if to make an attempt at conversation, but said nothing.

Vinny began crying again. Bryon had taken a toy from the box and Vinny wanted it. Bryon handed it over, but Vinny kept crying, his head bowed like his father's. It wasn't the toy, Carl thought. None of it was the play, the objects. Vinny needed the comfort of his mother. The comfort of Kara. Of having their family intact as it was.

Bryon got up and came to Carl. Carl lifted him and buried his face for a brief moment in the tender fragrance of the little boy's neck. Bryon relaxed against him, curving to Carl's chest, melting there.

Vinny came and stood looking at them, his mouth open, tears running down his cheeks, his eyes veiled with tears. Carl held out his hand toward Vinny.

Holly turned back from the window. "Daddy, shouldn't I put the boys to bed?"

"Yeah, I suppose. Maybe they'd sleep."

Carl kissed them both goodnight, and watched them leave the room. Three now, instead of four. How had this terrible thing happened to the family?

Carl rose too. "You go to bed too, Brent. Better get some rest."

Always, to Brent, at the end of day, at closing time, at the moment of their departure, he said the same thing to his hard-working son. "Better get some rest."

Brent nodded and told him good night, but made no effort yet to move.

Carl had started down the back stairs when Holly came from somewhere. He made a motion to kiss her goodnight. Tears burned the back of his eyes, a sudden reaction that had been coming on him unexpectedly since he had learned of Kara's death.

Holly said, "I'll walk down with you, Grandpa."

They went down the stairs in silence, her fingers thin and cool and smooth, coiled tightly around his rough stubs. She held on to him as if never to let him go.

The kitchen and deck light above laid prison stripes beneath the deck, yet still he saw the dark place where Kara's blood had drained from her, and he thought he could see the nick in the concrete made by the handle of the knife as it pressed more deeply into Kara's body.

The day after her body had been taken away, he had come back and worked on cleaning up the blood. But even after he had painted over it, over the darkness that seemed to have seeped permanently into the concrete, he could still see it. Even in the striped light and dark of the night.

He thought of something suddenly that made chills clutch his spine. In order to back her car out, Louise would have to drive over the place where Kara's life was drained away.

If it was him, he'd get to work tearing that deck down. He'd permanently close the sliding doors.

"Grandpa," Holly said.

She was looking off toward the lights at the end of the driveway. The striped light that came through the deck cut her face.

He pulled her out of that light and closer to the back door. He didn't want to leave her outside where she would have no protection.

She said no more. She kept staring away, turning her gaze from the driveway lights to the woods where the dog's grave had been, to the hollow. Finally to the Rentons' house, somewhere in the darkness across the hollow.

No lights there. For reasons he, Beverly, and her son hadn't been able to find out. Had something to do with their religion, Mel had said. They didn't use utilities. Carl hoped it was that simple.

"Did you want to talk awhile, Holly?"

She looked at her feet. "No, I guess not."

"I'd rather you didn't stay out here, Holly. By yourself. After I leave."

She nodded and stepped into the hall.

"Goodnight, Grandpa."

He hesitated. He didn't want to leave her. He didn't want to leave any of the children.

But they had their mother and dad to look out for them.

"Take care, Holly," he said. "Call if you need me."

He left her there, swallowed by shadows, her hair haloed by the light at the top of the stairs.

"Better turn the stairway light on, Holly."

The light came on.

Carl hurried, through the spotted light and dark, to his pickup.

He had a strong feeling that Holly had tried to tell him something. Since the day of Kara's death, he had felt that.

*   *   *

Aeternita services had ended. As always it had whispered away, leaving the euphoria, the feeling that all had gone well. Visitors had drifted quietly away, and only the members were left. Louise felt surrounded by them, guarded by them, smiled upon, a part of the mystery of all that they were.

A tiny flame seemed to burn in the back of her mind, something not yet extinguished, that flamed up at times and gave her bad feelings. Bad feelings, not the delicious ones, the feelings of being part of this that was perfect.

Someone draped a black cloak over her head and shoulders. Pale faces smiled at her.

"It's time to go," someone whispered. "Come, Louise, it's time to bring Kara back."

The euphoria returned, edging the flame of doubt away.

She was taken as if she were a priestess of high standing, to be guarded and treasured. Voices murmured in her ears.

"It's time. The time has come to get Kara."

They had been angry at her, she remembered vaguely. They had frightened her with their cold fury. It was as if they had reburied her again, as they had the dog, Pepper, leaving her cold and forlorn, forever. Lost to all. They had been angry at her because they hadn't been called.

"Never, never do that again. When it happens again, bring your child to *us*."

It was a lesson she would never forget.

She sat in the back seat of the long sedan between Joyce and Bertha. Their cold hands covered hers. Their dark cloaks fused with the night and their oval faces were pale and visible like dying moons.

The black sedan moved silently through the night,

keeping to the quiet and empty streets. Ahead of it went another, and behind yet another.

That single question left burning in her mind was surprised at their destination. Once again, the cemetery.

The sedans pulled silently into the narrow road that dissected the old cemetery where Kara had been buried this past day.

She was guided out.

A pale, greenish light hovered over the grave. A stone had not yet been erected, but the dirt was soft and loose, and rounded. The light, not of the moon, but, it seemed, of those oval faces that peered out from the black cloaks, fell briefly on other tombstones as they silently surrounded the new grave.

Louise stood waiting. Fear, that question in the recesses of her mind turning cold, as if dying, asked what they were doing with her child's grave. Yet she felt the rightness. Of course. Wasn't this the reason for the death? Those human remnants, gone.

Hands dug into the soil. They bent, and the greenish light fell upon the pale blue rounded lid of the coffin. It opened as silently as they had moved and worked. The light touched upon Kara's face.

The other faces, the oval faces that emitted the strange light, Louise saw now were not human. Smooth, featureless, glossy, colorless as if they'd lain centuries buried in the earth. It was their phosphorescence that lighted the grave. As if they had emerged like blind worms, to coil and absorb, to glow. Beings more primitive than insects, something that was capable of metamorphoses, of change to their choosing.

A spark of natural life deep within Louise cried out in terror. Then was gone. The broken wing of a pale butterfly drifting to dust.

The body was lifted. Kara lay as if she had been made of an unyielding quality, straight and stiff on the hands that transferred her to the leading sedan.

In silence they returned to their places. The motors
moaned and whispered, and the sedans moved again,
slipping silently from the cemetery, across deserted
streets. Far away a police siren played with sound.

They drove away from sound through the deep quiet
of the night back to the church on the hill.

Lights reflected briefly in the stained glass of the
windows. The door opened, and the body was carried
in and placed on the altar.

Pale light came from the lamps along the wall.

The faces around Louise were beautiful again.
Human. Young. Smooth. All so different, yet so much
alike.

She was stationed at the head of the altar.

"She was your child," Joyce said, smiling. All around,
hoods pushed back, hair glowing in the flickering,
matchlike flames of the lamps, they smiled at Louise.
She understood she was the one being honored.

"You have been generous. You have brought us a
child. You understand her name will be different. She
will be the daughter of Bertha and Sydney."

Louise said nothing. She longed to reach out and
touch the hair of the child she had given birth to, the
child she had . . . *killed?*

"No, no," they cried, smiles gone, faces smooth and
glowing, the features receding. "*Don't touch her.* She
must never feel your touch."

Louise blinked, the light brightened, and she saw
them again, smiling, beautiful, waiting.

She lowered her head and nodded.

They bowed over Kara, touched her with moth
touches, murmured chants Louise hadn't learned. She,
in her apprenticeship hadn't been given the right. She
had more duties to perform. Albert had told her that.
More duties. More sacrifices to reach her exalted place
among them. More children were needed to complete
the growing families.

With her hand on the table at Kara's head, she sensed

the change. There was movement. Louise held her breath, gazing down upon the child who had been her daughter.

Kara rose slowly, as if she had been asleep a long time. They backed away from her, motioning her up, up.

She turned and swung her legs off the side of the altar. Then like an infant being born, just as she had that night in the delivery room eleven years ago, she looked around. Her eyes took in the lamps on the walls, the rows of pews, the windows, the cathedral ceiling and the exposed beams.

Her eyes touched upon each face and swung at last to Louise. That last part of Louise that struggled to live, longed toward her. A memory of tears lingered deep within and yearned to be released, even as she felt the permanent smile on her face. *I am your mother*, she wanted to say to Kara, *don't you remember me?*

Kara's eyes passed by her and came back to one in the crowd.

Bertha stepped forward. She had put aside her robe, and her pale dress shimmered in the erratic light.

"I am your mother," she said. "And your name is Portia. Come meet your father."

Kara slid off the altar obediently, and put her hand into Bertha's. From the crowd Bertha's husband joined them.

They went down the aisle toward the door, parents with child between.

At the doorway Kara stopped. With her hands held firmly in her new parents' she could turn only her head.

She looked back, straight into Louise's eyes.

Louise saw the remnants of life and pain. A silent cry for rescue. *Mama . . . save me.*

The buried emotions in Louise spoke in answer to the silent cry of her child. All that she had been, all the love she had given, was closed smaller and smaller into that dwindling spark of real life. She longed to run,

gather Kara into her arms and save her somehow from
this endless fate.

But she couldn't move.

The look in Kara's eyes was gone, as quickly as it
came. That smooth blankness that was theirs slid like a
reptile's inner lid over her eyes, and she was gone.

30.

Louise drove home slowly, her hands gripping the wheel. Kara wasn't dead. She hadn't killed her.

She pulled to the side of the dark street and covered her head with her hands.

She had murdered her own child. Killed her and given her to—to—what were they?

She put her head back and opened her mouth wide, trying to scream an anquish that bubbled to the surface like poison. She wanted to run and take Kara from those—whoever—*whatever* had her, and together she and Kara would die, somehow, a natural death that would, please merciful God, put them into the hands of God. Not this—not this—whatever it was.

No sound came from her throat. In the front of her mind, like residue of drugs, the euphoria rose again. *You have done the right thing. Kara will live forever.*

Who had told her that? What voice had made itself a replication of a human voice?

Bring us your children, Louise. Remove them from this life so they may enter Aeternita.

No, no, no.

Yet she had given them Kara.

Portia.

She uncovered her eyes and looked at the deep darkness in the hollow. Trees, touched by the glow of her headlights, were no longer trees. They hung in the air, thick growths of vines, weaving, like webs blown by a hurricane wind. They swept toward her. The ground tilted, the car rolled. There was no car. She felt the wind, that unknown subterranean force that was sucking her in.

She found a strong vine and clung to it, her eyes closed. The winds blew, pulling, leafy, rotted, slimy beings brushing the length of her body.

She clung, desperate, terrified of this strange unreality.

Then suddenly it was gone and her hands were clamped tightly around the steering wheel. The car engine was still idling.

She was afraid to open her eyes. This was her punishment. For killing her child. For abandoning her to forces beyond hell.

At last she looked. The trees stood tall and dark, stable. The car lights showed her the road home.

She drove, and found her way at last into the driveway. The button of the remote control opened the left garage door as it always had. She drove in, over the newly painted area of the concrete where Carl had tried to cover the evidence of what she had done, the spill of her daughter's blood.

She wanted to die. Find a permanent rest.

She turned on the lights in the garage and began looking at insecticides and pesticides rarely used.

Rat poison? It had been purchased years ago, when Kara was only nine. They'd had mice in the garage. But Kara and Holly had both cried. "Mama, do you know the agony those poor little things suffer before they die? Mama!"

So they had gone back to the store and purchased the kind of trap that only holds the mouse until it can be released somewhere in the woods. "Let them be free," Kara had said as she happily released one small frightened mouse into the woods outside of town. "Only," she said as she watched it scurry into hiding. "I hope nothing finds him until he's dead of old age."

Louise took the box of rat poison down from the shelf. She pulled the lid open. It was a granule blend, deadly, rough little bits of grey and white, like large-grained sand. She stared into the box.

Oblivion, please God. Not Aeternita. Release. A chance for redemption somewhere beyond. A chance of—her humanity returned, even for only a moment in death.

She went to the faucet in the basement wall and knelt. Her hand, digging into the box, felt the fine pebbles. She dug out a handful, forced it into her mouth. A handful of poison, a handful of water. *Force it down, swallow,* she told herself. Soon it will be over.

Fire, burning filled her mouth and throat. Though they felt paralyzed, on fire, she forced down more, more, until she could no longer swallow.

A rod of pain shot through her body, jerking her forward, then forcing her backwards. Her spine arched, whipping back and forth as the unreal wind had whipped the monstrous vines in the hollow. Blood pulled from her tissues, poured from her mouth, her nose, her ears. She screamed in agony, but it was only a squeak, as the rat would have cried.

Oh God, oh God, let me die.

Then she remembered—*must die violent death to enter Aeternita.* They had tricked her, programmed her to destroy herself, and her children. They needed her children.

Holly woke. Her cheek felt as if it had been glued to the glass of the door. She eased free and sat up, rubbing her skin.

She had sat down on the carpet, the sliding glass bedroom door shut, to watch for Mama.

Why hadn't she come home?

Or had she?

Holly got up and peered at the lighted face of her clock. Almost four.

Mama must have come home and gone to bed long ago. It had been just past midnight when Holly decided to sit by the door where she could watch.

She was so frightened since Kara died. Afraid to open her door and go out onto the deck. Afraid to go past Kara's closed door. Terrified of the dark. Frightened even of the light.

Afraid of Mama, yet afraid for her.

She had almost told Grandpa when he was here, several times. But it kept going through her mind . . . Grandpa would tell Daddy, and what could they do? The police would have to be told. Or Mama would have to be sent away to an asylum to live the rest of her life.

Holly had spent hours crying in the privacy of her room, wondering what to do. She loved Mama. More than anyone in the world, she supposed, if she had to choose one over the other. Mama always came first. Daddy too came first. As if they were one, Mom and Dad. She loved the kids, and Grandpa. She loved them all, but Mama and Daddy came first.

She opened her door, unlocking it quietly. The hall was dimly lighted with a tiny plug-in that stayed on during darkness. She looked first one way then the other.

Kara's door was still closed.

The hall was so silent.

Never again could she go to Kara and talk about something that bothered her.

She turned away from Kara's door, afraid to turn her back to it. Afraid . . . afraid . . .

She went softly and soundlessly to the front foyer.

The glass panels on each side of the door looked out onto a lighted front stoop. The door was double locked, though. Why was the front light on? Was Daddy afraid too?

Beyond the lighted porch was nothing but darkness, and a paler sky above the trees on the opposite hill. There were no lights on across the way. The Rentons never had lights.

She went soundlessly on into the hallway to the master bedroom. The overhead light was on. The bedroom door stood open.

It was never like this before.

She crossed the threshold.

A dresser lamp burned softly.

The large bed against the wall to her right had only one person in it.

Daddy lay on his back with his left arm up and covering his face.

"Daddy," she said softly.

He leaped up and blinked toward her. Then, even as he started questioning her, he put his legs out of bed and reached for a robe and put it on.

"What's wrong? Holly? What time is it? Are you all right? Where's your mother?"

Holly began to weep silently. Tears slid hot down her cheeks into the corners of her mouth. Her voice trembled.

"Daddy, hasn't she come home? It's past four o'clock."

"My God."

He reached for jeans, and yanked them on beneath his robe.

She let him lead the way.

They went to the central hall, past a dark dining room, a dark kitchen, and down the lighted stairway toward the outside entry. When he reached the foot of the stairs he opened the door into the garage.

Lights struck Holly full in the face, blinding her at first. Still, she saw the car. Mom's car, in its usual place. At first Holly felt weak with relief. Her tears dried quickly, and a warning turned her weak and cold. Mom's car was here . . . but where . . . ?

She stood on the step into the house, her eyes searching all visible sections of the garage. Brent walked around the family car and over to Louise's station wagon. He stopped and looked down.

In that instant Holly knew he had found her.

"Call nine-one-one," he shouted.

But as if she'd been programmed to go to her mother, Holly ran around the hoods of the automobiles.

Louise lay drawn together, arms and legs gathering within them her shrunken body, indrawn neck and head.

Holly heard her screaming, screaming.

Someone shouted.

Holly felt the strain in her own throat and knew the screams had not come from her mother, but from her.

She fell, her body covering and protecting the small, tight, tortured bones that had been her mother.

31.

Mel called as Beverly was getting dressed for the day. She stood with her skirt dangling, held by one hand. Her pantyhose had twisted uncomfortably as she'd responded to the ring by pulling them on hurriedly. This wasn't one of those calls where she could say, can you hold a minute?

"Mom, I have some things to tell you. I've done more investigating, had some good people looking into this on the side, nothing going into reports except on a few special files. Have you got a few minutes?"

"Of course."

"Then I'll be over."

She had thought it would be taken care of in a phone call. It gave her time to fasten her wrap skirt and adjust the fancy buttons that held it halfway down her left thigh. She had put on a long-sleeved white blouse with buttons that were similar enough in style to look good with the skirt. Carl hadn't called yet, but she supposed they would be doing some tramping again. Old cemeteries, old libraries. Though it seemed to be going nowhere.

Sometimes she felt as if they were paranoid. But then she remembered the old story, the tree that covered the grave, and all that Carl had seen. And especially Monte, and the empty grave.

Now there was the terrible, accidental death of Kara, across the road from Monte, and the others who lived there. Carl accepted Kara's death as accidental. Kara leaning too far over the railing, with a knife in her hand, falling, the knife slicing into her neck. He accepted it because Holly had seen it happen.

It was another of the strange coincidences. Too strange. Like Morey—how could another child be so much like one dead forty years? She had to quit thinking of it or she'd go mad.

She'd hardly had time to run a comb through her hair when she heard Mel's car in the driveway.

She looked out the big corner window of the master bedroom and saw him walking fast toward the kitchen.

She hurried downstairs to open the door for him, the cats running with her to greet him with a few meows and questioning looks as if they understood that something was different these days.

He offered two small brown candy-type treats to the cats and gave Beverly a quick grin. "Guaranteed to keep Mom's cats off my lap."

"Coffee?"

"No thanks. Had some. You go ahead."

Beverly poured coffee that had brewed automatically and was waiting. She sat down.

"Aren't you eating anything else?"

She shook her head. "Tell me."

"You're getting thin. Trying to get your teenage figure back again?"

She smiled faintly. "Not that." Carl wouldn't mind one way or the other, fat or slim or in-between, she thought. She had a feeling that he cared for her, as she did him, the inner them, the real them.

"What do you have?" she asked Mel.

"All right." He drew a small notebook out of his pocket. "These families are all members of Aeternita.

It is not called the Church of Aeternita or anything like that. I believe it's the Way of Aeternita. Some of their names are, Faith and Armond Jasper—Willard and Milicent Lear—Bertha and Sydney Petersen—The Rentons, of course. Here's the list, the names, and addresses.''

She glanced through the names. She knew only the Rentons.

"Most seem to have at least one child," he said. "Sometimes a second child will show up soon after they move into the neighborhood. They all have chosen separate developments, all new houses. Yet they attend the same church. But each couple in each housing development is starting the building of new churches. As if each couple plans to pastor—or whatever—each church.''

"Are they Satanists?" Yet the Satanist movement was not old enough, she thought even as she asked.

"No. It's something else. I haven't gone to any of their services, although it looks as though all visitors are welcome.''

He paused, and a look came over his face that sent the maternal warning into Beverly's heart. That almost-panic when a mother hears the cry of her child.

"Is something wrong, Mel?"

"No," he said quickly—and she knew he was lying. She knew him. She knew also she couldn't pry, it would do no good. He would tell her when he was ready, and not before.

He shuffled some note papers that were filled with his particular brand of unreadable bird tracks.

"An interesting thing," he said. "The children are not babies except in one case that happened a few days ago. One couple became the parents of a very small infant. I'll admit I spied on them a little and saw them only going in and out with the infant covered so it was impossible to see. But it must be newborn. That doesn't register with any of the local doctors or hospitals, so it's our belief that the infant was born at home. Of course there's no record of its birth, just as there are no records of any of them.''

She had figured as much. How could there be? She said nothing.

"Which," he added, "with this bunch might be expected.''

"How have you found these people among all the other newcomers in town?''

"They belong to Aeternita. There might be more.''

"More?'' It was a terrifying thought.

"They are all young. There are no middle-aged members of Aeternita that we've found. They're perfect, in form, face, behavior, and family size. Even those who seem to have only one child soon comes up with a second. They seem to have no more than two except in a couple of cases that still have only one. There's a pattern. The men don't hold jobs that we can find. No social security numbers, except, of course, for the new members.''

"New members? You mean there are people joining this—this cult?''

"Oh sure. They're expanding rapidly. Not everyone who goes to visit becomes a member—so far. But I notice they keep going back—to these—,'' He paused again. "Nightly revivals.''

"Who," Beverly asked carefully, thinking suddenly of Paula, who was never with Mel lately, "did you talk to anyone that has gone to their revival meetings?''

"Tom Roush,'' he said.

"Tom Roush!'' she exclaimed in surprise. "The man who works for Brent? Who bulldozed the tree? Whose wife was—,'' She stopped, a choking sensation in her throat for a moment.

"The same,'' he said. "Tom claims it's different, but you get a good feeling. He apparently has seen nothing wrong.''

Beverly drew a deep breath and looked at the list of names of "Aeternita" members he had given her.

Very few on the list meant anything to her. The Rentons, and a couple more sounded familiar. One address, she noticed, was next door to Tom's. She felt a rush of alarm. Next door to Tom's two small children. She pointed to their names.

"Does this couple have children?"

"Umm, I'm not sure about them, Tom said he didn't think so. I forgot them. They're the only ones who don't have at least one. They're excellent neighbors, Tom said. Offered to watch his kids while he works. Free."

"He—doesn't mind?"

"No, he's appreciative. Says they're nice people. He needs them now."

They were living children, Beverly thought. Would that somehow protect them? "I don't know if I'd let them."

Mel got up, left his chair sitting away from the table as he always had. Nowadays those old boyhood traits that had irritated her, merely gave her nostalgia. She walked with him to the door.

"We'll keep looking," he said. "Though so far, they seem to be—well, just as perfect as they look. Their children don't misbehave, not in trouble at all even with neighbors. Nothing like that. Of course they're all small. There are some young teens among them, and they're model children. Nothing to be alarmed about, for sure. But we'll keep looking, because there are some things that seem odd."

Beverly shook her head, deeply worried about Aeternita people looking after Tom's children. Yet if he approved, how could she object?

"None of them have paid utilities. Evidently they use kerosene. And water . . . ? Well, I don't know how they bathe, or—"

It could have been the beginning of a joke, but he only sighed.

"Is Paula helping you with this?" she asked, her feeling persisting that a problem had entered his relationship with her.

At that moment the phone rang.

She hesitated. It rang again.

"Better answer it," he said. "I'll talk to you later."

Beverly went back to the telephone. He had avoided the answer.

Mel didn't wait to see what the call was about. It might be something she'd want to pass along. If so, they could talk about it another time. He had to get to work. There were trials coming up, the normal things that made him feel almost comfortable, like muggings and stealings and general devilment. They were easier to handle than this other, which had all the indications of a developing cult.

He hadn't told her one thing that had been ripping through his heart like a dragline. No, Paula hadn't been helping him. He had told her about it at the beginning, and she seemed skeptical, disbelieving, and bemused. She wasn't open to any crazy suggestions that the old folks had thought up. Then he learned that a new couple had moved in nearby, a block or so away. Paula had met them, and he hadn't been able to talk to her about them.

She attended their nightly services, just as several others he had once thought were just regular guys.

In the beginning he hadn't liked her devotion to it. Now he didn't know what to make of it. She loved going there. She wanted to become a member. She had asked him to accompany her.

She had even suggested they be married at Aeternita. He didn't know.

The people of Aeternita seemed perfect in every way.

Maybe they were all being misjudged by a lot of otherwise good people. Just a case of misunderstanding.

Yet a feeling of distrust kept him from going with her. Not Mom's or Carl's crazy stories, but something deep within himself.

"Beverly," Carl's voice sounded as if it came from a deep well. "Beverly, I'm at the hospital. Louise tried to kill herself last night. Holly and Brent found her early this morning."

Tried to kill herself? Because of Kara's death, no doubt. Forgetting for a pain-filled moment living children who needed her?

"Is she—?"

"She's still alive. But . . ."

"Do you want me to come?"

"Yes, I do." His voice sounded boyishly desperate. "I need you."

He hung up, and then she remembered he hadn't given her the name of the hospital. The big one was probably most likely, but there were a couple of newer, smaller places that took emergencies. She hastily dialed Saint Mary's, and was told Louise Salisaw had been admitted early this morning.

She drove over quickly, found a spot to park in the crowded lot and hurried to the large first-floor waiting room.

Carl rose from a chair and came toward her.

He immediately took her arm and guided her back outside.

"Brent's in the waiting room up in ICU," he said, answering her unspoken questions. "I took Holly and the boys home, then called in a friend to stay with them. Brent just grabbed up the boys and followed the

ambulance because he couldn't leave them alone—and
Holly wanted to stay with her mother."

They came to the shade of a tree near the parking
lot where heat waves moved over the cars and pavement.

His face was thinner, strained, cheek bones sharp,
chin and nose sharper, eyes receding.

"Carl, you're not well!"

"Louise took poison," he said as if he hadn't heard
her. "They said she swallowed enough rat poison to kill
a dozen people. Brent and Holly found her. There's no
way she can survive this, the doctors said."

"Oh my God."

Beverly thought of the horror of a child finding her
mother dead, by a terrible poison that did awful things
to the body. Then she thought of Brent, left to rear his
small children alone, and then—two tragedies to bear.
The accidental death of a child and the suicide of a
wife.

She asked, "Was it because of Kara?"

He nodded, his hand warm and quivering on her
arm. He propelled her toward a bench and then on
around it. "Presumably. She hasn't spoken."

"Is she in a coma?"

"Seems to be. Doesn't know anyone."

She felt him stop suddenly, his hand tightening on
her arm. She followed his gaze.

The Rentons were going up the walk, he dressed in
a black suit, and she in a dress that hung full from a
small waist to her calves. Behind them, as if marching
in formation, came five other couples, all dressed simi-
larly to the Rentons. Beverly was struck then by their
beauty. There was a vague resemblance woman to
woman, man to man, though some were dark-haired
and others blond. They faced straight ahead with faint
smiles on their faces.

"Isn't that Brent's neighbors?" Carl whispered. His
hand tightened. "Who the hell are the others?"

Church members, she thought, but decided to say nothing. He probably suspected they were.

He didn't say anymore but as his hand grew tighter, his fingers digging unconsciously into her arm, she looked at him and saw a look of horrified recognition.

She moved her arm, and he seemed to become aware that he was hurting her, and loosened his grasp. His head leaned closer to hers.

"The third one," he said. "He looks like the one who passed by me that night. I saw his face . . . in the edge of the headlight. He was the first to crawl out . . ."

People paused to watch them walk past. They moved in silence, speaking to no one.

Beyond the glass of the lobby the group separated, all but the Rentons remaining in the lobby. Joyce and Albert Renton went on and out of sight toward the elevators.

Carl turned to watch, his hand fallen away from her. She reached for it, needing the comfort.

"Beverly, I have to get out of here. I have to go home and be with the kids until Brent can get there."

"I'll go with you."

Brent waited alone.

Across the room sat a couple waiting to see an elderly relative who'd had a heart attack. Most of the people just came at visiting time and left again. Sitting and waiting was emotionally exhausting, but he couldn't leave Louise here to die alone. For hours he had been expecting someone to tell him it was over.

He was thankful Dad had taken Holly and the boys home, though Holly hadn't wanted to go. It was too traumatic for a young girl to have seen so much.

"I don't see how she managed to live this long," the emergency room doctor had told them.

The nuns had come to offer him solace and asked

him if they had a minister they would need to call. He had shaken his head, thinking of the Rentons, and that Louise had just come home from her church when she swallowed the poison.

The room became quiet after the last nun left. Brent sat alone.

They came in silently.

Brent recognized Joyce and Albert Renton, but they appeared not to see him. He waited, watching. Not many acquaintances visited ICU. They waited or called first.

Joyce did the speaking, her voice soft as cream as she leaned over the nurse's desk.

"We're from Louise's church, and we're here to comfort her."

The nurse looked at Brent, then at the large clock on the wall. "It's several more minutes before you can go in, and her husband—"

"This is an urgent visit. We can help her. Please lead us to her, now."

"Is that all right with you, Mr. Salisaw?"

The Rentons glanced his way, and smiled and nodded.

"Yes," Brent said slowly. "It's all right."

The nurse rose and went to the wide double doors. They opened up a vista of small curtained rooms surrounding a long row of desks, equipment, nurses, and sounds. The ICU nurse led them straight to the third cubicle and opened the curtain just enough for them to crowd in. The curtain fell back and she remained standing, like a sentry. Brent sat, unable to move. Stunned. Sick at heart. If they could help her, he'd get down on his knees to them.

Time seemed to stand still.

Then the curtain opened again, and Joyce smiled and nodded her thanks to the sentry.

As they passed through the waiting room they nodded at Brent, but didn't pause or speak. The door closed with a whisper and they were gone.

Brent fought back a hysterical urge to laugh, or cry. He had a sudden feeling of faith that Louise wouldn't die. . . . He prayed in the silent depths of his being she would make it through this . . . that they had helped her.

The clock made a small ting on the hour. The ICU nurse said to Brent, "You can go in now for ten minutes."

Still battling a nervous need to either laugh with happiness or cry with despair, Brent entered the double doors and went to Louise's room.

He stopped the moment the curtains parted, staring.

She lay straight and normal in her flat bed. Her eyes roamed the room as if she had never seen it before, as if she had never seen the world before.

Like a newborn she gazed about her.

It was as if they had actually brought her back to life.

She looked at him the same way she looked at objects in the room. But it was all right. Her body was no longer horribly cramped.

Her eyes were open, looking about. It was all right if she didn't acknowledge him.

Carl answered the phone on the first ring. It could be a call from Beverly, who had gone home a few minutes ago, or from Brent at the hospital. He was expecting at any time to hear that Louise had died. He didn't want Holly to hear it over the phone.

"Dad?" Brent sounded far away.

"Yeah."

"Dad—she's going to be okay. She's going to live."

Carl closed his eyes a moment in vast relief. "She's—," He had almost asked, *she's not dead?* He had been so certain she would die.

Brent's voice was suddenly louder and stronger. "She's okay! She's alive! They're moving her out of ICU. But they want to keep her overnight to run some tests. I thought I'd stay here at the hospital too, if you can stay with the kids."

"She's going to be well?" It was unbelievable. A few hours ago they had expressed no hope for her.

"She's okay." Brent made a sound deep in his throat, half laughter, half sob.

"Well, sure I'll stay with the kids."

"See you sometime tomorrow then. You'll tell Holly—the boys—their mother will be home tomorrow?"

"Of course I'll—"

But Brent had hung up. Carl almost collapsed in relief. He felt emptied, like an old balloon that had slowly floated to the ground. But the only thing that mattered now was Louise had survived.

"Clearly," the doctor told Brent, "it's a miracle. There was no way this woman could have lived. And yet, she's not only alive, she has no side affects that we can find."

Brent breathed a long sigh of relief. *Thank God.* Thank God for those strange neighbors.

"How did this happen, Doctor?" he asked. "Is this what's called faith healing?"

He made a short laughing sound. "Maybe. Who knows miracles? Anyway they're getting her ready to go home. We'd like to see her in a day or two, though."

Brent paced the floor, waiting. It seemed hours, yet only minutes had passed when the double doors opened and a nurse pushed a wheelchair through. Louise sat in the chair, looking calmly ahead. She still didn't look at him. Her face wore a slight smile, as if she were dreaming faraway thoughts.

He had started toward her, but he stopped.

She was so beautiful. He had always thought her attractive, but she'd been only human with what she considered her flaws. Freckles across her nose and cheeks that she used to try to cover with makeup, early wrinkles at the corners of her eyes. She used to complain as she sat in front of the mirror early in their marriage before the babies started coming. "My face is too fat. My eyes too buggy. And look at these cheeks and freckles! Chipmunk cheeks, too."

She'd apply darker makeup on her rounded cheeks to try to make them look hollow. He loved her cheeks. It gave her what his dad had called a baby face, and he loved it. As for her eyes, they were large and blue and lovely. What did she mean, buggy?

Perhaps she'd lost weight. The chipmunk cheeks were curved inward now. Her eyes looked darker, more deep-set. All those traits she'd considered flaws had changed, it seemed, to exactly what she had wanted. Where were those cute freckles? Maybe it was the lighting that made her look like ivory.

Her hair had grown, it seemed. Had he not looked at her lately? What was happening? She'd turned into a beautiful lady overnight.

32.

Davey came running suddenly into the driveway to meet the pickup as Tom made the turn off the street. Tom slammed on the brakes. Davey dodged around the hood as the pickup screeched to a stop. Tom, trembling, yelled at his son.

"What the hell are you trying to do, kill yourself?"

Davey had a look on his face that was somehow different from the somber, sad expression that had been a part of him since his mother's death. He looked ... elated? Excited?

He opened the pickup door and climbed in.

"Dad! Dad, guess what?"

"Davey," Tom, still trembling, shouted, "don't you know not to run into the path of an automobile? Where's your head?"

His mother dead less than a week, killed in a car, and now Davey ... good God, what if he'd hit Davey?

"Dad," Davey cried, "did you know that Sydney and Bertha have a kid of their own? I mean, a real daughter of their own?"

"What?" Tom wiped his hand across his face. Sydney and Bertha had a daughter? Tom hadn't seen Davey so excited in a long time. "What the hell does that have to do with you just about getting killed?"

"Dad! Don't you see? Now they don't need Ali!"

Tom took a couple of long breaths, then put the pickup in gear. He eased forward, looking into the shrubbery, making sure that Ali hadn't been running behind Davey.

"Where is Ali?" he asked. "Is she still with the neighbors?"

"Yeah. Dad, but did you hear? They've got a daughter! She came home. She's there. Now they don't need Ali."

"Davey, they're only taking care of Ali. I don't know what you're talking about."

He drove into the garage, got out, and left the garage door up. As he did every evening after work during these past few days since the neighbors had been keeping Ali, he walked out of the garage and across the strip of lawn to the neighbor's back door.

Davey came with him, as always. Davey said no more, his piece said evidently. Tom didn't know what'd he'd meant exactly, but he was too nervous and tired to ask. He was hungry, too, and wanted to get settled down for the night. Get his kids in the house for supper. See that they both were all right.

He reached out and put his hand on the back of Davey's neck and pulled him close. Tom was still shaking, thinking of how close he had come to killing his own son. He hugged the little boy against his side, and they walked together to the Petersen's back door.

Davey was silent.

Tom knocked. He was grateful for the care the Petersens were giving his kids. He didn't understand Davey's reluctance to be around them. They were great people. They were trying to help him all anyone could, or more. He thought he might even like their church, if Davey would just relent. He didn't want to force Davey to go yet. It was hard enough on the boy to lose his mother, without making life harder by making him do something he didn't want to do. But the part about Ali being cared for by the neighbors, and Davey himself being looked after by them was a help that Davey didn't seem to understand. Davey just had to hang on.

Tom knocked again.

Then Davey said, "When school starts, can Ali go instead of staying here?"

He started to remind Davey that Ali was only three. But of course there was nursery school. The only thing was, he couldn't take time off to take her in and go get her three hours later.

Still, he said, "Could be."

Less trouble that way. Davey was too worried about Ali all the time for his own good.

The door opened. Bertha, smiling, said, "Come in, Tom. Ali is playing with Portia. She's having a great time."

"Thanks, but it's pretty late. I appreciate your keeping Ali . . ."

He said it every day. He felt guilty and slightly uneasy about imposing on them. If they'd only let him pay, but—they refused to talk about money. They wanted nothing from him.

Bertha turned toward the interior of the house and called, "Ali? Your daddy's here."

Tom heard the footsteps. Ali running. His heart warmed with gratitude. The most precious sound in all the world. The footsteps of his children.

"Davey said you've got a daughter of your own," Tom offered, wanting to ask, did you adopt a child? He'd been under the impression that they had no children.

"Oh yes, Portia's been with relatives for a few weeks while we got settled. We're so happy to have her home."

The girl came walking into the room behind Ali. He hadn't heard her.

"Hello, Portia," he said.

She stared at him in silence. She was a pretty girl, which wasn't surprising considering the exceptional looks of her parents. She looked vaguely familiar. She kept staring at him, and yet . . . her eyes somehow didn't

seem to connect with his. It was as if she were looking
through him, beyond him, or perhaps not seeing him
at all.

Was she blind?

Ali came with her arms up, and he lifted her. Bertha
had brushed her long hair into curls that hung smoothly
over her shoulders. Bertha took better care of her, it
seemed, than her own mother had. He counted himself
very fortunate to have accidentally acquired such neighbors.

He said, "Anything I can do for you, just let me
know." He didn't add, for looking after my kids. Bertha
knew what he meant. They had gone through it too
many times for her not to know.

"Just come to services," she said. "We need you, you
need us."

He nodded. "All right."

He carried Ali out of their yard, across the driveway
before he put her down. She lifted a hand to cling to
his. Davey walked on the other side.

"Dad," Davey began, "do we have to?"

"We owe them a lot, Davey. I think it's a small price
to pay, don't you?"

Davey hung his head. Then, "I guess. But there's
something about it. You can't understand anything they
say. They don't even have Sunday school. Just those
crazy words that don't mean anything."

Tom said nothing. It was true that after leaving the
church he could never remember exactly what he had
heard. It was not like any church he'd ever attended.
Instead of a preacher getting up front and yelling his
message, or, at the larger churches, standing behind
his microphone and speaking his message, at Aeternita,
as they called it, several speakers mingled through the
crowd, all talking at once, until it sounded more like a
chant. They touched, their hands cold, brushing softly.
And the feeling of comfort came.

It was the feeling that was good. That sense of having

been transported from all your problems. It hadn't mattered to him what they said. It was the feeling.

"How did you like Portia?" Tom asked. He didn't want to think about their church, because after he got home he felt as if he should take his kids and run, run as fast as he could.

Davey shrugged, said nothing. They walked through the backyard gate and toward the kitchen door. He remembered the garage door was still open, entered the back door of the garage instead and pressed the button that shut the door.

Tom said, "She ought to make a pretty good playmate."

"She's eleven."

"That's only two years older than you."

"She's a girl."

"Bet she can ride a bike."

"No, she can't."

"She can't?"

"I asked her, and she didn't even answer. She just looked at me. Then, do you know what she said, Dad?"

"What did she say?"

Tom helped Ali up the steps into the house.

"She asked me what a bike is. She's dumb."

"Hey, don't call anyone dumb. That's not very nice. How'd you get along with Portia, Ali? Did you have fun?"

"Yes, we cut out paper dolls."

Then Portia wasn't blind.

He went into the kitchen. First, he wanted a bath. He hated even to walk through the house, losing dust off his clothes. He always tried to brush it away before he left the construction site, but dust clung.

Tom led the way into the living room and turned the television to children's cartoons.

"Okay, Daddy has to clean up. I'll be back in a few minutes."

They both sat down on the floor in front of the TV.

They would sit there, he knew, until he dragged them away again.

As he showered it suddenly came to him. He hadn't even been thinking of the child next door. His mind had been wandering, jumping from one thing to the next, hitting on everything from the bulldozing of the tree, to the funerals he had attended this past week. His wife—his ex-wife—and then the tragic funeral of Brent's middle child. He thought of her in the coffin. That was the only time he had ever seen her that he recalled, though he had gone by Brent's house a few times and noticed the children. His mind drew back the picture of that eleven-year-old girl, with her head nestled on the pink satin pillow, the lace hanging down over the raised lid of the coffin and shielding her from life, it seemed . . .

Portia.

Portia, who had looked familiar in an unfamiliar way, was the image of that other child. Brent's child. What had been her name . . . ? Kara.

He turned off the shower and stood with water dripping down over his face, his hair washed into a long bang that half covered his eyes.

The two children, so much alike.

He grew chilled. The water had turned cold without him being aware, or the air was cooling, or . . .

He shook his head, as a dog would shake water from its fur.

A coincidence. A strange, disturbing coincidence.

Brent's wife attended the church. Would she notice the similarity? Would it bother her?

He hoped not.

He reached for the towel and began to dry.

Since he was making Davey go to church tonight when the kid didn't want to, since Davey was sad and lonely and unhappy now anyway, tonight he'd take the kids to MacDonalds again. What the heck? A little more junk food might be good for the soul.

33.

"I really don't need any help," Louise said, for the third time since the nurse had insisted she be pushed in a wheelchair from the hospital bed. At the car she said it again, ignoring Brent's hand. Showing no signs of weakness or tremors, as Brent had feared, she moved gracefully from the wheelchair to the passenger seat of the chair.

The nurse who had brought her out looked at Brent and said, "She's a strong lady."

Brent nodded. He felt as though he were the weak one, almost crushed with thankulness that not only had she lived through a devastating amount of poison, but that she showed no ill effects. But he began now to be afraid. Would she try to do it again later?

The car turned smoothly under his guidance, through the crowded lanes of the hospital parking area and out into the street. He saw that Louise was staring out her window, avoiding his eyes. She was silent.

"Want to talk?" he asked.

She shrugged. "No."

"I think we should."

"Why?"

"We can't just pretend it didn't happen. We can't lose you, Louise. The kids and I need you."

She said nothing.

"I feel like I know why you did it," he said. "But we have to remember we have three other children. It isn't fair to them. They desperately need you."

She turned her face forward. He saw her profile etched against the street lights, the lights in the windows of the homes that hadn't yet closed for the night. She was smiling.

"But they have me," she said softly. "They have me forever. I will always be with them. I am doing what is best for them. I'm taking them with me, all of them."

"What?" He wasn't sure what she had said, there at the last. Her voice was so low. But still she smiled, a secret little smile that was hers alone.

She didn't answer him.

They were nearing the street that led home. Traffic had dropped back. Houses were larger and set farther back from the street. Trees veiled lights from the houses. Brent drove slowly.

"I've decided something, Louise."

"Oh?"

"Yes. I'm going to church with you."

He had thought she would be delighted. In the beginning she had asked him to go. Now she said nothing.

"We'll all go," he said. "We'll take the kids. The Rentons take their kids, don't they?"

"Oh yes," she said. "All of the families include the children."

"Then that's what we'll do."

He settled himself more comfortably, not aware until then how he had sat in a strain, trying to watch both Louise and the road. He felt as if a load had been removed from his shoulders. This was the culmination of what had been inevitable since the day the Rentons had moved in across the hollow.

He guided the car into the driveway, and drove past Carl's pickup. He pressed the button of the remote control and the left garage door began its quiet slide upward. The garage light came on. He drove in and stopped, turning off the engine.

Before he could get around to the other side of the car, Louise had opened her own door and was getting out. At the same time the door leading into the house burst open and the kids came running. They hit Louise all at once it seemed, Vinny allowed to come first, Bryon next. Holly looked both delighted and tearful.

Louise stooped and hugged Vinny, then Bryon. Brent noticed, with that old tug in his heart, that her attention to Vinny was less distracted than to Bryon. But—she was home.

Carl held the door open for them all to enter ahead of him.

"Glad to have you home, Louise."

She paused to kiss him on the cheek. "Thanks for being here with the kids, Carl."

Holly had prepared a supper. Brent kept his smile to himself as he sat down at the table. Potato chips. Plenty of pickles and olives. Big black olives with the pits, the kind Holly liked to nibble on. She had also made a pitcher of punch that caught the overhead kitchen light in ruby brightness.

Like blood, Brent thought, seeing as always the blood on the cement where Kara had fallen.

Eating was something he had to force. For Holly's sake, for the boys, for Louise. And for Dad, too. Carl wasn't as strong and tough as he tried to be. He'd almost had a stroke, or heart attack or *something* that Friday night. Carl could have died then, as Louise had almost died a couple of nights ago.

A thought came to him. His reluctance to go to church with Louise . . . this new one that she preferred . . . was he being punished? Was Kara's death, still a living, burning pain in his heart, a punishment for not taking the children and going with Louise to her church?

He would have reasoned a week ago that God did not punish like that. Kara was only a child. To take her as punishment against him was . . . cruel.

Now he wasn't sure of anything.

The evenings were no longer the same. Since Kara's death they no longer went to the television room. Would they ever again settle down together for entertainment?

Louise rose from the table and went to their room. To get ready for church? He followed her. She was standing in front of the full length mirror in the walk-in closet. Just standing, just looking at her image.

"Shall I get the children ready for church?" He heard his own voice, timid and pleading. He sensed within himself a fear of her, of rejection. As if all her love had been removed from him. "Whatever you want me to do . . ."

"No." She moved, waking from her own image. She took down a robe and a nightgown. "Not tonight. I'm going to bed."

A sensation almost of panic shot through him. He followed her into the bathroom.

"Are you sick?"

Was she not as well as the doctor claimed? Should he take her back to the hospital? She had told him earlier she was going to church, that never again would she miss a service.

"I'm fine," she said in a strange, impatient voice. "I wish people would stop asking me that. I changed my mind about taking my kids to church tonight, okay?" She looked sharply at him. "May I have some privacy now?"

"Oh sure."

He backed out, and she closed the bathroom door in his face.

He stood a moment, confused. Somewhere in the

house Vinny was crying, his voice dimmed by the walls. Inside the bathroom the shower rushed. He was glad Louise couldn't hear Vinny.

He left the bedroom to get the kids settled down and into bed. To take the burden off of Holly.

Brent tried to rest. The house had been quiet for a while now, the boys in bed sleeping, Holly in her wing of the house that now held an empty room next to hers. Louise had been in bed, the room darkened, when he came back from putting the boys to bed. He hadn't disturbed her, even to give her a kiss on the cheek. He had wanted to, but his new timidity kept him from it. Let her rest, he had told himself. She had suffered through so much in these past few days. Kara's death and funeral. Her own attempt at suicide.

Let her rest.

God knew she needed relief from the anguish she must be suffering.

He finally slept, disturbed by vague dreams in which Kara smiled at him in chilling contempt. Smiled, in a way she never had during her life.

He woke and turned over, trying to escape the memory of that strange, terrible smile on Kara's face.

He sought comfort on his right side, facing Louise but separated from her by an arm's length. She was still lying on her back, as if she'd never moved. A pale light from the bathroom put her profile in silhouette. He saw her face as though through a mist that separated them.

He gazed at her, gazed and felt the fear come again that he would lose her. He wanted to touch her, but again was afraid he would disturb her. *Let her rest.*

He slept.

Louise lay still. He woke and sat up and looked down upon her. A heavenly light bathed her face. Her eyes were open, staring at nothing, glazed with death.

Dead.

Dead.

He had brought her home from the hospital, and all the time she was dead.

He jolted awake, terror like writhing snakes in his body. He sat up, struggling to get his breath. Another bad dream. He sagged in relief.

She lay as she had the last time he had looked at her, still and unmoving, but veiled now in reality by the muted bathroom light. Then he jerked up and stared down at her.

He saw the shape of a head but there was no face, no features. Thin hair fell back from what should have been her forehead, like grooves in soft, spongy flesh. The rounded face was smooth, mushy, glistening with its peculiar skin.

The tree . . . the grave beneath the tree . . . a glimpse of something like huge worms . . .

The beings there, pale as if forever sentenced to darkness, something that was capable of wriggling when light came, opened by the destruction of the tree. The things buried beneath the tree, features developing as he watched, budding, as an insect's wings spread . . .

He stared at her, trapped by sights he hadn't been aware of seeing in the dimming hole beneath the tree, that opened grave that had not been a grave afterall, according to the investigating officers. He stared at her and saw the maggot skin, stretched tight and glistening where her features should have been.

He closed his eyes and looked again and saw that she was there, lovely and real. He brushed one shaking hand across his eyes. She was real. She was there.

He turned on the bedside light and gazed at her. His Louise. The mother of his children. Breathing.

God, what a nightmare. It had seemed to have no end.

He got up, went to the bathroom and tried to relieve himself. A couple of dribbles.

He drank a sip of water and looked at the clock. It was still early. Still only ten-thirty. The time of night when he usually turned off the television. But he was exhausted, and fell back into bed with a deep sigh. Louise had turned over, her back to him. He turned out the bedside lamp so that only the nightlight in the bathroom made its usual dim trek into the large bedroom.

He covered his head with a pillow and sought the oblivion of sleep. It danced away from him. Every nerve in his body felt as if it had been attacked by tiny worms that wriggled and ate at him. His head edged toward bursting with something like messages, garbled, too many at one time trying to make his conscious mind understand.

He couldn't take it anymore.

She didn't move when he again slipped out of bed. The clothes he had removed just before he showered were still thrown over the rack in the bathroom. In the semi-darkness he grabbed them on, and left the room quietly, shoes in one hand, the other still buttoning his shirt.

In the central hall he listened. All quiet down the halls toward the childrens' bedrooms.

He went on to the rear of the house and down the stairs to the garage.

One whiskey, a beer chaser. Or two or three. They'd be all right here at home—Holly, Bryon, and Vinny. They were with their mother.

It was the only night she had stayed at home for how long? He couldn't remember. It seemed months. Yet it had been only weeks, two perhaps, no more.

Holly heard her daddy leave. When the footsteps first came quietly into the central hall she had lain tense and terrified. Mama? It was so hard to tell. That one board in the hall that made a tiny squeak, the squeak that her mother had said in the beginning was the only flaw in the new house, had been stepped on. One squeaky board. Holly had never thought the sound of it in the night would scare her so much.

Then, as silence filled the house again, she heard the soft closing of a door, below, in the family room, or the garage. Then, an engine started. A soft hum, but audible from her room. Daddy? He was using his pickup. Parked at night out under the trees, it had a distinctive sound different from the cars. Louder. Larger. The engine of a truck.

She listened to it move out the driveway and drift to silence. Where was he going? Why was he leaving her alone?

The lighted face of her clock changed slowly from ten minutes to eleven to straight up eleven.

The silence in the house was like a heartbeat heard only in the depths of her brain. Yet someone was moving. Someone had risen from bed, and was slipping in complete silence along a hall, coming closer to the bedroom wing.

Holly listened, drawn tight with fear.

What would she do, if her mother came into her room with that sharp, serrated steak knife? What would she do?

Why had Mama killed Kara?

Why couldn't she tell Daddy or Grandpa what she had seen?

Why did Daddy leave her and the boys alone with Mama? Because he didn't know.

Daddy didn't know about Mama and Kara or he wouldn't have gone away in the night. He hadn't been told what Mama had done because Holly couldn't believe what she had seen. . . . She couldn't believe it though she had seen it.

She had been so glad when Mama came home, yet she couldn't stop her fear.

She waited, moistening her dry lips, listening.

She waited for her door to open. Her room was dark except for the lighted face of her clock. Even the drapery on the sliding door was closed. She felt safer in the dark. Now, since Kara.

Mama can see in the dark.

The words came to her mind as if they'd been spoken aloud.

Holly sat up, trembling. Someone stood next to her. Someone for whom the dark was natural and safe.

She reached for the lamp on the bedside table, her arm cold and unprotected. She fumbled for the switch, and light suddenly filled the room.

No one.

The door was still closed. No one had entered her room.

She sat still a moment in bed, her teeth chattering.

If her imagination had made her feel someone was in her room, wasn't it probable that she had imagined hearing someone slipping through the house?

She put her feet on the floor. The terror subsided, and she was able to breathe. She took several deep breaths, and tried to rub the chill off her arms.

She went to her bedroom door and opened it. A tiny nightlight in the hall showed an emptiness, a closed door at Kara's room, the foyer at the front a shadowy square where no one stood.

Holly moved soundlessly into the hallway and stood listening.

Nothing.

She started back to her room when the sound came, softly. Vinny, having one of his night terrors. Those sudden cries that lasted until Mama, or Daddy, or lately herself, went to comfort him. He never woke. Never remembered. He only screamed and clung and shook as she was shaking now.

Then suddenly, Vinny's cry choked off. Too quickly, as if someone had put a hand over his mouth.

She hurried toward the boys' rooms, her footsteps quiet on the carpeted floors.

At the doorway to Vinny's room she stopped. In the shadows of his bed Mama bent. There was a sound now of bedclothes thrown, of small arms and legs thrashing against the bed. Holly saw vaguely in the deep shadows of the bed the struggle. Mama was holding something over his face. *The pillow.*

Holly stood paralyzed, her throat filled with pressure, her head thundering. *No! No!*

She moved, but backwards, not forwards. She felt the wall against her back, the corner of the hall. To her right Bryon's bedroom door stood open. She was aware that he turned over restlessly and moaned in his sleep. Time ticked slowly, and held her in its grip.

Vinny's struggles stopped. Louise picked him up, pulling around him the small blanket he had slept with since he was a baby.

Holly felt invisible. A part of the wall. A part of . . . nothing. As if she were disembodied and floated in the air without voice, she watched her mother carry Vinny down the bedroom hall and disappear into the hall toward the kitchen.

Her senses so strangely alert, yet her body not functioning, Holly was aware of the closing door below, of the car door being shut, of the starting of the engine. She heard the garage door rise, and the car back out and drive away.

Then, as if a spring had been released, Holly was running. As if she were directed by something beyond thought, she ran to her room, pulled on her jeans, and ran out of the house.

At the bicycle rack she yanked out her bicycle and running, pushed it down the front yard to Shady Hollow Road.

The Rentons' house was dark, as always.

She mounted her bike and rode, down the middle

of the street. Car lights flashed past her, coming from
behind, dim and distant. Mama's car. She had driven
up to the street that connected to the hollow road, just
as Holly had known she would. She was taking Vinny
to church.

Why?

She had smothered Vinny—*to death?* Yet now she was
taking him to them. Why? Her mind asked the question
only peripherally as she hurriedly pushed her bike into
the cover of darkness in the trees.

Her mother's station wagon passed by. The car lights
flashed on toward dark trees and dark pavement.

Holly pushed her bike into the road again and began
to pump hard. She thought of Bryon home alone. She
thought of the door she had run through in her hurry
to leave the house. Unlocked.

But he was safe. Safer now than he had been when
Mama was in the house. Her heart knew, but didn't
understand. Tears of blood felt as if they were draining
from her heart. Fear held her tense. But she had to
reach Vinny.

He's dead . . . it's too late . . .

"No, no," she cried softly aloud in rhythm with the
tires on the pavement.

She should have told about Kara. But she hadn't.
Now Vinny was gone too, and it was all her fault because
. . . she couldn't hurt her mother.

34.

The wind created by the swift movement of her bike blew Holly's hair off her shoulders, lifted it into the air, slivering the pale lights that fell onto the narrow hollow road. Her shadow raced ahead of her, a crazy angle of shadows. The taillights of her mother's car appeared, disappeared, and appeared again as Holly pedaled. Disjointed images flitted through Holly's mind.

... The strangers across the hollow. The children coming, first Heidi, then Monte ... Pepper, suddenly dead, no marks on his body ... the Rentons, so beautiful ...

... Kara saying, "They're like perfect. Their family. Do you notice how they treat one another? They never fight like we do."

... Pepper, there, in the neighbor's yard ... the Renton's dog. Then, back in his grave.

... Kara saying, "That Monte, I don't like him. He was mean to his dog. Said he didn't like him."

... Pepper, in his grave ... disliked ... not needed afterall ... for the perfect family ...

... Kara dead ... Mama washing off her blood ...

... Mama ... curled beside the empty rat poison box as if all her bones had tried to desolve back to an amoebae ...

. . . The Aeternita people going to see Mama at the hospital . . . bending over her . . . the nurses not saying, "Only two at a time please," as if they were zapped by a force that turned them to zombies or suspended them in time.

Several of the Aeternita members had gone in, Daddy had told her, and her mother lived, a miracle, and Holly was filled with thankfulness. Such an immense thankfulness she could only put back her head, close her eyes against the mighty presence of God and feel thanks. There were no words. Only a feeling. Thank you—God. God? Someone. Thank you. Her mother lived. She was here, seemingly better than ever. Yet . . . there was the change, the feeling of closeness gone, of mother–daughter ties, those closest bonds—stretching thin—thinner . . .

And the awful fear. That Mama was destroying all she had once loved. She was killing her children.

What had happened to the happiness they'd had? Before they moved to this new house?

. . . and new neighbors . . .

"It's a miracle." Daddy's voice, repeating the doctor's words. A miracle that Mama lived.

Ahead of Holly the brake lights came on, and she applied her own brakes. She had been riding her ten-speed as fast as Mama had been driving, keeping the car in sight as much as she dared. Now she stopped and pulled to the side of the street.

The car turned and crept slowly up the hill.

Above, pale, colored lights glowed faintly among the trees like stars clustered together among clouds.

Holly dropped her bike and ran up the hillside. Brush grabbed her jeans. She stumbled over rocks and fell to one knee.

By the time she reached the top of the hill, Mama's car sat dark and silent in front of the church door. It was as if the other cars had parked especially to make room for hers.

The door opened. Light glowed past Mama. She carried Vinny in her arms. Inside, dark-robed figures greeted her in low voices.

Holly hurried around the car and stood undecided. Beyond the closed door a strange chant was rising.

Praying they would not notice her, she turned the door knob and found it was not locked. She slipped through.

The church was only partly occupied. Toward the front a few people sat on the solid wood benches. Holly slipped toward them. No one seemed to be looking at her. The chant was like music, words she felt she should understand but was unable to. The people in the pews swayed back and forth as if mesmerized. Their faces reflected a dreamy look of ecstasy.

Holly wanted to run after her mother, take Vinny from her arms, and run away again. But she stopped instead, unable to move against her.

Several people in dark robes gathered around Louise as if guiding her forward. Someone draped a robe over Louise's shoulders. Other hands took Vinny.

His arms and legs hung limp.

Unconscious, Holly told herself. *He's only unconscious.* She couldn't just do nothing, the second time, while her mother murdered her baby brother. She would try at least to stop her.

Then she saw his face. One clear, unobstructed view as he was laid on the strange, long table that was draped to the floor with a black velvet cloth.

Her heart stopped. *Dead.* It was too late. *Vinny was dead.* His eyes stared in flat blankness at the ceiling, and for just a moment, before his head was placed straight, his eyes stared toward her. It was the flatness of death. The same look she had seen in Kara's eyes. In Pepper's.

Barely aware of her movements, she walked forward along the aisle. Joyce Renton stood to the side of the altar on which Vinny lay. She raised her arms, tilted her face back and began a frightening, rhythmic chanting.

Louise stood at the end of the altar.

Others moved in, their tall figures hidden beneath the long dark velvet robes. Their cries rose softly, their arms raised, and then they lowered. Their heads bowed.

They seemed to be praying. Holly couldn't understand the words. It was a language foreign to her, if it was a language at all. It seemed somehow very primitive and gutteral, as if somewhere in the past it was connected to a different kind of communication.

She turned, desperate, looking at the crowd.

They seemed to be asleep. Their eyes were closed. Their bodies swayed gently back and forth, in unison.

A child's face stared at her. Her own glance slid past him, and then back again.

She knew him.

He sat with a man and a little girl. The little girl appeared to be asleep, really asleep. She lay with her head on the man's lap.

Familiar faces. Where had she seen them?

Tom! Davey! And the beautiful little girl . . . ? Her name escaped Holly. She could only stare. The little boy returned her stare. She saw in his eyes a desperation similiar to the one she felt. She should take him, she thought, grab his hand and pull him out of here.

She had seen pseudo devil worshipping among some of the kids at school. One night at a party they had done some things with candles and tried to conjure up a spirit. But that was just silly play. This was the real thing . . . *the real thing.*

And she was terrified.

She had to get out.

Then her eyes were caught by the face of another child, sitting with other children on the front pew. Sitting calmly, her hands folded in her lap, her face frozen in a picture of pleasantry, like a doll's face. Holly recognized the small nose and sharply cut lips, the dark bangs that came almost to her eyebrows, the rounded cheeks.

Holly clutched the end of a pew and stared.

Kara.

The girl turned, as if drawn by Holly's eyes. Kara's dark eyes looked steadily into Holly's.

"Kara!" Holly cried, her voice drowning beneath the rising chants at the altar. *"Kara!"*

Kara smiled faintly, then turned her face forward again to watch the ritual at the altar.

No recognition. The dim, fluttering lights of the lamps added to the unreal scene. Kara had not known Holly.

But it didn't matter. Kara was not dead. Kara was not in the coffin, not in the grave Holly had seen the coffin lowered into. Kara was here. *Here.*

It didn't matter that she no longer recognized her own sister.

Holly's gaze flicked down the row of children with whom Kara sat. Heidi, Monte, others she didn't know. But the expressions were all the same.

Only Davey, sitting in another pew with his father, showed the terror that Holly herself felt.

She was torn between wanting to run, and wanting to stay. Here was Kara, her beloved little sister. And here was Vinny . . . and Mama . . .

A cry of joy and satisfaction rose in the building. The children on the front pew stood up in unison, as one. Holly saw them clapping their hands.

The robed figures at the altar parted and drifted away.

On the altar Vinny sat up. His eyes blinked, as if he had been asleep. Only asleep.

Holly started to rush forward, then stopped. Vinny's eyes met hers briefly as he looked around, and she saw the change.

He did not know her. Like Kara, he had left her world.

What had they done?

Mama had killed Kara and Vinny. Holly had seen it, known it. But now they were alive again. Yet not really alive.

She began backing toward the door. She had slipped in unobserved, she had to slip out the same way. Only Davey had seen her, and knew she was there. Really seen her. She didn't belong. He didn't belong.

She motioned toward him to follow her, but he only watched, wide-eyed, lips parted. His eyes pleaded for her to stay. But she kept backing toward the door.

When she reached the door she saw she was being watched by the others too. They had known she was there afterall.

"Stay, Holly," Joyce Renton said. "We've been expecting you. Come and join in on this joyous occasion."

Louise was helping Vinny down from the altar. He stood on his small legs and looked about as if the world he saw was new. As if he had been born again.

Holly slipped through the door into blessed darkness and ran down the hill. No one came to stop her. She had left her bike behind a tree. Oh God, which tree? The hill, the roadside was lined by trees.

Then she stumbled over something and fell. She heard a wheel spinning and reached out. The bike. Thank God, the bike!

Lights would be coming down the hill any moment, following her. They couldn't let her get away. Even now the dark figures might be in the trees, along the roadside. *They couldn't let her get away.*

She rode home down the edge of the pavement. The pale light of the stars was an enemy tonight. Yet did it matter? Darkness was their friend. The Rentons used no electricity. There was none in the church, only dim lamps along the walls. Perhaps none of the church people needed light.

She rode feeling that hands followed at her back, reaching for her. She didn't dare look back.

When she reached the mailbox at the edge of the street, she dropped her bike and ran up the steps to the house. She tried the front door. Locked. She screamed, "Daddy!" But there was no answer.

She ran around the house to the door she had left unlocked. It was still open. With shaking hands she locked it behind her, then ran upstairs and to the master bedroom.

Daddy!

She turned on the overhead light, and saw the large bed empty, covers thrown back. Daddy was still gone.

She whirled and ran to Bryon's room.

In the shadows of his bed, half on his stomach, one arm and leg curved outward, he slept soundly. She laid her cheek against his back and heard his heart beating, heard his soft breathing.

She gathered him up into her arms. He stirred, mumbled something incoherent, but didn't wake. He curled against her, into the cradle of her arms. He was heavy. Much heavier than Vinny. But she ran with him to her room, feeling as if she were being dragged back. Back to them . . . even to her mother. Mama, who scared her now. Scared her so much she felt smothered by her fear.

She laid Bryon in her bed, then hurried back to the door and locked it.

She checked the locks on the windows, and the lock on the sliding door. Then she sat against the glass door and looked out into the night.

Brent sat at the darker end of the bar turning the bottle of beer in his hands, staring at the reflections of the neon lights in the brown glass. Behind him music from a three-piece band competed with voices. Dancing feet sounded like a herd of cattle stampeding across a plain. The sounds were a jumble that were getting on his nerves. His thoughts seemed as shattered as the sounds. What had he thought to accomplish by coming here, tonight?

He pushed the half-empty beer bottle toward the other side of the bar and started to get up. The bartender picked up the ringing phone.

Brent laid out a couple of extra dollars on the bar and turned to leave.

"Hey, Brent, you here?" the bartender asked.

Brent paused, surprised. A ribbon of fear fluttered through his chest. He had occasionally stopped in to have a beer at this particular bar with some of the guys after work, but who knew he had left the house? They all had been asleep. What tragedy had struck now? Who at home would have known to call him here?

"Yeah sure." He reached for the phone the man handed over the bar.

The voice was a mumble of words he only half understood. Not Holly, not Louise. A man's voice. Not Dad's.

"What?" he said. "I can't hear you."

"Trouble," the voice said more clearly. "At the site. Better hurry."

The caller hung up.

Trouble at the site. That meant only one thing. Something wrong out where all the machinery was shut down for the night. He hurried, half running, through the crowd against the bar, toward the door.

He ran to his pickup and pulled out of the parking area, tires spinning gravel to the rear. Tom? No, not Tom's voice he was sure. One of the other guys, someone whose voice was not familiar over the phone.

He drove straight out, across the southern edge of town and onto the street to the construction site. The pickup's headlights cut through a dark night as he bounced onto the dirt track into the field. Not much had been accomplished since the bulldozing of the tree. Some land leveling, some digging where the building of the mall would be. He hadn't been on the job much. There had been too many other things. Kara's death. Kara's funeral. Louise's attempted suicide. He almost didn't give a damn what was wrong at the site. Only the fact that he still had a family to take care of made it important.

He drove onto an empty field. Headlights ranged over the parked machinery. He drove past it slowly, the lights covering for a moment the tractors, the big bulldozer, the backhoes, all of it lined neatly together. Some of Tom's work, probably, grouping it, making it less likely to be hauled off by someone in a flatbed truck.

He drove slowly past the machinery, around it, and stopped, the lights angled past it across the field.

Nothing.

Who had called him?

Then, in the edge of the light, several hundred yards away, he saw a dark figure. He squinted, a cold sensation of having been dropped into space entering his body.

Someone standing where the tree had been?

More than one, he now saw.

He slowly backed the pickup away from the line of machinery and drifted toward the group, his foot off the accelerator. He started to reach out and lock the doors, but suddenly the lights dimmed. The engine stalled.

The pickup stopped, and the dark night closed in on him. In the darkness he saw them, surrounding his truck. The pale, distant starlight gave him an impression of dark-robed figures.

He reached again to lock the doors, but it was too late.

He thought he saw her face again as he had seen it in his nightmare. Pale, smooth, glistening, featureless, with only a long, dark slit that opened, closed, opened, moving as if taking in food, a primordial amphibian-type of being, long lost in the depths of the earth's seas.

*   *   *

Holly remembered her telephone. Here in her room
Given to her when they had moved into the new house

She could call Daddy. But she didn't know where h
was. In a bar somewhere, she thought. Lately. Sinc
Mama had started going to that place, he'd been goin
at night to bars. He didn't know she knew.

Grandpa!

She crept across the floor on her hands and knee
and fumbled on the table for the small princess phone
It fell, clunking on the carpet. Bryon didn't wake.

She took the phone with her and went back to he
station at the glass door.

The numbers on the telephone were lighted, and sh
dialed, missed a number and dialed again. She didn'
know what time it was. Late. Maybe midnight. As th
phone rang she wondered, what could Grandpa do
They would kill him too, make him into one of them
If Daddy knew, if anyone knew, they would kill them
make them into one of them.

She started to hang up, but on the second ring h
answered.

She hesitated, not speaking. She should hang up
Never tell. What could he do? Daddy, Grandpa, both
would be taken and she would be alone, she and Bryon

"Hello? Hello?"

She should just take Bryon tonight, and run away.

Run away? They would find her. They wanted her
They would keep on until both she and Bryon were par
of them. Unless . . . somehow . . . they could get away.

"Hello?" he said again.

"Grandpa!" She felt desperate relief for this tenuous
connection with him. "Grandpa."

"Holly! What's wrong?"

She began to cry soundlessly, tears rushing down her
cheeks and into the corners of her mouth. But she had
to be careful what she said to him. She didn't want him
to go to . . . *Aeternita.*

Eternity. A place, a time, from which no one ever returned.
Suddenly she knew. It had just been a crazy latin name
that meant nothing, a name for a strange churchlike
place. But now she understood. Oh God, what if they
had Daddy?

"Grandpa, I don't know where Daddy is."

There was a silence on the line. She could almost see
her grandfather thinking of possibilities.

"It's almost three o'clock," he said, "and he's not
home?"

"No. Just Bryon and me."

"Just you—where's Louise and Vinny? Where'd they
all go?"

"Mama—Vinny—" Still, she couldn't say it. Even
now. "Asleep," she finally lied. "But Grandpa—where's
my daddy?"

"Holly—calm down, sweetheart. When did he leave?"

"I don't know."

She had to tell Grandpa about Mama. She had to.
Even though it was her own mother. Yet she couldn't
make her voice work.

"I'll be right there, Holly. In a few minutes."

"No wait! Grandpa . . . I saw—Kara."

"Kara?" he repeated harshly. "What are you talking
about?"

She couldn't tell. She had to protect her mother above
all.

"She's . . . not dead. She . . . it looked like her."

For a few heartbeats she felt as if she had lost the
connection to him. Then he spoke again.

"I'm on my way over."

Car lights at that moment swept into the driveway.
She recognized the higher beams of the pickup her dad
drove.

"No, wait! Grandpa, Dad's coming. He's driving in
now. I have to go now, Grandpa."

She hung up and ran to the bedroom door. She

couldn't see, and switched on the overhead light. She unlocked the door and ran to the central hall and back toward the stairway.

She stopped.

Not Daddy, but Mama. Holly took a step backwards.

Louise began climbing the stairs. She was alone. Vinny was not in her arms. Kara was not with her.

She looked up, her eyes reaching Holly.

Holly backed farther away, and tried to flatten herself against the wall.

It hadn't been the pickup lights afterall. Not Dad, but Mama. Coming toward her.

Holly's voice trembled when she asked, "Where's Vinny?"

"Why didn't you wait?" Louise replied pleasantly. "You could have ridden with me. We could have put your bike in the back."

She came nearer up the stairs, so slowly it seemed, one foot lifting in a slow motion to a higher step, then the other . . .

Holly pushed back against the wall, her palms flat against the cool surface.

"Mama, where's Vinny?" She heard a sob in her voice. "What did you do with him?"

"You and Bryon, you must go with me too, you know, Holly."

"Mama!" Holly screamed, moving away from the wall, trying to block her mother's way. Trying to keep her away from Bryon. *"What did you do with Vinny? What have you done to Kara?"*

"It's all right, Holly. You know I would never do anything to hurt my children. They're in a better place, Holly. We'll all be together. Forever."

"Mama! You killed Kara! I saw you kill Kara! And now you've done something terrible to Vinny! He was dead! Dead! Can't you understand anything anymore Mama?"

Tears streamed down Holly's face. Her voice shook. She held out her hands to stop her mother, beseaching her.

"What has happened to you, Mother? *Where are you?* It's like I don't know you anymore! Mama! You scare me. Mama, where are you? You're like them. I don't know who you are!"

Louise stopped, inches away from Holly. Standing on a lower step, Louise's eyes were level with Holly's. Holly's eyes, dimmed by the tears that raged from her heart, saw her mother as though through a heavy fog.

She saw the smile. Those cold, perfect smiles that belonged to the women of Aeternita. Smiles that were only a facial expression expected of them as they pretended to be human. A smile that had nothing behind it.

Holly pressed back again against the wall. She felt herself weakening, folding beneath a force she couldn't win. "Daddy's gone too, Mama," Holly said softly, tiredly. "He's gone. And I have a feeling he's never coming back. What did they do with him, Mama? Where's my daddy?"

For just a flash a strange anger showed in Louise's face. A frown, like a thought, reaching somewhere to the past. She shook her head slightly.

"He is not one of us," she said. "He would never have complied. There are those who are lost."

Holly wept in silence, making no effort to wipe the tears from her face. They dampened the collar of her pajama top.

"You've taken everything away," she whispered. Everything. Everyone but Bryon and Grandpa. But even to mention their names she felt would put them in danger.

Louise spoke as if programmed. Her voice was soft and patient, the kind she had rarely used when one of her children talked back to her.

"You'll understand, Holly. I'll take you with me, and then you'll understand. Now, it's beyond you. But in a few days you'll see that what I have done is to save you. You and the other children. I have saved you, and you will be grateful."

Her mother passed by without touching her.

35.

Carl dressed hurriedly. Three-fifteen. He wanted to call Beverly, take her with him, but decided against it.

Brent was home now, thank God.

Holly had seen *Kara*? Or someone who looked enough like her that Holly had called, her voice quivering with emotion . . . with terror?

The streets were quiet, almost all traffic left only to the few trucks that delivered at night, to an occasional taxi or car. Carl drove without regard to the low speed limits, keeping his eyes open for the cat or dog that might have slipped its yard in search of adventure.

He drove to the cemetery where most of the family was buried. His grandparents, parents, an older brother, two younger sisters who had died in infancy. The cemetery where his wife and their two babies lay in the small family plot, where his own name was engraved on the double tombstone. Where, two plots away, Kara had been buried.

The day after the funeral he had gone there again, and placed a fresh bouquet of flowers near the head of her grave. There was no stone yet. It was to be delivered later in the week. A burial not planned for. A death unexpected. A terrible tragedy.

He parked in the deserted driveway that curled

through the cemetery, took his flashlight from the truck and walked straight to the gravesite, going over other graves. Something he wouldn't have done a week ago.

The flowers were tossed aside. All the flowers that had been laid on the rounded top of the fresh grave had been thrown haphazardly to the sides as the grave had been opened. In the depths his light shined upon the empty coffin. Its lid stood open. Clods of dirt had fallen in and lay like wounds on the pink satin.

They had made no effort to conceal their work.

It must have been done within the past three or four nights.

With the flashlight beam lighting his way, he walked slowly through the graveyard, checking the graves in the nearby area. At the outer edge he found three more that had been opened. The stones, undisturbed, described young children born and buried a hundred years ago. One of them was an infant, dead the day it was born.

He went back to his pickup and sat in the dark, trying to think. Gradually, the outlines of the stones became visible. Ghosts in the darkness. Trees, large, black in the starlight threw a deeper darkness onto the stones, but still they stood, and appeared to move as he stared at them.

He was further from an answer now than ever.

He needed to talk to Beverly. But it was now almost four o'clock. He'd wait until morning. Let her rest, if she could. He had been calling on her too much lately for emotional strength.

Should he go to Brent?

No. Yes. *No.*

Yes.

Brent had to know all Carl knew, eventually. All Carl had seen, that first night. He had to know Kara's grave was among those robbed.

He drove to the first all-night convenience store he saw, got out, left the truck door open, the engine running. The only lights, at the pumps, at the front of the store, shone down on emptiness. Few people out this time of night. But it was the darkness, the shadows in the places behind the store that made him uneasy, as if every shadow now contained danger.

He dialed Brent's number. Brent might not understand the call. He might be tempted to put Carl back in the hospital. Worse, he might want to throw him headfirst into a mental ward. But that was the chance he had to take.

The phone was picked up on the first ring, and Holly whispered eagerly, "Dad?"

For a long heartbeat Carl couldn't answer her. Holly too was silent. The night was so far gone now that a dim, pinkish light was beginning to expand in the east.

"Holly," he finally said, "this is grandpa. I need to talk to your daddy," he added, although her answer had told him something that hadn't even entered his mind. Brent still was not there.

"Grandpa, it wasn't him that came home when I was talking to you. It was . . . I just thought I heard his truck. I don't know where Daddy is. Find him, Grandpa!"

Her voice was husky, whispering, as if she'd been crying all night. As if she were afraid of being heard.

"Are Louise and the boys all right?"

"Yes," she whispered.

"Holly, if I send Beverly over to your street, would you get your mother and brothers to come to my house with her? While I see if I can find Brent?"

There was a long hesitation, then Holly said in a stronger voice. "No, it's okay. I can't leave Mama, Grandpa. She'd want to wait here."

He stood looking into the shadows on the other side of the big dumpster behind the convenience store, but seeing the split-level house in the woods above the hollow road. Seeing his three grandchildren who were there. He had to get Louise and the surviving children safely away.

But first he had to find Brent.

He hung up the phone and turned in a circle, distraught and worried. He wondered if he had said goodbye to Holly, warned her to be careful.

The sky had lightened. A few stars and planets lay in the mysterious expanse above like tiny bits of bright moon left over from a dark night. But the real mystery was here, in the earth, untouched by light.

He turned back to the phone, dropped in another coin and called the police station. Undecided, he almost hung up. What could they do? He didn't want to be detained to answer any questions. What could he say? Four more graves have been robbed, this time in a city cemetery. One of them my granddaughter, buried four days ago.

Someone, a female, announced the police station for a third time. Carl hung up without speaking.

He felt weak and disoriented. Coffee, he thought. The little shops would be opening. Coffee was available in the convenience store, he remembered, just as he was backing out of the lot. He left the truck running, door open, an easy target for anyone passing by who might want transportation. But the petty thieves were nothing. He wondered if they knew exactly how nothing they were, compared to this other thing? *Things.* The theives could only steal your property. They might even steal your life. But they couldn't steal your soul, as he feared was the way of the people of Aeternita.

He sat at a small booth in the store and poured down three cups of coffee, his mind a whirl of confusion. Mel, trying to find a logical answer to the preachers, the church, the background. Beverly, torn between the world she knew and understood and the memories of an old great-grandfather. Then Carl's own visions, of faces buried in the dirt beneath an uprooted tree, of arms and legs visible. Even one old shoe, half rotten.

Figures . . . rising from that terrible old grave and walking past his pickup. Dressed in black, hooded robes.

A face, two, three, perfect, beautiful, etched forever in his memory. Yet also, other faces, still in the dirt, smooth, glistening, no features . . . like overgrown maggots, something that lived in the soil, burrowed, were at home there in the vastness that lay beneath the surface of the earth. An area more mysterious and less explored than outer space.

The guys would be showing up at the site now. Maybe one of them might know where Brent had spent the night. Carl knew that at times his son stopped by different bars or restaurants that served liquor, sometimes on business with someone who was more comfortable in that setting, sometimes just to relax. But he had never known him to stay out all night.

It might be that in his grieving for Kara, he had simply tried to lose himself last night.

At the site . . .

The thought came to him like words spoken from the shadows of his own mind. Brent . . . at the site.

Traffic had grown suddenly, it seemed, with the coming of dawn. Delivery trucks, taking up too much space. Smaller commuting cars squeezing in wherever they could. Carl drove as fast as he dared among them, cutting lanes with the best.

A couple of pickups were already at the site. One of the men Carl saw standing in the middle of the leveled land was Tom, hands on hips. Near him stood Jimmy Andersen. They both were staring at one of the backhoes that had been moved out of the line of machinery.

Carl drove up to them, stopped, and looked around. "What's up?"

Brent was not in sight. Yet Brent's truck was parked almost in line with the machinery that hadn't been moved. He was around here somewhere, maybe on the other side of the big pile of dirt that had been dug out of what would be the foundation of the mall.

"Don't know," Tom said. "When I left last night this backhoe was over there with the rest of the machines.

Someone's moved it. Thought Brent must have, for
some reason, but we haven't seen him. There's his truck,
though.''

"He's somewhere around," Carl said. "Unless . . ."

Unless he went off with someone else.

Carl walked away from them, turning automatically
toward the place, now smoothed, where the sycamore
tree had stood. He went toward the grave that was now
covered. Only a few roots, thin, spidery, revealed where
the grave had been.

A few roots . . .

One of them thicker than he had noticed a few days
ago, the last time he had walked near here.

. . . Thicker . . .

He walked nearer, nearer, stopped. The scream was
in his head, buried in silence, exploding.

Not a root, but a hand, reaching . . .

36.

Carl recognized the wedding ring. He recognized the hair on the backs of Brent's fingers, so different from his own smooth hands. Brent's hand reached from the covered grave pleading for help, but it was stiff and still as if made of clay, a horrible joke. The fingers reached, unbending, the cry for help lasting forever.

Behind Carl a voice cried out.

"Jesus Christ!"

As if it propelled Carl to action he fell on his knees and began to dig with his hands. The dirt fell back as fast as he dug. He grasped his son's hand and struggled to pull him bodily from that horror of a grave. In one part of his awareness he felt the utter cold of his son's flesh, the rigidity of the arm. As if it were only a mannequin, buried.

Footsteps pounded behind him. Tom pulled him away. With shovels both Jimmy and Tom began to dig. Carl was aware that others of the crew were pulling off the street, heading across the field toward them. Men came running.

Someone tried to pull Carl away, but he flung them off. Words shouted, cries in the air, went over his head, his awareness.

His son was dead.

They had killed him.

But he'd fight them to the depths of hell before he'd let them have Brent's body.

Carl realized later there was a gap in his memory. He had stubbornly stood by his son, among police, rescue workers, even the press until he saw the funeral home director take Brent's body away. Everts. Don Everts. The man who had buried his wife, his granddaughter. Someone he trusted. But he remembered following Don to the funeral home, directing Beverly where he wanted to go, insisting that he speak with Don—he wasn't even sure how Beverly had come to him, who had called her—but she was there, and she listened to him.

He remembered telling Don, "Cremation. I want cremation."

Don had looked at him with sympathy, but no understanding. Then he had said in that soft voice, the voice Carl had always thought of as his funeral voice, "You know, of course, Carl, that his wife will have to be consulted on that. You know it will be her choice. Also, you know, since this is a homocide, there had to be an autopsy."

He gave up. Something within him snapped. He became easy to lead. He became silent.

Beverly said softly, "I'm taking you home, Carl."

She took him to his own house, took his keys and unlocked the door. He looked at her and pleaded, "Don't go. Beverly, don't leave me."

"I'll never leave you, Carl."

He was aware of her moving about in the house, doing the things in the kitchen that his wife had done. She came to him with a cup of coffee and a sandwich.

He took them, set them aside, then reached his arms for her.

They held each other, his head lowered against hers. Minutes passed, then he raised his head.

"Someone has to tell Louise and the children. I have to go to them."

"No, Carl. Sit down, eat your sandwich and drink that coffee. Right now you need rest and nourishment. The police will tell them."

"I want them to come over here. Where they'll be safe."

The doorbell rang. Carl sat slumped in his chair while Beverly left him to answer the door. He heard the soft murmurs of familiar voices. Neighbors, friends, relatives. Word had reached them, sometime during the hours past.

They came into the living room quietly, each touching him gently, speaking words he barely heard and wouldn't remember later. It didn't matter. Just their presence was comforting.

He smelled the odors of fresh-cooked food, and heard women going to the kitchen, taking over, putting away, storing for tomorrow, the next day when the house would be filled again with the folks who did all they could to help get through the loss of his only son. So soon after the death of Kara.

Beverly came and bent to say softly, "I'm going over now to see about Louise and the children."

Carl nodded, relieved that someone he trusted with his life would be there to help his son's family.

Deputy Gary Crowell saw a doorbell on the door at the back of the house. He looked around. The driveway came in the rear, to a double garage. He walked around the side yard and found the front of the house. A pebbled walk angled down the hill to a mailbox at the edge of the street below. The front door was solid steel, painted a deep burgundy, with a couple of fancy strips of pebbled glass gracing each side. But he had a hunch that most of the callers came to the back door. The family probably had a room back there in which they spent most of their time.

He walked back around the house. There were decks above with sliding doors. Two of them, one on the side and one over the garage.

Brent Salisaw's home.

He hated this job. It was the worst thing he had to do. Go tell a family that the dad had been killed. He wouldn't even be able to tell them how. It was too horrible. Not a car wreck this time, like a couple of cases last week. But murder. The most horrible kind of murder imaginable. Buried alive. At least that was the way it looked to him. Of course there was no official report yet, and wouldn't be for several days. But how could that expression on the man's face be explained? And the mouth filled with soil, as if he'd tried desperately to breathe. The reaching out of the hand . . . had he managed that himself, or had it been deliberately left that way by whoever had done this thing? One thing was for certain. It had taken more than one person to put that man in the ground.

I'm sorry, but your husband, your daddy, has been killed . . .

He'd had too many of these jobs lately. There was a rash of things going on that seemed oddly coincidental. There were also grave robbings in the county cemeteries mainly, but a few closer in.

Just a few days ago one of the children of this family had died accidentally. He looked up at the deck. The one that extended over the driveway, over the garage. She had fallen, on a knife.

Somehow, it just didn't ring true, even though there were witnesses.

He hadn't been here. He had only read the reports and heard some of the city policemen talking about it.

But this time the job was his, because Brent Salisaw

had died in the part of the county the town was trying to annex.

The same damned place where he was called to one evening about dark with the report that a grave had been uncovered beneath a tree that was bulldozed over.

He'd laughed then, even though he felt sorry for the dad . . . the man who'd stayed in the pickup. He'd had a heart attack or a stroke.

Yet today he was there, on the ground where he'd found his son buried, digging at the dirt with his bare hands.

Too many coincidences. Too many strings that had seemed to unravel from the same ball.

Crowell didn't understand. It made his brain feel as if somebody had knocked all the sense out of him.

He had a wife and three kids at home. He had parents and grandparents, brothers and a sister, nieces and nephews. He was beginning to worry about them all the time, as if whatever had invaded the area would reach them too, eventually.

He started to push the doorbell, then drew his hand back.

Why him?

Somebody had to do the job.

He pushed the doorbell in and held it.

When he released it he heard footsteps coming down a stairway beyond the door. To his right a sliding door opened out onto a patio. But no one came to that door.

A flower garden just beyond the patio looked untended. It had once been very pretty, but now needed dying blossoms picked off before they went to seed, and some weeds pulled.

No dog or cat came to greet him, even though there was a small doghouse under one of the decks.

The door opened.

The woman was gorgeous. Her hair was the most lustrous golden brown he'd ever seen. Her skin perfect. She wore no makeup, but needed none. She looked at him with calm eyes, the color dark but not brown. They were grey perhaps, or green. They shone, almost glittered. It must be the light. The way it fell on her. The thoughts zipped through his mind even as he was wondering how to tell her.

On the stairs behind her was a young girl, perhaps thirteen or fourteen, and at her side, as if trying to hide behind her, a boy about five. He saw the girl was holding the boy. Keeping him from going down the stairs ahead of her. Her hand clutched his arm. She came down slow, step by step, still keeping the child at her side as if protecting him. From falling, perhaps. Probably, after the fatal fall of her sister, she was terrified her little brother would fall. And now he had to tell her about her daddy.

"Mrs. Salisaw?" Crowell tried dampening his dry lips with a raspy tongue.

The beautiful young woman smiled faintly. "Yes." She didn't look concerned that a deputy sheriff stood at her door.

Crowell saw the look on the girl's face. The contrast to her mother was crushing. The kid was scared half to death. So was the little boy. Neither of them looked as if they'd seen the sun this summer.

"Ma'am, I'm sorry to have to tell you this . . ."

The girl came on down a couple of steps, pulling the boy with her. Her lips parted. The wild terror in her eyes increased.

Crowell licked his lips again. The contrast between the faces . . . so . . . wrong, somehow. Better to just get this over.

"Your husband, Brent Salisaw, has been . . . killed."

For a couple of heartbeats there was silence. Then the girl began to scream.

The girl's cries shattered the stillness, gasping, shrieking, as if each breath tore the heart from her. No tears appeared in her eyes. She stared at him, and screamed. He started into the house toward her. But her mother blocked his way, turned, and slapped her sharply across the face.

The girl silenced abruptly, although her throat continued to jerk and move as if the screams continued deep within her. The mother turned back to him. The pleasant, beautiful mask of her face hadn't changed. It was, he thought, just like a mask. Hiding something he didn't understand. How could a mother slap a child who was already in pain? And don't give him the shit about knocking her out of shock. He wished he could slap a child abuse charge on her.

The woman said, "She'll be all right. She'll be fine. Thanks for coming."

She shut the door in his face.

Crowell stood stunned. From beyond the door were movements, steps, climbing. Then he heard the soft cries and gasps of the girl. There were no sounds from the little boy. Probably he didn't understand.

He heard the woman speaking softly to the girl, but could not understand what she said.

Their steps reached the top of the stairs and silenced.

He moved back, turned away, and hurried toward his cruiser.

Further investigation was needed here, he thought, and in a hurry. Look into the possibility of the little girl being killed by her mother. Or was it shock, too many tragedies for the mother to bear that made her act in that strange, unfeeling way?

"It's all right," Louise said. "It's better this way."

Holly heard her mother's voice, felt her arms, the touch of her cold hand patting her cheek.

She shoved away.

"How—how did he die?" Holly demanded on a sob.

"I don't know."

"You do know!" Holly screamed. "You do know! He didn't come home last night! He went with you!"

"No—"

"Yes! He wanted to go to church with you. You killed him too, the way you did Kara and Vinny! You killed him! *You killed my daddy and I hate you for it*!"

"Holly—"

Holly attacked her, shoving, scratching at her perfect face, fury boiling beyond the love that had been so strong. It tore Holly apart, hatred mingling with love. That love that had always carried so much trust, until now, until Kara died.

"Bring him back! Bring him back!"

Holly felt her hands grabbed and held. Louise's grip was like iron, holding her prisoner.

"Listen to me! Kara and Vinny are not dead! You saw them yourself. They are not dead."

"You killed them."

Holly weakened, sinking, held up by the incredible strength of her mother.

"It's better that this life was replaced by the other. This life is fragile, Holly, and leaves quickly, and our bodies rot and become part of earth. This other way we command the earth, it's our servant. There is no longer death, or weakness, or illness or pain. Don't you see?"

Holly stared at her through tears. Her mother's face seemed featureless, gleaming and smooth and tight. In total terror Holly tried to release herself, but the strength that held her hands made her helpless.

"We'll all be part of it, you'll see. The earth will become ours, eternally," Louise said, her voice sounding like a distant recording. "You want your father back? Then obey Aeternita."

Obey Aeternita? Holly's head lowered. She didn't ask what it meant. Death, she knew, for one. But . . . perhaps a certain kind of death. She closed her eyes.

Only Bryon was left, and Grandpa. Maybe her mother was right. Maybe the people of Aeternita were superior, and some day the whole world would be theirs, and there would no longer be a condition called life. And without life, no more death. Maybe Mama was right.

But she felt a desperate need to keep Bryon away from it. He was all that was left of her family. Bryon and Grandpa.

She lifted her head.

"All right. I'll go with you." She hesitated, her heart aching for Bryon. "If—you'll let Bryon stay with Grandpa."

Louise nodded, smiled. "Of course. If that's what you want."

Louise's face no longer looked unfamiliar and strange, but now Holly wondered if that outer perfection was only an illusion. Something acceptable, something not questioned by those who didn't know this thing that was taking over the world.

Holly turned, looking for Bryon.

He was huddled in the corner of the hallway near the kitchen door. Hunkered down in the shadows, his small face a white blur beyond the tears that rushed into Holly's eyes.

She reached for him, but he remained where he was, looking from Holly to their mother.

The doorbell rang again.

Louise muttered something about the policeman. "I thought he had gone. Why don't they just leave us alone?" She started down the stairs.

Holly stooped to Bryon and whispered, "I'll get you out of here, somehow. Don't be afraid. It's okay."

He reached up, his arms clasping her neck. She straightened, his weight bearing her sideways. But she held to him.

At the foot of the stairs Louise opened the door.

Beverly! Not the police at all. Grandpa's lady friend. Holly had seen her only a few times, but her pleasant face was like the face of a friend. It was as if her unspoken prayers had been answered.

"Mrs. Inness," Louise acknowledged, but she didn't open the door wider nor invite her in.

"Are you and the children all right, Louise?"

"Yes, thank you. Is Carl with you?"

"No, he's at home. He's very concerned about you, and wants you to come and be with him."

"Yes, well . . . tomorrow. Tell him we'll be over tomorrow. You understand the shock we're in just now."

"Of course. Carl is devastated, as you must also be. I wish I could help."

Holly hurried down the steps, Bryon in her arms. She set him down and held one of his hands toward Beverly.

"Take him with you, please?"

She felt Louise's eyes on her, but it didn't matter. Louise would do nothing to arouse suspicion in Beverly. Holly didn't understand the purpose behind Aeternita, but she could see that it was important to them to insert themselves insidiously into human society. At least now, at his stage. She was counting on that.

Holly felt Bryon pull back from Beverly. She bent and hugged him and whispered, "Mrs. Inness will take you to Grandpa. Go stay with Grandpa. Please. Stay with Grandpa."

Bryon reluctantly moved, away from Holly to Beverly. Holly put his hand in hers. Beverly smiled down at him.

"Are you coming with me back to your grandpa's?"

Bryon nodded.

Holly did not look at her mother.

"I'll walk you out to your car."

They crossed the patio, Louise coming with them. Holly would have no chance to warn her, to tell her to tell Grandpa that Louise was already part of Aeternita. That she had killed Kara and Vinny, but that somehow they had been revived. Only now they were different. They looked like Kara, like Vinny, but they weren't. They had been made to create what appeared to be perfect families of Aeternita people, and Holly had a terror in her heart that it would always be that way. That

Vinny and Kara would never change from what they were now. That consciousness was gone. That growth and change were gone. Feelings and love . . . gone.

That mustn't happen to Bryon.

Daddy would be brought back, like Kara and Vinny. Like Mama? Mama too, was part of that strange existence that was not life but something else.

But . . . it was better, maybe, than losing him completely. She didn't know. She only knew she had made a promise. Bryon was free.

If she could believe the words of her mother. Of the shell that had been her mother.

She stood and watched the car drive away, down the driveway to the street, then out of sight beyond the trees. Bryon's small face kept looking back.

Go, she prayed in silence. *Don't look back.*

37.

The voices came gently to Carl from other rooms. Soft, floating murmurs, comforting, letting him know he wasn't alone. Beverly was there, and her son Mel. A few of the neighbors drifted in, stayed awhile, left, and were replaced by others. Some of the visitors were relatives, ready to stay as long as Carl needed someone.

He sat in the bedroom, Bryon in his arms. In the soft light of the room they were alone. The sound of the rocking chair as Carl rocked his grandson was like a heartbeat, steady and soothing. The little boy's head rested against Carl's chest, his pudgy hand held to Carl's wrist. Carl's memories went back to times long ago when he had held Brent like this, rocking him in this same old chair. Trying then, as he tried now, to rock a beloved child to sleep.

Bryon seemed unable to fall asleep. Every time Carl looked down he saw those blue eyes open.

Carl had thought Louise, Holly, and Vinny would be over by now. Perhaps they had company too. Or perhaps they had gone to friends or relatives.

Beverly hadn't seen Vinny, she'd said.

Carl had asked Bryon, when Beverly returned with only him, "Where are the others? Where's Vinny and Holly?"

He hadn't answered. He had seemed almost in shock, unable to answer. He had wondered if he should take Bryon to a doctor, but what could a doctor do? A tranquillizer for a small child? No. Just love and comfort. Carl had taken him and held him closely.

"Does he know?" he asked Beverly.

Beverly shook her head. "I don't know. I suppose he must. Louise and Holly knew. A policeman had come by, Louise said."

"Are they coming over?"

"Tomorrow, Louise said."

He didn't ask why Bryon was sent and not Vinny.

Now they rocked. It seemed hours since they had come into the bedroom where, when Bryon went to sleep, Carl would put him into his own big bed. The dark seemed to have fallen like a curtain, the first day gone that no longer held his son. Carl stared at the window, and was comforted by the warm life of the child in his arms, and the murmuring voices from other rooms in the house.

Suddenly Bryon spoke.

"Holly is going to go to the church and be one of them."

At first his words were only sounds, startling because this was the first time he had spoken since his arrival. Then the meaning struck Carl. A moment of utter shock and disbelief.

Carl stopped rocking.

"What?"

"She's going with Mama to church."

The Baptist church, or the Episcopalian, or whatever church they attended. Carl didn't know if they even went to church regularly. But now, at this time of grief, it would be understandable. Yet . . . within him was the sound that came with the falling of the tree. The muted drum, where no drum played.

"Church? What Church?"

"The Rentons' church. Where Mama goes."

The Rentons' church. Where Mama goes.

Carl's grip tightened on the child, but he was unaware of it until Bryon squirmed. Carl loosened his hold, but he sat forward in the rocking chair, still, his heart pounding, every muscle in his body tight and throbbing.

"Your mother has been going to the Rentons' church?"

"Yeah, all the time."

Oh my God.

"Holly—Holly has been going?"

Easy, an inner voice warned. Don't scare Bryon.

"No. Not till now. Now she's going with Mama."

Carl sat still. Time stood still. He couldn't move.

Bryon said, "Vinny's there, too. He went to stay with someone. And Kara."

Kara.

Carl wasn't sure if he had spoken. Bryon's voice, soft and trusting, speaking of things he had only heard, continued.

"Holly said Mama killed Kara and Vinny. But Mama said it's all right, because it's better to be killed, and then be part of them. Kara's not in the coffin now. And Daddy won't be dead. Daddy died. Did you know Daddy died? But he won't be dead now."

Oh God. They had let Bryon go. Was it because they thought he was too young to understand what he had heard? That he would not pass it on?

Or—more frightening—that it didn't matter if he did?

How long would he be protected?

Holly . . . he had to get Holly . . .

But he must not alarm Bryon.

"Bryon, listen to Grandpa, all right?"

"All right."

"I want you to stay here, in Grandpa's bed. I want you to try very hard to go to sleep. Will you?"

Bryon's fingers pinched suddenly into Carl's arm.

"Where are you going?"

"I'm just going—" *Where?* What would be acceptable

to Bryon? A place he wouldn't ask to go along? "I'm just going to the bathroom. I'll be back soon. But I want you to stay in my bed, and close your eyes, and try to go to sleep. Will you? While Grandpa goes to the bathroom? It's just down the hall, and you'll be fine. You can listen to the voices of the nice people who've come to be with us tonight."

"All right."

Carl carried Bryon to the bed and tucked him in. He tried to conceal the shaking of his hands, the need to hurry that pushed him. He leaned over and kissed Bryon's forehead.

"You stay here now. Grandpa's getting old, and it takes a long time sometimes to take a bath and get ready for bed. So you just wait for me."

"All right, Grandpa."

Carl slipped out of the room and closed the door, then he hurried toward the murmur of voices.

The few who remained were in the kitchen, at the table, cups of coffee or tea in front of them. His cousin Ruthy was still there, and her husband Clarence. They would be spending the night.

Beverly too was there.

All three hushed and looked up at him. Ruthy asked, "Coffee, Carl? Or a warm glass of—"

Carl grabbed his truck keys off the peg at the bottom of the letter holder.

"You'll take care of Bryon if he comes out?" he stated, more of a command than a question. "He'll sleep, I hope. Beverly—"

He didn't know what to say. Ruthy and Clarence had no idea of the problems. They knew nothing beyond the tragedies of two terrible deaths in Carl's family in the past week. One accidental, the other an unsolved murder.

As if Beverly read his face, his thoughts, she stood up.

"I'm going with you," she stated firmly.

"No," he said. He wanted to tell her more. That it was dangerous. That he would probably die in the process of trying to rescue Holly and Vinny. That he didn't want Beverly in danger. "I'll be back in a few minutes. I'm only going—to the store. I thought maybe I could pick up something that would comfort Bryon."

The lies slipped out naturally, without thought. He *must* get away without Beverly.

He had no plans. Only to get Holly and Vinny out of that place. Kara? It wasn't possible that somehow she was there, even though her grave had been robbed. What had they wanted with the child's body? He remembered Monte. The grave robbed, the child returned to life—if not life, animation of some terrible kind.

A deep and terrible anger filled him. How dare they do . . . whatever . . . they had done.

Even his imagination failed.

In the back of his pickup window was a rack that held one rifle and one shotgun. Never used. He had long ago lost his taste for shooting at deer. Or any other animal. The last time he'd shot at a deer, he had stood and watched as it fled unharmed across a field and into the woods. Afterwards he realized he'd had a grin of satisfaction on his face. On that last day of hunting he put the gun back in its rack and it had collected dust. The guns wouldn't help tonight either.

The driveway was half lighted, streaks of darkness like forbidden paths through the streaks of lights that filtered through the trees from the street lamp.

He ran to the pickup parked in its usual place beneath a tree, and heard the echo of its slamming door.

Beverly was already in the passenger seat.

She looked straight ahead.

"I'm going with you," she stated positively. "Something happened. I don't know what, but you're not going alone."

"Then you have to stay in the truck."

He started it and pulled straight ahead into the street,

whirling to the right, picking up speed. He had never been to the church, but he knew where it was. He and Beverly had seen it on the hill, nearly hidden behind trees.

"Where are you going?" she demanded. "I could see on your face that something—"

"Bryon told me. His mother is part of the church now. She had taken Vinny there and left him, and tonight Holly is going. They're going to bring Brent back." He laughed hollowly, to keep from screaming. "It's as though they plan to be a family again. With three children?"

Beverly said nothing. Lights from the dash sharpened her features. Her mouth pinched tight.

"Bryon said Kara is there. I don't know why they didn't take Bryon. Why they sent him over to me instead." He hooted again. "I suppose eventually they'll have to have a granddad."

"Holly was scared, Carl. I didn't want to tell you. She almost pushed Bryon at me."

They talked no more.

Carl concentrated on driving, on getting away from the downtown traffic as fast as he could and into Shady Hollow.

It no longer seemed a quiet, peaceful strip of pavement that was rarely traveled. Now it was lonely and dark, and filled with horrors that slipped along just outside the range of the lights.

The terror that had made Holly tremble was gone. When she had walked into the church it had looked so normal. What had she expected tonight?

Along the walls lamps fluttered dimly. Flames glowed within glass globes, little tongues of light. Dimness was everywhere, softening outlines and faces.

There were benches of oak, solid backs and seats. A high, peaked roof. Long, narrow windows, very widely

spaced, of stained glass. At the front was a larger arrange-
ment of stained-glass windows that took her eye and held
her gaze for a long moment. It was beautiful. Beneath it
was a long table, about the size of a coffin, with black
velvet draped over it and folded onto the floor.

It was as if she'd never seen it before. What had she
thought so scary about it?

Several of the people stood smiling in aisles outside
the benches. They all wore long black robes. They all
were beautiful and young. She recognized among them
the Rentons. They came toward her smiling, and guided
her slowly down the aisle between the benches as if it
were a kind of wedding march. They held her gently,
one on each side.

Many people sat on the benches, their faces turned
toward her, watching.

"Holly is becoming one of us tonight," someone said.
The voice, though very soft, carried clearly through the
church.

A child's head turned.

Holly stumbled.

Kara!

Kara. Holly wanted to run to her, throw her arms
around her little sister and hold her, hug her, laugh
with her. She felt as if she were in a dream.

Then she noticed the look on Kara's face. Though
pleasant, with a smile that reminded her of Heidi, there
was no recognition.

Kara didn't know her.

A thought flashed through Holly's mind.

Kara had no memory of her life. Her real life. She
was here. But . . . like a plant that moved with the wind,
that turned with the sun . . . there was nothing. Nothing.

Vinny, there . . . the same expression in his small,
blank face.

Holly swung back, pulling away from the Rentons.
She looked at Louise, coming along the aisle behind
her.

The blankness flattened her eyes. It had destroyed the soul that used to be there.

My God, get me out of here.

Hands clutched her harder.

Louise draped a black robe over her shoulders. Its touch was soft and heavy and the folds fell to her feet, as if it had been made just for her.

A strange peace settled over her. Her soul soared, as if flying away to wonders she had never known existed. She felt like lifting her voice in a heavenly song, even as something within the back of her mind screamed against what was happening to her. The terrible fear that was buried somewhere beneath the euphoria weakened.

She walked slowly, and saw they were guiding her toward the table beneath the windows. And she knew. Tonight she would die. She would leave forever the life she had known and enter another.

The unknown.

Aeternita.

From which there would be no escape.

Her daddy would be there and her mother. Her brother Vinny and Kara, her sister.

But they would not know one another. Or love one another, anymore. All the qualities that make a real family would be gone.

38.

Carl drove up the hill, following the dirt trail that wound through the trees. Above, narrow strips of colored lights grew dimly visible. He had turned off the pickup lights once, to hide their arrival, but couldn't see a damned thing, not even the trees that crowded the sides of the narrow trail.

He muttered under his breath, "Got to keep the goddamned things on."

Yet as soon as the light touched the automobiles parked in front of the church, he stopped and turned off the lights again. Darkness swooped down like a vulture. In the darkness were the mixed colors of lights coming like pale flutterings through narrow, long windows. It was a larger church than it had seemed from the bottom of the hill. Starlight brightened as they sat for a moment in the dark, touching the tops of dozens of cars.

Beverly hissed suddenly, "Listen!"

Her hearing was sharper than his. He rolled down the pickup window.

Then he heard it.

A chanting, almost like singing. Yet like nothing he had ever heard.

"I'm going in," he said.

He opened the pickup door and the overhead light came on. Beverly also opened her door. He reached down and pressed the button that held the light off.

"You are *not* going with me," he stated firmly. "I need you here. I'm going to be bringing Holly and the kids out if I have to shoot the whole damned bunch . . ."

He reached for the shotgun, and then drew his hand back.

Beverly expressed his thought.

"Guns will do no good."

"No. You can't kill something that's not alive."

He closed the door softly. On the other side of the pickup Beverly closed her door.

"The blowtorch!" he hissed in a loud whisper. "I'll set them back with that . . . if God's willing. Just long enough to get those kids out. Then—"

Then? He couldn't think beyond that. There was nothing beyond that.

But it hardly mattered at the moment that the world itself might be powerless against what lay beyond those walls, beneath the soil itself. Carl had only one goal.

Get Holly and Vinny out.

He reached into the darkness of the pickup bed and into the big tool box. His hand fell on the blowtorch.

With it held like a weapon he gave one last look toward Beverly.

She stood at the side of the pickup, a shadow within shadows. She didn't follow him.

He headed toward the front door.

A thought entered his mind. Locked.

If they were, he'd blow the damned things off their hinges.

His hand shook when he found the knob. It wasn't locked.

Double doors, but he opened only one and threw it back. It banged against the wall and the chanting within the church stopped abruptly.

He entered, holding the blow torch in front of him, a weapon, the only one he had.

A sweeping glance took in pews, dark and glossy, in rows through the length of the building as in any church. Long, stained glass windows reached high at the far end. Lights along the walls, fluttered dim and soft. Faces turned toward him in surprise.

Some of them he recognized with a shock that ran deep like a vein of blood.

Tom. Tom's children.

My God.

Kara. *Kara.*

Beautiful faces of perfect families, sitting together. Vinny, with a couple and another child, as if he were part of them.

Kara, with a couple and another child.

Families, perfect families—one boy, one girl, a father, a mother.

Draped figures began moving toward him. At the front, wearing a long black robe, lying on a kind of altar beneath stained glass windows . . . *Holly.*

"Holly!" Carl screamed. "Get out of here! Get out! Tom! Get your kids out of here! Holly! Goddamnit, get out of here!"

The atmosphere changed abruptly. People in the pews rose. Holly stood up, looking as if she had just awakened. Even in the distance and the pale light Carl could see her face. She blinked.

Then, fear whitened her skin. Her eyes rounded, her mouth rounded.

Carl went down the aisle.

Dark robed figures rushed toward him. Faces that had been perfect changed instantly and became rounded, glossy, smooth, featureless, with wide mouths that stretched from one side of the black hoods to the others. Sounds came from them, a deep rumbling, a deep disturbance that turned Carl weak with terror.

"Holly!" he screamed again.

He pressed the switch that turned on the blow torch and the flame shot forward. It touched one of the strange faces within a hooded robe, and Carl heard a sizzle, as if fat were frying. The figure in black dodged away.

Carl glanced backwards toward the door. It was still open. But the hooded creatures were surrounding the interior of the church. Suddenly it seemed as if there were dozens of them, everywhere, as if most of the families that had sat in the pews were now robed and closing him in.

But the blue flame of the blowtorch kept them away. Carl swept the blaze in a continuous circle as he, holding them back, went down the aisle.

Visitors to the church ran, crowding down the aisle behind him, their faces twisted masks of horror. But human. *Human.*

"Holly!" Carl screamed in desperation. Where was she? "Holly! Get Vinny! Tom, get your kids out of here!"

Holly came toward him. The black robe slipped off one shoulder, and dragged onto the floor away from her. As if it had held some power over her but now she could run.

Carl turned the blow torch toward the faceless figures that tried to stop her, and she rushed down the pew toward Kara.

Then she drew back. She came backing toward Carl, and he turned, and looked.

The child that had been Kara was now faceless, its head turning right, left, blindly. There were no eyes, no nose, only the wide slit of mouth. Like the mouth of a subterranean worm that eats its way through the soil, creating its own tunnel, closing the tunnel behind.

Carl moved over, the blowtorch aimed at every black-robed figure that approached. Holly ran past him toward the door.

He caught a glimpse of Vinny . . . not Vinny, not now. The child with his face was in the arms of one of the robed, and in the one glance Carl saw his features begin to recede.

In shock he paused. They approached, crowding toward him, swelling within the robes.

Holding the flame forward, Carl backed away. He saw Tom, carrying his little girl in one arm and his son in the other. Tom, looking pale, the strange lights crossing his face like muted rainbows.

Carl swept the blowtorch around as he turned to follow, to reach the door before the black-robed figures closed him in forever. He saw that Holly had gone now, and Tom was going out backwards, his eyes on Carl, his mouth open, his voice silent. The two children clung to him, both too frightened to cry.

Carl looked for other faces, and saw nothing but that glossy, featurelessness that characterized whatever they were.

Something squishy soft and cold swept with terrible force against Carl. His grip on the blow-torch loosened. The torch was jerked from his hands as he fell. The back of his head struck the hard threshold of the door. Light flashed, blazed.

A lamp on the wall exploded. Shards of glass flew through the air. Explosions ripped through the building, from lamp to lamp.

Carl felt himself touched, and dragged.

Terror filled his lungs, heavier than the smoke and flames. He was being dragged back into the exploding, burning church.

He heard a scream, but it was far away, and hushed almost immediately. He felt the roughness of being pulled downward, over sharp objects.

Then he smelled fresh air, and saw above him a sprinkling of stars.

Someone was still pulling him down the church steps and onto the ground, not back into the burning building.

He looked up, eyes burning. He saw the familiar outline of a head, a face . . .

Tom.

"Get up, Carl! Run, goddamnit!" Tom shouted above the roar of the burning building. "Come on, get to your feet and run!"

Carl tried to get up, but he was too weak to stand. He felt himself grabbed again, hauled up like a sack of potatoes. Other hands tugged at his arm.

"Grandpa!" Holly cried. "Grandpa, come on!"

Tom carried him into the yard before the weight became too much. Then, dragging, Tom on one side, Holly on the other, the cool of the night pushed back the heat of the burning building, and Carl regained his feet.

Sirens.

Sirens, the most beautiful sound in the world.

Last week he had cringed at the sound of a siren, but tonight, as they came up the hill, it was like music from heaven.

Lights bathed them. From the burning church, from the twirling lights on police cars and fire trucks.

On shaky legs Carl ran between Holly and Tom.

Epilogue

The next morning at dawn Carl went back.

Several police cars were parked near the black sedans that hadn't yet been towed away. The cars that had been parked there last night, cars that belonged to the members of the church, had not been moved except those closest to the building had been pushed out of the way. The paint scorched and curling, they sat like automobiles abandoned to a junk yard.

Carl counted three fire trucks still in attendance. Men dressed in fireproof suits and heavy boots walked through the burned rubble of what had been the church of Aeternita.

The faces of the men and women who searched were solemn and closed, the way of people who cleaned up after a terrible tragedy.

One of the policemen came to Carl again, as he and others had before him.

"You're sure people were in there? They didn't leave by a back door?"

Carl shook his head. "I didn't see any other doors. No one left. Just my granddaughter and Tom. Tom and his two kids. A few more. I don't know how many, but just a few."

They were there, accounted for. Most of them had

spent the night watching the church burn. Carl had
gone home because of the children who lived, to be
sure they were safe.

Behind Carl Tom spoke.

"Eight of us came out," he said. "Only eight."

He looked dazed. The other two couples also wore a
dazed look. One of the women appeared exhausted,
injured somehow. Her husband said something about
taking her home if he could get his car out.

Carl listened to the spates of conversation. Several
people had joined the church. Folks that were known
by Tom, and the other two couples who escaped the
fire. Carl knew none of them.

"They didn't get out," the man named Steve Lawson
said. "I knew those people personally. They were neighbors. They didn't get out. There sits their cars."

The search continued. Puffs of smoke and black dust
rose when half-burned timbers were moved. The foundation of the building, cement blocks, had crumbled.
Carl watched as searchers kicked them aside.

He had taken Beverly and the children home as
the church burned. In the night heated by fire that
seemed to rage beyond reason, Tom asked him to
take his kids too. Leave them in Carl's house, if he
would, with Holly and Beverly and the other women
who would be there.

Carl had taken them home, and then left again. He
went first to the police station and asked if his son's
body was still where it was safe.

"Safe?"

They didn't know what he was talking about. He
couldn't tell them.

"It's in the morgue, sir. The medical examiner will
be here tomorrow."

He left, relieved that Brent was there. That he hadn't
been taken to—to whatever existence Louise, Vinny,
and Kara now were part of.

He went back to the church on the hill, and with the

others stood watching. It had burned rapidly, Tom told him.

"I never saw anything generate so much heat and go so fast."

Carl nodded. At that time, with the dawn breaking in the east, spots glowed within the rubble, struggling to shoot to life again.

"Nobody . . ." Tom said. "They can't find anybody."

The sun rose. People came and stood with Tom and Carl. Firemen and policemen roamed the area.

Several detectives from the city police and a couple of deputies, one of whom Carl recognized as Deputy Crowell came to Carl, Tom and those of the men who had escaped and had gathered in a group to stand together.

"Do you know how this started?" the fire chief asked.

Yes. It was my blowtorch. But he couldn't tell them what had happened. *One of them knocked it away from me.*

Tom said quickly, stepping closer to Carl. "It was an accident. There were kerosene lamps on the walls for light. One of them exploded."

Another of the men pushed close. It was as if they were trying to surround Carl, to protect him.

"Gasoline," the man corrected. Carl didn't even know his name, but he could see the gratitude in his eyes. A glance from the man told Carl, thank God . . . we didn't know . . . thank God you came when you did. "Gasoline, not kerosene."

The third man said, "Very volatile. It just happened."

Carl licked dried lips. Vinny was in there somewhere, and Kara. Louise was there. Burned to death. At the moment he couldn't say, "I killed them." But later, when their bodies were found and identified, he would have to speak up. His consolation was that Holly and Bryon and Tom's children were safe.

Yet, had he killed them?

He had seen Kara buried. She was dead. And then
. . . she had been brought up . . .

He didn't understand. Yet he couldn't stop the feelings of guilt.

All day he waited. With the others he waited, until
the rubble was gone. Sifted.

People from various news sources shot videos and
took pictures. Late in the day the fire chief and chief
of police gave out the information.

"There are no bodies. Nothing. There's no sign of a
sliver of bone. Those people escaped. Somehow, they
escaped."

Carl heard, and relief filled him. Thank God. There
were no deaths, no bodies. Then the coldness came.
The puzzlement. The memories of a grave beneath a
tree pushed over, and the rising of bodies, and the
perfect faces of those who walked past him one night
not long ago.

Vinny, Kara, Louise. They hadn't been burned. Thank
God, they hadn't been burned.

Yet . . .

The conversations of the firemen and police drifted back to Carl, Tom, and the two men who had
stayed.

The last group of searchers who came forward, dusty,
darkened with soot, faces soiled, eyes white from goggles
that had protected them, spoke.

"There was a tunnel beneath the floor of that church.
Did any of you know that?"

They stared at him. No one answered.

A tunnel.

An escape route. Perhaps an opening that allowed
many others to emerge. Carl listened, barely able to
assimilate what he was hearing.

Then, another searcher said, "The only thing is it's

not big enough for a human, even a child. It's only about ten inches in diameter.''

One hole in the ground ten inches in diameter.

Carl stood at the window in his bedroom and stared out into darkness. Hours had passed. He hadn't slept in so long he couldn't remember.

Beverly had stayed. She had insisted, and he loved her for it. How could he possibly live without her now?

She was in the guest room. Asleep, he hoped. Holly slept in the third bedroom. Bryon was asleep in Carl's big bed, spread wide, arms and legs flung out. If Carl listened carefully he could hear the soft, even breathing of the child.

Tom had taken his children home.

One narrow hole in the ground beneath what had been the church of Aeternita.

Engineers had dug down and found that it went straight down for twenty feet, like the spoke of a wheel. From that narrow hole in the ground a dozen small tunnels branched in different directions.

They found it a strange puzzle.

The small tunnels were as clean of debris as animal passageways.

It was three o'clock in the morning. Night before last the church had burned.

Carl started back to bed.

He sat down, and then the sound reached him, like an echo from the falling of the tree.

Drummm, drummm, drummmm . . .

Soft, close, eerily musical and rhythmic.

Carl hurried to the window and looked out, but saw only the driveway with his old pickup truck parked under the tree and the doors to the garage where the sedan was parked, and his wife's favorite little car.

He ran from the bedroom and down the hall. It was

lighted dimly by a four watt bulb that came on at a certain point of darkness, and went out with light.

He ran on to the big window in the front of the house.

The sound was still there, so close.

Drummmm . . . rrummm . . .

He looked out.

A dark figure, tall with a black robe covering its head and falling full length, stood in the street.

It was looking at the house.

Carl heard a movement behind him and turned.

Holly stood in the doorway. Street light through the trees fell softly across her face. She was smiling faintly. An incredible beauty came with the light and shadows that wavered across her face. She was wearing a long gown or robe. Dark.

"They're calling."

Her voice was soft, almost a whisper, as rhythmic and musical as the drifting sounds of the drum. She seemed unafraid.

She knew, Carl sensed. She knew about the wormlike tunnels beneath the church, and where they led.

And she heard the beat of the drum.

HAUTALA'S HORROR AND
SUPERNATURAL SUSPENSE

GHOST LIGHT (4320, $4.99)
Alex Harris is searching for his kidnapped children, but only the ghost of their dead mother can save them from his murderous rage.

DARK SILENCE (3923, $5.99)
Dianne Fraser is trying desperately to keep her family—and her own sanity—from being pulled apart by the malevolent forces that haunt the abandoned mill on their property.

COLD WHISPER (3464, $5.95)
Tully can make Sarah's every wish come true, but Sarah lives in teror because Tully doesn't understand that some wishes aren't meant to come true.

LITTLE BROTHERS (4020, $4.50)
The "little brothers" have returned, and this time there will be no escape for the boy who saw them kill his mother.

NIGHT STONE (3681, $4.99)
Their new house was a place of darkness, shadows, long-buried secrets, and a force of unspeakable evil.

MOONBOG (3356, $4.95)
Someone—or something—is killing the children in the little town of Holland, Maine.

MOONDEATH (1844, $3.95)
When the full moon rises in Cooper Falls, a beast driven by bloodlust and savage evil stalks the night.

Prepare Yourself for

PATRICIA WALLACE

LULLABYE   (2917, $3.95/$4.95)
Eight-year-old Bronwyn knew she wasn't like other girls. She didn't have a mother. At least, not a real one. Her mother had been in a coma at the hospital for as long as Bronwyn could remember. She couldn't feel any pain, her father said. But when Bronwyn sat with her mother, she knew her mother was angry—angry at the nurses and doctors, and her own helplessness. Soon, she would show them all the true meaning of suffering . . .

MONDAY'S CHILD   (2760, $3.95/$4.95)
Jill Baker was such a pretty little girl, with long, honey-blond hair and haunting gray-green eyes. Just one look at her angelic features could dispel all the nasty rumors that had been spreading around town. There were all those terrible accidents that had begun to plague the community, too. But the fact that each accident occurred after little Jill had been angered had to be coincidence . . .

SEE NO EVIL   (2429, $3.95/$4.95)
For young Caryn Dearborn, the cornea operation enabled her to see more than light and shadow for the first time. For Todd Reynolds, it was his chance to run and play like other little boys. For these two children, the sudden death of another child had been the miracle they had been waiting for. But with their eyesight came another kind of vision—of evil, horror, destruction. They could see into other people's minds, their worst fears and deepest terrors. And they could see the gruesome deaths that awaited the unwary . . .

THRILL   (3142, $4.50/$5.50)
It was an amusement park like no other in the world. A tri-level marvel of modern technology enhanced by the special effects wizardry of holograms, lasers, and advanced robotics. Nothing could go wrong—until it did. As the crowds swarmed through the gates on Opening Day, they were unprepared for the disaster about to strike. Rich and poor, young and old would be taken for the ride of their lives, trapped in a game of epic proportions where only the winners survived . . .

Available wherever paperbacks are sold, or order direct from the Publisher. Send cover price plus 50¢ per copy for mailing and handling to Penguin USA, P.O. Box 999, c/o Dept. 17109, Bergenfield, NJ 07621.Residents of New York and Tennessee must include sales tax. DO NOT SEND CASH.